PRAISE

"Tobin masterfully takes us deeper and deeper into the minds and hearts of
her characters... You finish, wanting a sequel."
DAN MULHERN, J.D., FORMER FIRST GENTLEMAN OF MICHIGAN

"Tobin tackles HUGE subjects: grief, homosexuality, priest abuse, family
denial, parental guilt, the AIDS crisis, hypermasculinity, and feminine
stereotyping with a clear sense of unity and emotional richness."
BETH GYLYS, PH.D., AUTHOR OF *BODY BRAILLE*,
ENGLISH LITERATURE PROFESSOR AT GEORGIA STATE

"A poignant, funny, inspiring exploration of the healing power of empathy
and common humanity."
JOHN NEAFSEY, PSYCHOLOGIST, AUTHOR OF *A SACRED VOICE IS CALLING*

ABOUT THE AUTHOR

Michelle Tobin is a Licensed Clinical Social Worker who works with adults, including her city's refugee population. She also writes psychological assessments for annulments. Michelle trained as a chef at the internationally acclaimed Ballymaloe Cookery School in Ireland. Most recently she earned certification in Integrative Medicine and Nutrition for Mental Health. Her clinical work includes cooking therapy as part of the treatment protocol. In addition to writing, she is an avid lap swimmer, dog walker, reader, fabric artist, and volunteer cook for a soup kitchen. Michelle is married and raised three children. Like one of her characters, Michelle is one of twelve children.

michelle-tobin.com

HOME
FOR THE
BEWILDERED

MICHELLE
TOBIN

www.vineleavespress.com

It's a joy to be hidden; it's a disaster not to be found.
D.W. Winnicott

The mind that is not baffled is not employed.
Wendell Berry

In loving memory of my parents, Nobyn and Dorothy D'Haene.

For my husband Gerry—always my big red bow.

AUTHOR'S NOTE

This book is set in 1974 and reflects the language and terminology of the time.

PROLOGUE

1983

THOMAS

Love is our steady guide on this road full of hardships. —Rumi

Oh, Jesus, my Savior, my Solace, my Hope. My comfort when I sorrow, my compass when lost...

"Goddammit, Ruth!" Thomas muttered before he even opened his eyes. He woke to the sound of the other residents moving about and starting their day: toilets flushing, showers running, the smell of the morning's first cigarettes wafting in the air. A shaft of early morning sunlight pried open his eyes, an insult to the senses. Thomas had that scary second or two of disorientation where he didn't know where he was. It took a beat before he realized he hadn't heard Ruth sing in years. And he was nowhere near St. Lawrence.

Still, he played along, "What are you doing here, Ruth?" The lines between past and present, reality and illusion blurred every morning now.

I told you, Thomas, get yourself out of that bed and go find Dr. Morrissey.

Unless the weight of his full bladder became unbearable, he would not get out of bed. He preferred to wait out the other men. He didn't want to talk to anyone, least of all Ruth. He was not interested in making friends with total losers such as himself, just like he'd told her when they were at St. Lawrence Asylum together. "You never were very good at listening," he accused her now. He clung to every shred of dignity that his vanity could muster by keeping his distance. Gone were the days when he sought the approving gaze of other men by parading around in finery. And gone were the days when he had to put up with Ruth's singing.

As he listened to the lament of the mourning doves outside his window, snippets of another of Ruth's damn spirituals grew louder. *Sometimes I feel like a motherless child. A long way from home.*

"Shut up, Ruth!" he shouted.

I'm not shutting up 'til you get yourself outta that bed. She started teasing him in a *nahnah, nenahnah* tune. *I know where your sash is, I know where your sash is.*

"How many times do I have to tell you?" Thomas wagged his finger. "It's not a sash, it's an obi." But she had piqued his curiosity. "Where is my obi? You know I don't like my stuff hanging out for everyone to see."

Dr. Morrissey's got it.

Dr. Morrissey whom he liked to think of as his real mother. She never would have allowed his father to lay a hand on him. Ruth had just reminded him of the first time he met Dr. Morrissey. Really, he only remembered how upset he was. Thomas thought, *if those damn nurses hadn't taken my obi, I could have shown them what a proper kimono looks like.*

Dust motes danced about blurring with the floaters his eyes recently acquired. Outside of using the bathroom, he hadn't left the room in three days. In a moment of clarity, Thomas thought, *I need to go to the hospital.* The thought dismissed itself, drifted away on the sea of darkness that pulled Thomas under as if the very act of thinking sapped his energy. He'd been traumatized by what he'd seen and was grief-stricken by the loss of Regis yet again. The way Regis had moved in and out of his life made Thomas wonder if he'd made him up. Regis came into his life like a ray of sunshine after his brother JW left. Thomas kept his favorite pictures of JW and Regis, side by side, in his wallet, but the effort to get up and fish the wallet from under the dresser where he hid it from the liars and thieves in this hellhole was too much. He tried to conjure an image of JW in his mind. It occurred to Thomas that becoming an actor gave JW a way to pretend and dress up just like he had as a drag queen, albeit in a more socially acceptable way. He'd played the "Artful Dodger" from *Oliver* in their community theater. JW went from lord and protector to artful dodger. JW never wanted to play dress-up with Mother and me though he didn't stop us either. But then he ran off just like the artful dodger. The role pretty much summed up JW; that was for sure. Thomas ran through JW's performance in his mind. He had to admit he was pretty good. Maybe his brother had made it in Hollywood after all.

When he ran into Regis again after moving to Detroit, he felt the gods had finally smiled on him. Their reunion was proof that all his suffering had been worthwhile. Reunited with his one true love. The stars had aligned. Hope abounded. *If only Dr. Morrissey could see me now,* he remembered thinking, *she'd have to agree that I did the right thing when I discharged myself from St. Lawrence. Medication and therapy be damned! I'm in love, and that's all the medicine I need!* Now Regis was gone. Why wasn't he here talking to me instead of that infernal Ruth? Thomas couldn't remember just now if Regis had died or if JW was alive or dead. Was JW a dream too? His past didn't seem real, and a future didn't feel possible. He began to cry.

Sometimes I feel like I'm almost done. A long, long way from home.

"Ruth, will you please shut up? I'm not a card-carrying groupie, remember?"

I'm not shutting up until you get yourself to Dr. Morrissey.

"You had entirely too much influence on Dr. Morrissey," Thomas replied. "Music therapy, my ass. What the hell was wrong with a couple of bolts to the brain like the good ole days?"

I'm not the one who had her decorating the whole place.

He looked about the drab room; cinder block walls, green linoleum floors, a cheap dresser in the corner probably from Montgomery Ward. He smiled thinking about when Dr. Morrissey populated the common area with cheap Montgomery Ward furniture after he'd told her the room depressed him. Speaking of, depression pushed at his temples like a dull headache. Everything hurt. He rubbed at his neck, taut with tension that ran down his back muscles, his limbs felt heavy, his stomach ached with hunger, but the thought of eating made him feel nauseated. Even his eyelids hurt, and he hated the idea of rising from the discomfort of the YMCA's cheap, urine-stained mattress even though he could feel the metal springs poking his back.

"She probably hates me now anyway, or she's forgotten all about me," Thomas bemoaned. He guiltily recalled how he'd discharged against medical advice during the Christmas holiday while Dr. Morrissey was gone. Some non-descript intern was filling in for her. He'd promised her that he'd wait until she returned. Then again, Dr. Morrissey had not informed him of a prolonged absence. He'd been angry, and he'd felt abandoned. What did she care if her crazy, manic-depressive client checked out? She hadn't bothered enough to inform her patients of her whereabouts. He suspected she'd taken a position somewhere new. Rumors ran rampant about an elopement or severe illness waylaying her.

That was then, this is now, Ruth said. Thomas's eyes stung, and his throat was coated with the stale taste of cigarettes and sleep. He could feel a cough coming on and struggled to sit up. He reached for a hankie. There was the familiar tightness in his chest a warning that the iron-ore taste of blood would soon follow. *Get out of this hellhole. Go see Dr. Morrissey,* his need desperate, urgent. There was a knock on the door.

PART ONE:
INTAKE ANXIETY

CHAPTER ONE

WINTER 1974
DOROTHY AND KENNETH
PROTESTANT NEW YEAR

"Do your parents know that I've moved in with you?" Dorothy asked her boyfriend, Kenneth. The couple parked themselves where Kenneth's mother directed, having just come down the main staircase into the foyer. Gusts of cold air chilled Dorothy's nose and fingers with each entry of partygoers. The place tingled with excitement and hope as the guests gathered to welcome 1974, the atmosphere accentuated by the sparkling cut crystal chandelier above them. Champagne flutes clinking in salutation all around her.

"Do your parents know that we're dating yet?" Kenneth retorted.

"Fair enough," Dorothy replied, looking around at the guests.

"You look lovely, by the way," said Kenneth, squeezing Dorothy's hand. Dorothy wore a bright red, satin a-line dress with three-quarter length sleeves, for which she was especially grateful for now since she hadn't thought to bring a shawl. She loved that the dress had pockets because she didn't like carrying a clutch, but she needed her tissue and lipstick. "My god, your hands are like ice. Let's move away from the door." He guided her further into the foyer. Cold drafts plagued her even further in, tousling her hair and tickling her nose.

"You don't look so bad yourself," Dorothy said with a smile. Kenneth wore a black tux with satin lapels and a red satin tie. He was easy on the eyes. Her first thought when she'd met him was *Oh, what a beautiful man.* Kenneth possessed the waspy good looks of his Protestant lineage: blonde, blue-eyed, slightly Roman nose with a bump that was not too prominent. Nothing exotic, like the coal-black hair and freckles of her Irish-Catholic family. Only Tess had gotten blonde hair and it had been more strawberry than blonde. Like their mother, the girls had slight overbites and dimples in their chins. From their father, high color in the cheeks when embarrassed or drinking (it only took one glass of wine or spirits to set Dorothy's cheeks aflame). She hadn't needed much convincing to date Kenneth but introducing him to her parents was another story. "Last year's party, you introduced me to your parents and this year we've moved in together. Just don't announce our new status to the whole room." Not that Dorothy need worry. Kenneth was the consummate introvert, worse than she was. On the other hand, these were his people. This was his element. The annual Nelson New Year's Eve gala was an elegant and lavish affair replete with state politicians and their wives, CEOs and their wives, heads of non-profits and their wives, all the types that made the "Who's Who of Michigan." Everyone who was anyone in Lansing was in attendance. All of whom Dorothy found exceedingly boring. Kenneth's parents threw the best party in town according to the hoity-toity, and if you wanted to have any influence at the Capitol, you needed to be there. The mood was festive among the partygoers who were happy to see friends and colleagues for the last hoorah before flying off to exotic destinations for extended winter vacations.

The only similarity between the Nelson's and Morrissey's holiday celebrations was the free-flowing alcohol. She couldn't imagine her parents' reactions to this shindig. Holidays were religious and exclusively family affairs for the Morrisseys. No one came to the house who wasn't a relation by blood or marriage. Nor could they afford the luxury of a getaway to warmer climes. The thought would never have crossed their minds. Dorothy had just returned to Lansing after spending Christmas in Detroit with her family. Compared to holidays in the Morrissey household, admittedly plebian, this New Year's event at the Nelson's was a staid affair, snooty, boring, and dripping with wealth.

Kenneth's mother had been consumed with preparations for this year's party. Preservationists had recently completed the renovations of the old Turner Mansion and she wanted to showcase the restoration, which, as Dorothy could just now overhear his mother describing to a guest, had been *meticulously preserved with an eye to its Victorian roots.* Outside, wide concrete steps led up to an enormous portico covering the width of the house with steps on either side. Double doors led into a grand foyer with a view to a winding staircase past walnut wainscoting, dark but original to the building. The entryway was massive (Dorothy's parents raised nine children in a house that could fit inside it), flanked on both sides by open parlors perfect for entertaining opposing political parties. Congregated on the left side were the Democrats and the right the Republicans. Dorothy and Kenneth were told to stand in between, albeit awkwardly, to best not offend. The rooms were elegantly appointed with rugs, ceramics, and glassware, souvenirs from Mr. Nelson's posts abroad. Each room was a showcase for artifacts from their travels. "When this estate came on the market, I immediately saw its potential." Dorothy overheard Mrs. Nelson say. "I've committed every waking hour and untold amounts of money to overseeing the renovation. It had to be just right." Dorothy didn't understand the need for so much space for just two people. Kenneth was an only child and a grown man. They bought the place long after he'd gone to college. Was its only purpose to show it off? Conspicuous consumption came to mind. The scent of pine was in the air from the Christmas trees, wreaths and garlands over the mantels that anchored the open space of the first floor where guests chatted in small groups or moved about inspecting the art and books. The soft light fluttering from candles dotting the mantles and tables added a festive feel.

In any case, the gala was a long-standing tradition. When his father "retired" to work stateside for General Motors, they decided their home in Lansing would be the New Year's Eve destination. Lansing's upper class set their holiday travel around the party. Kenneth's father wielded significant influence in Lansing's civic and corporate affairs. He was a prominent member of the Board of Trustees at Michigan State University and the United Way. Kenneth's mother volunteered for the Daughters of the American Revolution, United Episcopal Women, and the PTA as well as other local causes.

Precisely the type of situation and people that provided potential landmines for Dorothy. Dorothy was psychologically astute, a good listener, and had a way of intuiting the secrets of other people without realizing it. This was a valuable skill in a therapist, creating a safe place for patients to confide in her because they "just knew" she understood them. However, in social situations like this party, her social anxiety fueled intuition became a liability. She was never sure if it was her own anxiety or an inability to connect with people in group settings. As Carl Jung would say, she became animus possessed. For some reason, seemingly beyond her control, she'd blurt out a name or a phrase or an opinion that might just miss the mark but was close enough that they both became uncomfortable. As if it was her job to expose the sins of those in power, the faux pas might exert itself in her sudden need to moralize about infidelity to the serial cheater or fraud to the embezzling bank executive. As Kenneth teased, there wasn't a pile of shit that she missed stepping in. She tried to laugh at herself but usually walked away feeling embarrassed. Regardless, this could prove to be a sticking point for Kenneth's parents inviting her into the fold since the Nelsons often rubbed shoulders with these types. The Nelsons were these types.

Standing there, listening in on their conversations, Dorothy thought how so few understood the work she did day after day. The suffering of the mentally ill did not register for a moment among this crowd. In fact, some of the politicians in attendance wrote the legislation that underfunded or outright denied funds for community mental health facilities, which had been promised as far back as the Kennedy administration, while at the same time shuttering the asylums. Dorothy suspected that even those who might be struggling with a mental illness would be hard-pressed to admit the fact to their friends and acquaintances here. Most of the guests, from where Dorothy stood, appeared puffed up with bravado, confident in their esteemed positions and contributions to the community.

"I don't know a soul here," Dorothy whispered to Kenneth.

"You know me and my parents," Kenneth said, squeezing her hand. "Besides, you talk to strangers at the hospital all the time."

"Yeah, that's when I'm in charge. I don't mind people-watching but that only goes so far."

"You don't fool me, Dr. Morrissey," Kenneth teased. "You'll be analyzing every last person in the room." Of course, he was right. She was already busy listening in on the self-congratulatory boasts as one high-powered person tried to outdo the next. As she did, Dorothy felt a bit of her working-class father's chip on the shoulder. She might be smart, but she was working class in her core. What did these people know of struggle, hard work, and suffering, really? Most were born, like Kenneth, with silver spoons in their mouths. Try as she might to give these titans of Lansing the benefit of the doubt—weren't they just better at protecting their vulnerability, after all? And, didn't they have as much need to be heard as her patients did?—she found most of them to be insufferable. If she had to choose, she'd stick with her patients any day. She took Kenneth's hand and gave it a squeeze reassuring herself that he was the exception to the rule.

Servers made their rounds with small platters of hors-d'oeuvres and glasses of champagne. Like a secret handshake, Kenneth executed a skillful eye-roll Dorothy's way, followed by a long-suffering sigh to let her know that he, too, found the command performance excruciating. As accustomed as he was to his parents' socialite status, his introverted nature chaffed when called upon to join in.

They stuck together in a corner with an eye to the crowd, gamely tasting whatever delicious canapés floated by while trying to figure out how to politely eat and hold a glass of champagne simultaneously. As much as she enjoyed Medjool dates wrapped in bacon, carpaccio of beef on rye toasts with small dollops of horseradish mayonnaise, and mini quiches, she couldn't help the derisive thought in the voice of her father that floated to consciousness: *What the hell is a can-ape?* "I don't know where to set down my plate," she whispered.

A pro, Kenneth laughed and hailed one of the servers. "Can you take these from us and bring us more champagne?" he asked.

"Certainly, sir," the young man replied. Gracious guests paused to congratulate Kenneth and chat amiably with the hosts' son and his girlfriend long enough to inquire about their future. Soon it became evident to Dorothy that all anyone appeared to be interested in was Kenneth's post-doctorate ambitions. She became increasingly annoyed by all the questions she fielded about Kenneth's future as a university professor or economist for local, state, or federal government. Older, established, and well-meaning couples each genially turned to their younger counterparts to inquire about marriage and Kenneth's aspirations. She'd just as genially albeit insincerely deferred questions about Kenneth's career to Kenneth since everyone she met at the soiree appeared to assume that she was just waiting for Kenneth to finish his Ph.D. so they could get married. Only one person, a woman, asked her what she did for a living. "I'm a psychologist," Dorothy responded.

"Your parents must be very proud," the woman said before moving on. *I wish,* Dorothy thought. Her parents had barely acknowledged, let alone celebrated, Dorothy's accomplishments. Since she had yet to snag a rich Catholic husband, she might as well have done nothing.

Had she not been drinking champagne, which she knew went straight to her head, she might have recognized the landmines before stepping on them. Still, with each annoying query about Kenneth's plans, Dorothy took another sip, and pretty soon, she began, perhaps a bit loudly, to introduce herself as Dr. Morrissey with barely a nod toward Kenneth just to see the supercilious eyebrow lift in surprise. If she drank much more, she would dispense with propriety altogether and start swearing like a longshoreman and asking where she might find a hamburger. She didn't have to wait much longer. She and Kenneth were approached by State Senator Mitch Kelley, a Republican and former car salesman known for being a blowhard. A stout man, he wore an ill-fitted, overly large suit, his tie emblazoned with Notre Dame and shamrocks hanging well below his belt. His comb-over made his fat, florid cheeks and bulbous nose look clownish, and he had small, meaty hands, one of which held a cigar and the other a bourbon on the rocks. He stood too close to her, his moist bourbon and smoke exhalations making her want to gag. He gave Kenneth a hearty slap on the back, congratulating him for his promising future as an academic. "And who is this young lady?" he asked Kenneth.

"This is my girlfriend, Dorothy. Dorothy, State Senator Mitch Kelley."

"Hello, Senator, I'm Dr. Morrissey." Dorothy recognized the land-mine posed by the senator. She was mad that Kenneth didn't let any of the people he'd introduced to her know that she was a doctor even as they asked him when he would earn his doctorate. And of all the people who needed to know she was a doctor in psychology, it was Kelley. Kelley, Dorothy knew, had drafted the legislation that cut funding to the mentally ill and was behind the yearly shrinkage of St. Lawrence Asylum from a stand-alone facility situated on scenic acres in the country to a ward within a hospital where she now worked. He'd forcefully condemned the abuses in asylums, taking his talking points from the book *One Flew Over the Cuckoo's Nest,* without proposing or funding an alternative. She would not be surprised if a car dealership would soon be built on the old property. Consequently, Dorothy was not well disposed to him in the first place, and once he opened his mouth, less so. "I'm assuming the recent legislation you sponsored isn't reflective of Notre Dame's values," she said, pointing at his tie.

"Which piece are we talking about, little lady?" Oh, how she wanted to kick him.

"I'm a psychologist at St. Lawrence Asylum," Dorothy said. "The place you've reduced to a few beds on a ward."

"So, you're not a real doctor, eh, sweetheart? Aren't you glad you don't have to play Nurse Ratched to those people anymore?" He smirked, enjoying his humor.

"Those people are human beings."

"Perhaps we shelve this conversation for another time," Kenneth interjected. He had a pained look on his face, as if unsure of whose toes he was stepping on. Then the senator brought up Nixon, defending the man's right to do whatever he wanted as the president. "The Salem witches got a better deal than poor Richard Nixon," Kelley said.

"Are you feckin kidding?" Dorothy said, taken aback. Her Irish grandmother always said feckin. Her father always said feckin. In her professional life, she never said feckin but just now the twitch developing in her eye sought cover behind her crass language. She looked at Kenneth to back her up, but he kept quiet, searching for the nearest exit. "How can you possibly compare the torturing and burning of innocent girls with an investigation into the criminal activity and abuse of power of a President of the United States?"

"That from the witch doctor herself," Kelley said with a sneer. Dorothy rubbed at her eye as if trying to remove the plank as she'd been taught by the Church. The woman who had asked Dorothy what she did for a living earlier walked up and took Senator Kelley by the arm.

"Let's get you home, dear," she said to him. Dorothy's mouth fell agape.

"You got a feisty one there, Kenneth," he said, dismissively. "But I don't need to endure this feminist quackery during my holidays." He used his heft to exhale one last smoky bourbon breath into her face before being led away.

"I'd rather be a witch doctor than a horse's ass," Dorothy said, maybe a tad too loudly. A hush fell over the room at just that moment. Flustered, she walked briskly away in search of a bathroom to regain her composure. Blinking back angry tears, she locked the door behind her, which was no easy task given the maple doors were original to the house. Kenneth would have some explaining to do. She'd been stewing before Senator Kelley approached them. There was just something about the disingenuous solicitude of this group that got under her skin. She could hardly blame Kenneth for basking in the attention, but to stand idly by while that horse's ass called her a witch doctor? *I should have stayed in Detroit,* she thought. She longed for the raucous, Jameson-fueled jollity of her more down-to-earth family. She took a few deep breaths, wiped any hint of crying from her cheeks, and walked out of the bathroom to find a drink. Kenneth came up to her as she waited for the bartender to make her a Jameson and Ginger.

As if nothing at all was amiss, Kenneth whispered in her ear. "When will this night be over?" he said.

"Not soon enough," she hissed. "I can't believe you didn't stand up for me."

"What are you talking about?" Kenneth said, defensively.

"With Kelley," Dorothy replied, exasperated.

"You handled him pretty well all by yourself."

"He called me 'little lady,' not to mention 'sweetheart.'"

"You can't let guys like that bother you," Kenneth said.

"And then he called me a witch doctor," Dorothy said, taking a large gulp of her drink.

"Everybody knows he's just a blowhard."

"That doesn't make it okay."

"You're overreacting, Dorothy. Let's walk around, calm down a bit."

"You should know by now, Kenneth, that I hate nothing more than a man telling me that I'm overreacting. How about you find my coat? I'm leaving."

"We agreed we'd spend the night here, remember?"

"I'm just going for a walk."

"Shall I join you?"

"I can handle it all by myself."

Dorothy didn't want to embarrass Kenneth's parents any more than she already had, so once she had her coat in hand, she let it drop. She really needed some fresh air. She was sure Senator Kelley would spout off about her to the Nelsons, and she didn't want to be around for that. "I'm just going to take a walk and look at Christmas lights. I need to calm down like you said. Go on and enjoy your parents' friends."

✦

"Happy New Year," Kenneth said, turning toward Dorothy and giving her a kiss. "Can you forgive me for not sticking up for you last night?"

"Happy New Year to you," she smiled at him. "Water under the bridge." It really wasn't but Dorothy was nothing if not a peacemaker. Blowhards were one thing, but in her personal relationships, she was conflict avoidant. Dorothy and Kenneth lingered in bed while his parents went off to mass at St. Paul's Episcopal of Lansing. Another strike against Kenneth if her father ever learned that she was dating him. She could hear her father now, *Are you feckin joking me? Bad enough you're dating a Protestant but the feckin Church of England!! Get him out of here!* As if reading her mind, Kenneth snuggled in closer. "Now that you've gotten the IUD, we can start the New Year off right." He moved his hand over her breasts, slowing making his way down her stomach. She tensed up and Kenneth sensed it. She moved his hand away.

"So, you haven't forgiven me," he said.

"That's not it. I thought we agreed that we're waiting until we get married," she said.

"Then why did you have the IUD put in? We've moved in together," Kenneth said. "I thought this meant you were ready to take the next step."

"I thought I was too but I'm not," Dorothy replied, color rising in her cheeks. The very thought of the pain she felt having the Dalkon Shield inserted was enough to turn her off from sex for a lifetime. The whole experience set off a cascade of guilt and shame in her that she would never be able to explain to Kenneth. There were no words that were sufficient just overwhelming feelings and the faces of priests and nuns looming over her, fingers pointing at her and calling her horrible names. He would never understand.

Just then, they heard his parents' car pull up in front of the house. The mood passed; Kenneth rolled out of bed. "I'll go take a shower," he said with a persecuted sigh that annoyed Dorothy and confirmed that he did not, in fact, understand. She made up the bed while she waited her turn for the shower. His mother had provided plush robes for both and an assortment of his and her toiletries for them to use. She inspected the contents of her basket. Dorothy imagined this must be what it felt like to stay in a fancy hotel. She found it odd that his parents just assumed they were sleeping together. She felt she was in a lose/lose situation. No matter what choice she made she would be guilty of something. Kenneth came out of the bathroom, towel wrapped around his waist, clean shaven, beads of sweat glistening on his furrowed brow. He said, "I'll do whatever you want, Dorothy, I really will. I'm just having a hard time understanding your motives."

"I don't want to hurt you, Kenneth. If it helps, I don't understand me either."

"It's like you're a half-hearted nonconformist," he said, "You want to go up against your parents but then it's too much and you sit back down. You won't tell them we're dating but you move in with me. You don't go to church but pretend you do. We sleep in the same bed, but you won't have sex. Like, why, in God's name would you put yourself through getting an IUD if you don't intend to have sex?"

"I want to be prepared," she said. "The only thing worse than having sex before marriage is getting pregnant out of wedlock."

Kenneth chuckled dismissively. "Dorothy it's 1974, for crying out loud."

Dorothy wrapped the robe more tightly around her. She didn't much appreciate his pointing out her contradictions. His words stung even though she knew he was right. Still, how would he like it if she rattled off all his shortcomings? Criticism was familiar to her. She'd spent a lifetime fending off mean comments from parents and sisters, friends, priests, and nuns. His only child bubble would burst if he ever had to endure half the slights to his person that she'd already suffered. She had herself a good cry in the shower, then took her time getting dressed. By the time she emerged from the bathroom, he'd already gone down to have a cup of coffee with his parents.

Dorothy joined the Nelsons in the kitchen. All unpleasantness was forgotten from the night before (and this morning), thrown out like the half-eaten canapes. The Nelson home was immaculate with no evidence of the holiday party. A small buffet of baked goods, juices, and coffee was laid out in the kitchen as if by elves. Dorothy filled her plate with a luscious-looking Danish and a *pain au chocolat*. She wondered where Mrs. Nelson found the pastries, because Dorothy knew for a fact that there were no French bakeries in Lansing. If there had been, she'd have discovered them.

She was relieved that Kenneth's parents were no more interested in bringing up her altercation with Mitch Kelley than she was. Instead, Mr. Nelson went to the refrigerator and brought out a bottle of champagne. "Kenneth tells us you've moved in with him," he said to Dorothy as he poured champagne into the four crystal flutes. "I think that deserves a New Year's toast. Here's to the happiest of New Years to the two of you!" Raising her glass, Dorothy smiled but thought how differently her parents would react to such news. She'd be eating crow, not drinking champagne.

CHAPTER TWO

THOMAS PERFECT

IT'S NOT A SASH, YOU NUMBNUT!

Patients always sound worse on paper when a more senior colleague wants to get rid of them than they actually are in person. On the other hand, some patients could really test one's mettle. So, when the nurse told her she drew the short straw, Dr. Dorothy Morrissey's anxiety kicked in.

"You're being summoned," Nurse Martin said to the new psychologist. "One of our regulars is in the emergency room. He's the revolving door of the psych unit."

Dorothy turned her notes face-down on the desk. "So, you're familiar?"

"Oh, yes, but I'll let you meet him before I weigh in," Nurse Martin said. "Oh, and by the way, your mother called. She said don't forget to buy Deirdre's coat."

Dorothy rolled her eyes. "I'm so sorry, I've told her not to call here."

"Not a bother," Nurse Martin smiled. "My mother is no different."

Daylight was already fading when Dr. Morrissey made her way over to the emergency wing in St. Lawrence Hospital. Over the years, the asylum had steadily shrunk from its own building out in the country to an entire wing of the hospital to an annex of the wing attached by a sky bridge surrounding a courtyard. The nurses were whispering that more shrinkage was coming. Apparently, the orthopedics division was growing and psychiatric would lose their second floor. Regardless, all patients, including the mentally ill, had to be evaluated in the emergency room first if they entered without a previously arranged appointment. People did not schedule their psychotic breaks. The policy made the situation that much more traumatizing for both the patient and the doctor. Feeling like the only bull in the china shop only aggravated an already intense and scary experience.

Dorothy was already very familiar with the emergency room staff. When she did her pre-doctoral internship at Michigan State University, she'd escorted more than a dozen suicidal undergraduates there. The ER nurse ushered her quickly toward her future patient's intake room. A low steady buzz of misery filled the waiting room accentuated by the steady thrum of the industrial rotating mop pushed along the edges of the tile floor by an expressionless janitor accustomed to shutting out the chaos. Flu season was at its peak, crowding the ER more than usual, pallid faces with vacant eyes, people too miserable to complain about the wait, crying feverish babies in their mothers' arms, groaning frail-looking elderly, and young athletes with broken bones. An ear-piercing scream rose above the drone of illness and sterility. At the center of the storm was a young man, scantily clad in a silk robe and scrub bottoms. He was skirted away to a private room by the police who'd brought him in. Dorothy's new patient was shrieking at everyone and anyone within spitting distance. Dorothy liked to believe that every patient had something to teach her, but just now the screaming she heard made her heart pound in her chest. She was aware of the color draining from her cheeks and an ashen wary visage taken up residence. Any spiritual connection she might have imagined with this patient flew out the window, making her wonder why she wanted to do this job. This guy was out of control.

"Give me back my obi! You can't have it!" He bellowed at a nearby nurse who was holding what looked like a satin belt. He was pulling against the grips of police officers as they tried to propel him to a private room. "Stop manhandling me, you Neanderthals! I'm perfectly capable!" he said. "Sooey, sooey, sooey, sooey, sooeeeey." His voice was hoarse as if he'd been at this rant all day, yet he still drowned out the high-pitched wails of babies in pain. The kohl seeping from around his eyes looked like black tears streaking his cheeks. His long stringy hair flinging into the faces of the police officers as they shouldered him toward a room away from the other patients.

Dorothy waited at the nurses' station reviewing the police report while a nurse hooked him up to an IV sedative. She had to hit the sweet spot of evaluating him after he calmed down, but before he became too drowsy. The harried staff whispered a gamut of negative attributions about him: that peculiar fellow, that pervert, that faggot pain-in-the-ass. She turned a deaf ear to their opinions so as not to cloud her judgment, but his screeching wasn't exactly helping his case any.

"Whatever you do," the nurse informed her, "do not call what he's wearing a robe. It's a kimono. We took away his sash for safety." She started to leave, but turned back and said, "He's stronger than he looks, so be careful." At least the nurse had given him scrubs to wear. Dorothy took a deep breath. She knew well enough to heed the nurses' warning. There was no chance of giving him a fair assessment if she couldn't calm her own nerves and keep an open mind. *Patients always sound worse than they are in person.* She whispered like a mantra. She took another deep breath and went in.

"Hello," Dorothy began. "I'm Dr. Morrissey. I understand you're having a difficult day."

"That's an understatement if I've ever heard one," Thomas retorted. He had the posture of a ballroom dancer, ramrod straight, head thrown back like he was more likely auditioning for a dance role on *Lawrence Welk* than sitting in an emergency room. He swung his legs back and forth. He had the stench of someone who had not showered in days. His facial hair, patchy in places, appeared to be about three days growth, and his dirty blond, shoulder-length hair was dank and disheveled. Hands and fingernails were also dirty. Poor grooming was diagnostic, and, as Dorothy would come to learn, not at all characteristic of this young man, who valued his personal appearance above all else.

Dorothy immediately did a quick mental status assessment. Was he oriented times three, person, place, and time? She'd begin with his name.

"Can you tell me your full name?"

He rolled his eyes at her. "Here, we go again. Thomas Patrick Perfect. Or, as the tormentors from my childhood called me, Toilet Paper."

Dorothy suppressed a smile. "We can discuss that later if you'd like, but for now, do you know where you are, Thomas?"

"Yes," he responded, "of course, I do." He stretched his arms in front as if blind and seeking a door frame, so he could make his escape. "I used to be able to walk these halls with my eyes closed."

"Can you elaborate?" Dr. Morrissey asked. Something about this young man made her want to smile and with that, her anxiety walked out the door that he'd been looking for.

"I thought I was being taken to St. Lawrence Asylum, but it doesn't look the same."

"You are right, Thomas," Dorothy said, "we're in the emergency room. The hospital changed the policy. All walk-ins must be evaluated in the emergency room."

"That's a pity," Thomas replied. "I've never been so humiliated in my life," he added with an aggrieved huff.

"So, you've been to St. Lawrence Asylum before?" Dorothy asked.

"You could say I'm a regular."

"Do you know what year it is?"

"Why do I have to go through this Every. Single. Time?"

"I'm sorry, Thomas, I must ask. Do you know what year it is?"

"1974." *Sigh.*

"How about the month?" A bit of hesitation.

"I know it's cold out," he said. "Give me a minute." Pause.

"February?" So, he was oriented to person and place, and slightly less oriented to time.

"Feels more like January. See, I'm not crazy!" His kohl-rimmed eyes darted wildly about the room, and he fidgeted with a loose thread on his kimono. He sat up straight as if trying to maintain composure, but the harder he worked, the more his hands and feet became a flurry of activity. He was like a puppy on its first walk outdoors. Every sound distracted him away from the interview; he followed the comings and goings of nurses, doctors, and conversations in the hallway. He jumped when a bedpan dropped behind the closed curtain across the hall. He flinched when a nurse approached to draw blood. What was most intriguing to Dorothy, however, was his outfit. She tried not to stare, but a kimono-clad Caucasian man was an aberration even in an asylum.

"I see there is a tear in your kimono." Her instinct told her that ignoring his outfit could be detrimental to forming an alliance. "Would you like to tell me what happened?"

Thomas looked down at his clothes as if this was new information. "Well, that's a fine 'how do you do'," he said. His kimono was open in front, and he wasn't wearing a shirt beneath. He became agitated, rummaging beneath the sheet, then behind him, then reaching underneath the roll-away bed he was perched on. Dorothy put a hand up to stop him, as he was about to jump off the bed. "What happened to my obi?" he cried.

"Would that be the sash? The nurses said they had to confiscate it."

"It's not a sash. It's an obi. I need it to tie my garment," Thomas said. He shot her a look of disdain, exasperated by her ignorance. "Unless you get a thrill looking at my bare chest."

"Oh, I'm sorry, Thomas," Dorothy said. "I'll make sure they put your obi in a safe place, but, as I'm sure you remember, belts are not allowed."

"It's not a belt, you dimwit," he said. "First Mickey, now my obi."

"Mickey?" she asked.

"My dog, you numbnut. The cops took Mickey away. I've got nothing left." He covered his face with his hands.

She sought to reassure him. "Listen, Thomas," she said. "I will put your obi in my office. And I'll make sure the police take your dog home. Does that help?"

"They'll probably stick him in a kennel just like they stuck me in here," he said. "I'm holding you personally responsible."

"I'll do my best," she said. Thomas seemed satisfied for the moment.

Just then, he tugged on the IV. Dorothy was afraid he'd pull it out. "This thing itches like the dickens," he said.

"I'll tell the nurses, Thomas, but it's to help you with fluids and medication."

"I hope it's the good stuff," he said, smiling impishly.

"I'd like to ask a few questions now."

"Fire away," he said.

"Okay, can you tell me what happened?" Dorothy asked. Thomas's legs continued swinging vigorously. Though his eyes had a wild look about them, she could tell that on good days they'd be "soft," as her grandmother liked to say, which assuaged some of Dorothy's anxiety. She relaxed into the intake as she realized that though he might lash out, it wouldn't be a deliberate attempt to hurt anyone. He worked to maintain a dignified posture by propping his right arm akimbo as if posing for a magazine. Still, the strain in his face belied his effort. Thomas cocked his head as if dubious of her questions and suspicious of her interest in him. Haughtiness aside, she could see he was bursting to talk, and, sure enough, the words suddenly overflowed like champagne from a freshly corked bottle.

He turned his head toward the ceiling and placing his hand alongside his mouth like a farmer calling his animals, he shouted like he'd done earlier, "Sooey, sooey, sooey, sooeeey!"

What on earth? Dorothy thought.

"The pigs," Thomas responded to her confused face in answer to the question she did not ask. "Out in the hall, the police. Do you live in a cave? I was arrested and sent here for public urination and indecent exposure. Those Neanderthals ripped my kimono when they tried to take me into custody." He nodded toward the hallway, where the police officers flirted with the nurses while they waited in case the patient acted up again. "I tried to explain that it was all a misunderstanding, but they were itching to lock one of us up. Of course, they'd choose me since I'm the most prominent member of our group. And somebody confiscated my obi. Do I look like I'm a danger to myself?" He asked, incredulous, but not waiting for an answer.

Dorothy quickly jotted notes on her intake checklist: *Affect—inappropriate e.g. name-calling. Agitated and Anxious—eyes skirting about, pulling at his clothes and skin, Mood—changeable, petulant then somber, laughing then crying. Grooming—Unkempt, hasn't showered. Wearing a kimono. Mud caked hands and feet. Very concerned about obi. Significant Symptoms—pressured speech, impulsivity, inflated self-esteem.*

Yes, you do, Dorothy thought. She stopped him. "I'm confused, where did all this happen? What do you mean by 'prominent member'? Of what group? And how did they rip your kimono?" She was curious about how he viewed himself. She was listening for more signs of grandiosity a symptom of manic depression.

"Hold your horses! I was about to get to that," Thomas replied, batting away her questions with an urgency that suggested she had better keep up. "I was at home. My roommates and I are all of the same bent if you know what I mean."

Dorothy shrugged slightly, prompting him to elaborate.

"You know, homosexuals with distinct tastes for feminine attire," he went on. "We rent a large house on Shiawassee not far from Lansing Community College, but the neighborhood has experienced some blight, and is full of miscreants and ne'er-do-wells. A proper young woman such as you would never venture to our neck of the woods. We're the most upstanding citizens in the neighborhood, I assure you. All kinds of vagrants sleeping on benches and urinating in alleyways, but the police bother with me?" Thomas huffed with indignation.

"Any whoooo," he said, stretching out the vowel sound for emphasis, "we have two pit bulls, Mickey and Miles. You need good guard dogs in our neighborhood. They're great big lovable pooches, but they scare away prying eyes and fingers from our front door. You can take Mickey home with you if you want. One needs protection."

"No thank you," Dorothy said.

"What? No thank you, what?"

"You just offered me your dog."

"I did not. Where was I?"

"You were telling me about your roommates."

"Oh, yes. Believe you me. We do not deliberately draw attention to ourselves. Inside the house is another matter. There are all kinds of shenanigans and rigmarole. We like to call ourselves the bare-assed boys."

Dorothy raised an eyebrow, which, to her surprise, Thomas noticed.

"Oh, don't be so uptight. It's all in good fun. Bare-assed boys, bare-assed boys, bare-assed boys," he grinned in a cross between impish and demonic. "On the morning in question…"

"Earlier this morning?" Dorothy interjected.

"Was it? Seems like a lifetime ago, but if you continue to interrupt me, how will I ever finish my story? Where was I?"

"You mentioned something about bare-asses," Dorothy prompted.

"Oh yes, I was indeed bare-assed. I don't know where these came from," Thomas said, pointing to the blue scrub bottoms. "I was in bed when suddenly Mickey barked in his way that means only one thing. He was either going to shit or vomit. I don't have the stomach for either, so I jumped up in a hurry and grabbed his leash. He was chomping at the bit, but we don't have a fenced yard. If I'd had more time, I'd have been fully clothed. Scouts' honor," he said, holding up two fingers and placing them over his heart. "I must apologize for my appearance. This," he said, his hand gesturing over his form, "is not proper kimono attire."

"Oh," Dorothy began.

"Do you mind?" Thomas admonished her. "I need to explain! He yanked me down the stairs and out the door off of the kitchen. I had just enough time to unlock the deadbolt, but I must have forgotten to unlock the doorknob. He pulled away and ran, but the door caught on the obi and sleeve of my kimono, and I was stuck. Mickey ran off. My roommates were passed out upstairs as I would have been had Mickey not woken me up. I was pounding on the door, but no one heard me. I had to pee like the dickens. I couldn't hold it any longer, so when the cops came by with the dog, there I was, in all my glory, peeing on the driveway. If I had been a buck-naked straight guy with his tattered terry cloth robe stuck in the door, I sure as hell wouldn't be sitting here right now. You know, in a slap on the back, 'Is this your dog, Sir?' kind of way. I heard one of the officers say 'faggot' when they walked up with my dog. I don't suppose they wrote that in their report. I'll admit I went a little ballistic when one of the officers said, 'What are you doing out here jacking off?' I slapped him," he said coyly. "I even surprised myself. Truth be told, it was no more than a pat on the cheek—nothing like what I used to get from my father."

Take a breath, Dorothy thought. More evidence of pressured speech and impaired judgment she mentally noted.

"There was not much I could say after that. The cops ripped my kimono as they dragged me away, and it's my favorite one too. Somehow, I ended up here instead of taken to jail. Evidently, a cross-dressing homosexual is considered a mental illness. I don't know what they did with Mickey," he said. His eyes became glassy and full of water. He smudged the delicate skin beneath his eye with a dirty hand.

"Don't worry, Thomas, like I said, I'll make sure Mickey gets home safely."

"There you go again, trying to take my dog!"

Thomas looked about the room, furrowing his brow, suddenly distracted, looking about the evaluation room. He took a deep breath, shook his hair out of his eyes.

"What are you trying to do here—freeze your patients to death?"

"You're right about that, it's cold in here." Sterility and cold went hand in hand.

"I'm right about a lot of things. What happened to Dr. Malpet?"

"He moved to Pittsburgh. There's a blanket there if you want it."

"I'm fine. Aren't you a bit young to be a doctor?"

"I'm old enough..."

"Hells bells, you like to interrupt. In any event, I didn't like Malpet. That's why I left. He wasn't helping me. Do you know what I could do with this space? Give me a couple of hours and a few dollars to spend, and voilà, this place will shine! May I have a glass of water? I'm parched!"

"Certainly," Dorothy replied. Her head was swimming.

Keeping up with Thomas was tricky. His face and frame were ravaged by the effect of significant weight loss and his manic state made him look much older than he was. He'd likely not eaten in days. His symptoms could as easily be the effects of drugs and alcohol. Amphetamines and alcohol abuse could trigger a psychotic episode. Regardless, Thomas needed to stabilize before he would be lucid enough to provide a more definitive history. In his current state, he was the only person who believed his behavior was within the bounds of normalcy. Although, normalcy was an overrated and a moving target to Dorothy's mind.

She got up to pour him a glass of water and used the opportunity to introduce what she read from the intake file.

"Just to clarify, the police report says that your roommates called the police." The flash of distress that crossed his face told her to proceed with caution as she did not want to upset him further. "There seems to be some disagreement about the Bare-assed Boys. There was a suggestion that perhaps you took what began as a joke too far?"

Thomas's face turned from hurt to petulant. He snorted. "I can only imagine that Seth started that ball rolling," he said. "I took it too far, my word! He's just jealous because I slept with Don. Don is gorgeous! I mean, Cybil Shepherd-gorgeous. He's not so pretty when he's angry though, like when he found me with our friend Jorge. Before I know it, they're all talking behind my back." Petulance turned to confusion. "Where's my obi?" He said pulling at his chin with his thumb and forefinger, as if doing so would help him remember. Dorothy made another notation—*symptom promiscuity.*

"As I said, Thomas, the nurses put it away for safekeeping," Dorothy said.

"Those Neanderthals tore my kimono when they put me in the cuffs and dragged me away," he said again.

Dorothy wondered if the sedative or psychosis was behind the forget-fulness and repetition. According to the roommates, over the course of a week or so, Thomas's behavior had become increasingly erratic, ending with a bender of amphetamines and alcohol. His roommates locked him out of the house and called the police, which they insisted was a last resort. The police officers said he resisted arrest, confirming his account of slapping a law enforcement officer. They didn't call him any names in her presence but that didn't mean they hadn't. When they could not subdue him, they brought him to St. Lawrence's ER. A few days in the asylum would allow time to rule out a substance-induced mania before making a definitive diagnosis of manic depression.

"Are you currently taking any medications?" Dorothy asked. Manic episodes could be triggered by anti-depressant medication in the case of a misdiagnosis. Due diligence required she be thorough. A quick scan of his chart revealed his last hospitalization was due to an altercation as well and had been a long one. A history of altercations resulting in hospitalization was indeed diagnostic but didn't mean he instigated. She'd learned early on that the mentally ill were often the victims of violence. His history suggested similar treatment at the hands of "sane people."

Thomas batted Dorothy's question away. "That stuff was awful. Did I tell you I was born in Japan?"

Hence the kimono, Dorothy thought. Nothing about Thomas suggested Japanese ancestry with his height, dirty-blond hair, and hazel eyes. But she knew better than to challenge him on that point just now. "You hadn't mentioned it," she said.

"My mother said we're related to royalty on her side," he continued. Dorothy skimmed the notes in his folder for any useful history. "If you'd listened," he chastised, as if she'd contradicted him, "I'm not a liar. I said I was born in Japan, and I was," he muttered inaudibly as if he'd decided she wasn't worth the time of day.

"I just have a few more questions, Thomas," Dorothy said.

"As you wish," he said, straightening his kimono with a loving pat.

"You mentioned Dr. Malpet? Was he your therapist during your last hospitalization?"

"Yes," Thomas replied.

"Do you remember what medication he prescribed?"

"Yes, Thora-something."

"Thorazine?"

"Bingo."

"And he believed you were ready to be discharged?"

"Not exactly," Thomas said. "He was going to do that shocky-thing torture therapy. I decided that I was tired of being here."

"Electroconvulsive therapy?"

"That's the one." He yawned loudly and stared at the door leading out of the room like a well-trained puppy hinting to its owner that it needed to go out. "Are we done?" he asked, yawning markedly again.

"Of course, Thomas," she said, "I just have one more question."

"Shoot."

"Are you now or have you recently felt suicidal?"

"Suicidal Ideation—been there, done that, don't want to do it again." He said with a mocking tone.

"Meaning?"

"Meaning this isn't my first rodeo. I'm not suicidal."

"Thank you, Thomas, but I would like you to stay for observation. We'll get you settled over in the asylum."

"Oh, all right," Thomas said with a sigh. He flounced dramatically and rolled his eyes. "I don't suppose the food has gotten any better?"

"I doubt it," Dorothy said with a smile.

Once Thomas was safely transferred to his room in the asylum, Dorothy went to her office and reviewed his file. Dr. Malpet had, as Thomas reported, prescribed Thorazine. He had not diagnosed Thomas with manic-depression and made no mention of manic-depressive episodes. Dorothy began a new page for Thomas's file, writing out a clinical note in a neat script.

2/8/74 *Emergency intake for Thomas Perfect. DOB -/-/48 Patient presented as oriented X 3 with prompting, poor hygiene, lack of self-control, agitation, and exhibited symptoms of mania, drug-induced psychosis, and lack of insight. Speech was pressured and multiple loose associations. Roommates report erratic behavior, sleeplessness (at least three days), angry outbursts, all of which, TP endorsed. Past history of depression, drug, and alcohol abuse. Prior hospitalization prescribed Thorazine and referred for ECT. Discharged self against medical advisement. Rule out organic psychosis. A diagnosis of manic depression requires further evaluation once the patient has detoxed. Investigate family history. Denied SI.*

✦

The next morning, Dorothy went to see how Thomas had gotten through the night. He sat up slowly when she entered his room. Evidently, the sedative had done its work. His agitation had subsided.

"Good morning, Thomas," she said.

"Who might you be?" He looked at her suspiciously. "Are you here to clean the bathroom?"

She smiled at him. "I'm Dr. Morrissey. We met last night in the ER."

"Ah, yes, it's coming back to me now. You're the new Malpet. You look too young to be a doctor, me thinks. And you smell like chlorine. That's why I thought you were planning to clean the bathroom."

"Funny you should mention that," Dorothy said, "I hate the smell of Clorox but oddly enough, I've never associated that with chlorine from the pool."

"Well, maybe you should." He picked at his cuticles. As the grogginess wore off, his agitation would return. "Why am I here?"

"There was an incident yesterday. The police brought you in."

"Where's Mickey?" he shouted. He sat up straight, a look of panic on his face.

"He's back at home, safe and sound."

"That's where I should be."

"Do you mind if I just ask a couple of questions?"

"Again?"

"So, you do remember me?"

He returned her smile with an impish grin.

"I want to formulate the best treatment plan possible for you."

"You need me for that?" Thomas wasn't going to make it easy on her.

"Yes, I just need a bit of information about your history. Then we can get you settled and off to breakfast."

"I could write a book on psychiatric intakes," he said, throwing his head back. "I'll call it, *Beating a Dead Horse by Toilet Paper.*"

Dorothy tried her best to not laugh out loud but he was funny. "Besides your roommates, do you have any other connections in Lansing?" she said, keeping a serious look on her face.

"Like what?"

"Work, for instance?"

"That would be two jobs. I work at Spencer Gifts and JoAnn Fabrics. Between them, I can five-finger discount my way to stardom!"

Dorothy raised an eyebrow. That was a quick shift in mood by any standards.

"I'm joking, don't get your panties in a bunch."

"You may have to call in sick for a while," Dorothy said. "How about a family?"

He stared at her blankly.

"Parents or siblings live in Lansing?" she asked.

"My parents moved back up north to Alpena," Thomas said.

"Oh, did they retire there?"

"You could say that. They grew up there—high school sweethearts. After my dad got out of jail, they went back."

"And why was he in jail?" Dorothy asked.

"He was involved in a hit-and-run while driving under the influence. Third time's the charm. That was the last straw for JW."

"My goodness," Dorothy said. "And who is JW?"

"My brother, John Wayne Perfect."

"So, you have a brother in Lansing?"

"If you'd let me finish," Thomas responded testily. "I *had* a brother here. Now I don't. He left after Dad's DUI, on JW's eighteenth birthday no less. Haven't seen him since. Dad had a way of destroying everything, especially birthdays. Can I wash my hands? They didn't even let me shower last night. I'm filthy."

"Sure," Dorothy said. Thomas eased off the bed and went to the tiny sink. He scrubbed every bit of dirt off with the small bar of soap. Then he slowly made his way back to the bed. He leveled his eyes at her with irritation. She was touching upon sensitive subjects. Once he was stabilized, they could explore the family dynamics in more detail, but she hoped to get a bit of information about parents and siblings.

"Do you mean JW left for college?" Dorothy knew it was a stretch but wondered if Thomas was exaggerating.

"No, I mean, HE UP and LEFT. He went to Hollywood. Gonna be a big star," he said sarcastically. "We never heard from him again," he said, abruptly standing. He started to pace and blew the air out his nose in a short burst of frustration. He eyed the door as if he was going to make a run for it.

"Thank you, Thomas, for clarifying for me," Dorothy responded, trying to maintain her composure. "I didn't mean to upset you." Though outbursts were common, she never got used to them. "Can you sit? I'll try to finish up here soon. How old were you when this happened?"

He reluctantly settled into a seated position. He was still agitated but unlike last night his feet did not swing back and forth. "I was sixteen."

"What happened after JW left?"

Thomas's eyes skittered about the room, and Dorothy noted trembling in his hands. "My father went to state prison in Jackson, and my mother went to her bed. Can we stop talking about this? I could really use a shower."

"Sure, thank you, Thomas. We can talk more later." She turned to leave.

"Dr. Morrissey?"

"Yes, Thomas."

"Dr. Malpet never asked me about my family." He looked away, hands shaking as if he were nervous or in withdrawal. Dorothy hoped she hadn't overstepped.

CHAPTER THREE

THE MORRISSEYS

"You're late, Dottie." Her sister Deirdre was standing, hands on hips, in the foyer when Dorothy walked through the door, drawn in by the aromas of Sunday dinner and the promise of warmth to thaw her nose and fingers from the bitter February winds. Too bad nothing could warm the frosty reception.

"I know, Deirdre," Dorothy mimicked Deirdre's tone of disgust. Dorothy had driven around the block five times before finding a parking space. Her parents' driveway was already filled with cars at the two-story red brick on Richter Street in Detroit. She'd dutifully made the drive every Sunday from Lansing. Richter was always full of cars, and parking ever a hassle. Once the middle of the Irish Ghetto, Richter Street was dubbed *Catholic Alley* during Dorothy's childhood with the addition of Italian, Polish, and German Catholics. St. Ambrose Church flanked Richter Street on one end and the Convent for the Sisters of St. Joseph on the other, with a dozen or so large Catholic families in between. All of Dorothy's childhood friends lived a stone's throw from her front porch and were from big families. The Morrissey family of nine children was small by comparison. Her best friend, MaryAnne lived across the street and was one of ten. The Cusacks also had ten kids. On the other side, the Fatas had twelve. One family, the McCabes, had eighteen children. Even other devout Catholics thought that was going too far. Dorothy was the fourth of seven girls roughly fifteen months apart. After the seven girls, by the look of it, her parents were done. They'd be the smallest family on the block, but still respectable by Catholic standards. Then her mother had twin boys, Aiden and Declan, just before Dorothy's twelfth birthday. With the "little miracles," her father's dream for sons was fulfilled, though at a very high cost. They'd probably not been born at all had the oldest girl, Tess, not died.

Breathless from rushing up the street in the cold February air, she'd slowed her pace as she climbed the steps to the family home. A sense of dread, and Deirdre's scowling face, arrested Dorothy's momentum at the door. Her nose was trying to steer her toward the kitchen, seeking the warm familiarity of her mother's roast. Sunday dinner was a command performance if you were within a 200-mile radius of home, a tradition both loved and loathed by Dorothy as nothing could ruin an appetite like the running commentary on your life by your family. Dorothy brushed the snow off her camel hair, part of her shopping spree after her first paycheck as a psychologist.

"Did you buy my coat like Mom said?" Her request sounded more like an accusation. Dorothy handed the shopping bag over to Deirdre before giving the Brigid's Cross a pat over the front hall closet where she'd tucked her camel hair, pocketbook, and gloves. She would have sent up a prayer for protection but clearly St. Brigid had already failed her.

"How could I forget? Mom called me three times at work to remind me."

"Better be the right size," Deirdre said, always one to look a gift horse in the mouth.

"Go try it on," Dorothy said to Deirdre's back since Deirdre had already pulled the winter coat from the bag and was heading toward the kitchen.

Dorothy followed her older sister down the hall. *So much for avoiding the piles of shit,* she thought. Those were Kenneth's parting words as she walked out of their apartment in Lansing without him again.

As she'd gotten ready, he'd said, "You don't have to go."

"I'll never hear the end of it if I don't," she replied. As it was, she'd already called home and lied about going to the eleven o'clock mass instead of the nine-thirty morning mass. Dorothy hadn't lived at home in almost ten years, yet she still woke on Sundays to the phantom stomping of her mother's feet. Her mother wore her piety around her shoulders like the fur coat draped over them every Sunday morning when she stood clad in nightgown, slippers, and fur coat, stomping her feet until all nine Morrisseys, and now some of their spouses, lined up to head out the door to Sunday mass at St. Ambrose Catholic Church. Just the thought made Dorothy glad she lived in Lansing. As her family trailed down the street, Mrs. Morrissey went back to bed, said fur draped over the loose bloated torso, secure in her ability to lord over her children and earn her hard-won place in heaven. The rules didn't apply to her as long as her children went to Sunday mass. Dorothy no longer went to mass either, but not without fear of being found out. Kenneth didn't understand the pressure she was under. His parents showered him, their only child, with unconditional love like it was going out of style. Nothing was required of him but to do what made him happy.

"I can go with you," he'd offered, though he knew what she'd say.

"Maybe next time," she'd said, which they both knew was an empty promise. "You know what I would love to do?"

"What's that?"

"Ice skate on the Red Cedar like we did when we first met."

"It's cold enough. Let's go next weekend if you can break away from your family."

"We'll go on Saturday," she had said, giving Kenneth a kiss before heading out.

✦

She walked past the parlor, where a Detroit Red Wings game blared on the television, toward the kitchen. Her father, younger brothers, and Sheila's husband sat glued there, ignoring the goings-on around the kitchen and dining room. The boys knew they didn't have to get up until their father stood to head to the table. *I'm not that late,* she thought.

Dorothy walked into the dining room where younger sisters, Norah and Nell, were already piling heaping platters of comfort foods: roast pork shoulder, mashed potatoes, buttered carrots, cooked red cabbage, and applesauce. Dorothy made her way around the massive mahogany table, navigating around Deirdre, to kiss her grandmother. "Hello, darlin'," her grandmother greeted her with a soft pat on the cheek. "Sit here next to me."

"You're late, Dottie," Dorothy's mother scolded by way of greeting, coming in from the kitchen with a bowl of homemade applesauce in one hand and the newspaper in the other. She still wore her apron, which meant dinner was not yet served. She reached across the table to hand Dorothy *the Detroit Free Press* opened to the *Pre-Cana* announcements.

"What's this?" Dorothy asked.

"If you'd been here earlier, you'd already know," Deirdre took up where her mother left off. "Taking your good, sweet time, as usual."

"It's a two-hour drive."

"You just don't want to help with dinner." She was busy unbuttoning the coat with her back to their mother.

"I don't see you helping, Deirdre," Dorothy said dismissively.

"Leave Deirdre alone, Dorothy. She's got all she can do, managing her Lupus. You know how tired she gets," her mother scolded. To Dorothy, Deirdre looked frantic to get the coat on. *What's that about?* she wondered, regarding her sister's harried efforts. Her interest piqued.

"If it weren't for the Lupus, I'd be a medical doctor, not some fake doctor like you," Deirdre said, still with her back to their mother, shoving her arms inside the sleeves, patting the front into place, trembling fingers working the buttons.

"You barely got through high school," Dorothy said. She couldn't help herself. She was so tired of Deirdre's comments. Deirdre pulled the fur-lined hood over her head, missing the eye-roll shared between

Dorothy and Sheila, who nursed her one-year-old. Sheila looked ready to burst with her second baby. Next in line after Deirdre, Sheila and Dorothy had tired long ago of the special treatment she received from their mother. Dorothy suspected her mother was over-compensating. Once Deirdre had the gray wool fully buttoned (Dorothy was relieved that she'd chosen the perfect size), she slowly turned toward their mother, her face filled with such expectation that Dorothy's retort stuck in her throat. She noticed that Sheila also saw Deirdre's desperate need for a "*You look beautiful*" from their mother. They shared a rare moment of sympathy for their older sister. God, hadn't she learned by now that their mother rationed compliments like there was a national shortage? Time stood still as even Grandma Morrissey seemed to hold her breath as she watched her oblivious daughter-in-law miss the moment. Younger sister, Louise, and her fiancé, Mike, absorbed in a world of French kissing, missed it all. Newly engaged, they whispered sweet nothings between kisses as if they'd invented love. Once Louise was married, Deirdre and Dorothy would be the only Morrissey girls still single.

Their preoccupied mother gave Deirdre a quick scan which also encompassed the dining room table. "Fits perfectly. Did you thank your sister for picking it up?" she said, removing her apron. The omission of the desired "*You look pretty*" recalled for Dorothy what the oldest Tess had written in her journal ages ago—*Deirdre the sorrowful*. Discombobulated by an unexpected wave of sadness for her sister, she plopped down next to her grandmother. She dropped the newspaper on the table.

"Leslie Anders is getting married in June," Norah and Nell said, coming from behind their mother, one with the water pitcher, the other with the gravy boat. Nell nodded toward the newspaper.

Louise took her mouth off Mike's for a moment and said, "She had a Valentine's Day Engagement party. Isn't that romantic? At the Detroit Yacht Club, no less. I bet the wedding will be dreamy. We decided to have a Christmas wedding." Mike grinned his agreement.

The mere mention of Leslie Ander's name had the potential to ruin Dorothy's appetite. She was not about to let that happen, so she quickly redirected the conversation by noting the absence of Norah and Nell's husbands. "Where are your husbands?" she asked. She stored the newspaper under her seat without looking at it.

"Ice fishing," Deirdre said, derisively. "We're not waiting for them," she said, giving her married sisters the evil eye.

"Why aren't you in the wedding party, Dottie?" Mrs. Morrissey asked. Before she could answer, her mother yelled above the cheers emanating from the parlor. "Dinner!" Then turned to Deirdre. "Go hang up your coat now." A collective groan issued from the men as the competing desires of food and sports played out just as the Red Wings scored a goal. The boys rushed in, shoving aside their sisters to fill their plates. Dorothy's father followed.

"No one takes a bite until your mother sits down," he roared, although Dorothy sensed his eagerness to get started on the meal, so he could get back to the game. The boys put their forks down. Finally, their mother sans apron took her place between her husband and Deirdre. "Dottie, you can say grace," he said, bowing his head.

"Bless us O, Lord, and these thy gifts, which we are about to receive from thy bounty through Christ our Lord, Amen," Dorothy trailed off, as the others took up the prayer, ending with, "May her soul and all the souls of the faithfully departed through the mercy of God, rest in peace." Every Sunday, this was the one and only way Tess's life and death were acknowledged.

If Dorothy thought her mother would forget about Leslie Anders, she was sorely mistaken. "So, Dorothy, all your friends are in the wedding party," Mrs. Morrissey said. "Why aren't you?"

"I doubt I'll even be invited to the wedding," Dorothy responded.

"What do you mean, not invited?" Dorothy's mother said now over the clattering of knives and forks.

"Leslie and I have never been friends."

"Did you see she's marrying a doctor?" Mrs. Morrissey asked.

"Not just any doctor," Norah gushed.

"He's the doctor for the *Detroit Tigers*!" Nell added.

"I heard he's a Protestant," Louise said.

Dorothy felt annoyed that all her sisters had to weigh in. Norah was fifteen months younger than Louise, who was fifteen months younger than Dorothy, Nell was only ten months younger than Norah, so they were called Irish twins. Hence, the competition for their mother's love and attention was fierce among the girls. Only the boys, born four years after Tess's death, could feel confident of their parents' affections. They lapped up the lion's share of their mother's love and their father's hopes and dreams for the future like the gravy they poured all over their mashed potatoes.

Their father took a long swallow of his scotch. "None of my girls will marry a feckin WASP. I don't care what he does for a living."

"Oh, I didn't know he was a Protestant," Mrs. Morrissey said, frowning. "Well, I'm sure they'll be able to afford a divorce when the time comes."

"Far be it from me to defend Leslie Anders, Dad, but what is so wrong with marrying a Protestant?" Dorothy asked, against her better judgment, compelled to test the waters for the unlikely chance she could introduce Kenneth to the family.

"How does a supposed doctor like you not have a better grasp of her history? Do you not remember The Potato Famine? The Protestants forced the starving Irish Catholics to convert before they'd give them the shite they called soup." Dorothy's siblings glared at her for getting him started. "This after stealing Ireland's bounty for themselves. They raped the country! Raped, I tell you!" He shoved a piece of potato in his mouth as if to emphasize his point. "Does that answer your question?" John Patrick Morrissey was a working-class factory lineman at Ford Motor. He was a first-generation Irish-American. Besides his Irish heritage, taking care of his family was all that mattered to him. He identified with his role as a provider in every sense of the word. His only tasks were to feed his growing family and keep them safe. If he worked hard and prayed harder, he would be rewarded. God had already failed him by taking his oldest and most beloved daughter to be with Him in heaven. The least the Good Lord could do was make sure the rest of his daughters marry good Catholic boys and not ask for money. Oh, and he hated Protestants.

"He's got you there, darlin'," her grandmother said, patting Dorothy's hand. Dorothy stared at her plate and sighed. Kenneth would not be meeting her father anytime soon.

"Why did you have to upset your father, Dottie?" Mrs. Morrissey said. "Did you get enough roast, Dear?" she asked, turning to her husband. Mr. Morrissey nodded his mouth full.

"Stop chewing with your mouths open," Deirdre said to the boys.

Declan opened his mouth to reveal chewed-up pot roast. "You're not my mother," he said.

"Disgusting," Deirdre said.

Both boys laughed.

"Then don't look," Aidan said.

"Do as she says," her mother said. She turned her attention back to Dorothy. "Why can't you find yourself a nice Catholic doctor?"

"I don't need to, Mother, I am a doctor."

"Not a real one."

"That's for sure," Deirdre said, a look of triumph on her face. "Dorothy's not smart enough to be a real doctor."

"Not like you, Dear." Mrs. Morrissey patted Deirdre's hand.

"How many times do I have to tell you, Mother? I might not be a medical doctor, but I am a doctor, nonetheless. I have a doctorate in psychology. Everyone at the hospital calls me Dr. Morrissey."

"Well, you'll always be Dottie to us," her mother said.

Now it was her father's turn. "I don't understand all this psychology crap. Whatever happened to getting down on your knees and praying when you have a problem?"

If that worked, maybe we'd be able to talk about Tess without you getting up and leaving the room, Dorothy thought but did not say.

"I work with the mentally ill. Sometimes, praying is not enough. I've explained this to you a million times."

As always, Deirdre had to put in her two cents worth. "I don't get why anybody would want to work in an Insane Asylum."

"It's called St. Lawrence Asylum. Where else should people go who need long-term care?" Deirdre wasn't listening, having had her say, but Dorothy pressed on. "Asylums are closing all over the country, and the mentally ill are abandoned to the streets. It's a sin. With all the funding cuts, we've gone from a stand-alone institution to a wing of the hospital." She looked around the table. Everyone but her grandmother had already tuned her out. Louise was whispering in her fiancé's ear. Sheila was now nursing her two-year-old who'd just woken up from a nap. The boys were punching each other. Nell and Norah whispered an inside joke. And her father was contemplating the bottom of his empty glass.

"Jesus, Mary, and Joseph, Deirdre's right. Why would you want to go and work in an asylum with all those crazy people?" her mother said.

"You know," Grandma Morrissey added, "in Ireland, we don't call these places where you work asylums. We call them Homes for the Bewildered."

"Really?" Dorothy responded. "Why is that?"

"Because aren't we all just?" Grandma Morrissey said as if that was all the explanation needed.

"Move back home, Dottie," Dorothy's mother said, ignoring the wisdom just dispensed. "I'll set you up with Mary Flannigan's son, Rory. You should be settling down and having a family of your own. You're wasting your life."

"You'll never find a man dressed like that," Norah said.

"What are you talking about?" Dorothy said. "I like how I dress."

"For the 1950s," Nell said. Nell always held the same opinion as Norah.

Dorothy did appreciate the vintage styles that had an air of 1950s Hollywood glamour. The only shocking thing about her tastes now was that she'd abhorred hand-me-downs growing up. Even with her mother's liberal use of Clorox, she could never fully remove the armpit stains from Deidre's blouses, which inevitably found their way to

Dorothy. She liked her clothes and loved dressing with the seasons. Her sisters Louise, Norah and Nell, wore much shorter skirts, and long hair, straight and parted down the middle. Sheila went with the floor-length, loose-flowing peasant styles preferred by the hippies. Deirdre wore overalls no matter the season and always had her hair in thin pigtails, which made not washing her hair easier to get away with. Dorothy cultivated a style all her own wearing vintage dresses and her hair in a bob of loose curls.

"I wouldn't be caught dead in a mini-skirt," she said to the Irish twins.

"Why not?" Norah and Nell asked.

"Jinx," Nell said, punching Norah playfully in the arm.

"They're unprofessional," Dorothy said. "Besides, someone I know and love laughed at my thick calves," she said pointedly at Norah. "I'd look awful in a miniskirt, and they make a mockery of trying to sit down let alone picking up a dropped pencil." As far as she was concerned, the mid-calf fifties styles struck the right note between feminine and professional. It didn't hurt that her grandmother had given her many of her favorite dresses. Lucky for her she was the only one of her sisters who was the same size.

"Well, you look like an old lady," Nell said.

"For crying out loud, get off her," Grandma Morrissey chided the rest of them. "You're a brave girl," she said, turning to Dorothy. "You get your gumption from me," she said, taking a sip of her sherry. "How do you think I got here in the first place?" She looked pointedly at her daughter-in-law. "When I left my home and family to get on a ship to this place I'd never been before, feckin scared the dickens out of me. I worked years as a domestic before I met your grandfather. God rest his soul," she said, making the sign of the cross. Dorothy's mother sighed audibly. They'd heard the story a million times, but Dorothy was grateful that her grandmother took her side.

"I can't imagine," Dorothy said. She was about to say more, but out of the corner of her eye, she saw that her mother patted Deirdre's hand again in a soothing manner.

"No one's bravery holds a candle to Deirdre's," her mother said. "Facing her illness with such courage."

That was the last straw for Dorothy. Her mother had managed to insult three people with one sentence. Deirdre didn't want to be brave, she wanted to be pretty. As much as Dorothy disliked Deirdre, she still felt sorry for her. Tess, dead now more than twenty years, was the pretty one and the artist, so being either was off-limits to the other Morrissey girls. Just like Dorothy's smarts would never be acknowledged because somehow in her mother's mixed-up calculations, Deirdre was the smart, and now brave, one. An audible sigh escaped her (which she hated because she knew this made her like her mother) as she stood to clear her dish, tucking the newspaper under her arm. Tomorrow would be soon enough to indulge her curiosity. She kissed her grandmother on the head. Dorothy had had enough of the conversation. As she set about clearing the table, she thought how "Homes for the Bewildered" resonated deeply with her view of her calling as a psychologist. At least, her grandmother understood. From then on, St. Lawrence Home for the Bewildered it would be, if only for her benefit. There was civility in the term that was missing from the cultural connotation of asylums as places where you locked up "crazy people," and threw away the key despite asylum's meaning as a place of sanctuary. The wisdom inherent in the Irish phrase was that one tragedy could be the difference between the patient in the Home for the Bewildered and the person on the street or even their therapist for that matter.

After clearing the table, Dorothy washed the dishes while Norah and Nell made tea and took out the cherry pie and dessert plates. Doing the dishes had always served as an escape for her, an acceptable way to avoid just such unpleasant conversations as she'd just experienced. When she was finished cleaning up, she went and grabbed her coat and boots from the closet. She popped her head into the dining room. "I need to get going," she said to no one in particular.

"You're not staying for dessert?" her mother asked. "It's your favorite."

"I've got a long drive," Dorothy said as she turned away. She still had to face round two when she returned to Lansing, where Kenneth would be waiting in their apartment, hurt that she hadn't brought him with her. Her lovely, innocent, optimistic, only child, Protestant boyfriend—how could he ever understand?

Mrs. Morrissey practically tackled her daughter as Dorothy reached for the doorknob. "Dottie, take a piece of pie with you," she said. "And, here, take this scarf. You'll catch your death of cold."

CHAPTER FOUR

GEORGE EAVEY
NOT GUILTY BY REASON OF INSANITY

"I've never met a woman doctor before," George's mother, Helen Eavey, said to Dorothy. She wore a hip-length, peach-colored wool flared coat over a paisley dress and navy cardigan. The incongruent pink signature of Bonnie Bell, likely borrowed from a daughter, shone noticeably on her lips. She removed galoshes from over low heels and left them at the entrance to Dorothy's office. The overall effect was dowdy made worse by swollen ankles and a plump midsection. She reminded Dorothy of her own mother. "You must be very smart." Dorothy guided Mrs. Eavey and George to the loveseat across from her chair.

"It's 1974, Mom," George said. "There are lots of women doctors."

"There were a lot of hurdles," Dorothy said, aware that she was teetering on a fine line between George and his mother. George was never forthcoming. His mother could fill in the blanks. She hoped to help Mrs. Eavey feel comfortable, so she would open up without pushing George further into his protective shell. Dorothy could feel in the sudden weight on her chest the strain created by this mother's incessant approach to the son's avoidance, her chasing his hiding. Her story hopelessly entwined with his like the rubber band ball in Dorothy's junk drawer. There was no way to tease it apart. His defensive retreat punishing to her. The weight of the words not being spoken suffocating until the burden shared and visible in Mrs. Eavey's hunched shoulders, tears threatening to spill, and a jaw that clicked when she brushed her teeth. Years of this had aged his mother prematurely. Of that fact, he was unaware. *I'm never having kids,* Dorothy thought.

"Is this your office?" Mrs. Eavey said, looking about. "You could probably use some plants."

"Jesus, Ma," George said.

"I'm sorry. I don't mean to insult you," Mrs. Eavey said. "Plants brighten up dull spaces is all."

"So I've been told," Dorothy said. "No need to apologize." She recognized a woman raised to apologize from the time she could toddle, she wanted to tell this mother; don't ever apologize again. "Can I get you some coffee or a glass of water?"

"No, thanks."

"Well, how can I help?" Dorothy asked. "I understand you have some concerns about George?"

"I had a dream about Georgie last night," Mrs. Eavey said. She perched awkwardly on the edge of the loveseat. Then pulled at a loose thread on her sweater. Patches of red mottled her neck and moved up her cheeks in case Dorothy missed just how nervous she felt. "I worry that George isn't representing himself in the best light. If he had been, wouldn't you have released him by now?"

George sat impassively, resigned to his fate, staring straight ahead. "That's not how it works, Mom."

"Don't the patients get released for good behavior? I don't think he's trying to get out of here. It's like he's given up."

The way George unconsciously worked his bottom lip and fingered the unlit cigarette in his hand contradicted his outward resignation. In fact, his display seemed to be for his mother's benefit. A former athlete and angry to boot, his posture was usually taut, muscles tensed, hypervigilant, as if always ready to defend himself.

Mrs. Eavey reached into her purse. She pulled out a handkerchief and dabbed at her nose.

"I'm afraid George is right, Mrs. Eavey," Dorothy said. "It's really not up to me. You said you had dreamt about him last night. Would you like to share?"

Helen Eavey closed her eyes as if that would help her conjure the images from the dream more accurately. She had a soft face, Dorothy observed, a kind person, who, no doubt, had trusted in the goodness of people. At least until her son's life fell apart. *A woman after my own heart,* Dorothy thought, *bringing a dream up right away.*

Dorothy could see the resemblance between George and his mother. They both had hints of curls and streaks of copper in their chestnut hair, though hers was full of worried gray. Their cheeks stood out on their round faces, with freckles lightly smattered across the nose and the apples that inflamed when nervous or upset. Wide brown eyes were soulful, hinting at introspective natures. The major difference was the sadness marking Helen's and the bitterness marking George's. Different renderings of the shared tragedy.

"In the dream, he must have been four or five years old. I pulled him onto my lap and mussed his hair. God, I loved his hair full of curls. I couldn't bear to cut it. He was eighteen months old before he had his first haircut," she said dreamily. "His father started complaining that he looked like a girl, so I gave in. He took little George to a barbershop. Thank God, George looked even cuter with a crew cut. Where was I?"

"You were telling me about a dream," Dorothy said.

"Oh, yes, in the dream, I was sitting in my parents' kitchen. You know how that is?" she asked Dorothy. "I haven't lived in my parents' home in fifty years, yet that's the kitchen I dream about." She shook her head. "Anyway, he snuggled into my chest, enjoying the undivided attention. I could even smell the top of his head like I did when he was a child. I was reciting the rhyme, *Georgie, Porgy, Pudding, and Pie, kissed the girls and made them cry.* He would laugh and laugh. The way George's face lit up when he was a little fella made my heart sing."

Dorothy couldn't imagine anything lighting up her patient's face. She could barely coax a smile from him. Nor could she ever imagine making this mother's heart sing. Didn't he know how good he'd had it? Even when George was in a good space, he held his emotions in check. Despair and resignation had drained the light from his eyes long before Dorothy met him.

Mrs. Eavey paused, looking for the right words. Her gaze was begging the doctor to understand the delight she felt. Someone as cute as her son doesn't hurt another person for no reason. "He was so sweet. When his father tossed him in the air, he'd laugh and laugh. He adored his father. I remember his father saying to me once, 'I've never felt love like this in my life.' He was a precious child. I couldn't get enough of him. He was so damn cute." Her hand went to her mouth. "Pardon my French," she said apologetically. "Do you have children, Dr. Morrissey?"

Dorothy shook her head. "No, I'm not married." A rush of annoyance and guilt washed over her. She hated herself for finding George's mother so annoying in her love for her son. With all that love, how did he do what he did? On the other hand, she agreed with Mrs. Eavey. One didn't do what he'd done for no reason.

"Then, you can't possibly understand my joy raising him or my agony seeing him here."

Dorothy jotted a quick note. *George's mother devoted to him, bewildered over the whole situation. Certainly, no indication of abusive home life.* Dorothy wrote. She'd thought for sure he'd come from an abusive home. She hated herself for thinking like those in the psychiatric community who attributed blame for a person's mental illness to a schizophrenogenic mother especially when fault was more likely with the father.

George was staring at the floor. He shifted forward on the couch and rested his elbows on his knees, letting his mother have her say.

"How long do you plan to keep him here? He already spent two years in prison before his case came up for trial. Shouldn't that count as time served?"

"I don't think that's up to me," Dorothy responded. "That would be up to the courts. From what I hear, these cases can languish for years."

"So, there's no hope?" Mrs. Eavey asked.

"There's always hope, Mrs. Eavey," Dorothy said, "I just don't want to mislead you, and I don't want you to think it's because of something George is or isn't doing."

Helen pressed on, "We must have failed him somehow. There is no other explanation. I always thought George would make a great father. He'd have a beautiful wife and cherub-faced children with cheeks round as apples, just like his." She paused as if lost in her imaginings of how things should have been. "This was not how I pictured getting older."

George finally looked up. "You're hardly old, Mom."

"Can he take back the insanity plea?" she asked Dorothy.

"For Chrissakes, Mom. It'll be a cold day in hell before they let me out of here. You've got to give it up."

"I guess you're right. Beating up our parish priest like that and all."

"I don't know," Dorothy said. "The next time his case comes up, I will be sure to express my confidence that he will be able to make a positive contribution to society."

George looked at his mother. "We agree on one thing. I shouldn't have pleaded NGRI. I'd probably be a free man by now if I'd pleaded guilty and just done my time."

His mother took his hand. He let her hold it.

"Don't worry, Georgie; we'll get you out of here."

George shook his head. "Nobody gives a shit, Mom. You can't even get Dad or the girls to come visit."

"Don't say that, George. Your father and sisters love you very much. It's been hard on everyone."

Mrs. Eavey looked at Dorothy. "Are you Catholic, Dr. Morrissey?"

"I grew up Catholic, yes," Dorothy said.

"Wouldn't your father be upset with you if you beat up your pastor?"

"You've got a point," Dorothy said.

"You have to understand, Dr. Morrissey," Mrs. Eavey's eyes pleading. "We were at the center of everything that happened in our parish. We'd been one of the first couples to build a home in the new suburb. We left our home parish in the city to move to the suburbs to give our kids a better life, but we didn't have a church within walking distance."

"I do get it," Dorothy said. "My parents stayed in the city. The church and school were a hop, skip, and a jump away."

"We missed that closeness, so twenty-five couples banded together to request a new church with George's father at the helm. He designed the church we go..." She stumbled here, holding back tears. "Went to every Sunday." She drew a breath. "We did everything from the Scouts to the school board. We served on guilds, cooked meals for weddings and funerals, took communion to the homes of the aged and infirm. We even opened our home as a host family for visiting priests and nuns from other countries. Little George folded bulletins and raked leaves."

"I folded bulletins one time," George countered.

"Well, you raked the convent yard often enough." She paused, looking embarrassed, but Dorothy wasn't sure if it was because Mrs. Eavey felt that she'd carried on or that George contradicted her. Dorothy thought they sounded just like her parents but better off. "I'm sorry," she said, "you probably aren't interested in all that. It's just, it's just, we were the lifeblood of our community. Now we're pariahs. We've moved to a new parish. Even there, as soon as anyone hears the name Eavey, they say, 'you related to the guy who beat up the priest?' I love my son, but he ruined our lives. We're as much prisoners in our home as George is here. Only, we don't get the support of doctors and therapists, and the like of that, or as his father likes to say, three hots and a cot," she said.

"Jesus, Ma, I'm not on a retreat," George grumbled. "This is no picnic, for Chrissakes."

She looked sideways at Dorothy as if to apologize on behalf of her son for his language. "I'm just saying you're not the only one who is suffering. And we don't have anyone to talk to like you have Dr. Morrissey here," she said, deferentially, extending her hand toward the therapist as if to show how good George had it.

"I'd be happy to set your family up with a therapist in the community," Dorothy said.

Helen Eavey ignored the offer. "I'm just saying we're all suffering. I want our lives to go back to normal."

Dorothy wrote in her notes, *family session illustrates the tragedy and cascading effect of one person's actions on multiple lives. What is the backstory? Drugs or not, blackout or not, where did all that anger come from? Be sure to address with George.*

"Sure, there were rumors that Father Miner had fiddled with George's friend, Brian, but why couldn't George mind his own business?" Mrs. Eavey said. George hadn't mentioned this piece to Dorothy and yet here was his mother acting as if it was common knowledge. George had learned of his friend's overdose on the night of the attack. If he'd known something about Father Miner and his friend, Dorothy thought that would have been worth mentioning especially since, for his mother, that was the end of their world. What else was he withholding?

"If only you could behave yourself here," she said. "Then maybe they'd let you out. Leave that poor man from Japan alone, for goodness' sake."

George laughed, an edgy devil-may-care look in his eyes. "Aw, c'mon, he knows I'm only teasing. I don't mean it, but seriously, he's such an easy target. I can't help myself. He's the only real entertainment in this place." This was the George that Dorothy recognized.

"That's not how I raised you," she said.

"I think that ship has sailed," George responded.

Dorothy made a note of their exchange. *Clearly, George talks to his mother about his day-to-day life.*

"You must have some influence, Dr. Morrissey," Helen Eavey said. "Can't you tell them how great he is?"

George looked at his mother. "Dr. Morrissey has to work with me. She doesn't like me any more than any of the other doctors. What judge is going to give me the benefit of the doubt, especially with Miner campaigning against me?"

"Is that true?" Mrs. Eavey asked Dorothy. Flustered, Dorothy was internally giving herself forty lashes. She'd thought she'd successfully held her feelings about George in check yet here he was calling her out.

"I like you," Dorothy said, turning toward George, with as much sincerity as a game show host.

George was one of Dorothy's first patients when she arrived at St. Lawrence. As the new psychologist, her caseload was made up of patients that the psychiatrists were trying to unload. The descriptions in his file regarding him ran the gamut of negative attributions such as "impaired judgment" and "exhibits limited insight" to "pathological tendencies" and "sociopath." So far, in their sessions, he had not exhibited any such tendencies outside of anger and hypervigilance. Yet, she was having a difficult time connecting with him. He seesawed between curiosity and resistance. She tried everything to forge an alliance. She inquired about both his day and night dreams as a way to break open his shell, but he wasn't having it. Now George revealed that he didn't trust his connection with Dorothy either. He'd be one to talk about in supervision with Dr. Keith.

"What matters is that George believes he can be rehabilitated," Dorothy said.

"We are a good family. He grew up in a loving home. We were all devastated to hear about Brian's overdose, but just because he was George's best friend, that's no reason to attack our priest," Mrs. Eavey was brought to tears.

George said, "If I knew, Mom, I'd tell you. I don't even remember doing it. None of it matters now. He's going to make sure I'm locked up forever."

"What do you work with him on then, if not to get out?"

Dorothy turned to George. He could disclose whatever he wanted, but she wouldn't without his permission. "I've told you, Mom, that's between Dr. Morrissey and me."

"Well, I don't understand all that. Keeping secrets from your family."

"I can tell you that typically I teach anger management to our patients, among other things," Dorothy said, taking pains not to break confidentiality.

"Can we meet again, Dr. Morrissey?" Mrs. Eavey asked.

"Certainly, perhaps Mr. Eavey will join us next time?" Dorothy said.

Mrs. Eavey's eyes lowered, and her mouth turned down in disappointment. She sighed, defeated. "I doubt it, he seems to be having one of those mid-life crisis thingies. Is that what you call it? Since this mess with Georgie happened, all he does is sit alone on the back porch, smoking cigars and drinking his Pabst Blue Ribbon. He barely talks to anyone, me included," she said, sadly.

"I'm very sorry for the pain all this has caused your family. If he changes his mind, he's always welcome," Dorothy said, "and like I said, I'd be happy to refer you to a therapist in the community." Dorothy stood, signaling the session was over.

"Would you like the door closed?" Mrs. Eavey asked as she and George were about to leave.

"You can leave it open," Dorothy said, "thanks."

As they walked out of her office, Dorothy heard Mrs. Eavey say to her son, "I liked her. She's awfully pretty, isn't she?" George didn't respond. Then she overheard Mrs. Eavey say, "Would you like me to bring you a fried Spam sandwich next time?" she said.

"That sounds great," he said. "Don't forget the mustard."

"I love you, Georgie."

"I love you too, Mom."

Before writing her note, Dorothy stood at her window and contemplated the sad turn of events for George and his family. She watched as Mrs. Eavey crossed the parking lot toward her car. The setting sun lit up the horizon. All that love. She shook her head. Her parents would have disowned her for much less. She thought about a recurring dream she'd been having ever since Thomas had mentioned Clorox to her. In the dream, she was trying to tell her mother something about her second-grade teacher, Sister Constance, sending her over to the rectory with a note. Dorothy didn't want to go to the rectory presumably because she'd miss out on Around the World, her favorite math game. Her mother was busy wiping down the kitchen counters with Clorox. The dream was so real, Dorothy felt she could smell the fumes. She was tugging on her mother's shirt sleeve trying to get her to listen. Deirdre was screaming from another room: *Mommy I need you this minute!* Dorothy's mother yanked her arm away. She said, *just do as you're told.* That's when Dorothy would wake up.

Dorothy sat down to write her note. *3/21/74 Met with George and his mother today. Mrs. Eavey expressed concern over George "misrepresenting" himself. She appeared devoted, worried, and showed a strong desire for her family's life to "return to normal." George participated, albeit allowed his mother to do most of the talking. He appeared resigned to his fate, "locked up here forever." Also, it seems mother and son talk regularly. Mrs. Eavey made reference to George's daily life. She alluded to conflict with her husband. Undersigned offered twice to refer the family for therapy. Mrs. Eavey declined. Address conflict with Father Miner in the next session with George. Mrs. Eavey alluded to rumored inappropriate behavior with George's friend. Why does this all sound so familiar?*

CHAPTER FIVE

SPRING 1974

THOMAS

Thomas was waiting outside of Dr. Morrissey's office when she returned from lunch with Kenneth. Seeing Thomas standing there, she'd felt a moment's panic thinking she was late. Dorothy and Kenneth had met at a deli across from the hospital. When Dorothy ordered pastrami with mayonnaise on white bread, the whole place fell into what felt to her as a stunned silence. The server said, "I beg you, anything but mayonnaise." His eyes crinkled with laughter. "I'll even put Thousand Island on it if you want but a nice mustard on rye is what you need."

Kenneth was laughing too. He whispered in her ear. "He's right, go with the mustard."

Cheeks flushed to have drawn so much attention to herself, Dorothy acquiesced. The server encouraged her to take a bite before she left the counter. He watched eagerly for her reaction. "Delicious!" She said with her mouth still full and wiping the mustard from the corners.

The server beamed. "Another convert!"

Afterward, they'd taken a walk to soak up the first hints of spring-like weather. "I never knew ordering a sandwich could be so complicated," Dorothy said, "but I'll admit, that was the best sandwich I've ever had."

"You haven't lived until you've had a good pastrami on rye," Kenneth agreed then added, "with mustard that is."

"Better than the bologna and cheese of my childhood," Dorothy laughed, "with mayonnaise on white bread."

"That's the stuff of nightmares," Kenneth said.

Now Dorothy glanced at her watch relieved that she wasn't late. "You're not late, Dr. Morrissey, I'm early," Thomas said, reading her mind. "Nowhere to go, nothing to do." Thomas sighed. Six weeks had gone by before his symptoms had stabilized enough that he could remain coherent and focused during sessions. Once the psychiatrists had found the right combination of medications, Dorothy incrementally increased session time and worked toward processing traumatic experiences. Once they managed his mania, he was able to relax and talk about his life.

The hall was quiet, given that most patients were still in the small cafeteria on the floor. A waft of fried foods clung to Thomas. Most days, Thomas hung around the cafeteria until the doors were shuttered. More than anything, he was a social being. He relished attention and would wait all day to get the kind and amount he needed to fill his well. She figured he must be eager to get started if he left the cafeteria before being kicked out, so she allowed him to come in a few minutes early. She liked to think she held to strict boundaries, but sometimes her patients nudged her to ease up.

"You look nice, Thomas," she said.

"Shit, showered, and shaved," Thomas said, smiling. "I have to tell you about my dream last night." He situated himself on the loveseat. His eagerness piqued her interest. He was well put together in his kimono and slippers. By now, he'd learned that the best way to capture her attention was to give her something juicy to analyze.

"Have you ever been sleeping and dreaming, but you also feel awake?" he asked. "Like part of you is awake and observing the dreaming you?"

"Yes, I have. It's called lucid dreaming."

"Well, that's new information," Thomas said, stroking his chin like Sigmund Freud.

"Would you like to share?" she asked, trying to remain focused. With Thomas she had a hard time keeping the smile off her face.

"I was in the house in Alpena, where we grew up before we moved to Lansing. I was in my parents' bathroom, sitting on the toilet. I felt like I was awake, but I wasn't. And I thought Dad is only trying to make mother happy. But, of course, she never was."

"You know, I'm from a big family, so the only place I could think my own thoughts was in the bathroom," Dorothy shared. "That's how this feels to me. Maybe, you recognized that your mother was unhappy."

"Melancholic was the most apt description of my mother. There was no happy to compare that would make us notice unhappy. She claimed she was happiest when we were in Japan. But I wouldn't know. I was just a baby then."

"Yes, you mentioned that she taught you about the kimono," Dorothy noted, letting him know that she'd listened.

"Yes, there was that," he said. "But there was a lot that she couldn't replicate. She had to improvise. She loved raw tuna, but we had to make do with cans of 'chicken of the sea.' And we couldn't find the green tea that she preferred. But it didn't matter to me. I didn't need the fancy stuff. It was enough to pretend. JW, not so much, he couldn't be bothered. JW was like a butterfly, always flitting beyond my mother's reach. But he kept our secret from my father."

"So, do you think she wasn't happy because she didn't have access to the delicacies from Japan or because JW wouldn't participate? Or that you all had to keep it a secret from your father?" Dorothy asked.

"I will be happy to get to that if you'll stop interrupting," Thomas said. He burrowed more comfortably into the cushions as if readying himself for a lengthy story. He wanted the floor without the therapist directing the conversation. Dorothy gave him some leeway as long as they made progress. "As my mother used to say, we are the Perfects, and we are perfect in every way! But it was far from perfect. I think once she had a taste of Japanese culture, everything about our life in Michigan became lackluster. Japan showed my mother what could have been. Hah, did I just have an insight?" He asked, brightening a bit.

Dorothy smiled. She wanted to reflect that perhaps Thomas felt he wasn't good enough to make his mother happy but inserting the observation might be hurtful if Thomas didn't come to that conclusion himself. So instead, she said, "That's why I like working with dreams. If we pay attention to them, we learn a lot about what we hold inside. Where did your family move after Japan?" Dorothy asked.

"My father was stationed north of Chicago at Great Lakes Naval Air Station. I don't remember that at all. JW and I were not aware until much later that Dad was dishonorably discharged. That came up after a DUI. Dad never said much, except when he was drunk. Then he'd blather on about his Navy days, and how misunderstood he was. His problems were always the fault of 'that asshole, so and so.' I kid you not, for the longest time, I thought 'that asshole' was somebody's first name."

Dorothy's laughter elicited a satisfied smile from Thomas. He was on a roll.

"We went back to Alpena after his discharge. We moved in with my grandparents. His dream was to own a couple of acres of land where he could have a view of Lake Huron in front where he could fish and woods in the back where he could hunt. Supposedly, living with my grandparents would save us money for his dream. He never got that far. I guess he liked drinking more. My grandparents kicked us out."

"Do you think your mother was disappointed that they didn't get a house on Lake Huron?"

"I don't know. She didn't say, but if I were to hazard a guess, I think she would have liked that. I don't think she liked Lansing at all," he said, an audible sigh accompanying a sudden slump in his shoulders as if to demonstrate her feelings.

"What makes you draw that conclusion?" Dorothy asked.

"Because, as JW was fond of pointing out, she never left the house once we moved here."

"What about you? Where was your favorite place to live?"

"I was only seven when we moved here, so I don't remember much before then. I liked that Dad was never home," he said, his shoulders returning to an upright position as if Dorothy were a stewardess instructing him to ready for landing. "He became a truck driver, which was better for everyone. When he came home, he brought us treats from the road to keep us busy while he and Mom got reacquainted. I hated him. I hated how he pawed at her, with his big meaty hands, as soon as he walked through the door." Shoulders down again, another audible sigh. Hers sagged just watching him. "Mother was so classy when Father wasn't home. He was a brute, and that was before he'd start drinking. All we could do was hope he'd pass out before he turned mean." Thomas was holding his breath now as he might have done as a fearful child. Another deep sigh escaped him before he continued his story. "Selfishly, I wish he would have gotten his cabin in the woods and gone to live there by himself." He paused. He took the rubber band from his ponytail and tied it up again. He smoothed the wrinkles in his kimono. "Dad never liked me," he said, dejection occupying the place his sighs had been. "If you could see how he looked at me. I was so nervous around him. He hated that I wanted to be near Mom. He was always shoving me outside. 'Get outside, go play. You shouldn't be cooped up playing dress-up like a little girl.'" He mocked his father's snarl and vocal growl, illustrating a rabid demeanor indeed. "He'd shoot daggers at my mother all the while."

"Are you saying that the dream is telling you that your mother wasn't happy because your father didn't like you?"

"She chose him in the end. So, it doesn't matter now."

"How did he feel about JW?"

"JW was everyone's favorite. And he knew how to read my father. He played sports. He enjoyed hunting. He tried to live up to his name-sake John Wayne, our father's favorite actor. Don't get me wrong, JW hated our father as much as I did, but he could spot trouble from a mile away, so he never got hit. I, on the other hand, could be standing in the middle of a firestorm before I knew a match was lit," he said. "If I had a nickel for every time JW said, 'Jesus, Thomas, keep your mouth shut!' I'd be a rich man." He mimicked JW by raising both arms as if directing traffic. "'Time and place, Thomas!'" He laughed.

Dorothy made a quick note: *Thomas claims to have trouble "reading other people," stated that his brother was much better at assessing parents' moods. According to Thomas, JW was his protector.*

"I don't know," Dorothy said. "It seems to me you are a very social person."

"Just because I like people doesn't mean they like me back." When Thomas's soft eyes skittered with hurt, Dorothy's heart followed.

Dorothy scribbled, in her notes to avoid joining him there: *Self-image shaped by family perceptions.* "So, your father hit you?"

"Yes," Thomas responded. "See this scar," he said, pushing loose hair away from his forehead. "That was from Dear ole Dad."

"I'm sorry, Thomas."

"Don't be, I'm over it." She knew he wasn't but decided not to challenge just now.

"Did your father hit JW?"

"Never JW. And he didn't hit me when JW was around. I think he was a little afraid of JW."

"And your mother? Did he hit her?"

"It was more like he threatened to hit her. He intimidated her, so she wouldn't stand in his way when he smacked me around. I was taking the hit for her. It was the least I could do. I'll admit, I wish she would have stood up for me just once."

"The least you could do, why?"

"My mother and JW accepted me. They protected me best they could. For every time I got hit, there were probably ten that John helped me wiggle out of. John Wayne was 'Perfect in Every Way.'" Thomas splayed his arms to each side as if to demonstrate why he gave up, saying, "As long as I had JW and Mom, I didn't care that my dad hated me. In the end, they both rejected me too. Once JW left, the rest of my life fell like dominoes."

"Why do you suppose JW has not been in touch?"

"I have my theories."

"Care to elaborate?"

"JW always held himself apart from the rest of us. I remember this one day after we moved to Lansing. He was probably eleven or so. Mom wanted to have a tea ceremony. She was tying my obi, the last bit of detail on my kimono. I was standing in front of the mirror. She said, 'Twirl for me, Eiji. Let's take a look at you.'" Thomas beamed as if the memory was so close, he was standing in front of the very mirror. "JW was standing in the doorway. I caught his eye. He rolled his eyes at her trying to get me to side with him. I remember he said to her, 'Why can't we just go to a movie for once.'"

"What did she say to that?"

"'Be a dear, JW, and get me my pills,'" Thomas said. "Which she promptly shared with me, I might add." A bit of a gleam still in his eyes from the memory.

"What kind of pills?"

"Oh, you know, the kind to keep our figures. I was chubby."

"But she didn't share them with JW?"

"He didn't need them. Even back then, he was already so handsome. He looked like you'd imagine Robert Redford might have looked like as a child. Sandy blond hair, tan, lean; I envied his natural beauty." Dorothy detected pride more than envy.

"But he didn't challenge your mother about sharing her pills with you?"

"Ha, you never challenged our mother."

"Why not?"

"She was delicate. She'd shut down, take to her bed that sort of thing."

"I guess I'm still confused about why JW has not been in touch with you," Dorothy said.

"He might have hated our father, but he did not hold our mother in high esteem either. I loved her, and I loved dressing up. I couldn't betray her. But I see it now. She was weak."

"That still doesn't explain why he wouldn't be in touch now."

"He wanted to make it big, like in Hollywood. We would drag him down. The hicks from Michigan, you know what I mean?"

Dorothy knew all too well. It was how she felt around Kenneth's parents. "You mentioned that your mother chose your father in the end? What happened?" Dorothy asked.

"When my father was released from prison, they moved back to Alpena. I guess I was just there to prop her up while my father was away."

"You didn't want to go with them?"

"Even if I'd been invited, which I wasn't, I wouldn't have gone."

"Do you ever talk with them?"

"Mother calls me once a month, always on a Sunday and always after 11:00 p.m. when it's cheapest. I never talk to my father. She'll make some excuse or another for him, but I'm sure he's out drinking. You ask a lot of questions," he said, despair settling in on face and shoulders.

"I'm trying to understand you," she said.

"Why aren't you trying to get me to change?"

"What do you mean?"

"Every other doctor has tried to get me to stop dressing up. I thought that's where you were going with this."

"Is that what you'd like me to do?"

"Of course not. I'm just wondering why you haven't."

"Because dressing up doesn't make you a danger to yourself or others."

Thomas nodded, satisfied in a *I could've told you that,* sort of way.

"I do have one more question before we finish," Dorothy said. "About your dream."

"Alrighty."

"In your dream, you noted that your father was trying to make your mother happy, but she was not. Let's say the people in your dream represent different parts of you. Could it be possible that, like your father, you tried but could never make your mother happy?"

"You are not insinuating that I'm like my father?" He huffed, flung his ponytail behind him, and stood up, "I'm nothing like him," his voice rose in anger. "He was a drunk. He was a mean SOB..."

"Not at all, Thomas," Dorothy said, instinctively leaning back away from him like he might have done as a child. "I was merely saying that perhaps the dream—"

Thomas cut her off with a wave of his hand and stormed out of the office.

DATE 4/8/1974: Family life unstable due to history of abuse, alcoholism, frequent moves, father's chronic unemployment, mother enlisting children in fantasy. Thomas's drug addiction might have started with his mother sharing her amphetamines with him during his childhood. Mental illness in both parents? No mention of an extended family being involved—chronic isolation. Thomas—oriented times 3, affect fluctuated from calm to testy depending on the line of questioning. Perhaps, treatment should move more slowly. He is willing to address family dynamics, but painful memories can overwhelm. Denied SI.

CHAPTER SIX

DOROTHY AND KENNETH

Kenneth nudged Dorothy awake with a gentle rub on her back. The morning light was already streaming in through the blinds. Their apartment was warm and cozy despite the drafty windows; standard for the older buildings on the edge of MSU's campus. Old but not dilapidated—no mice crawling through her walls, although a bat got in right after she moved in. When that happened, she ran screaming out of the apartment and wouldn't come back until Kenneth assured her it was gone.

She and Kenneth had met in graduate school. They maintained a long-distance relationship during Dorothy's postdoctoral internship at the Veteran's Affairs Hospital in Ann Arbor. When Dorothy accepted the position at St. Lawrence Asylum, Kenneth convinced her to move in with him. Kenneth's parents had already furnished the place, pieces bought new for him, the Nelson's one and only, or cast-offs saved for him as they restored the mansion they'd purchased. Anything that he didn't want went to the cottage in Pentwater on Lake Michigan.

She was curled in a tight fetal position as if she needed to protect herself even in sleep. Kenneth set down a cup of coffee. "Wake up, sunshine," he whispered. "Here's your coffee." She had worked all weekend and had a late night on-call. "Remember, you asked me to wake you so we can get errands done."

She moaned, rolling over. "I'm so tired."

"Tough night?" He sat down on the edge of the bed, sipping his coffee. Kenneth, Dorothy knew, had more than likely written two thousand words this morning while she slept. His ABD (all but dissertation) status at Michigan State kept him focused. She cozied up to him for reassurance as he bent over her and moved in for a kiss. They were like a study in opposites, which she found oddly soothing. Kenneth wore his wealth and only child's preciousness like an apology. He didn't have that hands-in-pockets confident amble of most rich kids she'd known. Rather, he entered rooms awkwardly; ducking like his five-foot eleven-inch frame was six-foot-seven as if to show how humbled he was by all he'd been given. He was smart, very smart. Learning came as easily to him as everything else. He never apologized for being smart. He reveled in his analytical mind and didn't shy away from expounding among their intellectual friends. Compared to him, Dorothy felt hard-scrabbled, like the middle child in a large family would have to be to survive. Kenneth pointed out her tenacity often enough. She was smart too, but perseverance was how she'd gotten as far as she had, clearing every hurdle placed in front of her since grade school.

"Exhausting, I had this poor kid from MSU, an international student who hadn't left his room in two weeks. No one noticed until his mother called from India."

"Yikes, that sounds awful."

"One of my old supervisors brought him in. He said the staff at MSU loves when I'm on-call." Dorothy sat up and propped herself against her pillows. "I'm flattered, but that means I get a lot of suicidal college students."

"Too bad there weren't any full-time positions at MSU."

"I like St. Lawrence. There's more variety."

"I don't know how you do it, Hon," he said. "Let's go out to breakfast before we do our errands."

"That sounds good. We can stop someplace on the way to Horrock's. I want you to help me pick out plants for my office."

"Let's just make sure we work out our errands before we head out. You know how I hate when you spring something on me." He smiled at her.

"Me? You're the one who adds unnecessary stops."

"Never, unless I need something from Builder's Square." Dorothy and Kenneth reliably found common ground in all the quotidian aspects of life in Lansing. They both hated going up Saginaw Highway for any reason other than a trip to Horrock's Market for fresh produce. They agreed before ever heading out the door where exactly they were going, and God forbid either one of them suggested an extra errand. There was no detour to the Lansing Mall on the way to Builder's Square or vice versa.

Dorothy swallowed the last of her coffee. "Give me ten minutes."

✦

Dorothy and Kenneth settled into a booth at Connor's, a diner off Saginaw that was on the way to Horrock's. A group of girls in Catholic school uniforms sat nearby, smoking cigarettes and chatting noisily while gesticulating enthusiastically, each vying for the last word.

"O'Rafferty girls," Kenneth, who grew up outside of Lansing when his family wasn't living in Europe, informed Dorothy. "They're closing the school after this year. They're merging with Gabriel's to become Catholic Central."

"Geesh, sounds like what's going on with St. Lawrence Asylum," Dorothy said.

"Down-sizing?"

"Yes, merging with the hospital. Everything centralized."

"I remember when St. Lawrence Asylum was in this old, scary-looking, brick mansion out on Tecumseh. We used to think it was haunted. Kids would go out there on Halloween and egg the place. See how many hits you could get before running for your life."

His story stung as if one of their eggs hit her full on the face. She wiped at her nose and eyes. "That sounds cruel to me. The mentally ill are not ghosts, you all probably scared them to death."

"I didn't say I was proud of it. We were assholes back then."

"Still, there has to be a happy medium between isolating the mentally ill in the middle of nowhere or leaving them out on the streets. They need a safe place to stay while they get help."

"We're talking about Senator Kelley again, aren't we?" The mere mention of Kelley's name made her eye twitch.

"I'm sorry, I can't help it. Pretty soon we'll be nothing more than a broom closet within the hospital. His callous budget cutting means that my clients could end up homeless or in jail. Their only crime being ill."

Just then, the hostess behind the counter called out to the girls in the booth nearby. "Is there a Mickey DeHane there?" One girl, cigarette dangling from the side of her mouth, slunk lower in the booth. "Your mother called. She said, and I quote, 'Get your ass back to school.'" The place erupted with laughter.

"That's so funny," Dorothy said. "Sheila was just like that in high school, always skipping class and smoking cigarettes. You'd get a kick out of her."

"I wouldn't know, now, would I?" Did she detect an edge in the chronically equanimous Kenneth?

"Can we not?" Dorothy was too tired to talk about why Kenneth had not met her family.

"Fine," Kenneth said, "I need to talk to you about something else anyway. I've got to start looking for a job. One of my advisors suggested I look at the government."

"State government? I thought you were planning on a postdoc position in your department."

"I've been offered a postdoc, yes, but I'm intrigued by the idea of working for the federal government." Equanimity restored for him at least.

"Federal government? What are you saying, Kenneth?"

"I'm saying we need to start talking about our future. Doesn't a big city sound nice? Get out of Lansing?"

"You don't like Lansing?"

"Do you?" She was reminded of Thomas's Michigan hicks comment in the way Kenneth's surprise seemed judgmental somehow.

"Yes, I find it quite manageable compared to Detroit."

"I'd rather live in a city where we can walk everywhere or take public transportation." Dorothy liked walking as much as the next person. She and Kenneth enjoyed long strolls through Michigan State's campus and along the Red Cedar River no matter the time of year. She could appreciate his desire to live in a place where everything was a walk away. Still, she was just getting established at St. Lawrence.

"There's nowhere like that in Michigan. Detroit is a big city, but it was built on cars."

"That's what I'm saying. Wouldn't you like to try someplace new? Have an adventure?" He knew better. Dorothy was a creature of habit. She had taken up swimming in graduate school, and, ever since, he liked to tease her that she met her thrill quotient by staring at the bottom of a pool.

"I would have thought you'd want to settle in one place after spending your childhood traveling," she said. To her mind, the postdoc at MSU was an ideal situation for both of them. She'd hoped that he planned to take it, so they could shelve this very conversation for another year.

"You know me, I love exploring new places," Kenneth was saying. He sopped his breakfast sausage and eggs in the syrup from his pancakes. "I think you'd love going to a bigger city," he said, shoving the lot in his mouth in one big bite. "There's so much out there to discover, Dorothy. Lansing is boring."

"I like Lansing."

"How? You stare at four walls all day long, and then for fun you stare at the bottom of a swimming pool."

Dorothy took a big swallow of her coffee. She did not understand how Kenneth could eat sausage or eggs doused in maple syrup. Syrup ruined eggs, which belonged with toast and only toast. She looked down at the demarcation on her plate. No food touching. "The beauty of my work is that I'm never bored. Working with the mentally ill, I feel I travel all over the place without ever leaving my office. And, swimming," she said pointedly, "gives me time to think."

"Swimming pools and the mentally ill are everywhere. You'll have no trouble finding either one. Regardless, we need to talk about our future."

"I agreed we'd talk about that after you are finished with your dissertation." No matter how many words he wrote each day on his dissertation, Dorothy knew, the process could take a long time. If his advisors were anything like her advisors, they'd demand rewrites right up to the end. She was counting on it.

"Okay, okay, but we can't avoid this discussion forever," he said, wiping his plate clean. "You haven't even touched your breakfast," he said.

"Thank you," she said relieved. She opened a packet of butter meant for his pancakes and added more to her sparsely buttered toast, then worked a bit of the heavily salted yolk from the white, placing it on the toast. She took a bite.

"I guess I should meet your family before we discuss our future together, anyway."

So much for the brief reprieve, she'd only gotten in the one bite. She sighed, chin sinking to chest. "I thought we'd talked about this."

"They can't be that bad, Dorothy."

"Oh, but they are."

"I know, I know, your father doesn't like Protestants. We can deal with that."

"No, Protestants are the Devil. And we're living in sin, so our relationship is doomed regardless of whether we decide to get married."

"I beg to differ," Kenneth said, "we're hardly living in sin. Can't you just explain that we're waiting to have sex until we're married?"

"My father will never accept you. We can't get married in the Church. You'd have to agree to become Catholic and raise our children as Catholics. We've already decided we don't want children. It's impossible." Her eggs were getting cold as she anxiously tried to defend her position.

"I'm not ruling out children just yet," Kenneth said. He reached over to take a piece of her bacon. He paused. "You know what I think, Dorothy?"

"I'm afraid to find out," Dorothy said. The smell of smoke coming from the high school girls' table was ruining her appetite.

"You're managing your life like your breakfast here," he said, pointing to her plate. "You're not comfortable unless you have a compartment for each part of your life. You have your family in one compartment, I'm in another, and your patients are in a third. I don't know where you put your friends, or your sister who died, or any past slights or hurt feelings. But no one compartment touches the next."

Dorothy's cheeks grew hot as if Kenneth had just slung an egg at her. He'd obviously been thinking about this for some time. "I thought I was the psychologist," she quipped in a sputtering attempt at a joke to hold her back tears. The little bit of toast she'd not swallowed caught in her throat. She couldn't say more for the coughing fit. Of course, he was right. She had incrementally divided her life into separate pieces in the years after Tess's death. Before and after—how could she help it? School life became separated from family life. Sisters became arranged according to whether she liked, tolerated, or took care of them, in that order. But Kenneth didn't know why. She barely understood her reasons. Hadn't she allowed him in, telling him about Tess's death? Still, she hid from him the more shameful aspects of her family. She just couldn't parse out whether she was more worried about Kenneth meeting her family or her family meeting Kenneth.

Her flushing cheeks made her think of Deirdre's Lupus diagnosis, the butterfly rash on Deirdre's face the telltale symptom. She made no mention of Deirdre to Kenneth. She would never speak of Tess and Deirdre in the same sentence. Sick or not, Deirdre had always been the opposite of Tess. She felt simultaneously justified and ashamed for the hateful feelings she harbored for Deirdre that tarnished the loving memories of Tess.

Tess had been the star of the family. Bright and beautiful, kind, and funny, the rest of the Morrissey girls looked up to her, and she was clearly the favorite of their parents. Tess had been blessed with a winning smile with perfectly straight teeth, expressive blue eyes, and thick strawberry blond hair.

With her death, what Deirdre lacked became more evident to all but Mr. and Mrs. Morrissey, who acted as if there was nothing wrong. Deirdre's overbite was pronounced over a weak chin. Her brown eyes bulged in a perpetual stare as if even sleep couldn't close them, and her thin black hair hung limply exposing her large ears. Though smart in the extreme (she was a whiz at any quiz show), she barely graduated from high school. Worst of all, she was moody, angry, and very needy of their mother. Deirdre always sat at the dinner table right next to their mother, parroting everything that came out of Mrs. Morrissey's mouth. Dorothy resented that her mother always compared her to Deirdre, especially regarding intellect and marriageability. "Boys don't like smart girls, Dorothy, just look at Deirdre."

"I've talked about my family with you," Dorothy said now in self-defense.

"I know that you loved your older sister, Tess, and then she died. I know your parents hate Protestants. I know you feel close to your grandmother and maybe two of your sisters. And I know your brothers are twins and were a surprise."

"That's a good start."

"Maybe for a first date," Kenneth said. "I'd like to meet them."

The truth was, Kenneth was right. Dorothy had reduced her parents to one dimension—staunch Catholics whose daughters' worth was dependent on marrying 'a good Catholic boy' and providing them with grandchildren. Her sisters were just there to harangue her. She'd thought Kenneth had accepted her explanations, albeit the missing and complicated family dynamics, that prevented her from taking him home. What he'd said just now indicated otherwise. She knew Kenneth hadn't meant to hurt her, but all she heard was more judgment and more reason to hide. Overwhelmed, she focused on the one comment he said that he probably wished she had missed. "You know I don't want children," she said. "You should have spoken up before I had the Dalkon Shield implanted." She pushed her plate aside, no longer hungry.

"I'm not trying to upset you," Kenneth said.

"Can we skip the errands?" Dorothy responded. "I need a swim."

"Can we take a walk instead? Maybe go up to campus?"

"Only if I can analyze you this time?" She smiled. Another place where they found common ground, neither Dorothy nor Kenneth could tolerate conflict.

He took the bait. "What could you possibly analyze about me?"

"How easy your life is as an only child."

"I would have taken lots of brothers and sisters any day of the week."

"Ha, ha, you don't know what you're missing," she said. With that they made their way to the car to head east toward Michigan State's campus, to let the topic drop for another day.

CHAPTER SEVEN

GEORGE

George needed a few moments to settle down before Dorothy would start the session with him. He'd obviously taken advantage of the opportunity to see the barber, who came in once a week to give haircuts and shaves to the residents. The clean shave made him look more innocent than usual. The smirk on his face when he entered the office said otherwise and prickled irritation. She wanted him to take his sessions seriously. She breathed deeply until she sensed he was ready to get down to business. Finally, he situated himself into a relaxed but alert position. He looked at her and smiled.

"You got a haircut," she said.

"That I did," he said. "And a shave with hot towels and everything." He slapped at his cheeks as if applying aftershave.

"What a treat," Dorothy said. "How's everything else?"

"Can't complain, given the circumstances. I was pretty bored most of the week, but I'm enjoying the books you let me borrow, so thank you."

"I'm glad to hear it." One day while swimming, she thought perhaps tapping into his intellect might help her like him more. So, she had lent George books from Harry Stack Sullivan and Erik Erikson about child development, hoping they'd elicit memories about his childhood.

"I thought you'd enjoy them. Has the reading sparked anything of interest for you?"

"I could relate to Erik Erikson's identity crisis, but I liked Sullivan's views of chumship."

Dorothy's instincts to lend him the books were confirmed with that statement. Reading from the masters would prepare him for the more probing questions that could uproot old fears or vulnerabilities that he preferred to keep buried.

Dorothy glanced out the window, distracted by pebble-sized hail spattering the panes. She turned back to George, "Speaking of, I like to explore childhood events through a practice I call, 'significant memories.' Looking back in small doses at our memories can make them feel more manageable. Can you describe a significant early memory for me? It doesn't matter if it's positive or negative, happiest, saddest, whatever comes to mind."

"Is this a parlor trick you use with all your crazy patients?" George said suspiciously, scrutinizing her face, searching for the lie.

"Each person's therapy is different according to their need. You'll just have to trust me."

"I'm not crazy like the others. I don't need therapy."

"Everyone can benefit from therapy, George. We all desire to be understood." Dorothy would not take the bait.

"What if I think it's stupid?"

"How about you humor me." She tried not to let annoyance get the better of her.

George ran his fingers through his newly cut hair. He inhaled deeply as if he were pondering whether to answer her question truthfully. Dorothy remained still and allowed the silence to sit between them. After a time, he let out a long sigh of acquiescence.

"So, the memory has to be significant? Like how?"

"It can be significant because it was one of your first distinct memories, like the one you told me about getting your tonsils out. Or maybe it was memorable because it was a particularly happy memory."

"Okay, of my early memories, my happiest and saddest both happened on the same day. And they both involve my father. It was the day I got the belt."

"Oh my," Dorothy said. "That doesn't sound very happy to me."

"The day started happy. My father was combing my hair. At my Catholic grade school, our uniform was navy pants, white shirt, and a blue or black tie. In the winter, we also wore navy blue sweaters. My dad would lift me up to stand me on the toilet and comb my hair with Brill Cream, just like he did his own. I was so proud to be like him. He'd also help me with my school uniform tie. I loved the attention. The neatness of my hair and uniform reminded me of his Navy uniform when he would get ready to go off for his weekend reserves. I wanted to be just like him. He was a commander, and his uniform had all these bars of colorful ribbons lined up and medals he earned in the war."

So infrequently did her own father make mention of his service, Dorothy couldn't remember if he was Army or Navy. Nor could she imagine her brothers wanting to serve. She couldn't imagine feeling this way about her father regardless.

"Dad always carried a comb in his breast pocket. He put a dab of Brill cream in my hair, pulled his comb from his pocket, and combed my hair neatly to the side, making sure every strand was in place with a straight part on the side. My mom came into the bathroom just as my dad held me up to the mirror over the sink. She told me I was a handsome devil and the spitting image of my dad. Dad looked over my shoulder and winked at me in the mirror. Meanwhile, I'm beaming my fool head off, huge ears all the more noticeable with the comb-over that no one seemed to take notice of, but that's blind love for you. I also loved it when my mother said that I was the spitting image of my dad because he was my hero."

"That's very sweet." She was put to mind of the pride she took in ironing the pleats of her school uniform.

George averted his gaze. Dorothy waited.

"Unfortunately," George continued, "this day was the last time my dad did my hair. By the end of that day, my hair was a mess, my shirt was ripped and dirty, and I hated my father."

She detected a shift in George's demeanor. There were no jokes. He wasn't trying to amuse her. She waited to see how he would proceed this time.

"I was a good kid, a bit of a spitfire, maybe, but I don't think I looked for trouble. I cannot explain my behavior. More than anything, I wanted to comport myself like I was wearing a Navy uniform. My dad was so regal when he wore his Navy whites. And Jesus, I was only eight years old. I loved going to school up until that point."

Obviously, something went very wrong, Dorothy thought.

"The school day went from bad to worse. We'd been practicing for our First Confessions. A storm had passed through, so the playground was muddy. Sister Joseph warned us that if we got our white shirts muddy, we would get a spanking. No matter how it happened, if someone pushed you into the mud or you pushed someone else, spanking was the consequence." Dorothy felt like her little Catholic school girl self was right there with him, and she wrote: *Reminds me of my Catholic school experience.* George paused.

"Go on."

"Of course, I got knocked down in the mud. I was so scared of the spanking that I wouldn't line up to go back to the building. Sister Joseph could turn on a dime. Beautiful and serene one minute, going ballistic the next when she was angry. We did not doubt that she'd make good on her promise to spank us. I stood frozen in place at the bottom of the hill even after my classmates entered the building, half of them crying, the other half calling us pansies. She came flying down the drive, grabbed me by my ear—as I said, my big ears made them easy to grab." He paused. Dorothy detected a hint of a smile in him. He obviously enjoyed his own humor.

"Go on," Dorothy prodded despite rising anxiety about what he would disclose.

"She dragged me to the rectory, kind of like the nuns' version of 'wait till your father gets home.'"

Dorothy didn't laugh. As a girl, she was terrified of her pastor and his story was beginning to hit too close to home.

"The rectory had the hushed silence of authority. No one spoke above a whisper. The foyer was massive with leaded glass windows. I could see dust motes floating around in the sunbeams. Everything looked old and valuable and breakable. I was afraid to move. But I remember the place smelled of stale cigarette smoke and lemon Pledge. Sister Joseph barely spoke above a whisper once we crossed into the foyer. My situation could only get worse."

"Sister told me not to embarrass her and to go straight back to the classroom when I was finished. She said, 'Don't think I've forgotten about your spanking.' Then she left me there by myself. Remember how scary it was getting sent to the rectory?" The skies darkened and the hail slammed against the windows as if for emphasis. Dorothy could feel his fear like it was her own.

"I do," Dorothy said.

He nodded. "I noticed a carton of cigarettes on a side table near the door. I don't know what got into me. Without thinking, I took them and ran out. Lo and behold, my friend Brian Moreland was on his way to the rectory. He was also a muddied mess and crying from the spanking he'd just received. I grabbed his arm, and I said, 'Let's go.' It didn't take much convincing." George was laughing like he was sitting on a barstool sharing a laugh with his buddies. Dorothy just knew he had taken a detour around the heart of the matter. She would not join him at the bar.

"Lucky for us, the good Father had a book of matches tucked into the carton. We took off running. We had no idea where we were going. There was a Woolworth's about a half-mile from the Church, which backed up to an alley. We ran there, hoping to score some pop and chips or candy. Brian was game by this point. He went into Woolworth's and got us a couple of bottles of pop. We sat in the alley behind the store and smoked cigarettes until we were sick. We wandered around. We sat on the swings on the playground. We started out thinking we were tough guys, but as the day drew on, we were terrified to go home, and the next thing we knew, it was getting dark. We were sitting up against a tree near the playground, trying to figure out our next move when Brian's dad drove up. 'Get in the car,' he said to Brian. To me, he said, 'Go home, George. Your father is looking for you.'"

George took a deep breath, laughter gone, bar and buddies nonexistent. "When I got home, my dad took one look at me and told me to go to the basement. I could hear him take off his belt as he followed me down. I don't think I'd ever been hit before that night, yet I knew what was coming. I deserved what I got from my dad, but still, I never forgave him. Trust me, even then, the irony was not lost on me that I could have avoided all of this had I just gotten in line for my spanking from Sister Joseph. I can't even describe how much that belt hurt on my backside, but I think I was more stunned by how angry he was. Then I was sent to bed without supper. My mother was so disappointed in me—that hurt. I never asked my dad to comb my hair again." Sadness for the little boy caught in Dorothy's throat. What a horrible thing to do to a child, but George could have been talking about eating an ice cream cone, no emotion, just an everyday occurrence. He couldn't hide the hurt little boy lingering in his eyes though.

"Do you have any recollection of why you took the cigarettes in the first place?"

"To this day, I don't know what possessed me. After that, nothing was the same. I ruined my chances to be an altar boy."

Dorothy wrote: *George's emotions not aligned with the intensity of the incident.*

"How would you feel about doing some writing about this incident for me?"

"Like how?"

"I'm thinking about whatever else you might remember about stealing the cigarettes. I can't help but wonder what could turn a little boy who adored his father, loved to please, was conscientious, and a good student, so quickly into a 'hooligan' when, from your recollection, you'd never looked for trouble before that. Because, as we both know, you found plenty of trouble after. It's like the whole trajectory of your life turned in one day."

"Are you looking for something specific?"

"I'm looking for your truth is all. You said yourself, you've been having nightmares that start out innocently enough, kids playing cops and robbers. Then somehow, grownups got involved and ruined everything." She looked out the window. "There's a storm brewing inside you, George, that has been too painful to remember, but that might account for your behavior. Also, you may find it easier to write about your experiences before you share them with me. Ask your mother to bring in family photos from early in your childhood and then from grade school to prompt some memories if that helps."

"I can do that."

As George left her office, Dorothy heard him shout, "Hey, Thomas-san! How about you be Cato, and I'll be Inspector Clouseau?"

Dorothy sat down to write her note. She was suddenly overwhelmed by emotion. She felt like she was overcome by the emotions George was refusing to allow. His second-grade experiences hit uncomfortably close to home, so much so that his blended into hers and she didn't like it. She got up and stretched, taking deep breaths to calm her nerves. *I'm feeling the feelings he should be feeling,* she thought. *Why?* Then she remembered the day she won the award for most candy bars sold on behalf of the Biafran babies. She had gone door to door after school to collect donations from their neighbors. She went to the grocers. She asked the milkman and the butcher. She deserved the award. Sister Constance had told her she would get a certificate and a chocolate bar.

Father Mayer came to the classroom to present the award. When she stood up to receive her certificate and candy bar, he looked down on her akin to what the eight-year-old could only interpret as hatred.

"Aren't you the greedy little girl," he said. The color rising in the second grader's cheeks became hot with shame. "I hardly believe a little girl could raise this much money."

"She did, Father." Sister Constance had stood to come to Dorothy's defense. Father Mayer fixed a cold stare upon her until she sat back down before he turned back to Dorothy.

"I believe the award for the most donations should go to Michael O'Shaughnessy, don't you, Dorothy?" His cold mean eyes bore through his thick lenses, burning a hole through the second grader's heart. "You win enough awards. Now go sit down." He called little Michael to the front.

Dorothy could still feel the confusion and humiliation that had filled her then. She was left feeling guilty and ashamed for nothing other than being a girl and doing as she was told.

Dorothy believed strongly in a parallel process. She was still plagued by strong feelings of dislike for George but felt she had made progress today. Still, the thought that inserted itself just now was *If I could move beyond it why couldn't he?*

She wrote in her notes: *4/22/74 George beginning to share more with Therapist. He shared a painful memory from his childhood. However, something is missing. Specifically, what happened that made George behave as he did? Did he feel guilty? What happens to the child when trying to do the right thing only gets her into trouble?* (She didn't notice her Freudian slip). *Assigned George writing exercise to help him access memories and his feelings. He denied SI.*

CHAPTER EIGHT

RUTH FITZGERALD JOHNSON
PUT ON A HAPPY FACE

Common sense dictated that Dorothy should be wandering the haunts of dreamland in REM sleep. Instead, she was peering through the wet windshield onto abandoned streets on her way to the hospital. Fortunately, there were no cars on the road, and she could sail through the traffic lights; she strained to see through the cold rain, and her eyes burned from exhaustion. Taking a weeklong turn each month as the on-call psychologist was part and parcel of the job, and reliably included at least one emergency in the middle of the night. Dorothy hated getting woken in the middle of a good dream. Startled by her pager, she flew out of bed, heart pounding, bleary-eyed, and unsure of what was happening. Kenneth was lying on his stomach, open-mouthed and drooling. He barely stirred. This call was unusual because she was being called to the hospital's maternity ward rather than the asylum or the ER. The maternity ward staff frantically described what sounded like post-partum psychosis. Before she left, she jotted him a note regarding her whereabouts and put it on his nightstand. She bent over his blissfully snoring self and kissed him on the top of his head.

By the time she arrived at the hospital, the adrenaline rush had retreated, and sleepiness made her slow to react. On the way down the hall, Dorothy heard someone singing a show tune. She was so tired and the singer's voice so lovely, she thought there was a radio blasting.

Oh, it was from *Bye, Bye Birdie.* She was singing "Put on a Happy Face." Whoever was singing could have rivaled Dick Van Dyke's rendition on Broadway.

Dorothy was met with a lingering stench of urine and disinfectant as she entered the maternity ward double occupancy room. The smell and accompanying scene triggered a new surge of adrenaline, alerting her to the situation at hand. She tried not to dry heave by turning her face away from the mess beneath the empty bed and toward the bed where a patient stood on top singing. From her bleary-eyed perspective, a ragtag group of nurses, doctors, and orderlies surrounded the bed arms stretched out as if to break the fall of the hefty black woman balanced precariously on top of her bed. The patient was in her hospital gown, but it was opened at the back in such a way that would make any woman with her wits about her cry in shame. If the woman's song hadn't admonished to 'put on a happy face,' Dorothy would have burst into tears on her behalf. The patient had her arms flung wide, her large breasts like weights pulling her forward, counterbalanced by sturdy thighs. She could have been Liza Minnelli the way her voice projected, making Dorothy wonder if she'd actually performed in *Bye, Bye Birdie.* Dorothy wouldn't have been surprised if the patient Rockette kicked an attendant in the face. She almost wished she would.

The room was lit up under the fluorescent lights, and apparently, the other occupant had been shuttled out because the sheets were wrinkled, and the blanket was thrown wide as if someone left in a hurry. An empty bassinet was next to the roommate's bed. Likely, a newborn had been in for a visit recently. Also, a bedpan with its contents spilled lay underneath the absent roommate's bed.

Everyone's arms extended toward the patient to catch her if she fell. Tension and concern held them in place as if the last trust fall patient had slipped through and hit the floor. If she fell, they would catch her, by God.

Despite the upbeat lyrics and tune, the patient's face was etched with sorrow, her eyes swollen from crying. Ruth Fitzgerald Johnson had recently lost a stillborn baby. By rights, she shouldn't have been up and walking yet, let alone standing on a hospital mattress singing. Yet, Ruth swung her arms up like she was about to start jumping up and down on the bed as a young child might. This was a first for Dorothy, who no longer felt tired, but the sleepiness that edged her eyes made her nose run. She could feel her heart beating in her chest from the adrenaline. The incongruity between the happy tune and the unhappy circumstances of the patient gave Dorothy a diagnostic clue but also threw her for a loop. *Hallucinating? Does she believe she's on stage?*

An equally tired but wired nurse stood by Dorothy's side and filled her in. "I shouldn't have taken my eyes off of her," she informed Dorothy. "She hasn't slept, and she's been behaving strangely. We suspect she's having some sort of post-partum crisis. I turned away to give her some privacy, and then I heard a crash. Ruth threw her full bedpan at Mrs. Ellis' bed because she was snoring."

Rather than mopping the mess, the janitor stood staring, distracted from his duties by the patient's alarming antics. The attending doctor, the nurses, and a security guard were trying to coax Ruth to sit. "Ruth, please, just sit down," the doctor said. "I've called Dr. Morrissey to talk to you." The patient would have none of it.

"You know what my brothers call these?" She shouted, slapping the tops of her legs. "Thunder-thighs. I can stay up here all night!" *So, she is oriented to place and time,* Dorothy thought.

Everyone turned to look at Dorothy with helpless expressions and fear. "We need to subdue her," the attending said. "This is fool-hardy. She just had a hysterectomy. She's hemorrhaged enough blood to kill a horse. I'm afraid she'll rip open her scar." His voice became shriller with every piece of information as if the psychologist needed convincing. Dorothy glanced at Ruth to see if she was listening, but Ruth commenced with another lyric about some girl so gloomy. Dorothy couldn't quite catch it but she got the gist, which was enough for her to be amazed at the power of the unconscious.

"And this isn't like her either, she's really more the long-suffering type," the nurse added, nodding her head in Ruth's direction. "It's like she's in a trance. She's only gotten worse since we called."

"Let me see if I can talk with her," Dorothy suggested. "Can I have a few minutes alone with her?"

"I suppose you'll catch her when she falls?" the attending asked impatiently. "What we need is for her to sit down so we can administer a sedative. You'll have plenty of time to talk with her later."

"You called me," Dorothy retorted, "so give me a minute. I understand the physical danger. I don't want her to be traumatized more than she is already. As you can see, she's losing momentum." While they'd been sniping over what to do, Ruth's singing had turned to a moan. Dr. Morrissey edged quietly toward the bed.

"Ruth," Dorothy gently coaxed. "My name is Dr. Morrissey. Can you do me a favor and sit? You've got everyone worried here."

Ruth glowered at Dr. Morrissey, no evidence of long-suffering there, but complied and slumped to the mattress. "I don't want to be a mean ole thing," she said. "Mama says, Aunt Sylvie's a mean ole thing." The attending moved quickly with the sedative.

"She needs to sleep," he said. "Come back in the morning, and you can have all the time you need." A frustrated sigh escaped Dorothy. *Just when we were getting somewhere,* she thought.

Though she didn't like the attending physician's attitude, Dorothy reluctantly agreed that the poor woman needed a good night's sleep. In Ruth's state, the most Dorothy could do was listen to what the song was revealing about Ruth's state of mind. And if she were honest, that would be more fun for her than Ruth. The power of the unconscious drew Dorothy like a moth to a flame. Everyone else in the room saw Ruth's singing as mere gibberish. Dorothy knew it meant something, but she'd have to wait until morning. In situations like this, however, Dr. Morrissey wondered why she was called in the first place. Why call her at two in the morning only to snap at her when she tried to help? The doctor certainly did not need her permission to administer a sedative. The sedative worked quickly. Ruth fell back on the pillows, and her eyelids became heavy. A nurse tucked her in, covering her with a sheet and blankets. The doctor ushered everyone else from the room. He turned to Dorothy, "I'm sorry I snapped. This has been a stressful night. Ruth's been on bed rest here for three months. We all feel close to her. I hate that she lost the baby."

"I understand," Dorothy said. "Everything's worse at two in the morning. I'll be in my office if you need me. No point in driving back home."

Dorothy had thrown on the skirt and blouse she had laid out before going to bed, assuming there would be no going home that night. She sat on the loveseat in her office with a clipboard and notepaper to begin her documentation of the night's events. Next thing she knew, Nurse Martin was shaking her awake. "Dr. Morrissey, the maternity ward at the hospital called. They're ready for you to evaluate Ruth Johnson."

"Thanks, I must've fallen asleep over my notes."

"That was some storm last night, eh?"

"Gosh, I didn't even hear it."

✦

When Dorothy returned to the maternity ward, the shifts were changing. She saw the attending with his overcoat on, filling in the day team about Ruth's late-night performance.

"With all that blood loss, I was surprised she could stand at all, let alone on top of the bed, singing like she was. I've never seen anything like it," the doctor said. The fedora perched on his head was covered in plastic and reminded Dorothy of her grandmother's couch cushion covers. His muffler was wrapped tightly against the cold morning, and his shoes were protected from inclement weather by black galoshes. If he had chanced a look outside, he'd have seen the rain had ended and the sun coming out.

Dorothy stood in the door of Ruth's room while the nursing staff attended to the patient. There was no trace of urine wafting beneath the strong disinfectant. The room was cleared of any evidence of the other patient. The bassinet was gone, and the roommate's bed was stripped of soiled linens and newly made with hospital corners. Early morning light peeked through the semi-closed blinds, inviting the room's sole occupant to avail herself of any ray of hope offered and gave Dorothy sufficient light to see her. Otherwise, the room was dark. The staff was busy readying Ruth for a transfer to the asylum. One had just finished helping her get into a pair of sweats and sweatshirt while the other worked to dry and pin back the front of Ruth's afro, which still dripped from a shower. For the first time, Dorothy could see that Ruth wasn't much older than she.

One of the nurses joined Dorothy at the door while the other finished Ruth's hair. "Ruth doesn't like fluorescent lighting," she said. The only other source of light came from above the empty bed next to Ruth's.

"Was she averse to fluorescent lighting before the stillbirth?"

"Yes, she said it bothered her. Why do you ask?"

"I wonder if she already had anxiety."

"She did say they made her nervous."

"Someone should have informed the night staff," Dr. Morrissey told the nurse, exasperation tightening around her mouth and straining her voice. "When I got here last night, every last light was on. No wonder she was agitated."

"Couldn't have helped," the nurse said. "She's had a terrible time of it, poor thing." Sympathy and her intimate knowledge of Ruth's preference soothed Dorothy's irritation. "She's been through a lot physically, and mentally she's not at all herself. We managed to get her into the shower, at least."

"I understand she's been here for three months on bed rest?"

"That's right. We all love Ruth. It's been so sad."

"Where's her husband?"

"Between you, me, and the bedpost, he must be some kind of horse's ass." Now, it was the nurse's turn to feel exasperated. "All I know is, he hasn't been around." They both looked to see if Ruth heard, but Ruth was in her own world, passively submitting to the hairstyling.

"What about immediate family?"

"She comes from a huge family."

I can work with that, Dorothy thought. She always sought a point of connection with her clients. That they were both from big families was just such a point.

"I've seen her brothers and an aunt, but her parents don't come in."
Sounds like my parents, Dorothy thought. "Ruth said they're afraid of
hospitals. She talks on the phone with her mother frequently, though."

"So, she has some support?"

"I would say so. Ruth also belongs to a church. And she has a beautiful
voice," the nurse said, her genuine fondness for Ruth soothed Dorothy
in its embrace. Dorothy imagined this nurse's patients becoming very
attached to her. "I'll let you talk with her. I should get back to my other
patients. Let me know if I can help."

"Thanks," Dorothy said, as the nurses left the room. She turned to
Ruth.

Ruth rocked back and forth, singing quietly. Dorothy didn't recognize the song, but it sounded like church music, though not the
Catholic hymns she was accustomed to hearing. She tried to concentrate on the lyrics, but Ruth sang so softly that the words were impossible to discern. Her head was upturned, but her eyes were closed like
she imagined a different place entirely. A single tear slipped from her
eye and down her cheek. Whatever the song, it sounded very sad to
Dorothy, like the songs from her sister's funeral. She hadn't known
those lyrics either, but the melodies could still bring tears to Dorothy's
eyes. She waited a few moments to see if Ruth would pause to look
at her, but Ruth kept on singing, ignoring Dorothy's presence. By all
accounts, Ruth had slept through the night, but defeat and grief exuded
from every cell that wouldn't be cured by one good night's sleep. Three
months of bed rest rendered her face slack and pallid, accentuating
the sorrow around her eyes and mouth. Swollen eyelids blended with
the dark circles beneath, making it look like she was squinting, and
obscuring large, dark brown eyes. Shoulders rounded and slumped as
if to protect a soft underbelly where once a baby had been.

Dorothy thought Ruth's singing might be her way of warding off
the prying questions from the nurses, doctors, and psychologists. Or
perhaps singing was the only way she knew how to express her grief.
Dorothy tried again.

"Ruth, what happened last night?" Dorothy was gentle and spoke just loud enough to be heard but stood firmly planted, suggesting, in her way, that she would not be leaving any time soon. She could be particularly stubborn when deprived of her beauty rest. The grieving patient finally opened her eyes and gazed at Dorothy. She stopped her singing. Her eyes looked vacant, responding to the cue but not really seeing her.

"They gave me a shot to dry up my milk," Ruth said.

Okay, lucid. Dorothy thought. Having never been pregnant, she wouldn't even try to pretend she understood how final that must have felt.

"They said I need to have a bowel movement before they can discharge me, but I'm all backed up. And Mrs. Ellis wouldn't stop snoring. I wasn't trying to hit her or anything. I just wanted her to shut up." What were they thinking, putting a new mother in with a bereaved mother? She felt an overwhelming urge to wrap her arms around the poor woman, who sat on the edge of her bed, head hung low over slumping shoulders, fat tears falling to her lap. She wore green Michigan State sweats. Despair enveloped the woman and sucked the air out of the room, threatening to swallow them both whole.

Dorothy wrote a quick note. *Ruth Fitzgerald Johnson grieving stillborn baby after three months of hospital bed rest. Indication of a post-partum psychotic episode, but currently lucid. Overwhelmed by grief.*

The physical and mental toll of three months of inactivity, the trauma and anguish of stillbirth, to say nothing of the hysterectomy, emptied any animation from Ruth's face and body like an emptied sack discarded on the ground. Filling her back up with hope would be a daunting task. Ruth hiccupped when she tried to catch her breath. Only the dimples in her cheeks hinted toward happier times. She wondered if Ruth remembered standing on the bed, and if so, she wanted to hear about the incident from Ruth's perspective.

Ruth began singing just loud enough for Dorothy to pick out some lyrics. *"Oh, Lord, in me, there lives a weeping..."*

Dorothy did not recognize the song but got the message. She stayed quiet to see if Ruth would look at her. Ruth continued singing between hiccups.

"Child of my waters swept away by the tide..."

After a few minutes, Dr. Morrissey tried again. "I can't help, Ruth, if you won't talk to me."

"Why'd they give my baby to Mrs. Ellis?" Ruth said suddenly.

Oh, no. Dorothy thought. *Not lucid.*

"Where'd they take her? They want to keep giving me shots, so I'll forget what they did to my baby," Ruth said.

Dorothy scrambled to see if she could steer Ruth toward clear thinking rather than allow a descent toward psychosis. She noticed the ring on Ruth's finger.

"And your husband? Where is he?"

"Wouldn't we all like to know!" Ruth shouted, suddenly riled.

Dorothy opened her mouth to speak but then thought better of it. She waited glad she'd asked the nurse already about Ruth's husband to give her a baseline to compare Ruth's grasp of reality.

"I only know what my brothers tell me, which is he's a lying, cheating, SOB. Couldn't even be bothered to sit with me these past three months."

"I'm so sorry, Ruth. You must feel very angry with him."

"Who am I to blame him? I can't give him a child."

"Forgive my bluntness, but at best that makes him an insensitive jerk." Outrage tightened around Dorothy's shoulders. She rubbed at them to loosen up. She saw that Ruth noticed. "Fell asleep at my desk last night," she explained, glad that Ruth was alert. "Has he been to see you since the baby died?"

"Nope."

"Now I understand why the nurse said he's a horse's ass." Dorothy was rewarded with a dimpled smile.

"Yeah, I fought so hard for this baby. Just lying here day in and day out while he's out there finding himself a new woman." Ruth fell back into a puddle of tears. Like her song, everything about her situation felt like drowning. Dorothy dove in after her.

"They said all I had to do was lie still and everything would be all right. For three months, not moving a muscle. Didn't matter, I lost her, and they take out my uterus. Why me? What do I have left?" She wiped at her nose with the sleeve of her sweatshirt.

Ruth's and maternity ward nurse's account of husband consistent, but Ruth also expressed a belief that her baby given to another patient. Dorothy wrote. *Discuss later after the patient gets more sleep before making a definitive diagnosis.* She looked at Ruth. "I don't get it either," she said.

"I've been a faithful servant my whole damn life. This was my second stillborn, you know. Twins the first time, twenty-six weeks, I didn't think it could get any worse. That's why they put me on bed rest."

"I'm so sorry," Dorothy said.

"All I have left is a horse's ass for a husband. What the hell am I supposed to do?"

"You know what, Ruth? I can't imagine anyone could hold up well under these circumstances," Dorothy said.

"Really?" Ruth said, looking Dorothy in the eye. "I said to God, I give up," What do you want from me? Is that wrong?"

"Anybody in their right mind would lose their faith," Dorothy assured her.

"So, I'm not crazy?"

"No, you've had an expected response to a traumatic situation."

"Does that mean you're sending me home?" Anxiety, not hope, replaced despair for a brief moment.

"Actually, no. I think you've had a post-partum psychotic episode," Dorothy said, glad to be able to console Ruth in this one instance. "Probably due to the trauma, the hormonal fluctuations, and grief. I'd like to keep you over for observation."

"Will they get my baby back from Mrs. Ellis?" Just now, Dorothy wanted to slap whoever had the bright idea to put a new mother and baby in the same room as Ruth. Regardless, Ruth's words confirmed the need for a transfer to SLA, where she could receive psychiatric help. At the very least, Ruth could rest and delay a return to the shambles of her upended life.

"Let's get you settled in a new bed, and we can talk later," Dorothy said. "Is that okay with you?" Ruth nodded and soon began to hum as if to mark the end of their conversation.

As Dorothy stood to leave, she said, "Thanks, Ruth, for talking with me."

Feeling dejected after absorbing the tragedy of Ruth's life, Dorothy returned to her office to set up a consult with the psychiatrist to treat Ruth's psychotic features, depression, and possible mania. Then she wrote a clinical note.

4/29/1974, New Patient: Ruth Fitzgerald Johnson. DOB 6/17/1939. The initial evaluation conducted on maternity ward following psychotic episodes with manic features. Ruth presented as irritable and grieving with delusions, including obsessive concern that her child had been given to roommate. No history of psychosis or mania before the episode. Working diagnosis, complicated grief due to stillbirth, physical, and emotional trauma. Emotional trauma complicated by husband's rumored affair while Ruth was on bed rest. Rule out post-partum psychosis, generalized anxiety, and dependence disorder. The patient denies suicidal ideation. Protective factors: religious, nurturing personality, resilience, large extended family.

CHAPTER NINE

SUPERVISION

Dorothy ducked out at lunch to go for a swim at the YWCA. She wanted to gather her thoughts before supervision with the psychiatrist, Dr. Keith. She needed to talk about Ruth, but George was niggling at her as well. Once in the water, she counted every stroke to keep track of her laps, but parallel thoughts about her clients floated above the rhythmic movement.

As she worked out the tension held in her body from the session with her new patient, she couldn't let go of the way Ruth excused her husband's behavior because she could not give him a child. Would Kenneth justify cheating on her because she refused to have children? Kenneth tried very hard to be a modern man. He'd read *The Feminine Mystique.* He wanted to support Dorothy as a career woman but, every now and then, he let slip disbelief in Dorothy's assertion that she didn't want children, which told Dorothy that he wanted children. And why didn't she? Dorothy's reasons for denying them were not clear to her outside of her experience as a middle child. She never saw her mother as particularly happy raising so many kids. There was no time. Dorothy remembered feeling so jealous of the way her best friend Mary Anne's mother would just pull Mary Anne onto her lap. Dorothy's mother never sat down long enough to pull a child in for a cuddle. Memories of her mother swirled within the strong odor of Clorox, her mother's go-to cleanser for kitchen counters and bathrooms. Having kids felt like a crap shoot. What if she had a child who turned out like Deirdre? Deirdre's moods ruled the roost. Dorothy couldn't stand her, and she could feel her parents' resentment toward Deidre as well, no matter how emphatic their praise. The only thing worse was losing a child. How have they gone on after losing Tess? Daunting challenges that inspired awe and dread all at once. Every bit of procreation scared her—the sex, the emotional intimacy, the vulnerability. To say nothing of the physical toll on the body.

Ruth felt her life was over because she couldn't have children. That must have taken some courage to try again after losing two. How was it that Ruth didn't feel afraid? Her thoughts, a jumble of concern, guilt, and worry, merged and smoothed out with every turn of her head for the inhale then back in the water blowing out the anxiety. As she counted and breathed, each stroke released a bit more of the tightness in her back and shoulders until, with the mile completed, she felt relaxed and ready to face the uncomfortable scrutiny of supervision. She'd let George go for another time.

✦

Supervision was a combination of therapy, training, and advice. Dorothy outlined a treatment plan for Ruth to talk with Dr. Keith about, hoping to stay off her personal life. Of the psychiatrists at St. Lawrence Asylum, she sought out Dr. Keith to clinically supervise her because he was the least condescending. Her father's age, he'd had a long career at St. Lawrence. He had extensive clinical training in psychodynamic theory. He even looked like Freud with his white hair and beard, and he smoked a pipe during consultations. She noticed the pipe and tobacco on his desk when she entered. He'd devoted his life to the care of the mentally ill and moved his office to the hospital wing with the patients. Most of all, he had a nice laugh. A laugh that made him seem innocent and impish at the same time.

In contrast, his colleagues were busy claiming new offices to set up a private practice in the newly renovated old asylum, now medical building, leaving the therapy in the residential treatment facility to the psychologists. Just as she'd thought, Mitch Kelley's company was clearing some of the land for a car dealership nearby. So, in an ironic plot twist, the residents in the old asylum had better views than the pampered egos of those treating them.

Dr. Keith wasn't exactly getting a raw deal. His office was large and well-appointed. His desk was a massive mahogany with a leather inlay on top and surrounded by leather desk chairs. A Smith-Corona typewriter sat on his desk as he preferred a typed written note. "My handwriting is atrocious," he'd said when she'd asked if she should be typing her notes. "I'm also writing a novel on the side." He winked after he'd told her, like *aren't we all?* A Persian rug framed a separate sitting area for treatment with a leather chair, a chaise lounge, and a full sofa. Floor-to-ceiling bookcases filled with books on Freudian, Jungian, Adlerian, Rogerian, you name it, warmed the room. She wondered if he painted his travels as a hobby because many unframed canvases of beachscapes and lighthouses hung on the walls. What she didn't see were pictures of a wife or children. She felt like she was entering an inner sanctum.

"Make yourself comfortable, Dr. Morrissey," he said. He motioned for Dorothy to sit across the desk in one of the leather chairs. Dorothy perched rather uncomfortably, still a bit nervous in his presence.

"Who are we talking about today?" he said. He lit a match and held it over the tobacco in his pipe, puffing at the stem to get it to take. The aroma served to sanctify the space like incense streaming from a thurible during mass.

"I want to start with a new patient. Her name is Ruth Johnson. African-American, early thirties, post-partum psychosis after a stillbirth. She was on three months of bed rest because she previously had stillborn twins and a couple of miscarriages. They had to give her a hysterectomy due to extensive hemorrhaging. They are still waiting on the pathology report. I'd like to rule out a heart condition as well."

"Always rule out the physical," he said. "How many psychotic episodes has she had?"

"I'm only aware of the one at this point, but her delusion that her baby was given to another patient has been intractable," Dorothy said. "We've admitted her, and we'll be monitoring her closely. I'd like to see how she is after she gets a few good nights' sleep." She kept her tone clinical, not disclosing how upsetting Ruth's situation was for her.

"I'll prescribe a sedative for now, but if the episodes persist, we may need to prescribe Haldol."

"Okay, I would like to give her a few days and proceed with grief counseling first."

"Group therapy?"

"I can get her into a group, yes."

"Good, keep me updated. If she needs medication, we'll get her on it, but I agree, she needs some time to grieve, and for her hormone levels to return to normal."

"Thank you, doctor," Dorothy said.

"By the way, I've heard good things about your work, albeit your methods are unconventional?"

"Really?" she said, pleased, sitting up a bit straighter. I try to adjust my approach according to patient needs."

"What's your theoretical orientation?" As he often said, he'd seen it all, but tried to stay abreast of current developments in the field.

"Whatever works," Dorothy said. "I like Winnicott, Carl Jung, Carl Rogers, Fritz Perls, Adler, Erikson," she said, leaning in, excited to be talking theory with Dr. Keith.

"Oh, an eclectic, are you? Is that because you can't decide?"

"Like I said, I do whatever works. I don't see the value in limiting myself to one theory if another works better."

"I wouldn't use Gestalt around here."

"I'll admit, I like it better in theory than in practice. I'm not comfortable encouraging someone to act out. However, once we move through some of the grief and trauma with Ruth, I do think trying to keep her in the present moment might be a good idea."

"I can agree with you there," Dr. Keith said. "Not a Freud fan?"

"He was ahead of his time, I'll give him that, but I prefer Jung."

"Watered down psychodynamic," he said, but there was that endearing laugh like he enjoyed his own humor.

"To each his own," she said, feeling her heart rate ramp up as she held her ground despite his laugh taking the sting out of the challenge. "Regardless, Freud isn't suitable for Ruth's treatment." Hands followed heart rate as Dorothy defended her position. She wasn't about to wax eloquent now about her interest in the archetypes or dream analysis because she wasn't sure if she was being tested or if he just wanted to talk.

"Let's move on," he said. "I hear you have been assigned George Eavey. How's that going?"

"Alright," Dorothy said. Sparring over theoretical orientation suddenly felt like a cakewalk.

"You don't sound very enthusiastic," Dr. Keith said. "Has he gotten violent?"

"No, nothing like that," Dorothy replied. "This is hard to admit but I just don't like him. And it's like an aversion. I can't put my finger on why. He's smart, cooperative even though everyone said he wouldn't be, went to Catholic school like I had, so I get him..."

"Ding, ding, ding," Dr. Keith said before she could finish her thought. "Projection is the obvious issue here. Have you and he discussed your similar upbringing?"

"I try to keep my personal life out of the therapy session," Dorothy replied.

"Good luck with that," Dr. Keith said laughing again. "It's impossible to keep your personal life and history out of the session. Everything that has ever happened to you, conscious or not, enters the therapy session."

"I'm trying everything I can to get him to open up about his life. I feel like I'd be taking away from his experience if I deflect with my own." Resistance restricted her breathing, stiffened her mind.

"Isn't it interesting that you both have ended up in the same place?"

"I chose to be here. He didn't." She pushed the pout down.

"Some would say there are no coincidences." Her resistance tightened the vise in her chest as her body tightened up. *So much for swimming*, she thought. If she knew she was resisting, Dr. Keith would certainly pick it up. "Let's try an exercise, Dorothy. I think you will find this useful for both you and your patients, perhaps most especially, George." Dr. Keith began an active imagination exercise with Dorothy. "Close your eyes and imagine George sitting on the other side of the room at a safe distance from you. Can you see him?" Dorothy nodded. "Okay, now tell me the very first thing that bugs you about George, not just a word but a phrase or full sentence."

"If he was so cherished by his parents how the hell did he end up in here?" Dorothy was shocked at how easily that came to mind.

"Does he tell you he was cherished by his parents?" Dr. Keith asked.

"No, his mother came to see me. She doesn't understand why he hasn't been released. She talked about how cute he was and how much they loved him. All I could think was, then why is he in here?"

"So, let me ask you this—how might this relate to you?"

"I wasn't cherished at all." Again, Dorothy was surprised at how easily that slipped from her mouth.

"So, in your mind, someone who is cherished shouldn't make the kinds of mistakes that George has made?"

"He had parents who would listen to him." She sputtered here. "They would have been there for him if he had a problem." Now she was trying to push down tears and the pout. A toddler could keep it more together. She recalled the belt story.

"So, you feel like your parents did not listen to you?"

"That is an understatement. Not at all. I'm fourth of nine."

Dr. Keith nodded.

She went on. "He has shared a story which would say otherwise if I'm honest. They didn't listen to him at all. But he hasn't provided me with any details, and he doesn't show any emotion."

"Perhaps, he doesn't fully trust you, Dorothy. If you let him in even a little bit, then maybe just maybe he will give you more. Find out what prevented him from going to his parents. It's worth pursuing. What's important for you and him in the therapy process is finding out why it feels threatening to you. You don't have to talk to George about that, but you do have to ponder why you don't feel like your parents were there for you and the connection to George's story. Okay, now take a breath and close your eyes again. Imagine you are looking over at George again from a safe distance. What do you see?"

"He's scowling. He's angry." This time she started laughing because she knew what Dr. Keith was going to say.

"Isn't that funny?" he said. "You're scowling and you're angry. Worth exploring, don't you think?"

"I can't imagine George would appreciate it if I told him that I understand his anger."

"You don't have to tell him you understand his anger, Dorothy," Dr. Keith said. "You just need to understand your own."

"What do I have to be angry about?" Dorothy asked.

"Anyone who didn't feel cherished as a child is bound to feel angry." He smiled at her, and she suddenly felt able to relax again as if the benefits of her earlier swim had just kicked in. "I think you'd find it helpful to do some writing around these themes especially when you can't account for your reactions to patients or anyone else for that matter."

"I will," Dorothy agreed. "This was very helpful, Dr. Keith."

"I'm glad, Dr. Morrissey," he said. "Keep me posted on them both."

"Thank you, Doctor." She left his office, feeling invigorated and ready to get back to her patients.

CHAPTER TEN

MARCELLA MAFOUD
PERSONALITY DISORDER—THERAPIST SUFFERS

The atmosphere tingled like static as soon as Dorothy walked in as if she brought the lightning in with her from the storm that had just blown through. She knew something was amiss that morning before she ever met Marcella Mafoud. Nurse Martin caught Dorothy in the hallway as she walked onto the floor. Dorothy, soaked from head to foot by a sudden downpour as she walked from the parking garage to the hospital, held her umbrella at arm's length to avoid dripping on Nurse Martin's feet while she filled Dorothy in on the situation. Her own feet squished inside sodden nylon stockings and shoes. This was the very reason she left her first appointment on Mondays open.

Marcella, an undergraduate from Michigan State, was another patient well-known to the psychiatric staff. Marcella was described as "crisis-prone," when Dorothy was handed her file.

"Marcella had an accident," the nurse informed her with finger quotes. Certain patients fatigued the staff with their histrionics. Marcella was one of them. In and out of the hospital after injuring herself while on campus, her impulsive behavior followed by emphatic denials of suicide ideation or intent to harm herself was exhausting to all involved. The fluctuations in her parents' decisions regarding her care made matters worse. Just as Marcella began to make headway in her treatment, her parents would disrupt her progress by insisting she was stable and needed to get back to the university. Apparently, the whole family operated in crisis mode.

"What happened?" Dorothy asked, holding her breath and hoping it wasn't too bad.

"She cut herself. Slashed up her thighs with a nail file."

"That doesn't sound like an accident," Dorothy said. "And where, in God's name, did she get her hands on a nail file?"

"No clue. My goodness, she's still got her arm bandaged. Now this. Here's the other interesting piece," Nurse Martin whispered. "She said she was upset because you're mad at her."

"Oh, for crying out loud," Dorothy said. "I barely know her. How could I be mad at her? That's diagnostic, isn't it?"

"That's what I thought," Nurse Martin agreed. A psychiatric nurse for a long time, she'd learned a lot about how patients exhibited mental illness. "Are you thinking about borderline personality disorder?"

"The impulsivity, self-harm, putting me on a pedestal then knocking me off again—all signs. I hesitate to attach a label to a college student, but it's like she's read the handbook on borderline personality disorder."

"As Dr. Smith likes to say—Mood disorder, patient suffers. Personality disorder, therapist suffers."

"Ha, so true," Dorothy said. The erratic behavior and emotional push-pull—*You're the best, you're the worst*—was indicative of borderline personality disorder. Dorothy recoiled as much from the flattery so full of expectation that she could save someone as she braced herself for the fall when the client pushed her off the pedestal when they realized she couldn't. She could only accompany them on the journey. "I'll talk with her. Give me ten minutes."

"Will do, Dr. Morrissey," the nurse said. "One more thing, her parents want her released so she can finish up the semester. Do you think Marcella is trying to tell them something?" She smiled at her colleague.

"That would be my guess," Dorothy said, shaking her head.

"I'll fetch her in ten minutes," Nurse Martin walked back toward the desk.

"Thanks," Dorothy replied. She unlocked her office, took off the dripping coat, and hung that and the umbrella in the closet. Opening the window a crack for the fresh rain-soaked air, she took a deep breath and sent a prayer heavenward. "Help me, help her, God." Dorothy hedged her bets with difficult patients by praying for help. She couldn't save the client but maybe God could. Dr. Morrissey had not been angry with Marcella. She'd only just met her last week, but she could still feel how she inwardly recoiled from the flattery ("you're so much better than my counselor at school") just as she now braced for the fall from the pedestal. What was behind Marcella's disappointment in her? Of course, wasn't that the mindset, conscious or unconscious of the person with BPD? *If you're not saving me, you're abandoning me.* She took another deep breath, straightened the pillows on the loveseat, and turned on the overhead lights. The skies were very gray, and the room was dark. There was a soft knock. Nurse Martin entered with the patient. Marcella took her seat, looking coyly at Dr. Morrissey like the cat who swallowed the mouse. Dr. Morrissey took her place in the armchair across from her.

"Do you want to tell me what happened, Marcella?" Dr. Morrissey began, tamping down irritation.

"It was just an accident," Marcella responded innocently. She tucked her legs up beneath her, situating her slim body firmly against the arm of the loveseat. She smiled sweetly at Dorothy and brushed her long, straight hair from her eyes with her one good arm. The other was bandaged and in a sling.

"Who are you trying to kid, Marcella?" Dorothy said, bluntly.

"I wasn't trying to kill myself."

Marcella had a history of emergency room visits for presumed suicide attempts that she explained away as accidents. The tipping point for Marcella's last psychologist was when Marcella put her elbow through a window at a house party off-campus. Dorothy believed multiple therapists only added to Marcella's issues but took her case. Tall and thin that bordered on frail, Marcella's skin shone with a bronze glow. Her eyes were brown with green flecks. She appeared to be every bit the college student, with her silky black hair parted in the middle and cascading down her back. She typically wore mini-skirts and cowboy boots as she entered the hospital's emergency room door, which was why she usually cut her stomach or the very top of her thighs.

"Let's say I believe you, Marcella, and I do. I don't believe you're suicidal."

Marcella raised one eyebrow, her head tilted, and her lips turned up in a slight smile. "So, can I go back to school?"

"Just because you're not suicidal doesn't mean you're not a danger to yourself."

Marcella took a deep breath then shrunk down into the couch, making a pouty face. "Oh, poo! That's not fair. I don't even go that deep. Would you like to see?"

"Would I like to see what?" Dr. Morrissey responded. When her patient looked up, the doctor held her gaze.

"My cuts. You can see when you look at them that I wasn't trying to kill myself."

"I'll take your word for it," Dr. Morrissey said. Seeing the wounds did not serve a purpose. What she wanted to see were the emotional wounds. "I worry that one day you will go too far. You might not mean to kill yourself, but you could accidentally go too deep or hit an artery. You could easily die even if you don't intend to."

"My mom says I've always been accident-prone," the young woman responded, cavalier in her dismissal of Dorothy's concern.

Dorothy leaned toward Marcella with a steady gaze, so there would be no mistaking what she was about to say. "Cutting is not an accident. In fact, it's quite deliberate. I believe it's a cry for help or an expression of emotional pain. I guess what I'd like to focus on is why. What is beneath the self-harm?"

"Are you going to make me do trust falls or something?" Marcella deflected with sarcasm. "Can I smoke in here?"

Dorothy sat back as if to indicate that she was not going to work harder than Marcella. "No to both questions, but that reminds me. Before we can proceed, we need to clear something up."

"What's that?" She shifted her weight but leaning into the bandaged arm was clearly painful, so she shifted back to her original position.

"I understand you think I'm angry with you?" Dorothy said. She was not about to tiptoe around the pedestal she'd apparently fallen from.

Marcella exhaled, blowing the hair out of her eyes. "I didn't mean it," Marcella responded. "I was just upset because I thought you'd be mad at me after I put my elbow through the window."

"When you put your elbow through the window, you were not my patient. Perhaps you're upset that you have a new therapist?" Dr. Morrissey asked.

"No, that guy was weird," Marcella responded. "But that meant ..." she trailed off, looking out the window as if trying to remember the window in question.

"Meant what?"

"That you had to take me," Marcella said. She looked away. Marcella's acts were like desperate messages, smoke signals, SOS, *somebody help me*. Perhaps, there was a secondary gain she sought from the self-harm. Someone would have to notice.

"I was more than happy to take you on as a client," Dorothy said.

"Everyone thinks I'm a pain in the ass," Marcella said. "No one likes me." By this time, the rain had stopped, and more light was filtering into the room. A cool breeze dissipated the mustiness that had built up over the long weekend.

"Look at me, Marcella," Dorothy said. "We can like you, yet, not like your behavior. Of course, I don't want you to self-harm, but I'm not angry with you. I want to find out why you harm yourself. Can you accept that?"

Marcella nodded, a tad bit reluctantly. "You're my shrink, so you have to like me," she said.

"No, actually, I don't," Dr. Morrissey responded, "nor can I make you want to get better. That's up to you." She moved slightly forward again, testing the waters.

"What if I told you that I don't know how to stop?"

"That's why I hope you can learn to trust me. I believe you are trying to get your parents to listen to you. Most people act out when they feel misunderstood. We want someone to hear us. Self-harm feels, to me, like you're desperate for someone to listen."

"I don't think they will ever listen to me," Marcella screwed her lips to one side in an endearing effort to hold back her tears.

"Unfortunately, all too often, it is those to whom we are closest, who misunderstand us the most," Dorothy said more gently. *I should know,* she thought.

"Then what do I do?" Marcella asked.

"If you let me, we can work together. You tell your story, and I will listen."

"Where do I start?" She leaned toward Dorothy, hope replaced sarcasm.

"First, we need to set some guidelines. Self-harm keeps all of us in crisis mode. It's like there's a big hole in your roof, and no one thinks to fix it until there's a storm overhead. So, I would like you to try as best you can to not harm yourself, so we can begin to patch the roof while the sun is shining."

"How do I do that?"

Dorothy didn't want to get her hopes up, but there was earnestness in Marcella's question. "How about we start with delaying when you feel an urge to hurt yourself."

"Delay how?"

"Breathing, writing, drawing, jumping jacks, talk to a friend, whatever works for you. Just try to distract away from the impulse to harm. See if the urge will pass."

"What if it doesn't work?" She started to work a piece of her hair.

"Pay attention to your thoughts and feelings. Where are you feeling them in your body? What thoughts are running through your head? Ask yourself if the thoughts have any basis in fact, like would they hold in court of law? For instance, Marcella, why is it you are so ready to believe that I would be mad at you?"

"I don't know," Marcella responded. "I guess I always feel like I've done something wrong."

"But?" Dorothy prompted. She believed there was more to say on this.

"My mom says I have nine lives, but I don't feel like she's glad about it. Like she says, I've cheated death, but my twin didn't. So, it's not a compliment. You know?"

"So, you and your twin were involved in an accident, and she died?"

"Yes," she nodded toward the arm in a sling. "I lost my thumb from the accident. I barely remember her or what happened. My parents won't talk about it except, like I said, my mother will make comments."

"I'm so sorry, Marcella. Identical twin?"

"Yes, we were really young when she died."

"What was her name?"

"Marissa."

Marcella's monotone contrasted sharply with the sling and cuts, so Dorothy thought now was as good a time as any to demonstrate what she wanted Marcella to do. "Take a deep breath and tell me where in your body do you feel the loss of your sister?"

"I feel throbbing where my thumb should be," Marcella looked at Dr. Morrissey with wonder and curiosity.

"Where else do you feel throbbing?" Dorothy prodded gently. Marcella's free hand moved to her heart. She let it linger.

"Now let's examine a persistent belief. You said you feel like your mother blames you?"

"Only for being the one who lived."

"Well, that feels very hurtful to me, Marcella. But could there be another explanation? I'm guessing your mother's comments are more about her than you."

"Like, maybe she blames herself? Like she thinks she was a bad mother or something?" Again, a light bulb turned on in her head.

"Yes, something like that. I think this is a good place for us to start."

"I was ten before they even admitted I had a twin who died. I thought she was my imaginary friend."

Dorothy was very familiar with this complicity of silence in her own family. Her parents never talked about Tess outside of the nod they gave their oldest child during the blessing before dinner. This information provided her with the backstory that helped to explain Marcella's behavior.

"There's another problem," Marcella said.

"What's that?" Dorothy held her breath, bracing for another fall.

"It's the end of semester and my parents want me to return to MSU as soon as possible."

"I don't think that's a good idea. Being on campus probably adds to your stress. And we need time to work together to uncover more of your story."

"I can't afford to miss any more school," Marcella said, toeing the line that her parents had drawn. "My mother said that she's tired of my shenanigans." She began chewing on her cuticles. Dr. Morrissey noted her fingernail beds were raw from chewing on them. *Her anxiety must be through the roof,* she thought.

"Do you suppose they would change their minds if I spoke with them?"

"You wouldn't be the first therapist to tell them I need to be locked up."

"That's not how I would put it, but I do believe long-term treatment is the only way to move from crisis intervention to healing the trauma behind your behavior."

"I'll be fine, Dr. Morrissey. I promise. I'll go back to my therapist at MSU."

"Then, I'd like you to sign a release of information, so I can talk with your therapist there." Dorothy tried to shrug off her disappointment. "Listen, try the exercises I gave you. Don't give up."

"Sure, no problem." She looked relieved to be escaping Dorothy's scrutiny.

"And what will you do over the summer?"

"I usually do pretty well when I'm with my family. My younger sister keeps me company. She's in high school."

"Do me a favor," Dorothy said. "Before you leave for the summer, come back for the group sessions. That way, I can have eyes on you."

"Okay, I like group." With that, Marcella swung her long dark hair back off her shoulders and stood to leave. "Don't worry, Dr. Morrissey, I'll be fine, but I really need to get back to school."

After their session, Dr. Morrissey went to discuss the situation with Nurse Martin. "You were right, Marcella said her parents want her to go back to campus." She rubbed at the frustration pinching her forehead.

"I'll make sure to include in the paperwork that discharge was against medical advisement."

"Did you explain to Marcella and her parents what that meant?"

"Oh, yes," Nurse Martin said. "This isn't my first rodeo. I'll get you the discharge paperwork to sign."

"It's so frustrating," Dorothy said. "I don't know how they expect her to get better when all we are doing is crisis intervention."

Dorothy stood at the nurses' station chatting with Nurse Martin while they waited for Marcella and her parents to discharge. Dorothy hoped to catch them on their way out. Mr. Mafoud put up his hand to block Dorothy's protestations, grabbing the paperwork with the other, as Mrs. Mafoud hurried Marcella out the door. Nurse Martin turned to Dorothy and whispered, "I give her two weeks."

"I just hope she'll come for group." Shaking her head in dismay, Dr. Morrissey walked back to her office to write her note.

Dorothy's Note: *Date: 05/02/1974 Patient: Marcella Mafoud. DOB 11/30/54*

Marcella presented to the therapist after cutting her legs with a nail file. A junior at MSU, Marcella has been a frequent short-term patient due to self-harm episodes on campus. The most recent incident involved putting her elbow through a window at a house party off-campus. At which time, the patient transferred to this psychologist by senior psychologist Dr. Smith, who described the patient as "a handful" and "resistant to treatment." Marcella presented as oriented X 3, exhibiting borderline features, and anxiety. Despite multiple incidents of self-harm patient denies suicide ideation.

This therapist recommended long-term treatment to address symptoms and explore family history of trauma from an accident involving Marcella and her twin. According to Marcella, her twin died in the accident. She stated that her parents won't discuss the incident with her outside of "comments," e.g., "You are accident-prone." Parents discharged Marcella back to the MSU campus against medical advisement.

CHAPTER ELEVEN

GROUP THERAPY

Dorothy was finalizing her treatment plan for a group session when Dr. Smith stepped into her office. "Can you do me a huge favor?" he asked.

"Sure," Dorothy responded. "What do you need?"

"I have two intensive out-patient clients that need to be placed in group therapy, both female. One is a nun and the other a young adult female. Dr. Keith said you could probably add to your group."

"They won't be too disruptive?"

"These two will be a walk in the park compared to Marcella."

"Okay, we meet tomorrow." Dorothy regretted her decision as soon as the words came out of her mouth. Group therapy was integral to SLA patients' treatment, but group therapy was not Dorothy's cup of tea. In fact, she preferred one-to-one in any interaction, whether social or professional. Large gatherings made her profoundly uncomfortable. She believed that growing up in her large family was the reason she found groups overwhelming. Years of fending off barbs from sisters and parents compounded by the rejection she suffered from her friends created an internal narrative whereby she held a working (albeit irrational) assumption that people did not like her. She worried in group situations that she'd offend someone by saying the wrong thing, which made the faux pas more likely. Small and manageable was the only way to go.

This was also Ruth's first group session. The treatment plan that Dorothy had worked out with Dr. Keith was to see how Ruth interacted with Dorothy's other long-term patients. Now Dr. Smith messed up Dorothy's best-laid plans. Dr. Smith dropped the two patients' files on Dorothy's desk and quickly left before she could change her mind. As she looked over the files, Dorothy berated herself for her inability to say no. She wanted to make Ruth's introduction a gentle one because she didn't want to overwhelm her. Adding two patients would change the dynamic even more. What if they were disruptive? What was a nun doing here?

By the time the group met the next morning, Dorothy was feeling anxious. She barely slept trying to plan for every eventuality. Her morning swim did nothing to calm her anticipatory anxiety. Even more than individual sessions, groups necessitated she keep a strict time boundary no matter what came up. Many clients had a way of introducing sensitive material at the last minute, dropping a secret like a bomb, daring her to abandon them when they've just divulged the crux of their issue. Or they might lob a verbal assault on another member just as Dorothy was about to wrap up with a summary of the session's content. Today was shaping up to be no exception as she'd gotten wind of a storm brewing on the floor.

Across the expanse of the circle from Dorothy, Marcella sat on the sofa next to Ruth. Ruth's face was relaxed as if she was easily warming up to Marcella, who was whispering something to her. Next to Marcella, in a wheelchair off to the side, "Grandpa Elliot," sat closed in on himself. At seventy-five, Elliot was the oldest person in the unit. Elliot suffered from dementia, which, in its progression, made his posture slump forward so that he was curling in toward his lap. His presence at SLA was a bit of a mystery to everyone. Hailing from New York City, his family, for all intents and purposes, dumped him in Lansing, claiming they needed to protect his privacy, but they never returned to visit him. Dr. Smith spent hours in the library searching newspaper articles on microfiche about the man.

"He might just be a doddering old man to us, but he was a piece of shit," Dr. Smith told Dorothy. "No wonder his family doesn't visit." Apparently, before his diagnosis, Elliot Singer made millions as a rogue investor. "Whatever that means," Dr. Smith said. "It's all Greek to me. The bottom line, he ruined people's lives. I wonder if he remembers any of that now."

Elliot was welcomed without judgment by the other patients. He didn't actively participate as he had lost a lot of ground cognitively, but Dorothy included him because his quiet presence had a soothing effect on the other members. And to be honest, he took up a spot without demanding anything from her.

Next to Ruth in an armchair, Thomas sat with his arms crossed tightly against his chest, looking peeved. Apparently, he was still upset that no one had been paying him much attention of late. Finally, George, unlit cigarette cradled above his ear, was seated in the chair closest to Grandpa Elliot. Thomas and George observed the newcomers warily as they took their seats. One of the newcomers eyed Grandpa Elliot suspiciously as if she was among those whose lives he ruined.

"We have some new members in our group today," Dorothy said, "but before I invite them to tell us more about themselves, I'd like to review the ground rules. Remember the session lasts for one hour, and I would like to give each one of you a chance to speak, so please allow time for everyone's input, and be respectful of each other's feelings. No shouting or name-calling or assaulting of any kind. After each person has had a chance to speak, we may focus on a particular issue. As always, we respect confidentiality by not speaking about what we discuss to others outside of the group." Dorothy looked across the circle to Ruth. "Ruth? Would you like to tell the group a bit about yourself?"

"I'm Ruth. I like to sing."

"So, we've heard," Thomas said. Ruth's face fell.

"I like singing," Marcella said. "Don't let him bother you."

Dorothy turned to Krystal on her left. "Would you like to introduce yourself?"

Barely out of her teens, she was short and stocky with curly close-cropped brown hair except for the mohawk atop her head dyed a bright pink. A tattoo of an anchor peeked from beneath her sleeve. She wore a thick leather strap with three metal snaps around each wrist. From experience, the other group members assumed she was covering up the scars from previous suicide attempts, and they were right. She wore tight black jeans over black, lace-up ankle boots and a baggy tee-shirt. Nothing about her suggested an embrace of her more feminine attributes. And the brass knuckles, studded leather choker, and Swiss army knife that were confiscated upon admission served to reinforce the masculine biker stereotype she sought to portray.

"My name is Krystal Dawn Porter. That's Krystal with a K." She scoured the room for a reaction like a Doberman on the lookout for an intruder.

"Can you share with the group a bit about yourself, Krystal?"

"Sure, I tried to kill myself, end of story." Krystal stared out at the rest of the group. "Why the hell are you all staring at me?"

"Doesn't your get-up invite scrutiny?" Thomas asked.

"I would like to finish the introductions before we start any discussion," Dorothy stated. "Sister Mary Claire, would you like to tell the group a bit about yourself?"

No one needed to be told that Sister Mary Claire was a nun. She wore the traditional white and black habit of the Adrian Dominicans like armor. Dorothy hadn't seen a nun in a full habit in a long time. Most sisters had abandoned the habit after Vatican II and dressed in more modern styles with shorter hemlines just below the knee and veils that sat back on the head with bangs or short cropped hair, a statement of hoped-for power sharing in the Church. Not Sister Mary Claire. She hid beneath the full habit as if the memo of changing times had failed to reach her.

Dorothy found this curious and wondered how Dr. Smith was managing with her in individual treatment. She appeared mortified to be there at all. She looked at the floor, cheeks aflame with the attention on her. Her habit seemed to have swallowed her whole, covering every part of her except her face, which retained a youthful innocence that belied years of working in the trenches among the poor and forgotten both at home and abroad. In her sixties, Sister Mary Claire looked to Dorothy to have been quite fetching in her youth.

Dorothy knew that Mary Claire's Mother Superior found her in the bathroom with razor blades. She denied any thoughts of suicide because it's a mortal sin. However, Mother Superior indicated that was exactly what Sister Mary Claire was doing. Intensive outpatient seemed insufficient for both the sister and the biker girl, but who was Dorothy to judge?

"My name is Sister Mary Claire. I don't belong here." She barely spoke above a whisper.

"Join the club!" Thomas sniffed. Mary Claire retreated into herself.

Dorothy ignored Thomas's statement and asked if Mary Claire would like to share more.

"No."

"Are we done with the introductions?" Krystal asked sarcastically.

"Yes, we are. Would you like to discuss something?" Dorothy asked, keeping her tone neutral.

"I liked to know why you're all staring at me."

"Everything about your get-up shouts stare at me," Thomas said. "And I should know."

"Yeah, Thomas," George said. "How's her get-up any worse than you parading around in a robe and velvet slippers?"

"It's not a robe, it's a kimono, you dimwit."

"Watch the name-calling, Thomas," Dorothy said. "I'm sure you can think of a nicer way to correct George."

"I didn't say her outfit was any worse than mine, George. I said, she's asking people to stare at her. Same as Sister," he said, pointing at Sister Mary Claire, who squinted against the sun pouring in from the southern-facing windows. It encircled her like a halo, imbuing her with resplendence, and thwarting her efforts to disappear beneath the layers of holy armor. Dorothy stood up and adjusted the vertical metal blinds.

"I'd rather we talk about what is bothering us or what is going well rather than point fingers at our fellow patients," Dorothy said. "For instance, I appreciate your sense of style, Thomas. I can say that if it weren't for your input, this room wouldn't look as nice as it does." His suggestions had prompted Dorothy to request (or badger, depending on differing perspectives) a budget to allow her to purchase the reasonably priced but homey furniture from Montgomery Ward that they were now sitting on.

"Is Thomas the teacher's pet?" Krystal teased.

"What I'm saying is that we all have something to contribute."

"I do have a sense of style," Thomas said.

George looked up from his dogged-eared copy of *The Communist Manifesto*. He addressed newcomer Krystal.

"So, Krystal with a K, what's with the tattoo? Were you in the Navy?" Apparently, they'd moved on from Thomas.

"What's it to you?" Krystal replied.

"Just curious," George replied, shaking his head. "My father was a commander."

"My father was in the Navy too!" Thomas said, standing up excitedly, looking at George. "He was stationed in Japan. I was born there."

"You don't say." George was mocking him. "Is that where you got your kimono?"

Thomas sat back down, deflated. "Say what you want. I was born there."

"George, that's the second time you've made a negative comment toward Thomas and his kimonos," Dorothy said. "I think you owe him an apology."

Thomas looked at George, his face twisted with hurt feelings, waiting for the apology.

"Whoa, I was just kidding. Sorry, Kemosabe," George said.

"Are you always an asshole?" Krystal was staring at George with a gleam in her eye.

"Allow me to reiterate the ground rules," Dorothy said, "but before I do, George, I think Thomas's feelings are hurt." Thomas harrumphed and looked away.

"I'm sorry, Thomas," George appeared more sincere this time. "I didn't realize I hurt your feelings. Really, I'm just goofing around."

"Do you accept his apology, Thomas?" Dorothy asked.

"I suppose," Thomas said, with an exaggerated eye roll.

"Then let's move on," Dorothy redirected. She laid out the rules for the newcomers' express benefit, adding, "We do not volley profanities at each other. George," Dorothy said. "You had a question for Krystal?"

"I asked Krystal Dawn if she was in the Navy," he replied, eyeing Krystal.

"I just like anchors," Krystal retorted. "I don't like your attitude." Dr. Smith had told Dorothy that Krystal was wary of men. Just now, it appeared she was most wary of George.

"Why are you here?" she asked him.

"Drunk and disorderly," George lied, but Dorothy would not force anyone to disclose more than they were ready to share. Still, she noted he did not make eye contact with Sister Mary Claire at all.

"That doesn't make sense. So, what are you, a sociopath?" said Krystal.

"In a word," George responded coolly. Elliot's head was nodding too.

Dorothy interjected. "Krystal, attaching labels to people is a shortcut that ignores the complexity of the human being." Dorothy was not warming to this newcomer and hoped Smith's referral was not a ruse to get Dorothy to take her on individually. "Can all of the complexity of you and your life be summed up with one word?"

"Of course not," Krystal replied. "I was thinking about a method I learned in another group. We were asked to describe ourselves in one word. I chose 'ferocious' to describe me. And I'd just guessed that George is a sociopath."

"Do tell," George winked, accepting the challenge. "What makes you so ferocious?" Mary Claire continued to stare at the ground, but the hot red flame rising up her cheeks indicated she was paying close attention to the sparring.

"Give me a minute, and I'll sum up the rest of you in a word." Krystal looked around at the others.

Another harrumph issued from Thomas. Ruth and Marcella inched closer together, afraid Krystal might come flying across the room.

Dorothy looked at Krystal, "Rather than attaching a label to someone else," Dorothy said, "would you like to explain to us why you chose ferocity as an apt description for yourself?"

"No one messes with me," Krystal said. She lobbed the warning shot at all of them, but specifically at George. Before George could respond, Thomas jumped in. He wasn't buying her bravado for one second. He knew she was faking.

"If you're so tough, what are you hiding under those cuffs?" he asked, looking at her wrists.

"What do you know?" Krystal said. "My grand-pap would say you're a flaming fairy, wearing that dress and all." Dorothy started to say something, but Thomas put up his hand.

"I got this," he said. "It's a ki-mo-no." Thomas accentuated each syllable. "I'm from Japan, remember? You're deflecting."

"I already told you. I tried to kill myself." She said, holding up wrists to show the group. "That was a long time ago, and I just don't like you all staring at them."

Marcella sat up. "I think Thomas was saying that if you're so ferocious, why would you try to kill yourself?" She looked over Ruth to catch Thomas's eye.

"I take it, you know from experience," Krystal retorted, not giving an inch.

Marcella looked at Krystal squarely. "I've never wanted to die. Dr. Morrissey said I'm acting out to get my parents' attention." Dorothy hoped that she had put it more deftly, but let it go for the time being.

"About what?" Thomas asked.

"My sister just disappeared. I mean she died, I guess, but it felt as if she disappeared because no one explained to me what happened to her. We got electrocuted." She pulled her hand out of her pocket. "That's how I lost part of my thumb. If I hadn't lost my thumb, I would have thought I made her up. My parents won't talk about her. I feel crazy."

"That is why we're here," George laughed.

"Electrocuted?" Thomas asked, intrigued. Suddenly Marcella was more interesting to him. "How?"

"That's part of the mystery. I can't remember, and my parents won't talk to me about it." She looked across the circle at Dr. Morrissey. "Dr. Morrissey wants to help me, but my parents pulled me out of here."

"Aah, poor you," George said.

Thomas piped in. "My brother also disappeared. He left home right after he turned eighteen. Didn't tell any of us where he was going, and we never saw him again. I haven't been able to make sense of why he left me. It's like he never existed."

"At least there's a chance of being reunited," Marcella said. "Death and moving away are not the same."

"Right, she didn't reject you by abandoning you on purpose," Thomas said.

Now Marcella took a turn at leveling the evil eye. "You aren't seriously equating the death of my twin sister with your brother essentially running away from home." Thomas ignored her, refusing any culpability for insensitivity.

"If only I could stop the memories," Krystal said.

"From?" Marcella asked.

"My grand-pap. I mean, I don't live with him anymore, but I can't stop the memories and nightmares. I swear, it's gonna either be him or me," Krystal's tone became menacing in her resolve.

"You're probably safer in here then," George said. "And so is your grand-pap. Though I'm guessing he doesn't deserve it."

"I'm not inpatient anymore." Krystal spoke as if she suddenly missed the place. Dorothy noted a softening in Krystal's features as if she'd felt understood. She was proud of George's show of compassion.

"I wasn't trying to kill myself either," Sister Mary Claire said, looking at Marcella. "I was just trying to get the noise to stop."

"Oh, Sister, that is not going to help," Ruth spoke kindly. "What kind of noise?"

"Careful," Thomas said to Sister Mary Claire. "She's going to break into song. On second thought, maybe you two can sing together since all of her songs are about coming to Jesus." He resettled himself with a flounce and exhaled his signature sigh.

"Would you like to elaborate, Sister?" Dr. Morrissey asked. Sister Mary Claire shook her head vigorously as if embarrassed that she was at fault for starting something.

"I'm not upset with you, Thomas. Go on and make fun," Ruth asserted as Marcella patted her hand. "My songs help me figure out who I am just like your kimonos help you."

"That's an excellent point, Ruth," Dorothy said. "We often are not able to come up with the words to express how we feel, so we find other ways to express our pain or our identity, or our hopes. Do you all understand what I mean?" she said, looking around at the group. She could see they followed. "Hymns express for Ruth what she's feeling inside." Sister Mary Claire nodded her recognition of Ruth's coping mechanism. "They are consoling. You, Thomas, find comfort, and, I dare say, your identity, through Japanese culture. The kimono speaks for you. However, we sometimes find unhealthy ways to express our emotions, such as self-injury or substance abuse. I hope that we can use our time here to find healthy forms of expression to understand ourselves better and heal our wounds. Make sense?" Dorothy was met with blank stares, but she pressed on. "For homework this week, I'd like each of you to choose a song that expresses your feelings. You can choose any genre you want from religious to Motown but take it seriously."

"I can't hear songs on the radio because that's how Denny McClain gets in touch with me," Ruth said suddenly. Something was off in her delivery.

"The former Detroit Tigers pitcher?" George asked, startled.

"Yes," Ruth said, matter-of-factly, but lobbing the verbal grenade Dorothy always feared as she closed a group session. "He's been talking to me ever since my baby died."

"What does he say?" George asked, sitting up straight.

"Three strikes, you're out," Ruth replied.

"And I thought I was nuts," Thomas muttered.

Uh, oh, Dorothy thought, hoping her alarm did not show on her face. "Thank you for sharing, Ruth, but I'm sorry our time is up for today. You and I can talk in my office as soon as we wrap up here." Her plan had been to pull Sister Mary Claire aside to pursue what she'd mentioned about the noise, but Ruth was her patient. Disappointment was written all over the other group members' faces, their prurient interest getting the better of them.

"But this was just getting interesting," George said. Ruth's face was a blank. She did not meet Dorothy's gaze.

Dorothy maintained quiet control. "Obviously, you all have trusted the group to share some very sensitive information. As you all know, we can also follow up during individual sessions. To reiterate, for homework, I would like each of you to ponder how you manage painful memories and events, and to think about what songs might express how you feel."

Thomas and Marcella hung back watching as Dorothy escorted Ruth from the room.

"Poor Ruth," Marcella said. "But that Krystal Dawn scares me."

"She's putting on a show," Thomas replied. "She doesn't scare me. Who names their child Krystal Dawn? What kind of name is that? Her mama was begging for her to cut herself up, naming her after cut glass."

CHAPTER TWELVE

RUTH

Dr. Morrissey escorted Ruth back to her office. She wasn't sure meeting was a good idea. Talking could be too taxing on Ruth, since Ruth had appeared to be in the middle of a hallucination just minutes ago. Dorothy decided to take the risk because she thought it would help her better understand what was going on if she could unravel the content of the hallucinations while they were still fresh. The time could be ideal to make some headway. At the very least, she could provide a steady presence for her patient. Dorothy helped Ruth to a seat, pulled her chair close to her so she could speak in soft tones and took a deep breath. A patient who was hallucinating was capable of anything or nothing, one never knew. They might be talking gibberish one minute, head lolling and incoherent, then make perfect sense the next. By the looks of it, Ruth had returned to herself, depressed but clear-headed.

Before she began, she apologized for the overhead lights. "I know you don't like fluorescent lights, Ruth. Table lamps are on the top of my to-do list." Ruth nodded. Dr. Morrissey began with the treatment recommendations to assess whether Ruth understood before addressing what she'd said in the group. She outlined what she and Dr. Keith had discussed, emphasizing sleep, talk therapy, and if all else failed, medication.

"I'm not taking medication," Ruth said.

"Dr. Keith will only prescribe medication if the psychotic episodes persist," Dr. Morrissey said. "I promise we'll give it time. Let's see how you are after some consistently sound sleep." Sleep was essential, but so far, Ruth's sleep was spotty at best, and, if the psychotic episodes persisted, she would need to convince Ruth of the efficacy of medications before a decision was made for her.

Ruth was having none of it. "You're trying to trick me. My momma says never to trust white men in white coats," Ruth said. Dr. Morrissey saw the muscles tighten around Ruth's mouth as she dug in her heels.

"First of all, I hope I can earn your trust. I'm not a man. And I'm not wearing a white coat, so that's a start." Did she detect a slight smile? "Did your mother have a bad experience with a doctor? Is that why she says that?"

"I don't know," Ruth said. She began to sing quietly, the same sorrowful song about the child of her waters swept away by the tide. Ruth sang soft and low, but unlike the first time, loud enough for Dr. Morrissey to discern the meaning. Perhaps Ruth wanted her to listen?

Spirituals as a defense mechanism, or is she trying to tell me something? Dorothy wrote.

Dr. Morrissey decided on a different tack since pursuing the subject of medications was met with such resistance. Trust needed to be established before any real work could get done. She decided to address the incident in the maternity ward.

"You know, Ruth," she said. "I'd like to discuss the song you sang the other night."

"What song?"

When you were jumping on the bed up in maternity," Dorothy said. "'Put on a Happy Face.'" Given Ruth's depressed affect and her new choice of music, it was inconceivable that she would sing "Put on a Happy Face."

"You were there?" Ruth asked. Color rose in her cheeks. She looked to the door like she wanted to get out of there.

"Don't be embarrassed," Dr. Morrissey said. "There was a lot of commotion. And we often don't register details when we're distraught.

You mentioned your Aunt Sylvie while you were singing. Do you remember? I'm wondering how your Aunt Sylvie relates to the lyrics in the song. Can you tell me about that?" Mentioning her aunt within the context was as significant as the song, so that was where she'd begin.

"My mother's name is Delta. My aunt Sylvie is my mother's older sister. She came to visit me while I was on bed rest. She told me Delta was married straight out of high school and had me a month later. I heard that and I called my mother right away. I asked her about my birth, she said, 'Don't listen to her. She's just jealous because she can't have children. Aunt Sylvie is a mean old thing.'"

"That sounds like a mean thing to say," Dr. Morrissey said. "Does she understand that you're not able to have any more children?"

"That was before the hysterectomy. Everyone called my mom, 'the Fertile Delta.' Everyone always said I was just like her. I just assumed I'd follow in her footsteps. Now I'm just a mean ole thing like my Aunt Sylvie."

Dorothy pulled the sheet music out of her desk drawer. She had run out to a music store to get a copy. "There seems to be a theme here for you," Dorothy said. "On the one hand, you're singing a show tune, 'Put on a Happy Face,' on the other a spiritual about losing a child. They seem all tied up together. I guess I'm wondering what's the connection? And what does your Aunt Sylvie have to do with any of it?"

"I guess because I'd hear it from my mom." She shrugged. Consciously maybe there was no connection, but Dorothy was interested in the unconscious. "I don't know," Ruth said. "My mom used to sing it whenever I was pouting. She said I was a sourpuss just like my Aunt Sylvie."

Dorothy tried again. "So, that's what you hear?" she asked.

"What I hear is I'm sick and tired of putting on a happy face when nothing is going my way," Ruth responded, her voice rising. "'Good ole Ruth. Can you watch the boys, Ruth? Can you do the dishes, Ruth? Bake me a cake, Ruth.'"

"It feels like there was no room for you to be sad or upset," Dr. Morrissey encouraged.

"Now, I find out I'm illegitimate. Maybe I was just a mistake all along." Ruth was scowling now, her body wound like a tight fist.

"Have you asked your parents about that?" Dorothy took a deep breath to prompt Ruth to do the same.

"My mother said that I shouldn't pay any attention to Aunt Sylvie. Besides, I've got bigger fish to fry."

"Like what?"

"Like Calvin, that's what. Like why I was such a fool to trust him again."

"Would you like to tell me more about Calvin?"

"Only that he's always been full of promises that he doesn't keep. I just wasted my time waiting for him to come home from college. He strung me along, cheating on me the whole time. While I should have been having my own kids, I was busy minding my little brothers. I waited and waited. My mother said she can't blame Calvin for leaving me. I failed him. He needs a woman who can give him a family."

"How do you feel about that?"

"She sure knows how to kick a gal when she's down."

"That's how it feels to me, Ruth. In fact, it makes me angry. Are you feeling angry?" Everything about Ruth communicated anger to Dorothy. Her brow was furrowed, her shoulders hunched, even her lipped curled. But she ignored the reflection.

"She doesn't get it. She popped all of us out without a problem."

"How many?"

"Twelve altogether."

"Holy cow," Dorothy said, "I thought my family was big."

Ruth blessed Dorothy with a dimpled smile as if she was glad to have something in common with the therapist. "You're from a big family too?"

"Yes, nine," Dorothy said. "Seven girls, two boys. When we have more time, we can talk about that. Right now, I want to ask about today. What's the connection to Denny McClain? You said, he talks to you through the radio?"

"My father listens to baseball on his transistor all the time." She moved her fist to her ear as if to demonstrate how he held the transistor when a game was on.

"What did you mean when you said, 'three strikes you're out'?"

"I've lost three babies. I struck out. I'll never be a mother." Anger shifted to despair, shoulders from scrunched to hunched, brow from furrowed to hooded and the saddest was in the way her mouth turned down as a fat tear slid over her cheeks.

"About that, let me circle back to the beginning of our conversation."

"I'm not taking medication." Good news, Ruth was following the thread of conversation.

"Not that. I'm talking about the song you started singing; you sang, 'child of my waters swept away by the tide,' remember?"

"What of it?" Ruth gave her a wary look.

"You've said that you will never be a mother, yet the song expresses what only a mother can know, and that is the sorrow of losing a child. You are a mother, Ruth. You just don't get to see your children grow up." Ruth considered the validity of what Dr. Morrissey just said.

"Then where's my baby?" she said. "I'm not crazy. I know she's dead. If I'd make such a good mother, then why are my arms empty? I should be potty-training the twins and complaining about sleepless nights. I'd be so happy." Wasn't hard to imagine. Ruth had the maternal body and instincts made to provide love and nurture to children. Dorothy could see Ruth puttering around a kitchen, little tykes throwing their arms around her legs, begging to be picked up.

"What I wanted to say, Ruth, is that only other mothers know the kind of pain you're experiencing. You are a mother, Ruth, a grieving mother. That's what your song is telling me."

Ruth nodded in tacit agreement.

"Don't make it hurt any less," Ruth said, folding her arms across her chest. "My arms are still empty."

"I can't imagine," Dr. Morrissey said. "But don't let anyone tell you that you're not a mother."

Tears welled in Ruth's eyes as she absorbed what her psychologist was saying.

"One last comment," Dorothy said. "You know, Ruth, the sum of your losses is great, the babies, Calvin, even God, yet there you were on the worst night of your life, singing a song that says there is hope. It's like you were telling yourself that gray skies *are* gonna clear up. Perhaps, deep down, you believe that's true?"

"Maybe," Ruth said. "As long as I don't turn into a mean ole thing."

"I know you're tired. Let's end for today. For now, I would like you to catch up on sleep. Would you like me to walk you to your room?"

"I'm okay. I can manage," Ruth said. She pulled herself up. "I like that Marcella, she's sweet." She smiled for the second time. The effect was endearing.

05/24/74: Ruth Fitzgerald Johnson: Brief session with Ruth immediately following group therapy session during which Ruth exhibited hallucinatory symptoms. Therapist took opportunity to explore content of hallucinations from the session and from emergency evaluation. Hallucinations reveal belief system regarding childbearing and self-worth as well as express Ruth's grief over loss of child and inability to have more. Pursue both in treatment. Sleep essential to healing and remitting symptoms. Plan to use music in treatment protocol as Ruth loves singing.

PART TWO: GOING DEEP

CHAPTER THIRTEEN

SUMMER 1974

DOROTHY AND KENNETH

Dorothy and Kenneth sat across from each other reading the newspaper and munching on donuts. Kenneth had a weakness for Dawn's Donuts and Dorothy had easily joined in his obsession. Her favorite was the nutty donut. She chewed hers thoughtfully followed by a sip of coffee while Kenneth dunked his straight into his coffee then shoved the donut in whole. Sundays always meant Dawn Donuts and the Sunday paper for the couple now. Kenneth was absorbed in *The Lansing State Journal*. Dorothy was staring at a section of *The Detroit Free Press* that her mother sent her even though she knew Dorothy subscribed.

The section, which she was now scowling at was the nuptials page of *The Detroit Free Press*. Dorothy looked down at the smiling faces of her childhood friends gathered around her old nemesis, Leslie Anders. She showed the picture to Kenneth. "This is my mother, Kenneth," she said, holding the paper out in front of him. He looked confused. "No, I mean this is what my mother does to me. She sends me the wedding pictures of the one girl I hated most in grade school. Why in God's name," she said, "does Mother insist on shoving this down my throat?"

"Are you sure that was her motive?" Kenneth asked. "Maybe she thought you'd be interested."

"I've already told her that I'm not interested in the least. I hate Leslie Anders," Dorothy said with a vehemence that surprised both. To Dorothy, it felt as if her mother and Leslie were in cahoots to make sure Dorothy never forgot how easily Leslie stole her friends with excursions only afforded by the wealthy, and her tactics on the playground that left Dorothy on the outside looking in.

Just then the phone rang. Kenneth reached behind him to answer. "For you," he said.

"This is Dr. Morrissey," she said, assuming it was a work call.

"Dottie? It's me, Louise. WHO WAS THAT?" she asked as if she'd just hit the jackpot, unwrapping the shroud around Dorothy's life.

"A friend," Dorothy said as coolly as she could muster. Kenneth gave her the side-eye.

"Invite him to the wedding!" Louise said enthusiastically. "By the way, I'm calling about the wedding. You can tell me all about *your friend* later." For once, Dorothy was relieved that Louise was so self-absorbed. "Got a minute?" her sister asked.

"Of course," Dorothy said. "Is everything alright?"

"Did you see my Banns of Marriage announcement in the paper?" Louise asked.

"I did not," she said to Louise.

"Mom said she sent you *The Detroit Free Press,*" Louise clarified as if Dorothy might have forgotten their hometown newspaper.

"Mom sent me Leslie Anders wedding announcement."

Louise laughed. "Jesus, Mary, and Joseph. She loves to rub it in, doesn't she?"

"I'll say."

"Speaking of Mom, I need a favor," Louise said.

"What's that?"

Louise paused for a deep intake of breath. "Can you talk to her about Deirdre?" She asked in her best little sister whine. "I really don't want her in the wedding."

"Why don't you tell her yourself?"

"C'mon, Dorothy, you're the psychologist. She'll listen to you."

"Since when?"

"Please, Dottie, if she pulls another stunt like she did at Norah and Nell's wedding, I'll be so embarrassed. She'll ruin everything."

"God help us if she starts drinking," Dorothy commiserated with her sister.

"That's the least of my problems. What if she won't shower?"

"Or starts screaming at us for God knows what?"

"So, you'll talk to Mom?" Louise asked, pleading.

"I still don't understand why you think that Mom cares what I say. She just sent me Leslie Anders' nuptials instead of your announcement. She's always trying to take me down a notch."

"Please, please, please, please?" Louise begged, employing the whine again.

"I'll try," Dorothy said, caving.

"Oh, thank you, Dottie, I owe you one."

"Yes, you do. No mention of my friend to anyone, got it?"

"Cross my heart and hope to die. You coming home for dinner?"

"Wouldn't miss it," Dorothy said. "You can show me the Banns of Marriage announcement then."

"Love you."

"Love you, too."

Kenneth looked up from his paper. "I feel like we just took a big step in our relationship," he laughed. "I've moved into friend territory."

"She caught me off guard," Dorothy said. "I didn't know what to say."

"I'm serious, Dorothy, it's better than being nonexistent. Next thing I know, you'll invite me to the wedding." He smiled broadly at her, his eyes laughing.

"You are pleased with yourself, aren't you?" Dorothy said. "I'm sorry, I'm just so thrown by this Leslie Anders picture," she said. "It brings up such bad memories."

"You want to talk about it?"

"I'm going to sound like a big baby," Dorothy said. She harbored an irrational association between the death of her sister, Tess, and Leslie Anders. The wedding picture reliably triggered a cascade of painful memories that reopened the wound.

"So, what else is new?" he smiled his devilish grin at her again. She playfully punched him in the arm but even though she felt secure confiding in Kenneth, a piece of donut still stuck in her throat. "Go on, I can handle it."

Dorothy took a large gulp of her coffee. "Right before Christmas break, the Christmas when Tess died, I was late getting to the playground because I was the last second-grader to go to confession."

"To confession?" Kenneth interjected. "What would a second grader have to confess?"

"Answers a lot of questions, doesn't it? Anyway, Tess was like Mighty Mouse swooping in to save the day whenever I was in trouble."

"*Here I come to save the day!*" sang Kenneth.

Dorothy smiled. There wasn't a show on television that Kenneth didn't know the theme song. "She was the perfect older sister. I ran out to the playground already upset because Father Mayer had yelled at me in the confessional then followed me out and yelled some more. He gave me about a thousand Hail Mary's and Our Father's and called me some awful names."

"Jesus, what did you confess?" Kenneth asked.

"I wish I could remember, but I can't. The day just kept getting worse. I ran out toward my friends but when Leslie saw me coming, she scooted the girls away from me. They linked arms in a tight circle, shutting me out. All I saw was a woolen barrier of coats, hats, and scarves. They looked like a public service advertisement for how to properly bundle up against the cold Michigan winter."

Kenneth nodded knowingly.

"My transgression was earning the role of Mary in the second grade Christmas pageant, but I'd also just been yelled at, so I was very upset and thought everyone knew what happened. Dorothy could still remember how Leslie humiliated her. 'I pick you, and you, and you, and you,' Leslie Anders said to all my friends. She was like a priest bestowing his favor upon the heads of Mary Anne, Katherine, Camilla, and Penny." She pointed to all the bridesmaids in the picture. "In fact, she was just like Father Mayer. For the life of me, I could never figure out what I'd done to offend her. So, anyway, to me she says, 'Go away, Dottie, you aren't invited.'"

Dorothy took a deep breath and went on with her story. "At first, I did not understand what was going on. As the square of my friends' bodies tightened around Leslie, I felt confused. Why were my closest friends shutting me out? Had they overheard Father Mayer yelling at me? My breath caught in my throat, making it difficult to breathe. I felt like my heart was coming out of my chest. I could feel beads of sweat on my forehead, yet I was shivering uncontrollably. I felt overwhelmed by the raucous hollers of the other kids on the playground. Now I know that I was having a panic attack, but, at the time, there was no such thing." So much made sense to Dorothy when she first learned about anxiety attacks during her graduate studies in psychology.

"Leslie loudly invited all the girls but me to Greenfield Village over Christmas break. Tess was striding toward us, as if a sixth sense told her I was hurting. Tess called Leslie a spoiled brat before hustling me toward home, wiping my tears with her mitten."

Kenneth was listening intently, nodding to Dorothy to keep going. "'They're just jealous, Dottie,' Tess shouted toward the group as she pulled me away. 'They'll never be as smart as you.' Then she shouted over my shoulder to Mary Anne who was my best friend at the time. 'Mary Anne—you Benedict Arnold! With friends like you, who needs enemies!' Walking away quickly with her arm around me, she said, 'Wait till I tell Mom.'"

"'Don't tell Mom.' I faced her and finally allowed the tears to flow. 'Please, Tess,' I said, 'I already tried to tell mom. She won't listen.' I started to panic again. Tess dragged me over to a corner away from the crowd and wiped away my tears. She soothed and soothed until I calmed down. 'Don't worry, Dottie, I won't tell anyone.' The sting of not being invited to Greenfield Village was lessened by the fact that I had the beautiful and popular older sister. Leslie was intensely jealous of that fact. I let Tess drag me home."

"Don't tell your mom what?" Kenneth asked. "Had Leslie bullied you before?"

"I don't know," Dorothy said. "Probably, but this was the most memorable because by the time we returned to school in January, Tess was dead. Leslie approached me at the front of the school. Mary Anne had walked with me to school and stood by my side. She knew well enough not to mention the Greenfield Village trip, but, of course, I didn't care anyway. Many of my classmates had offered hugs of condolence and I took heart that Leslie came to offer the same. 'Who will save you now, Dottie, fat Deirdre?' Leslie said before grabbing Mary Anne's hand and skipping away." Dorothy could feel the heat of childhood anger well up in her like it was yesterday.

To Kenneth she said, "That's why I hate Leslie Anders so much."

"I can understand why," he said. Dorothy took a bite of the "nutty" donut, coated in peanuts and sugar, and washed down the cakey goodness with a large swallow of coffee. She wasn't jealous that Leslie Anders had gotten married. Nor did she hold Leslie responsible for Tess's death. Yet, without fail, the mere mention of Leslie's name unleashed the eight-year-old Dottie's visceral emotions and dumped them in Dr. Dorothy's lap. And Dorothy would feel as shocked and bewildered as she had at eight years old when her parents came home that Christmas morning. Kenneth took her hand. "I really appreciate you trusting me with this, Dorothy." She let him hold it.

Chewing morosely on the last bits of donut and still staring at the photo, she thought, *why can't you just let it go? You're not in the second grade anymore.* When she was young, Tess taught her how to turn on her heels and walk away, never allowing any of them to see how the intended message hit its mark. Even so, Dorothy was unable to unstick her desires and accomplishments from the rejection and a nagging sense that she'd done something wrong. Whenever such memories surfaced, a box full of "uns"—unloved, unworthy, undeserving, unlikable, unwed, unable, and unsuccessful—assailed her. Whatever it was, she couldn't shake it. After Tess died, Dorothy's inferiority coalesced around the mysterious appendix. If beautiful Tess could die of a ruptured appendix, then anyone could. Then there was the shame of wishing it had been Deirdre who'd died. Even as the capable adult woman she was, every once in a while, the box of irrational guilt, shame, and fear spilled its contents, reminding her again of what was wrong with her. And that Tess was forever gone. And she was still getting excluded by her friends from home and criticized by her family. She didn't share any of these thoughts with Kenneth.

.

CHAPTER FOURTEEN

THOMAS

REENACTING CHILDHOOD TRAUMA

Thomas arrived, as he typically did, a few minutes early for his session. No matter his mood, he squeezed every minute out of his time with Dr. Morrissey. He lumbered into her office and dropped, like a lead balloon, into a chair. A tattered, blue terry cloth beltless robe hung lifelessly over tee-shirt and brown corduroy trousers, notably uncharacteristic for a man who relished parading around in finery. He hadn't pulled his hair back into a ponytail as he usually did, and some fell over his face. He also hadn't shaved. His shuffle toward the loveseat in brown slippers over white socks was more like an old man's and missing were his preferred velveteen sandals. This attire, in addition to his sagging posture, shouted depression. A deep furrow knotted his brow. A storm was brewing.

Dorothy jotted a note: *Change in grooming significant—sloppily dressed—a stark contrast to Thomas's fastidious attention to detail.* She welcomed him to sit. "How are you?"

"I'd like to know what you just wrote down." He moved as if to peek at her notes.

"I noted that you are wearing a different outfit from what you usually wear."

"So, you've got an iron-clad grasp on the obvious?" He huffed and rolled his eyes dramatically at her in case she missed how upset he was.

"Would you like to tell me what's going on?" She responded impassively, showing him she would not take the bait.

"Isn't that why I'm here?" Thomas sat, staring at his psychologist without speaking.

After a few moments when he still hadn't answered her question, she decided to make an observation. "Okay, Thomas, I can't help but notice that you didn't dress up today. To me, that means you must be upset. So, why don't you tell me what you're upset about? Are you upset with me?"

"No. Believe it or not, the world doesn't revolve around you."

She wanted to laugh but knew better. He was really trying to get a rise out of her.

Since he wasn't forthcoming, she ran through the requisite assessment questions with him. "Okay, how's your sleep?"

"Fine." Arms crossed, mouth in a straight line as if to fend the intrusion of understanding.

"How's your appetite?"

"Also fine." She noted the monotone, the slouching, and the loss of light in his eyes.

"Would you like to tell me what you are upset about?" Dorothy asked again in her unflappable way.

"Yesterday was my birthday."

"Oh, happy birthday!"

"Pfft, pfft." He dismissed the good wishes with a wave of his hands. He adjusted himself on the couch.

He sat upright, feet planted on the linoleum, shoulders rounded, eyes cast downward, his posture a notable shift from his typical stance on the loveseat with legs stretched off to the side and sandals falling to the floor. "You'd think I was invisible," he added after a few moments.

"What do you mean, invisible?" She leaned in slightly afraid he might retreat.

"Everyone, including you I might add, has commented on my robe and slippers today, but yesterday, when I looked my very best, not one person, not one, said a kind word." He looked away, took a tissue from his robe pocket, and wiped his nose. "I paraded around the floor in my most elegant kimono and sandals, looking very stylish. You'd think I'd get one glance, just one. *Somebody notice me! Can I get one happy birthday?*" He got up and took a stroll, albeit in a tight circle in the small space and without much enthusiasm, to demonstrate his best runway promenade, glancing from shoulder to shoulder to see who might be watching. "One glance would have been present enough. I just wanted someone to look at me. 'Be yourself, Thomas,' you say. Well, I did that, and they all ignored me! When I'm myself," he moved his fingers like quotations, "no one likes me."

"I'm sorry, Thomas." Being a middle child, Dorothy knew the feeling. "Did you tell anyone that it was your birthday?"

"Why should I? It's like I repel the others. They recoil when I get too close."

"Honestly, Thomas, you cannot expect people to wish you a happy birthday if they don't know it's your birthday."

"No, you know what the problem is?"

Dorothy knew immediately that Thomas was not about to indicate a "what" so much as a "who."

"That new gal, Ruth, she's the problem. You know the one that lost it in group. She's feeling better, I might add. Her maternity ward fan club came down and asked her to sing. She practically sold tickets. How can anyone pay attention to me what with her singing her damn church songs all the livelong day? What is she trying to do, bring us all to Jesus?"

"Could it be possible that you're upset because Ruth receives the very kind of attention with her singing that you hope to elicit from the kimonos?"

Thomas sneered at Dr. Morrissey. "I will not even dignify your question with a response." He folded his arms across his chest.

Dorothy liked Thomas, but she could see how other patients, who also stood on shaky ground, might be wary of him given his unpredictable mood swings and general flamboyance. She took a moment to jot another note: *Thomas caught between wanting certain other patients to like him and his unwillingness or inability to meet them where they are.*

"Are you saying that Ruth was deliberately trying to take attention away from you?"

"I wouldn't give her that much credit."

"That's a bit unfair, don't you think?" Dorothy challenged. "You're upset because no one is giving you the time of day, while at the same time demeaning another patient. I wonder, Thomas, if the attention Ruth receives feels similar to your experience growing up when JW received all the positive attention, specifically from your father."

Thomas ignored her interpretation. "I suppose you're going to tell me to get off my high horse too."

"Did someone say that to you?"

"Yes, Ruth." He jutted his chin in righteous condemnation.

"And what was your response?"

He drew his hands down across his outfit. "You're looking at it." Thomas rolled his eyes, but Dorothy could see the tears forming. "You're almost as annoying as she is." He shifted to pull the robe closer around his middle. "God forbid I get a proper belt in this stupid place."

"Can you elaborate?"

"The no belt policy—"

"Before that, you said I am as annoying as Ruth. What do you mean?"

"You're only keeping me here because I'm homosexual. I know that's what you doctors do," he accused.

"I would never recommend inpatient treatment for homosexuality, I assure you. But you're right, Thomas, historically, even in recent history, that may have been the case in the medical community. But the newest revision of the DSM no longer designates homosexuality as a mental illness, and neither do I."

Thomas would not make eye contact. He busied himself by tracing a figure eight on his thigh as if he were following a pattern.

"Thomas," she said, "can you look at me? I can't emphasize enough that I am primarily concerned about your ability to keep yourself safe. I worry that if you were to leave here, you would stop taking your medication, and reckless behavior will follow. I don't feel we have gotten to a stable place, Thomas. Can you understand why I may be concerned?"

"I'm not going to hurt anyone."

"You know that is not what I'm worried about." In Dorothy's assessment, Thomas did not pose a threat to others. "I'm more concerned that someone will hurt you." His recklessness drew danger to him like a moth to a flame, particularly because he failed to connect his actions with undesired outcomes. Unaware of his behaviors, he was inevitably bewildered by others' reactions.

"Right now, I'm concerned about depression," Dorothy said. "I feel like we've been able to tackle the mania, but now you've slipped into depression."

"What makes you say that?"

"Your outfit," she said, "to say nothing of the fact that you haven't shared one bit of floor gossip with me today." Thomas regaled in the floor gossip and routinely informed her of the goings-on.

"I did so, Ruth and her fan club."

"And Ruth hurt your feelings by telling you to get off your high horse?"

"If you must know, she said I needed to get good with God."

Now Dorothy understood his train of thought.

"She's one to talk. I think she had eyes for Marcella." The way Thomas looked at her, chin down, eyebrows raised, a hint of a smile, Dorothy thought he was daring her to comment and break confidentiality.

Instead, Dorothy asked, "Were you and Ruth arguing?"

"Not necessarily."

"What prompted her to say those things, do you think?"

"I might have said she thinks she's God's gift to music."

Dorothy suppressed a smile. "If you don't mind a bit of interpretation…"

"Not that it would stop you."

"I think your feelings were hurt, Thomas. It would have been nice if someone like Ruth had sung Happy Birthday to you. I also believe that most of the time, the other patients do accept you as you are, but perhaps, in this case, it worked against you because you were actively trying to get noticed."

Resisting the overture, Thomas took another swipe, as if his whole world had become as lackluster as his robe and slippers, and he wanted her to join him there. So, this time, he went after her, commenting on the drabness of her office.

"Still trying to bore us to death?" He asked, gesturing around the room.

"I thought you'd like the macramé." She and Kenneth had been in over the weekend to spiff up her office. "And did you notice the new plants? Believe it or not, it's been your influence that's gotten me to spruce this place up." There wasn't a lot she could do given the one large window and cinder block walls beyond plants and wall hangings. Thanks to Thomas's complaints about her furniture, she replaced the green vinyl office chairs with cozier cast-offs found in Kenneth's parents' basement. He made her think about the surroundings in ways she hadn't considered before. Accustomed as she was to living in her own head or in those of her patients, she never thought about décor. Thomas had style, and any upgrades to her space were thanks to his suggestions and Kenneth's execution of Thomas's ideas by doing the heavy lifting.

He grunted. "I suppose it's an improvement."

"You know what I think, Thomas?" Dr. Morrissey said.

"I know you will tell me."

"I think you're trying to get me to understand how you are feeling. Everything, the outfit, the accusations, the criticism about the décor, you're letting me know how you're feeling about being ignored, especially on your birthday. Your feelings are hurt. Does that sound accurate?"

"I'm just humiliated. I can't tell you how long I waited for someone to take notice of me yesterday," Thomas said, his voice thick with emotion. "I'm worn out. And I've got that 'O, Jesus My Redeemer' song stuck in my head. Damn thing kept me awake half the night."

"How long did you spend waiting?" Dorothy asked. She ignored his swipe at Ruth.

"Until after dinner," he replied. He coughed, trying to choke down a sob. "I would have been satisfied with one 'Konnichiwa' from George."

"So even negative attention is good attention?"

"Desperate times … I finally just sat with the rest of them and watched television. I can't remember what it was we watched. *Gunsmoke*, maybe, I don't know. At least Ruth shut her trap for a minute."

"Can I ask you something, Thomas? How would you feel about dressing up just for yourself?"

"What I enjoy is making people happy by wearing elegant attire. Asking me not to consider others' opinions when wearing my kimono is like asking a writer not to consider the reader or the actor his audience. What's the point of looking fabulous if there's no one to appreciate you? What else do I have in here?"

"Am I right in saying you want to share the joy that wearing beautiful garments brings you? And, how hurt you feel when no one appreciates the beauty? It wasn't so much that Ruth was singing, but that she had an audience, people appreciated her?"

"Bingo. My mom was the only one who appreciated how fabulous I looked. That's what she used to say. 'You wear it so well, Eiji. Twirl around for me again.' I could traipse around here all day, and no one would notice."

"You must miss your mother, Thomas."

He waved her off, but his lips quivered with the effort to hold back his tears. He took a breath. "I've said it before, and it bears repeating. She made her choice. But, like I said, she was the only one who appreciated me."

"Hey, I told you how fetching you looked just the other day."

"You don't count. You have to be nice."

"The point I would like to make, Thomas, is that I find you delightful. Wearing a kimono or not, or, whether you're attracted to men or women, makes no difference to me. You are lovable, period."

"Pishaww." His eyes skittered toward the door as if the glare of her compliment was too much exposure.

She understood. Last night over dinner, Kenneth had pointed out to her how she pulled away from him just when he was trying to express his love for her. He'd had a couple of drinks and was getting mushy. "I love you so much," he'd said, reaching for her hand. She'd chalked it up as maudlin due to the alcohol. He begged to differ. "It's like you don't believe me," he'd said. He was right. She didn't. The question was why? Helping Thomas gave her own suffering meaning. Hopefully, by convincing Thomas that he was lovable, she would also convince herself.

"I mean what I say, Thomas. Can you consider that might be the truth?"

He nodded, fists balled to his eyes, no longer able to hold back his tears.

"I'm sorry, I have to ask. I can see you are depressed. Have you had thoughts of suicide?"

Thomas snorted. "Then I'd really be invisible, wouldn't I?"

Dorothy raised her eyebrows.

"I'm not," he said with a heave signaling his exasperation with her. "I had my brush with death. It's not all it's cracked up to be."

July 17, 1974: Thomas arrived early. He presented as oriented X 3 and depressed. Uncharacteristic was his grooming. He was shabbily groomed, unshaven, hair on his face. Affect—sad, testy, glum, and it took him longer to open up to therapist. Depression could be situational in nature since, according to Thomas, no one remembered his birthday, "I might as well be invisible." This therapist wonders if his mother realized that she was setting Thomas up to be misunderstood. According to Thomas, she was "the only one" who appreciated how he looked in his kimono. Thomas stated that this Therapist "is keeping me here because I'm homosexual." Therapist denied and explained her worry about his ability to keep himself safe if we were to release him prematurely. He denied SI.

CHAPTER FIFTEEN

RUTH

DEPENDENT PERSONALITY

As the days grew warmer and longer, Ruth's psychotic symptoms abated. Each week Dr. Morrissey noticed less delusional content and more lucidity in her client. Ruth was able to pay attention and respond appropriately, she used her words more but reverted to singing when Dr. Morrissey addressed specific topics like how she was feeling. As the psychotic episodes abated so did any talk of antipsychotic medication, much to the relief of both. Dorothy felt she had gone a long way to establish trust with Ruth by respecting her wishes regarding the antipsychotics, and she felt rewarded every time Ruth shared more about her life.

Dorothy's treatment plan, now that Ruth's head was clear, was to seriously tackle the grief, and the post-partum depression, which was persistent and severe. As she waited for Ruth to arrive for her appointment, she jotted notes about how to address both. Dorothy understood that post-partum depression could last for months, but eventually, Ruth would need to contemplate living on her own, without Calvin. Dr. Morrissey thought that once Ruth's mood stabilized, she might be willing to entertain the open windows of her life. The doors of wife and motherhood had closed to her. Like it or not, this would be the reality Ruth would need to face sooner than later.

Ruth threw a curveball into Dr. Morrissey's plans minutes after she entered the office and sat down for her session. For the first time, since she'd been admitted, Ruth exhibited a light-hearted mood and increased energy. She wore a light weight paisley sweater, baggy pants and an MSU tee-shirt. Her afro was growing, which had the effect of making her round features even rounder. No longer relegated to bedrest, the color returned to Ruth's cheeks and tone to her muscles. She was clearly following Dr. Morrissey's advice to get outside in the courtyard to walk and enjoy the sunshine. Dorothy should have felt relieved but instead felt an instinctual foreboding. As if sensing this, Ruth plowed ahead before Dorothy had a chance to ask the perfunctory check-in questions ("How was your week? How's your appetite, sleep? Are you having thoughts of suicide?"), during which the psychologist assessed Ruth's demeanor as well as the details she shared.

Ruth had news.

"You'll never guess what happened," Ruth began. She bounced on the edge of her seat like a restless kindergartner.

"I'm all ears." Guessing the news accounted for Ruth's sudden elevated mood.

"Cal showed up," Ruth said, coyly. Alarm bells sounded in Dorothy.

"What did he want?"

"He said he'd take me back." She lifted her chin defiantly, as if to say don't even try to talk me out of it.

"Tell me more about the visit."

Ruth's face relaxed, chin settled down. "He brought me a basket of goodies from Kroger." Ruth noticed the confusion written on Dr. Morrissey's face. "He knows how much I like Kroger."

"The grocery store?" To Dorothy, grocery shopping was a necessary chore to be gotten over with quickly, like the laundry.

"I can get through the Kroger with my eyes closed," Ruth explained, perking up. Ruth sat up straighter, leaned forward. Such enthusiasm for a grocery store that wasn't Horrock's was hard to imagine. Dorothy was grateful to have landed in safe territory, but also suspected that Ruth was deflecting. "Growing up, I was responsible for the grocery shopping. My mother hated it. Took me two hours and two carts. You'd be shocked at how much eleven boys can eat." The way Dorothy's younger brothers shoveled food in their mouths, she could only imagine the size of the Fitzgerald's grocery bill.

"I remember going to the grocery store with my mother. She could easily fill a cart to the brim but two? Wow. Tell me more about Kroger."

"I'd take one of my brothers with me, usually Joseph because he knew how to behave. I'd go around the store once, fill one cart, park him near the magazines, and I'd go around again, filling another. My parents bought so much food from Kroger that the store manager gave us a holiday gift basket full of food with all the trimmings, including a turkey or a ham, every Christmas." Ruth spoke as if she were the proud parent of eleven boys who ate her out of house and home. "Christmas was the one time during the year when my mother came with me. She always did like a fuss made over her," Ruth said. "'It's the least we can do, Mrs. Fitzgerald, you're our best customer!'" Ruth mimicked. "Technically, I was their best customer."

"What does all this have to do with Calvin?"

"When I was twenty-five, Calvin came back to Lansing. He was working as a store manager for Kroger."

"So, he didn't go back to Lansing after college? Where was he before that?"

"He was working for Kroger in Cincinnati as a management trainee. I'd all but given up on him then there he was, standing in Customer Service, smiling his fool head off. He presented us with the Christmas gift basket. I don't know how I missed that he'd returned home. As soon as we walked out, my mother was on me like white on rice," Ruth said. "'That Cal is so handsome, Ruthie! Go back in there and say hello!' I stood there, frozen in the parking lot. I didn't know if I should be excited or angry. He came running after us and asked me out. It was like we never skipped a beat."

"You weren't aware of other girlfriends in all those years?"

"There were rumors." Ruth's expression put a stop to that line of inquiry.

"If I were to venture a guess, Calvin is hoping for a repeat performance."

"What are you saying?" Ruth's full lips flattened into a straight line.

"It seems to me that he left you after high school when you'd hoped to get married, but then he won you over with the Christmas gift basket once he returned home. Now he's hoping the gift basket will win you over again. My question is, what else does Calvin bring to the table?"

"What do you mean?"

"We've talked about how angry, sad, and disappointed you've felt because he cheated on you, and he wasn't there to support you during the loss of your child. Does a gift basket make up for all of that?"

"I don't know, he kicked me when I was down, but..." She let her thoughts trail off as if too much energy was involved in considering the alternative. But Dorothy detected warring factions of belief and doubt in the way Ruth looked to the heavens.

"But?"

"I'm not sure I can live without him."

"Actually, you've been living without him for several months." Dorothy worked to keep the frustration from her voice.

"He'll take care of me," Ruth said. "I don't have anywhere to go when I get out of here."

"What about moving back home?"

"I can't do that."

"Why not?" *Work with me Ruth*, was what she wanted to say.

"My mother has a saying—you burned your ass, now sit on the blisters. Cal will take me back as long as I agree to his list of demands."

"Demands? Like what?"

"Like, I let him step out when he wants."

Dorothy laughed out loud at the absurdity but quickly realized that Ruth wasn't joking.

"Oh, I'm sorry, Ruth, I thought you were kidding." Mortified, Dorothy's face flushed, and she inwardly berated herself for the indiscretion.

"To be honest, I thought he was joking too."

"But, seriously, Ruth, you talk as if you did something wrong. From my perspective, he should be begging you to take him back."

The astonishment of an idea that had never occurred to her written on Ruth's face. "You really think so?"

"Do you want him back?" Earnest in her question, because who was she to dispense relationship advice?

"I thought I did until I started talking to you."

"And what if you wanted to 'step out,' would he be okay with that?"

Now it was Ruth's turn to laugh, but there was no mirth in it. "Lord, no. That would be disrespecting him," Ruth said, with a hint of sarcasm that informed her psychologist that the irony was not missed. "But I can't give him the children he wants."

"What I'd like to know, Ruth," Dr. Morrissey paused, feeling exasperated for Ruth even if Ruth couldn't muster indignation. "What's in it for you?"

"He'll pay the bills. And I can stay in our apartment."

"So, he supports you financially while you wait on him—it's like that Neil Young song, 'A Man Needs a Maid.' Cal hardly sounds like a knight in shining armor, Ruth." Before Ruth, Dorothy hadn't consciously thought how songs symbolized relationship issues. In sessions with Ruth, songs floated to the surface naturally.

"Who else would have me when I can't have children? Cal said I should be grateful that he's willing to take me back." Dorothy wanted to wring this Cal's neck. But she kept quiet. "Cal's smart and popular. People like him. He has a good job at Kroger. Where am I going to find a better man?"

"You know what I didn't hear, Ruth?" Dorothy began. "I didn't hear anything about Calvin being kind, loving, nice, or treating you well. You left out all those descriptors. And, I might add, these are the very traits you possess. You are kind, loving, nice, and you treat people with respect."

"Calvin would say 'that and fifty cents will get me a cup of coffee.'" This time, Dorothy picked up a bit more doubt in Ruth's response.

"What do you think, Ruth? Do you believe kindness isn't worth a cup of coffee?"

"Cal says I have to be nice because I need him more than he needs me."

"That's an awful thing to say. Has Calvin always spoken to you this way?" Dorothy struggled to hide her indignance.

"Not in the beginning. He started getting mean after I miscarried the first time. I guess it went downhill from there."

Dorothy wondered how this Cal could look into the deep pools of Ruth's eyes and still mistreat her. "Has he ever hit you?"

"No, he just goes around slamming the kitchen cupboards."

"What do your parents think?"

"They love him. Everybody loves Calvin. I'm lucky to have him." She said as if by rote.

"Have you ever heard the saying, 'street angel, house devil'?" Dorothy asked.

This time, Ruth laughed out loud. "Now there's a perfect description of Calvin." She smiled at Dr. Morrissey. Behind the dimpled smile, Dorothy detected the tears forming in the corners of Ruth's eyes. She abruptly looked away from her doctor and began a tune, soft and low, which indicated that Dorothy touched upon sensitive material.

Dorothy wasn't going to let Ruth shut her out with a song. "I know we are talking about painful issues, Ruth. But I need you to stick with me. I love how you sing, but I think you sing when you don't want to talk about anger, sadness, or shame. What are you feeling right now?"

Ruth shrugged.

"Does everyone in your family sing?" Dorothy thought about how much joy she felt listening to her father sing with his brothers and sisters.

"No, just me," Ruth said. "I've been singing in my church choir since I was a child."

"Can you think of a song that can express anger?"

"Who said I was angry?" Ruth said, scowling at Dorothy.

"Believe me, I am not criticizing you, but I wonder if you sing at times when you don't have the words to express anger or upset. You started singing immediately after I asked about whether Cal was a street angel house devil. Does it bother you that your family is fooled by him?"

"Everybody is fooled by Cal."

"I'm not so sure about that," Dorothy said. "I don't think you're fooled by Cal."

"Okay, but what makes you think I'm angry?"

"So, you're not angry? It's only natural to feel angry after all you've been through. I know I feel angry when I hear how Calvin speaks to you."

"I didn't say that, but what good is it?"

"Expressing your feelings may not change him but it may change you. Certainly, talking does help, but if singing works better, by all means, let's use music."

"If singing worked, I probably wouldn't be here."

"Well, then talk to me."

"I just, I just, I'm just so tired," Ruth said. Her voice was choked with emotion. "All the time, I'm expected to do right by everyone, and when I need help, who's there for me? I can't move back home, but I heard that Darren and his pregnant girlfriend are moving in with my parents."

"So, the same rules don't apply to the boys?" Indignant again, Dorothy stumbled against what seemed like innumerable roadblocks in front of Ruth.

"I guess not."

"Why do you think that is?"

"I don't know. My mother has always spoiled Darren."

"Is it possible that your parents see you as stronger?"

"I'm not feeling too strong right now. But I'm not a drug addict."

"Your brother is an addict?"

"So is his girlfriend." The monotone of Ruth's response made Dorothy wish there was a song for that. Something like the new song, "When Will I Be Loved" by Linda Ronstadt.

"Then, they probably do see you as stronger, eh?"

Ruth's face contorted with emotion as if she heard Dorothy's need for a song. "I'm just a pushover. Why can't they see I need help too?"

"Big family thing," Dorothy said. She knew only too well. Maybe if she could get Ruth comfortable expressing her hurt feelings, then she'd learn herself.

"Nobody thinks of me until they want something." She lowered her voice the knowledge dawning on her. "I think Cal must be hankering for a skinny burger."

"Skinny burger?"

"I made 'em up when I was growing up. The boys always thought I was making something special, but it was my way of stretching the meat. With eleven brothers to feed, I had to make the burgers extra thin. I made these flat, skinny burgers, but I fried them in butter and soy or Worcestershire sauce, whatever we had on hand. They are pretty good if I say so myself. My brother Jerome used to wake me up in the middle of the night to make him a skinny burger. Cal loves them."

"Sounds delicious," Dorothy said. Ruth smiled big, dimples and everything.

"It also sounds like you are very nice, Ruth. Too bad other people aren't as nice as you."

"You know, the odd thing about bed rest? That was the first time in my life when someone waited on me. The nurses were so nice to me. I didn't want to leave."

"Nurses make all the difference, don't they?" Dorothy smiled. "Before you go, Ruth. I have a request. I heard you sing, 'O, Jesus My Redeemer,' it's beautiful, but I haven't caught the lyrics, would you mind singing a bit for me?"

Ruth complied, singing the first stanza.

"I love your voice, Ruth. Not only is this a song of solace for you, but it's also a perfect expression of how you've been feeling. And I think you're having an influence on me. Have you heard of Linda Ronstadt?"

"Oh yeah, my brothers say she's sizzling." She licked her finger and touched the top of her other hand and made a hissing sound. They both laughed, which Dorothy considered a small victory.

"All these Linda Ronstadt songs were coming to mind today as you talked. Like I was thinking about 'You're No Good,' when you talked about Calvin." Dorothy smiled, hoping Ruth wouldn't take offense.

"That about sums him up," Ruth said with more certainty than Dorothy expected.

"It seems to me that singing serves many purposes for you. If you're willing, write down for me the lyrics that speak to you. If it's spirituals, folk, or rock use whatever speaks to you, and we will see where they lead us. And do me a favor. Don't make Calvin any promises. I'd like you to wait until you're feeling stronger to make any life decisions."

"Okay," Ruth agreed begrudgingly, but Dorothy detected a trace of hope behind the skepticism. As the door shut behind her, Dorothy could hear Ruth picking up the thread of the spiritual where she'd left off. "*O, Jesus, my Redeemer...*"

Diagnosis of Dependent Personality Disorder supported. Per the patient report, the husband is verbally and, in this psychologist's opinion, emotionally abusive, which could escalate to physical abuse. Treatment plan: empower the patient to acknowledge strengths and become independent. Set achievable goals e.g., employment, housing, etc. Continue with support, grief counseling. Incorporate singing into treatment as a way for Ruth to express grief. Currently, singing appears as an unconscious way to avoid feelings. Treatment plan to make singing more conscious as a path to healing.

CHAPTER SIXTEEN

GEORGE

THE EMPTY CHAIR

George clutched a pile of photos, laying them on the table between them. He told Dorothy that he had enlisted his mother to help with the assignment, as she'd suggested. He'd availed himself of the barber again. His hair was cut close to his head, and his face was clean-shaven. Outside of that, he wore his usual sweatpants and a University of Michigan sweatshirt.

"I bet that made her happy," Dorothy said.

"She was thrilled," he said. "She brought two albums worth for us to go through." He handed two black and white pictures to Dorothy. "I think these will give you an idea of me as a little kid before my First Confession."

"Oh my, you were adorable," Dorothy said. "Tell me about this one."

"My father looks like he's entertaining us somehow. I clearly adored him." He bit back a wave of sentiment.

"Yes, it's like your mother said," Dorothy commented, "Your face is beaming. The tenderness is palpable." Dorothy looked at the other photograph. "Are these your sisters?"

"Yes, the older one is Lydia, and the younger is Alice. We loved to go ice-skating." Young George's mitten-clad hands held each sister's as they all looked to be precariously balanced on the ice, smiling and proud. Rosy-cheeked children bundled against a snowy Michigan winter day. Even with a black and white photo, one could detect George's chapped cheeks still full of lingering baby fat. And just like his mother had always claimed, his eyes were sparkling.

"I look so innocent," George said.

"Evidently, this is how your mother still sees you," Dorothy said. She'd been working hard in supervision with Dr. Keith about how she projected onto George because of their similar experiences. So, even though she had softened toward him, there was still something bothering her that she couldn't name.

"Yeah, it's hard to imagine how this little boy could end up in an insane asylum."

"I see you did some writing," Dorothy said. "How about you read what you wrote."

"It's pretty disturbing," George said, "and I was there." Back to his cynical self.

"I can handle it," Dorothy said.

George looked down at what he wrote. He took a deep breath before looking back up at Dorothy. "You went to Catholic school, right?"

"Yes, I sure did."

"Do you remember the Examination of Conscience?"

"How could I forget."

They both chuckled. There were certain things drilled into every child raised in a Catholic school.

"It seems absurd now that they would put second graders through this, doesn't it?" she asked.

"You're telling me."

"Go on," she prodded.

"George's First Confession," he began.

"Sister Joseph Rose gave the second graders the following instructions. 'Once you have completed your Examination of Conscience, and you have told God that you are deeply sorry for your sins; you will go to Father Miner for your First Confession.'"

He looked up and said, "Sister Joseph Rose could be an imposing figure when she wanted to impart the gravitas of a matter. Whatever we did, we would be in deep shit if we humiliated her in front of the priests. So, she went through the examination line by tortuous line." He and Dorothy both smiled. She understood completely.

"She said, 'How do we begin, boys and girls? 'Bless me, Father, for I have sinned. This is my first Confession,' we all said together. She looked around, scanning our faces to make sure we were listening. 'Then you might say one of the following: Since then, I do not recall committing any mortal sins, or since then I have committed the following mortal sins,' she instructed. She did not address what, exactly, constituted a mortal sin. She did the same with the venial sins in the same clipped sentences working on the assumption that we knew the difference between mortal and venial sins. Most of our eyes glazed over as Sister Joseph Rose droned on. My mind wandered off to more pleasant thoughts like recess."

"'Then you say,' Sister paused, then like a jackrabbit she was flying down the third row of desks, her long habit billowing behind her, ruler in hand. The ruler came down with a loud thwack on top of Patrick Doyle's hand. 'Patrick Doyle! Stop your doodling and pay attention!' He didn't know what hit him, poor bastard. 'Where was I,' she says like nothing happened, scared the bejesus out of us and poor Doyle crying his eyes out, but she just moves on, 'yes, then you say, for these and all the sins that I have committed during my life, I am deeply sorry.' Listen for your penance from Father Miner. When invited to do so, make an Act of Contrition.'" George looked up again at Dorothy. "What was penance, you ask? We didn't know."

"It's like they knew nothing about child development," Dorothy said. "Keep going."

"She made the sign of the cross, prompting us to follow. 'Say it with me now, children."

Dorothy joined George in the recitation: "O my God, I am heartily sorry for having offended Thee. I detest all my sins because they offend Thee, my God, who are all good and deserving of all my love. I firmly resolve, with the help of Thy grace to sin no more and to avoid the near occasions of sin. Amen."

They laughed.

"So, you know," George said to Dorothy, "that when the good Father says, 'Give thanks to the Lord for he is good,' you say—" he nodded to Dorothy to join him again—"'For His mercy endures forever.'" They laughed again. This was exactly what Dorothy had been trying to explain to Kenneth. This was why she was so messed up.

Dorothy said to George, "Brings back memories. I think my second-grade teacher even rapped some poor boy's knuckles."

"Well, before the recess incident," he said, "Sister Joseph Rose assigned me to be the first to go to First Confession. She could count on me to make an excellent first impression on behalf of the class." He took a quick look at his notes.

"I knew the Act of Contrition by heart; I had aspirations to be an altar boy. First in line for the girls was little Margaret Cook, the best student among the girls. She, too, would make an excellent first impression, despite the fact of her girlhood because, as Sister Joseph Rose knew well from personal experience, Father Miner was not a fan of girls. Poor Margaret suffered multiple public humiliations at the hands of the good Father so that he could put her in her place. God help the girl if her hand flew up to answer a question posed by him during his visits to the classroom. His distaste for smart girls written all over his face with every correct answer she provided."

Oh my God, Dorothy thought, *just like my experience.* "Jesus, they must teach a class on how to hate little girls in the seminary," Dorothy said.

He smiled at her like she was finally getting it.

"I was eager to make a good impression, and I felt spiffy with my white shirt, red Christmas tie, and neatly combed hair. My only worry was what to confess. As far as I knew, I'd had no occasion for sin. I wasn't even sure precisely what constituted a sin. I had practiced at home with my mother. When I asked her, she said, 'Oh, just make something up, Georgie. Say, *I stole a Twinkie.* Anything will do.'"

Just do as your told, was what Dorothy's mother had said to her, she was now remembering.

"All that changed after recess. Suddenly, I was guilty of insubordination, a word unfamiliar to me, but evidently not a compliment."

George was visibly trembling. He paused in his narrative.

Dorothy asked, "Would you like to stop, George?" She too was trembling as the similarities to her experience of confession were uncanny.

"No," he replied, "but suddenly I feel like I can't breathe. I remember trembling like this when I sat across from Miner."

Dorothy stood up. "I have an idea," she said. She needed an excuse to breathe herself. She walked to the corner and pulled another chair over and placed it in front of George. "There is a gestalt exercise called 'the empty chair,'" she explained. "Let's do a variation on it. Pretend this chair is the confessional where Father Miner is sitting as he was back then. If you feel overwhelmed or unable to proceed, let me know. You are safe here. If you need to stop, we stop. Are you willing to try?"

George nodded. He looked at the chair still trembling but with considerable courage, unwilling to turn back now. Then he took a deep breath. "'Take a seat, George,' Father Miner said. His sweaty hand grasped my elbow to situate me 'properly.'" George turned to Dorothy. "You'll need to put the chair closer to me. We sat face-to-face, knees touching."

"Really?" Dorothy asked. "What happened to the confessional?"

"Oh, Father Miner was, let's just say, ahead of his time. Ostensibly, he was trying to put us at ease by interviewing us in person for confession. I guess the idea was to make the sacrament less scary." George squirmed in his chair, as if the memory was still making him anxious, but motioned to Dorothy to move the empty chair to be right in front of him. "Father said, 'Relax, George. Just do as Sister instructed.' So, that's what I did. *Bless Me, Father, for I have sinned. This is my First Confession,*' I recited. Then Father Miner said, 'And what sins would you like to confess, George?'" George paused looking at Dorothy. "I think this is where it all went wrong," he said.

"Okay, keep going," she prodded.

George looked straight at the chair. "'I haven't sinned all week, Father.'"

Dorothy laughed. "I love that. Of, course, you were only eight. When you think about it, what could an eight-year-old possibly have to confess?"

Now I'm starting to remember, she thought. She tried to concentrate on his story.

"Right? I reasoned that since getting mud on my clothes was an accident, then it couldn't have been a sin. Secondly, if I made up something, then I would be lying and to lie was a sin, so I didn't want to sin by lying during my First Confession. I figured that if I lied, then I'd be embarking on a vicious cycle of needing to go to Confession forever because I lied during Confession just to satisfy the priest's need for sinners. I hadn't completely worked it out, but that was my train of thought."

"Sounds like you were pretty smart."

"Unfortunately, Father Miner didn't think so."

"Go on."

"Miner's eyes turned to slits, scrutinizing me. 'Surely, you can remember a venial sin, George.' I sat up straight. I was trying to prove with my neat attire and hairstyle, even if I was spattered with a bit of mud, that I was an upstanding citizen free of sin. But I detected the shift in Father's demeanor." George looked up like a little boy looking up into the eyes of a priest, trying to fathom what he had done wrong. "Father seemed angry with me rather than kind and forgiving, as I would have expected. Sister Joseph Rose must've told him I was bad. I thought, *brace yourself,*" he said to Dorothy.

"It's okay, George. I'm with you," she said, soothingly, seeing the contortions in his face.

George took in a deep intake of breath. Dorothy was bent forward, twirling a piece of her hair as she listened intently. She almost believed herself that Father Miner was sitting in the room with them. "'Let me show you what a little sinner you are, George. You are a little devil, young man.' This worried George, because hadn't his mother said he was a *handsome devil,* just this morning? Why did he get the feeling Father Miner didn't mean it in the same way? Something menacing was going on, but George had no experiences with which to compare and defend." Dorothy noted two things. George stared, as if in terror, at the empty chair and he'd begun referring to himself in the third person.

He froze in place. Father Miner grabbed George's head and pushed George's face into his lap, rubbing George's head around and messing up his hair. He mocked George for the Brill-creamed hairdo.

"'Who do you think you are with this hair, George, Elvis Presley? Now, look what you've done. You've made my hands greasy.' He pushed George's head back and exposed himself to George, rubbing himself off with the Brill-creamed hands from George's head." George's eyes were riveted with horror by a scene he did not understand. Dorothy watched as George's expression revealed the atrocity he described.

"When he finished, he said, 'Now let's begin again, shall we George? Say it with me, George, *Bless me, Father, for I have sinned.* This is my First Confession. I have committed the sin of pride. I sinned against Father Miner by tempting him with my vanity. I am a bad boy, and I beg God's forgiveness. I am a bad boy, and I beg God's forgiveness,'" George repeated again and again.

Dorothy felt like throwing up.

"Now let us say the Act of Contrition together, 'Oh, my God, I am heartily sorry …' Then Father said, 'Give thanks to the Lord, for he is good.'"

"'And his mercy endures forever,'" George said. The defeat in George's voice broke Dorothy's heart. A defeat so encompassing that she knew, George would never have faith in a merciful God.

"'For your penance, say five Hail Marys and five of The Lord's Prayer. Now, turn around,' he said."

George looked stricken when he turned away from the chair and at Dorothy. Dorothy realized she'd been holding her breath as if the air had gotten sucked out of the room, and as if God had, indeed, abandoned the little boy. "He placed a gold cross around my neck," George said to Dr. Morrissey. "I didn't want it, but I was afraid to take it off."

"The crowning blow," she said, breath held freezing her in place.

"Yeah, like he was blessing what he'd just done to me."

George looked down. He held his head with both hands. Dorothy gave him a moment to absorb what he'd just shared with her. They both exhaled as if Miner had just gotten up and left the room. Just to be sure, Dorothy stood up and moved the chair back to the corner. She felt an eight-year-old's fear. George raked his hand through his hair.

She sat back down. "Tell me what you're feeling, George."

"You know what I feel? I feel guilty," he said, recovering himself. "Brian hadn't been to Confession yet. While we sat smoking, he'd noticed my cross. He said, 'I want one of those.' We had to stand in front of the classroom and apologize to Father Miner, Sister Joseph, our parents, and classmates. Then Brian was led away by Father Miner for his First Confession. Before he took Brian away, Miner came over to me and ripped the cross from around my neck. I just stood there, mute. I knew what would happen to Brian, and I said nothing. I feel like a piece of shit." *Why does this feel so familiar?* Dorothy thought. She pushed the thought away.

"Do you know if Father Miner molested Brian too?"

"Oh yeah, I know all right. When Brian came back to the classroom, he was wearing a gold cross. A couple of other boys also had them, but none of the girls. Brian changed." George wiped the tears from his eyes as he struggled to keep his composure. "I can't forgive myself."

"I couldn't help but notice, George," Dorothy observed, "that you switched from first person to third person in your narrative. What do you make of that?"

"I have no idea," George said, confusion animating his features as if he'd just traveled through time back to the present moment.

"I wonder if putting it in the third person made it easier to get at the most painful memories? I also noticed that you assume responsibility for what Father Miner did to Brian as if your experience doesn't count. What I want to know is—how do you feel now that you've shared your story with me? About being molested, I mean."

George looked like he was witnessing the horrors of war firsthand. His eyes wide and glassy skirted about in disbelief reaching for an answer that could make sense of his experience. "It was way worse for Brian. I have no right to complain. I got him into the mess in the first place." He directed his gaze at her as he dismissed his feelings.

"That's not true, George. I'd wager Father Miner tested the waters with all the boys that day. As you said, a few boys wore crosses." Anger, disgust, outrage, and a strong desire to mete out justice on the hypocrite burned in her chest where the crosses would have been.

"I don't know how I feel. I hate myself. That's what I feel," his voice empty as he'd just handed her the urge to fight.

"Did you ever tell your parents?" She spoke gently to him, tamping down her outrage for the benefit of the traumatized child.

"No, I never told anyone. After I got the belt from my dad, I... I don't know, it was like I couldn't trust anyone. I shoved the whole incident away, and then Brian overdosed. You know the rest."

"How do you feel about what you've done now?" Dorothy asked.

"Well, I'm glad he didn't die, and I'm glad I can't drink. I never meant to kill him, I swear, but I do wish there was a way to make him pay for what he did to Brian." He was owning his anger now.

"And to you," Dorothy said. "You worked hard today, George," Dorothy said. "I know it must feel very traumatic, so I need to ask about thoughts of suicide." She coaxed them both back to present time.

"If I wasn't suicidal after that day, I won't ever be." His matter of fact response was edged with bitterness.

"So, you're not?"

"Right," he said, teetering on impatience with her.

"There is some good news," she said.

"What's that?"

"I bet the recurring nightmare will stop."

"Really? I hope so." His hope lifting his spirit a touch.

"I want you to do something nice for yourself."

"Like what?"

"I don't know exactly, maybe take a nap, something relaxing, but give yourself time to process the experience. The writing helped you to open up, so perhaps write some more."

"Whatever you say."

She could see he was both drained and lighter somehow.

George gathered his notebook and photographs and stood to leave.

"George," Dorothy said.

He looked at her. Pain still lingered in his eyes. "Yes?" he said.

"I'm really sorry about what happened to you."

He walked out the door.

08/14/74 George arrived on time, neatly groomed, and in good spirits. It appeared he felt good about completing the narrative assignment. Therapist utilized 'the empty chair' to facilitate recall. The patient revealed sexual molestation by a priest during First Confession. He became increasingly despondent. He stated that he felt guilty for his friend, Brian. He feels he should have warned him or protected him. Writing appears to be the right vehicle for George to express his feelings. We will continue to process the incident next session. He denied SI.

Dorothy had a sudden urge to get on her knees and pray. Instead, she pulled out another notebook from her drawer. Dr. Keith had pressed her about writing her personal reactions in her last supervision. She had bought the notebook but had resisted. She wrote now. *What happens to the child when he/she tries to do the right thing but gets into even more trouble?* That was as far as she could go. George's story was hitting too close to home. She took a walk toward the chapel.

CHAPTER SEVENTEEN

FALL 1974

MARCELLA

SELF–HARM

Marcella wasn't back on Michigan State University's campus two weeks before she came back to St. Lawrence. Dorothy was paged at two in the morning. When the pager sounded, Dorothy flew out of bed from a deep sleep, nearly falling and tripping over shoes and slippers. Disoriented, she stumbled in the dark toward the living room to the phone and dialed the unit.

"We should just reserve a weekend bed for her this semester," the attending nurse said when Dorothy phoned in, and Dorothy immediately knew she was referring to Marcella. From what the nurses could gather, Marcella had overdosed on a mix of over-the-counter pain medications. "They are just about to pump her stomach," she said. "Do you want to come in to talk to her?" Her tone was sympathetic, knowing how hard it was to work all day only to turn around and come back at night.

"I'll come in," Dorothy grumbled, trying to set aside the irritation from being woken up in the middle of a good dream. "I'd rather err on the safe side." She tiptoed back to the bedroom to dress. "Shit," she said, tripping over Kenneth's shoes in the dark.

Kenneth woke. "You okay?" he asked. His eyes remained closed, but he listened as Dorothy groused about the hour and having to be out on deserted roads in the middle of the night. "Boy, you get called out a lot," he mumbled before rolling over. Dorothy envied her boyfriend's career path, which didn't involve such rude awakenings. Dorothy kissed him and told him to go back to sleep.

"I'll be back," she said. Dorothy accepted that late-night calls were part of the job, but every middle-of-the-night call came as a shock to her system. Especially when all this could have been avoided had Marcella and her parents followed treatment recommendations last spring. Could they not see how their denial put Marcella's life at risk? Maybe now they would see with this attempt that Marcella was a danger to self and would heed her recommendation and admit Marcella to St. Lawrence for as long as it took. What good was her education if she wouldn't be alive to benefit from it?

As Dorothy approached the curtained-off room where Marcella was recovering, she saw her parents standing outside in the hall, talking with a nurse and Mr. Otto, from the counseling staff at MSU. "Hello, Mr. and Mrs. Mafoud. How's Marcella doing?"

"They've pumped her stomach," Mr. Mafoud, responded, his face filled with shame. Mrs. Mafoud wouldn't make eye contact, as if waiting for Dorothy to say, 'I told you so.' "She's with a nurse now," Mr. Mafoud went on. "Dr. Morrissey, this is Mr. Otto. He's Marcella's counselor at MSU."

"We met last spring," Dorothy said. "I was so upset to get the call. I hoped with the new semester she'd be doing better."

"I hoped so too," Mr. Otto replied. "But she did return to counseling, as we'd set up before she left. As I've just informed Mr. and Mrs. Mafoud, I'm sorry to say that Marcella is not allowed back on campus until you feel she's ready." He directed his gaze at the Mafouds to shut down any attempts at stonewalling.

Dorothy glanced over at the Mafouds. She set aside her frustrations with them because their distress was evident. "I have to agree with Mr. Otto," Dr. Morrissey said to them. "She's clearly a danger to herself.

Marcella needs extended care. I'm sure you understand." Exhausted and resigned, they conceded.

"When can we see her?" Mrs. Mafoud asked.

"Let me have a few minutes with her, and then you can sit with her while they prepare a room," Dorothy said.

"How about we go get a cup of coffee while Dr. Morrissey tends to Marcella?" Mr. Otto said to the Mafouds. "It's going to be a long night." He took Mrs. Mafoud by the elbow and led them down the hall.

Once Mr. Otto escorted the Mafouds toward the vending machines, Dorothy slipped past the curtain to check on Marcella. One look at the pitiable figure and all irritation slipped away. Marcella's bronze coloring had taken on a sickly shade of gray. Her eyes were tightly shut against the bright overheads in the ER. Her matted hair was no longer long and lustrous, cascading down her back, but dull and slick with sweat, sticking to her face and the pillow. No one could make heads or tails of Marcella's slurred muttering. Stomach pumped and mouth lined with charcoal, her head lolled fitfully as if she was dreaming or drunk. She took one look at Dorothy and began to cry. "Are you mad at me now?" she said.

"Oh, Marcella, I'm not mad at you. I'm worried about you. Do you want me to be mad at you?"

"No," Marcella responded weakly. "I'm sorry. I don't mean to disappoint you."

"Listen," Dr. Morrissey said, "What I want is for you to get some sleep tonight. We can talk about what happened tomorrow. Your parents are here, and they want to see you." Whatever happened would have to wait until morning. Marcella was in no shape to explain. "Do you remember Ruth from when you were here last?"

"Yeah, she was sweet," Marcella whispered.

"Well, I think I will put you in with her. I don't want you to be alone."

"That would be nice," Marcella said.

"Okay, then, I will see you in the morning. Get some sleep."

Dorothy went over to SLA psychiatric and stopped at the nurses' station. "Marcella Mafoud is in the ER. We need to prepare a bed for her."

"So, you got called out? You must be so tired," the nurse at the desk said sympathetically.

"I am," Dorothy said. "I've never understood why these things happen in the middle of the night. Anyway, I don't think we should leave her alone," Dorothy said. "Let's put her in with Ruth Fitzgerald."

"Will do, go home and get some sleep."

"Just got a note to write, then I'm on my way," relief that Marcella was safe, her parents cooperating, and that she could go home and get some sleep.

With that, she went back to her office and jotted a clinical note in the girl's file.

Date: 09/06/1974 Patient: Marcella Mafoud DOB: 11/30/1954 Crisis response after MM overdosed on a combination of OTC meds and alcohol. The patient had stomach pumped in ER, incoherent, drowsy. Poses a danger to self. Admitted for long-term treatment as the patient exhibits suicidal ideation, history of attempts. According to MSU's therapist, this was the second attempt in two weeks despite the consistent denial of SI. A working diagnosis of BPD—exhibits impulsivity, reckless behavior, emotional instability, and self-harm. The counselor from MSU present and informed parents that MM would not be allowed back to campus until treatment recommendations met. Rule out sexual abuse.

Dorothy was sitting quietly, eyes closed, half asleep, and half pondering Marcella's situation when a soft knock startled her out of the reverie. The night nurse poked her head in. "Still here?" she said.

"Just wrapping up," Dorothy said, disoriented from her suspension between dream and reality.

"Marcella is settled in Ruth's room. I tucked her in myself. She's snug as a bug in a rug. She should be good for the night. Now go home."

"Thank you. On my way."

The nurse turned to leave. "Oh, by the way, her parents signed the paperwork for extended inpatient treatment."

"That's a relief. Now I can go home and rest. Can you tell Nurse Martin I'll be in late?"

"Will do."

✦

A beleaguered Dorothy left the hospital and drove home. She mulled over the crisis as she drove, gliding through a long stretch of green lights just as Kenneth predicted. No one was on the road at this hour. Drained from the intensity of her patient's suffering and her parents' anguish, she fought against falling asleep at the wheel. She turned on the radio and sang along loudly to *When Will I See You Again,* a catchy tune that seemed to underscore her dilemma about her relationship with Kenneth. Had she already pushed him into the just friends limbo? A word he wouldn't consider valid anyway as a Protestant. She belted out about beginnings and ends long after the song was finished. Dr. Keith would have a field day with this one, she thought though she wasn't sure if she meant Marcella or herself.

By the time Dorothy crawled into bed, it was almost four in the morning, just about the time her grandmother got up to start her day. Her grandmother had always been an early riser, so she could sit quietly with a Sanka and read a book before the rest of the house woke up. What she wouldn't give to hear some pithy bit of Irish wisdom delivered in her grandmother's soft accent. Something like, *done and dusted* or *we'll get you sorted* or *end of.* How she would love to know when she was sorted, and her patients' problems were done and dusted. Even better would be the *end of...*End of what?

She plopped, exhausted but wired into bed next to her boyfriend. She welcomed his warmth and snuggled close, but when he reached for her amorously, she immediately tensed up. "Are you serious?" she said, wishing she had thought to bother her grandmother with a tearful phone call after all. Clearly, he did not understand the toll a late-night crisis took on her. Or maybe this was his way of showing her he did understand, she thought guiltily. Still, Dorothy turned her back to Kenneth, unable to relax. Can't a snuggle just be a snuggle, end of?

Kenneth was not going to let it go this time. He turned her back toward him. "Dorothy, you woke me up. Not the other way around."

"I just needed a little comfort," she said.

"What do you think I was trying to provide?"

"As the nuns would say, only one thing." She'd meant it as joke but that was not how it came off.

"Jesus," Kenneth said. "So, let me get this straight. Nothing is on the table before marriage, but once we are married you will suddenly desire me and enjoy sex?"

"Something like that," Dorothy said. "I didn't make the rules." She knew she was being ridiculous, but how could she explain all the guilt and shame she felt?

"Have you ever thought that you might be a lesbian?" Kenneth asked. She hadn't. If she felt so guilty about the prospect of sex with the man she loved, she couldn't imagine how guilty she would feel as a lesbian. She could only tolerate so much guilt.

"This is why it's so hard to date a Protestant," she said. "You don't understand."

"I think I'm beginning to," Kenneth said. "It's messed up."

"On that we can agree," Dorothy said.

"You're a therapist," he said. "Maybe we should go to a sex therapist."

"I would rather die," she said. "I mean, once we get married, if we are still having this problem, then I'd consider it, I guess."

"That's hardly a resounding yes, Dorothy. Oh, and yeah, you'll be totally into me then. Once we're married, I mean." Now Dorothy was really hurt. This was hardly the comfort she'd been seeking. She rolled up to go move to the couch. "Don't bother," Kenneth said, "I'm getting up anyway. Get some sleep."

End of Catholic guilt was her last thought before drifting off to sleep.

✦

Late the next morning, Nurse Martin escorted Marcella to Dr. Morrissey's office to ensure she did not find trouble along the way. Marcella needed to prove she could keep herself safe before the staff would allow her to be alone for any length of time. She took her seat, curling her legs beneath her. Not yet showered, she had the ill look about her of one who still felt sick to their stomach and depleted of all energy. Charcoal still outlined her lips. Her head rested on the back of the couch as if it was too heavy to hold up. She was already crying by the time Dr. Morrissey took her seat across from her. Still, despite sniffling and wiping at her eyes and nose with her sleeve, once she started to talk, Dorothy couldn't get a word in edgewise. She settled in with her pointer finger pressed on the indentation above her lip to remind herself to keep quiet and just listen.

"I'm sorry I dragged you in here again in the middle of the night," Marcella said. "Do I still have charcoal on my mouth? Ruth tried to get it off. She said I look like I have whiskers," she said, wiping at her chin. "I like Ruth. She's nice. She sang me a lullaby."

Dorothy listened while Marcella nervously chattered, waiting for her patient to pause and take a breath so she could delve into what led up to taking the pills.

"My head is killing me," Marcella said. "And I'm starving. Ruth said she'd wait for me to have breakfast. She said, 'you were gone, girl.' I don't even remember coming here. She told me she sang me, *Hush, Little Baby.* Put me right to sleep. All I know is I haven't slept that well in a long time. Do I get to stay with her? I felt safe. My mom used to sing us lullabies, Irish ones." *Now we're getting somewhere,* Dorothy thought.

Dorothy took advantage of the brief break in Marcella's voluble account. "You haven't been sleeping well?"

"Not since I left here, last time. Every time I'm just about to fall asleep my heart starts pounding and then I'm wide awake." She wiped her sleeve against her mouth, still self-conscious about the charcoal.

"Sounds like a panic attack," Dorothy said assuredly.

"That's what keeps happening. I feel like I'm losing my mind. I swear I'm not trying to kill myself. I just want it to stop." Frustration filling her voice.

"The panic?"

"Yes. I just wanted to sleep." She closed her eyes and rested her head on the cushion as if to dramatize her exhaustion.

"Let's look at it then. Can you remember what thoughts you've been having as you drift off?"

"This might sound weird, but I keep thinking about the bunk beds."

"The bunk beds?" Curious now.

"Yeah, in the new house, we were getting bunk beds, and we were really excited, but..." Marcella closed her eyes like she was trying to remember.

"But?" Dorothy prompted after a minute or so.

"But I liked it better at my grandma's when Marissa and I slept in the same bed."

Dorothy waited.

"My mom was okay then. Nicer. She used to sing us *Too-ra-loo ra-loo-ra.*"

"You felt safe then," Dorothy said, hoping that Marcella could tap into that feeling.

"Yes. I felt safe then all tucked in. Marissa would often take my hand and suck on my thumb instead of her own. I know it sounds strange, but it was oddly soothing for both of us. Off I'd go, snug as a bug in a rug. I hated the bunk beds." *End of,* Dorothy thought.

"That's funny, the night nurse said that she tucked you in snug as a bug in a rug." Marcella's story made Dorothy want to cry, so she thought it appropriate in this case to let her client know she felt her pain. "Your story makes me want to cry, Marcella. I can only imagine how sad the memory is for you."

"Funny you should say that," Marcella said. "I haven't been able to stop crying since I came back to school."

"Is that right?" Dorothy asked. "The last thing you mentioned was that you hated the bunk beds. What does that have to do with what's going on now?"

"I sleep on the top bunk in my dorm room."

"So, that's an association and quite possibly the trigger. That makes good sense."

"When we moved to our new house, our parents made a big deal about giving us bunk beds. Marissa always said that she wanted the top bunk. I know she was at the new house with me, but I don't ever remember her sharing the bunk beds. We never talk about her, like what happened. Sometimes I feel like she is with me and talking to me. Like before they found me last night."

"What did she say?" Dorothy was intrigued as she'd often felt Tess's presence.

"'We have to get you some help.'" Marcella laughed weakly at the thought. "Boy, that was an understatement, eh?"

"Did she say anything else? Dorothy asked.

"Yes, she said, 'I'm not leaving you,'" Marcella said as she relaxed into the thought.

"Is it possible that you are self-harming because you are trying to get Marissa to visit you?" Dorothy asked.

Marcella laid her head back against the couch again and closed her eyes. The crying had abated, but a few loose tears sneaked out the sides of her eyes and made her eyelashes shine. "Maybe, but I know she's dead. I don't know how to explain. It's like every time I want to go to sleep, I get this sense of impending doom. Like it's coming at me out of the clear blue. I know my parents are losing patience. I feel like everyone is beginning to wish I'd just get on with it. Can we talk about this later? I still don't feel well. I can't get the taste of charcoal out of my mouth. I need something to eat." She whined like a four-year-old.

"We'll wrap up soon, but I need to ask. Is this why you took the pills?"

"Yes, it's suffocating," Marcella began. "Like, I'm waiting to be struck, and that whatever is coming is going to happen so fast, I won't know what hit me, and I'll be dead, but then I wake up, and I'm still alive. But I guess that's when the panic sets in. I'm not even sure if I fell asleep at all." Her speech was pressured, as if Dr. Morrissey needed convincing.

"How do you feel when you realize you are still alive?"

"I'm relieved but scared. It's like I have amnesia or something."

"So, you're not disappointed?"

"No, I'm relieved, but lonely, like no one understands." She straightened up and looked longingly at Dr. Morrissey, eyes begging her to believe her.

"It feels to me, Marcella, that you are acting out a previous trauma. I'm guessing this is about you and Marissa. This is exactly why I want you to stay in treatment. You need to be able to have the time to unearth and share your story. I'm going to ask you to start writing. Write down whatever you can remember about your move to the new house. We'll take it from there. Okay?"

"Okay, but how do I do that?" she asked more hopeful now.

"I think it would be beneficial for you to write to Marissa like a letter. Perhaps try something like *Dear Marissa, Remember the first time we saw our bunk beds?* Something along those lines. See what comes up. Okay?"

"I guess so, but we were only four when she died."

"For our purposes, write to her no matter what age the memory is from. You can move forward or backward from her death. Just see what you remember."

"What if I feel like cutting, what do I do?" Her hands fidgeted as if the urge was powerful.

"I think the writing will help. Do anything that serves as a delay tactic, do some jumping jacks, bend over and touch your toes, ring Nurse Martin."

"Maybe I can ask Ruth to sing me a song?"

Dorothy smiled. "Whatever works."

"Right now, I just need something to eat."

"Sure, I think you've worked hard today," Dorothy said, tired herself.

"I owe you that much, eh?" She smiled as she rose from her seat, still looking a bit unsteady.

Dorothy returned her smile. "Go find Ruth and get some food in your stomach. We'll talk again soon."

Feeling better after making headway with Marcella, Dorothy called Kenneth. Louise had sent a picture of the bridesmaid dress that she chose with instructions for Dorothy to get fitted at once. She also thanked Dorothy for intervening with their mother on her behalf. "Whatever you said worked. Thanks, sis!" she wrote. It didn't matter that Dorothy had spoken to their mother about Deirdre. Nothing would stop her if she wanted to act out. All Dorothy had gotten for her trouble was: "How dare you, Dorothy Marie Morrissey? What's it to you if Louise wants her in the wedding?"

"Mother, that's what I'm trying to tell you," Dorothy said. "Louise asked me to talk to you. She doesn't want Deirdre to be a bridesmaid."

"You should keep your nose out of it," her mother had said. Dorothy sighed with the thought.

Kenneth picked up on the first ring. "Hello," he said.

"Hey, hon, what are doing?"

"Procrastinating," he said. "I haven't gotten much writing done today. I went for a jog though."

"I'm sorry about last night," Dorothy said, "I know I have a problem. It's not you." She dropped her voice to a whisper as if someone was listening on the other side of her closed door. "It's not that I'm not attracted to you, I am. But just when I feel the flame my shame and guilt throw a bucket of cold water all over it."

"As you've explained, Dorothy. I get it, no sex until marriage. What I don't get is why everything besides kissing is also off limits."

"I just told you. Because I might lose control." Her volume dropped even lower. "One thing leads to another."

"Why are you whispering?" Kenneth asked.

Dorothy drew a deep breath. Why was this so hard for him to understand? She could feel her heart racing and the all too familiar anxiety around her inability to please anyone cutting off her air. "I don't know. I'm sorry, ok? I'm calling to see if you want to go to Knapp's with me. I need to get fitted for the bridesmaid's dress. Do you want to meet me there? We can grab dinner afterwards."

"Does this mean I'm invited to the wedding?"

"Can I say, 'we'll see'?" Dorothy said. "She's having a big wedding. There will be so many people there that maybe my father won't sniff out the Protestant."

"Until that bolt of lightning strikes me," Kenneth laughed.

"There's that," Dorothy agreed, relieved they weren't fighting anymore. "He'll be too busy boasting how much he spent on the wedding to his siblings."

"Didn't you say that they couldn't help you with college because they didn't have the money?" Kenneth asked with what sounded like genuine curiosity. "How are they able to afford these big weddings for your sisters?"

"College for a girl would be throwing good money after bad, according to my father. Weddings are an investment in his daughters' futures." Dorothy couldn't quite conceal the hurt behind her sarcasm. Getting the air into her lungs was becoming a full-time job as the conversation veered again toward touchy subjects. She knew he was just trying to be supportive, but she just wanted to get some fresh air.

"Oh, so that's what it is," Kenneth said. "Seems hurtful to me. Do they realize how accomplished you are?"

"God, no. Until I find a good Catholic boy, I've wasted my life. So, meet me at Knapp's?" Dorothy said, trying to get off the phone before the walls closed in.

"Well, if this is the only way to see you in the dress, sure," he said.

"Twenty minutes?"

"With bells on!"

CHAPTER EIGHTEEN

THOMAS

UNCONDITIONAL POSITIVE REGARD

Dorothy was finishing up clinical notes before lunch when Nurse Martin knocked urgently on her door. When she entered, Dorothy was met with a strong aroma of fried fish. Fish was always on the menu on Fridays at St. Lawrence. Her senses piqued; Dorothy's mouth watered in anticipation of a deep-fried filet of sole sandwich slathered in tartar sauce.

"Dr. Morrissey, they need you in the cafeteria," Nurse Martin said. "Thomas won't move from the line. He's yelling for sushi, and there's a crowd gathering. Apparently, he shoved his way to the front and cut in front of George. George is up to his usual shenanigans with the *konichiwa* and *aah so* stuff. You know, making things worse. I'm worried they'll come to blows."

"There goes lunch." Dorothy sighed.

"I'll make sure to wrap up a plate for you," Nurse Martin said. Both women jumped to action.

Dorothy dashed toward the cafeteria. Other patients and staff fell in behind her to see what the ruckus was about. The situation was precisely as Nurse Martin had described. Thomas had his back to George, using his body to block any forward movement.

"This isn't even fresh!" Thomas shouted. "How can you possibly call this catch-of-the-day? This is a pedestrian attempt at fresh fish!"

"I said, move along, Kemosabe." George nudged him. "I'm getting hungry here."

"Don't touch me, George! Or you'll be sorry." In the state he was in, Thomas appeared surprisingly strong, situating his body to block his nemesis.

"Cato, just let the rest of us eat, for crying out loud," George said.

"I've been requesting sushi every day! Why can't you put it on the menu?" Thomas was yelling at the staff.

"I'm sorry, Thomas, we've never heard of sushi..."

"I've described it to you in detail. What do you mean you've never heard of it?" Thomas was shrill. The counter women, mostly women whose hairnets made them appear old, restrained any instincts to roll eyes or respond sarcastically.

"Our distributor doesn't know what we're talking about. We tried, Thomas, really."

"I suppose you call this tea?" Thomas shouted, perhaps realizing sushi was a lost cause, waving a Lipton teabag at the staff. The servers were definitely confused now.

By that time, Dorothy had pushed her way through the gathering throng of patients and staff who were accustomed to daily outbursts of all kinds but curious, nonetheless. The crowd parted quickly for her as she made her way to the cafeteria counter where Thomas stood. One look at him, and she knew he was manic.

"Thomas, what's going on?" she asked gently. "How about we go down to my office? We can talk more there." She made eye contact with him, and, as if her very presence soothed him, he exhaled deeply, and gave up the fight.

"I just want some sushi," he said. Dorothy lightly placed her hand to the back of his arm. He allowed her to steer him away from the counter among the snickers from his fellow patients. She heard one of them say, "Who does he think he is? Cock of the walk?" Thomas must have overheard the comment as well because, as Dr. Morrissey spirited him through the parting crowd, he yelled loudly enough for everyone to hear.

"How do you not know what sushi is? You morons!"

In Dorothy's assessment, Thomas's entire identity was rooted in the dynamics of his childhood home. Wearing kimonos and eating sushi could evoke for him the feelings of safety, love, curiosity, culture, and tenderness of his boyhood relationship with his mother and brother. But he also tended to unconsciously create situations that could repeat the violence he experienced at the hands of his father. Fortunately, none of the staff in the cafeteria took the bait, and George's ribbing never rose to a tipping point.

Once inside her office, Thomas paced, but Dorothy took her seat.

"Remember when you told me how your brother always said there's a time and place for everything, Thomas?" Dorothy asked, aiming to help him employ his brother's guidance to the outburst in the cafeteria.

"I know where you're going with this, Dr. Morrissey. I shouldn't have gotten so upset," Thomas said, moving around her office. He busily inspected all the items on her desk, picking up pencils, investigating a framed family photo. But she could tell he was listening.

"Let's just consider for a moment. How realistic is it, do you think, to expect sushi in a hospital cafeteria?" She watched him as he crossed from one side to the next.

Thomas sighed his signature sigh, deep with exhaled frustration.

"Not very," he muttered. Dorothy imagined that this encounter went along similar lines to his and JW's in years past when JW taught Thomas how to modify his expectations and behave appropriately in public. Moreover, as they talked, Dorothy hoped that Thomas was beginning to see, as she was, that his illness was separate from his inclinations, as he liked to say. Whatever he wore, or wanted to eat, he would continue to suffer from and need to learn to manage his manic depression.

"Tell me more about what happened after JW left," Dorothy said. "I remember you saying that everything turned upside down. Can you talk more about that?"

"The summer before my junior year, I got caught shoplifting," Thomas said. He handed her one of her pencils as if to demonstrate. Then he moved to the window and began twirling the cord of the blinds. "You want to know what the judge ordered me to do?" He looked over his shoulder at her, his face animated with an impish grin, relieved not to be talking about his outburst. "He said I had to join the football team. How do you like them apples?"

"You're kidding me?" Dorothy said.

"Yeah, his kid played, and he was a volunteer coach. He said I could join or sit in jail with my dad."

"Is this a true story?" Dorothy asked. With Thomas's build, it seemed a stretch to want him on the football team.

"Scouts' Honor." Thomas laughed, his fingers still twirling, enjoying Dorothy's response. "No one was that big back then. I suppose you could say, if it weren't for football, I would never have ended up here in the first place." Dorothy stayed alert to listen for more confirmation of her belief in Thomas's tendency toward repetition compulsion— the unconscious drive to reenact situations from his childhood. The trauma of John Wayne's departure and his father's incarceration likely instigated "the falling dominoes," as Thomas described. She waited to hear more, but she felt his outburst in the cafeteria was but a taste of the unconscious drive. Kimonos and sushi were just the preludes to how he put himself in situations where the violence of his youth played out again and again.

"I vowed I'd never grace the doors of this god-forsaken hellhole again, but here we are," Thomas said.

"Go on," Dorothy nudged.

"I'll never understand why that judge thought it was a good idea to put me on the football team, but little did he know how he changed my life—and his son's, I might add." Thomas smiled. "So ironic, nothing would have made Dad happier, and he was missing it. Besides, being on the football team, I felt closer to JW even though I mostly rode the bench."

"I can't help but see a connection," Dorothy said, "that your encounter with George today has led to a discussion about football. Perhaps it's because George reminds you of JW, and because of that, your feelings are more easily hurt when he teases or ignores you?"

"I don't know about that," Thomas replied, his fingers now thrumming the windowsill. "Can we leave George out of this? George is not JW." He moved away from the window and toward her shelves as if deciding the collection of psychology books looked more appealing. He pulled one from its neat alphabetic position, handed it to her as if for homework, and moved on.

"Sure, tell me more about football," Dorothy said, wishing he'd sit before a pile accumulated on her lap.

"Turns out the judge's son played football. His name was Regis Campbell." Thomas's tone was casual as he inspected a marble owl on Dorothy's bookshelf as if he'd practiced the delivery. "When I met Regis, it was love at first sight. We started to hang out. I had lots of free time because with Dad in jail and JW gone, all my mother did was lie on the couch and watch television. No more teatime for us. Regis was a sophomore, but his talent as a running back earned him a place on varsity. Once Regis and I found each other, we started, you know, exploring. He was the only person outside of my family who knew about my kimonos. He liked seeing me in them. And, with JW gone, he was the only person with whom I could truly be myself. I felt like I deserved a little happiness, you know? You can't imagine how happy I was then."

He was right; she couldn't. Happy was not an adjective she'd think to describe Thomas.

"We used to hang out in Grant Park. All the football players and cheerleaders used to go there. We'd build a bonfire and drink and smoke pot. I was accepted as part of the group because of Regis, and because I was JW's younger brother. Mind you, I still believed JW would come home. I talked about him all the time. They thought he was cool. And it didn't hurt that I could drink anyone under the table. But, if it weren't for bad luck, I wouldn't have any luck at all. Judge Campbell must have put two and two together, because all of a sudden, Regis was gone and the judge stopped volunteering, and I was kicked off the team with nary an explanation. Rumor had it, he sent Regis to military school in Ohio. I was heartbroken, but what could I do? Who was I going to tell? He was my one true love. Disappeared just like JW."

"Thomas. I'm so sorry," Dorothy said. As if the sadness of his tale was dissipating his energy, Thomas handed her the marble owl before finally plopping onto the loveseat. Dorothy was relieved. A pacing client made her nervous. "What did you do after that?"

"I was desperate after Regis was sent away. I'd just begun to accept that JW wasn't coming back. That's when I really started drinking. And that's how I found other cross-dressers and cocaine. We hung out at the bars around downtown Lansing. You had to be careful; there were a lot of meatheads around. I was always on the look-out for Regis. Time crept on, and neither JW nor Regis came back. Life began to feel like a roller coaster ride. I loved the cocaine. So, you could forgive me if my judgment sometimes failed me."

"Can you describe for me the feelings you had during that time?"

Thomas didn't hesitate. "Desperation," he said. "Before I knew it, I was up on another anniversary of the day Regis' father sent him away. The night before Thanksgiving. I went from bar to bar looking for Regis. I thought for sure the judge would let him come home for Thanksgiving, but I didn't dare go to his house. Regis knew where to find me. He knew what bars were safe for us. I drank a lot that night, but that's not a crime, is it?"

"Tell me what happened."

"The bars were crowded and hot. Everyone went out the night before Thanksgiving, so we couldn't squeeze into the bars where the friendlier sorts hung out."

"Who were you with?" Dorothy asked. "Football players?"

"God no, without Regis or JW, I was nothing to them."

"Then who were you with?"

"If you'd let me finish," Thomas said. "Mere acquaintances, nameless, if you will. I didn't have any real friends. Anywhooo, we landed in the only place we could find with empty seats. Even close to the door felt like a steam bath. I was never looking for trouble, but as the night went on, I might've gotten more belligerent. I don't know. The only piece of my father's clothing that I liked was his Navy pea coat, and I wore it that night over a smoking jacket of sorts hoping that if I ran into Regis,

I could surprise him. By the end of the night, I guess I forgot I had it on. The bar was so hot, and I was sweating like a pig. Looking back, taking off the pea coat was pretty stupid. I just didn't give a shit. Why should I? No one cared about me." Beads of sweat dotted Thomas's forehead as if he was sitting in the hot bar.

"The last thing I remember was this guy's yellow teeth and spittle. He had the worst breath and bulging eyes, but it took three of them to keep me down. I thought I was going to die. 'This is what we do to Japs,' the man said. He stripped off my kimono and my shoes and socks. I was reminded of my father. As far as I knew, those Neanderthals who left me lifeless on the cold concrete at two a.m. in downtown Lansing had not been charged with a crime. They certainly did not join me at St. Lawrence. Why was I locked up?" he asked Dorothy. "What is so fucking bad about wearing a kimono? I am not the one who beat the living shit out of someone."

"Point taken," Dorothy responded thoughtfully.

"No, really." Thomas's voice rose. "Why is it, these guys can beat the shit out of me, but I'm the crazy one? Why aren't they locked up like George is? He beat up the priest; he gets arrested, he gets locked up. Happens to me, I get beat up, I get arrested. They lock me up. I could have identified them if they gave me a chance."

"I don't know, Thomas," Dorothy said. He had a point. "I guess because he was a priest."

"So, a priest's life is more valuable than mine?"

"Not to my mind," Dorothy said.

"It's a rigged game," Thomas groaned.

"That it is," Dorothy said, shaking her head and feeling a bit dispirited herself. "I'm so sorry, Thomas," Dorothy reiterated. "I'm not surprised that you acted out. I, too, would have felt traumatized by your experiences, especially since so many awful events happened one right after another. Your dad goes to jail, JW and Regis leave never to return, and your mother shuts down. I'm feeling upset and angry, and it didn't even happen to me. And, frankly, if someone beat me up like that, well, I can't even imagine how devastating that would feel. Would you say that's an accurate reflection?"

"I suppose," Thomas replied half-heartedly. "But what could I do? I guess I didn't care anymore if someone wanted to kick the shit out of me. Have at it. That's how I felt. I just didn't care."

"I don't know," Dorothy observed. "You said yourself, you felt desperate. Can you tell me more about that?"

Thomas shrugged his shoulders. "Desperate to find just one person who really cared about me. Regis did. He was forced to leave. He didn't choose to leave me like JW. I just wanted to find him that night. Instead, look at what happened." He sighed.

"The men who assaulted you should have been charged with a crime. I can imagine how hard it must be to trust me after all of your experiences of betrayal before."

"Of course, I don't trust anyone," he said. "If my own family could so easily turn their backs on me, how can I expect you to care?" He said to Dorothy, "I think it would have been easier for me if my whole family had died in a car accident. Then I could be the tragic figure who is suddenly an orphan. I'd only remember the happy times. But no, they all *chose* to leave me."

The defeat in Thomas's voice and eyes belied the bravado of his words. His arms hung limply as they might have the night of the beating, his eyes cast downward as if he was afraid that if he looked up, she too would be gone. His bewilderment over their collective abandonment filled the space between them with such heaviness she felt her shoulders sag under the weight. She wasn't about to tell him to feel differently or question his version of events.

"Would you like me to contact your family?" Dorothy asked.

"Out of the question. I don't want them here."

"And what about Regis? Did you hear from him again?"

"Last I heard he moved to Detroit."

"As you said, Thomas, he did not choose to leave you," Dorothy said.

"True," Thomas said. "Hope springs eternal." He smiled, but his eyes were sad.

"I'm sorry, we have to end here, Thomas, I have another patient soon. But I'm surprised you haven't said anything about my tea set." He'd inspected almost all the contents of her office yet missed the tea set.

"What?" Thomas said, perking up and looking behind him to where she'd nodded toward the side table. "I love it!"

"You inspired me to go out and buy one," Dorothy said. "So, before you go, I have an idea."

Thomas burst into tears. "You want to do a tea ceremony?" He said as if he couldn't believe his ears. "Who will do it?" He reached for a tissue and wiped at his eyes and nose.

"You, Thomas, I'm hoping you are willing to do one for our next group. I think a tea ceremony would be a nice change of pace and an interesting learning opportunity for everyone."

Thomas stared at her agape. "You want me to do the ceremony? Like, be in charge? You would trust me? You're not mad at me for having a hissy fit?"

"I think you're more than capable. I will help you, of course. But I'll need you to tell me what to do."

Thomas stood and resumed his pacing, but there was a difference from earlier in the session. She could see by the light in his eyes that the idea was exciting to him and that he was already planning. "I knew I liked you, Dr. Morrissey," he said. "Even though you remind me of that Coca-Cola commercial with all your peace, love, and joy talk."

Dorothy smiled. "You mean the one where they're all singing?"

"That's the one."

"Does that mean you'll think about it?"

"The mere thought makes me giddy, but what if the others laugh at me?"

"Take a day to think about it, Thomas, but I think the others will love a tea ceremony."

"I don't need to think. I'll do it. If you still believe in me after I've been so difficult, who am I to say no." He headed for the door. As he was about to open it, he turned back and smiled. "Thank you, Dr. Morrissey. I'm sorry I was in such a mood today, you know, no sushi." With that, pangs of hunger propelled Dorothy from her seat and out the door to the nurse's station to see if there was fish sandwich with her name on it. Thomas's note would have to wait.

CHAPTER NINETEEN

GEORGE

PARALLEL PROCESS

Dorothy went to the pool for a long swim before going into work. She'd taken the morning off after an exhausting on-call weekend. Swimming was the only time Dorothy felt comfortable in her body. Kenneth was clearly tiring of her "Catholic guilt," and was done tiptoeing around the subject of sex. He'd confronted her again this morning after Dorothy allowed him to stroke her back but as soon as he moved to the front of her body she recoiled. "Honestly, Dorothy, what is going on with you?" he'd said.

"What do you mean?" she asked.

"The longer we've lived together, the more distant you've become."

Though she appreciated the euphemism, Dorothy knew he was trying to say nicely what they both knew. She was uptight. There were places she didn't know how to go, and when he tried to take her there like this morning, she shut down. "It's like you've set it up so that you're damned if you do, and damned if you don't," he said.

"Now you are beginning to understand," Dorothy said. "Have you ever once been made to feel guilty about anything? It's so easy for you to point out my shortcomings from your perfect perch."

"You're just avoiding my question, Dorothy."

"I didn't hear a question I heard a statement and a judgmental one at that. How many ways can I explain this to you?" she asked. "You say you understand, but then you keep bringing it up."

What did Kenneth know about Catholic guilt? She'd had urges just like everyone else. But from the time she could toddle, she learned that any expression of sexuality outside of a good Catholic marriage constituted a mortal sin. How many times had she and her sisters heard, "Why buy the cow when you can get the milk for free?" from their father? She couldn't count. And, in case she missed his meaning, the priests drove it home. The priests let her know early and often that female sexuality was the root of all evil. "Wayward girls" were somehow responsible for the boys' bad behavior, and they made very public examples of girls who got pregnant all on their own apparently.

Consequently, self-loathing ran alongside her blossoming sexuality. From her very first crush as a teenager, she was always at odds with herself. During the week she could be bookish, smart, and over-achieving. Asexual nuns in her all-girl academy expressed high hopes for her, suggesting even the University of Michigan as a possibility. But when the weekends came, and the Catholic Youth Organization hosted mixers, Dorothy would foolishly cast aside her ambitions in favor of a hoped-for romance with some dreamy upperclassman from Detroit Jesuit. But, God forbid, she mentions her Michigan aspirations. While trying to feel her up, Dorothy's male peers would joke— "nine out of ten girls are pretty, the tenth goes to Michigan," using the joke like a weapon when they didn't get their way. The "Good Catholic boys" her parents hoped she'd find to marry were the very ones who were either trying to feel her up or busy putting her down.

What was a girl supposed to do? The only conclusion to young Dorothy's mind was that her choices were ugly but smart, liked but slutty, or uptight and marriageable until the wedding night at which time, she could let loose without being a slut. She tried to explain all this to Kenneth.

"Personally, I find it absurd that a bunch of celibate males can dictate how people should use their bodies," Kenneth said.

"I agree intellectually, but the damage was done a long time ago."

✦

Dorothy inhaled the deep soothing breaths required to move seamlessly through the water as she mulled over their conversation. Of course, Kenneth was right, but she found it maddening how easily he could move through life. He was so confident about his place in the world order. He didn't understand her predicament, why she was such a contradiction, as he put it. He didn't know the meaning of shame. She was damned no matter what.

She felt guilty about Kenneth too. She could only enjoy sex with Kenneth if they were married and to marry him would kill her father. Even if her father had been the man he was before her sister died, the possibility would have been remote at best that he might begrudgingly have accepted Kenneth into the fold. Kenneth was a Protestant. Catholics did not marry Protestants. The Church was one thing. She could walk away from an institution buttressed by exclusionary tactics. Her father was another story altogether.

As she rolled back and forth, taking deep, cleansing breaths, her mind emptied as the tension rippled down her spine and released into the water. She wondered how the morning's conflict with Kenneth would play out in her sessions because uncannily her patients always seemed to hold a mirror up to her issues as they worked on their own.

✦

By the time George entered Dorothy's office and sat down, she felt of calm mind and body. The September sun shone through Dorothy's window, accentuating the sadness around George's eyes and the dark shadow of his unshaven face. He hadn't made it to the barber as his hair was getting long, and his curls were more disheveled than she'd noticed in a while. "What's going on, George?" Dorothy asked. "You look upset."

"You're not married, are you?" he said.

A laugh escaped from her before she could stop it.

"What's so funny?" George asked, unaccustomed to any show of emotion in Dorothy.

"To answer your question, I am not. I'm sorry I laughed but I'd just been thinking about that in the pool."

"Boyfriend?" He inched forward, curious now.

"Yes." She sat back, guarded.

"Do you have sex with him?"

She laughed again. She couldn't help it. George kept hitting the mark of her ruminations this morning.

"None of your business, George, but I'm interested in why you ask. Where are we headed with this?"

"If Miner hadn't abused me, I'd be married or at least have a girl-friend. Do you know I've never had sex?"

Neither have I, she thought. The hard shell that had swirled around her from the morning's conversation with Kenneth was threatening again. She felt a need to jump back in the pool.

"Again, I'm not laughing, but I was thinking this morning about how abuse steals from your future especially future relationships. You've had so much stolen from you, George," she said.

"Did I tell you I had a visitor? Besides my mom, that is."

"You did not. Tell me more about that."

"Of all people, Margaret Cook, my nemesis in grade school."

"Really?" Dorothy said. "The girl who Father Miner liked to take down a notch or two?"

"The very same. She came to see me. She's a lawyer now." Did she detect a blush moving up his cheeks?

"And why did she come to visit?" Dorothy asked.

George took a deep breath. "She wants to represent me as part of a class-action lawsuit against our parish and Father Miner."

"Are you serious?"

"She had a younger brother who recently committed suicide. In his suicide note, he made very detailed allegations against Miner."

"Oh, my goodness. Who knows how many children he has abused," Dorothy said, shaking her head in disbelief.

"Her blood is boiling. She hated Miner to begin with, but now she wants him to pay."

"That's good news, don't you think?"

"I suppose. Won't do me any good."

"She's going to have a fight on her hands going up against the Catholic Church."

"She's like a dog on a meat wagon," George said. "She feels she has enough for a class-action lawsuit. She said she thinks she can get the charges against me dropped or reversed. I don't know. I'm not getting my hopes up."

"You must feel vindicated," Dorothy said.

"I guess I do, but what good is that now? I'm stuck. Miner's still the pastor of my parents' church, and Brian is still dead."

"I don't know how they get away with it," Dorothy said. She noticed immediately the Freudian slip, but George seemed to miss the "they" in her sentence.

"Margaret was pretty funny. She said, 'Let's see who's a smarty-pants now.'"

"Speaking of," Dorothy said. "You said she was your nemesis. Can you tell me what you meant?"

"We were number one and number two—the smart boy and the smart girl. She became a lawyer, and here I am."

Dorothy said. "I wonder if seeing Margaret has given you a glimmer of hope?"

"I'll believe it when I see it." He turned away, as if his hopes sat close to Dorothy.

She leaned closer, speaking gently. A hunched-over-head-down shame replaced the 'I dare you' jutted chin of early sessions. Treading lightly, she kept digging.

"Remember, you once told me you were a sullen shit?" Dorothy prodded. "I think being a 'sullen shit,' saved you from more abuse." A memory intruded unbidden as Dorothy tried to concentrate on George: *You think you're so clever, do you?*

"I guess, but now that I remember exactly what happened, I can't let go of something Miner said."

"What was that?" Dorothy asked, trying to keep her focus.

"Miner said I'd committed the sin of pride. He made it his job to shame me into nothing. I felt I deserved what I got. I was proud. I was proud of my dad being in the Navy. I was proud of how my dad combed my hair. I wanted to be neatly pressed and 'look sharp,' like my mom always said about my dad when he was in his uniform. I didn't know it was a sin. By the end of the day, I didn't want to be like my father anymore. I lost everything, and somehow my pride was at the center."

His frustration and sorrow were palpable. It was uncanny to Dorothy how similar George's experiences were to hers. He brought to life the second grader inside of her, who had also been made to feel ashamed. Why was it so awful, in the eyes of the Church, for a blossoming child to feel some self-worth? She had an uncomfortable feeling there was something lurking at the edges of her consciousness that must be too overwhelming to let surface. The session was being derailed by her own mind, so, she asked a question to refocus on George.

"Can you remember what you felt back then, George?"

George closed his eyes. Dorothy observed him take a deep intake of breath as if he needed to dive deep.

"It fried my ass, even as a child, that I had to apologize to him for stealing a pack of cigarettes when what he did was so much worse. I'm so mad." His hands balled up in tight fists.

"I agree, George. I can't fathom why he would defile a son's pride in his father."

Rather than comment, George said, "How come Margaret could go on to become a lawyer, and I ended up here?"

"For one thing, Father Miner did not sexually abuse Margaret. Even when he tried to shame her publicly, it is not the same. There were witnesses. Her friends could console her." *My friends didn't console me,* she thought. "She could run home crying to her parents." Another thought popped into Dorothy's mind. *I tried to tell my mom.* "Father Miner ambushed you, and he shamed you, and you were only eight years old." *Just like Father Mayer.* She was annoying herself with all the intrusive thoughts by this point. "An eight-year-old does not have the cognitive ability to begin to interpret or explain to other grown-ups what had happened to you, George." *I tried to tell Father Mayer and look where that got me.* "He might as well have been feeding you poison." Dorothy's voice rose in shrill anger and frustration that they both noticed. "How does an eight-year-old comprehend the fact of sexual abuse? Within a matter of minutes, Father Miner alienated you from your parents, your peers, teachers, and yourself. What were you to do, George?"

George hung his head down and wept. He gathered himself before he spoke. "I played right into it. I shouldn't have let my anger get the best of me."

Just then, Dorothy would have liked nothing more than to punch Father Miner in his groin. She felt her anger boil up inside of her. The injustice was crushing. How could a man such as Father Miner exist in the world? How could he look into an innocent child's eyes then destroy his young life? It was incomprehensible. And what kind of system propped up such evil? That George didn't do worse damage to the priest was a testimony to his character. These were her thoughts when suddenly, she realized the reason she'd been reacting to George as she had.

"Oh, my God!" she blurted out. "I don't dislike you, George." She laughed again, a bit hysterically this time. He looked at her quizzically. "I'm so sorry, I know I'm not making any sense." Tears had sprung to her eyes. She quickly brushed them away. "Remember when you said you thought I didn't like you?"

"Yes," he said, suspiciously.

"It's not that I don't like you, I was projecting."

"Projecting?" Curiosity dried his tears.

"I was seeing in you what I didn't want to see in myself."

"So, you beat up a priest?" he said facetiously.

"I almost wish I had," she said. Dorothy took a deep breath, trying to pull it together so she wouldn't steal George's time. She brought her focus back to her patient.

"Well, that's a relief," he smiled.

"What is?" she asked, losing track.

"That you like me."

"I do, George. Let's just say, we have a lot in common." She was flustered by her inappropriate disclosure. This was so unlike her. *Get it together, Dorothy,* she thought. "Let's get back to you," she said. "Though your actions were misguided, honestly, George, I'm so sickened by what he did, I'm sitting here wishing you'd finished the job." George wiped away any lingering tears and shot her a surprised smile. "Can I ask, George, what are you most sorry for?"

George didn't hesitate. "I'm most sorry for the loss of my dad. I might not have had the words to explain what Father Miner did to me, but I knew he was a hateful man. My father was a good man, and I loved and admired him. That he didn't think to question why I behaved as I did before he took off his belt and dragged me to the basement is inconceivable to me to this day. Why didn't my parents think it through? Why didn't they wonder what happened to their good little boy suddenly doing something so out of character? Of course, I shouldn't have stolen the cigarettes or run away, but wouldn't you, as a parent, wonder what might have precipitated my behavior?" He shook his head in disbelief.

"For what it's worth, my parents never questioned the authority of the parish priest," Dorothy said. "So, you're disappointed in them too?"

"I guess I am."

"Hopefully, Margaret's lawsuit will provide an opportunity to mend fences," Dorothy said.

"I'm not ready," George said.

Dorothy took a sip of water. George followed suit.

"Well, it's not up to me whether you tell your parents, George, but I'd like you to think about what's stopping you. Remember what I said. Abuse steals your future relationships too. Perhaps, we can put an end to that."

"What could I possibly do now?" His habitual cynicism sneaking in.

"Write your parents a letter, maybe? Listen, our time is up. Before you go, let's say, worst-case scenario, you spend the rest of your life in here. How would you like to spend it?"

"I hope Margaret comes back to visit."

"That would be nice, wouldn't it?"

George blushed. "I mean to take a statement. She wouldn't touch me with a ten-foot pole."

"I wouldn't be so sure about that, George," Dorothy said with a smile. "What about the best-case scenario? What does that look like for you? Let's say, Margaret is successful, and you're released. Then what?"

"I'd do what you're doing." George didn't hesitate. "But maybe not in an asylum. I've had enough of this place." Dorothy smiled. He'd just answered her question about how he felt about their process together.

"I think that's entirely possible, George," she said. "Just don't lose it in the middle of a session like I did today," she said sheepishly.

"Honestly, I'm glad you did," he said. "Thanks, Dr. Morrissey."

Once the door was closed behind George, Dorothy burst into tears.

September 3, 1974, George indicated that a childhood friend, MC, visited, which prompted questions of sexuality. George worked very hard to uncover the many layers of disappointment, grief, and sadness. He is making significant progress. Interesting to this therapist, George hasn't brought a nightmare to a session for a long-time. Monitor mood for depression as he continues to uncover unconscious content.

Dorothy pulled her private notebook from the drawer. *Therapist experienced a breakthrough (breakdown) today in session with George. Childhood memories intruded upon the session. Unfortunately, Dr. Keith is on a long Labor Day holiday. Need to make an appointment with him as soon as he returns. Monitor mood for depression as therapist continues to uncover unconscious content.*

CHAPTER TWENTY

DOROTHY

HYPNOSIS

"Okay, Dorothy, I want you to lay back comfortably on the chaise and we will start counting back from one hundred." There was a hush to his office that belied her knowledge that they were in the busy hospital. Though very self-conscious, Dorothy did as he said, doing her best to relax. Dorothy had tearfully apprised Dr. Keith about George's treatment and how her unconscious content from her childhood spilled into the last session. Mortified by the intrusive thoughts, she was desperate to figure out what was behind them. She lay back and placed her arms comfortably on her lap.

Dr. Keith instructed her to take deep, controlled breaths. He convinced Dorothy that hypnotherapy was the best intervention for someone like her whose understanding of traditional psychotherapy was the very thing that got in her way. She could anticipate a line of questioning and take pains to avoid it. Hypnotherapy was his work-around to her resistance. "Relax, Dorothy, you are safe," he said. His voice was calm and soothing. "When you are comfortable, close your eyes. Breathe in, breathe out," he instructed quietly and at a snail's pace. Though skeptical, Dorothy followed suit. She took deep breaths and exhaled slowly while she counted backwards. "Take me back to the year your sister died. Remember, you are safe. Whatever happened is over now. You are just looking."

Somewhere outside of her peripheral vision there was a metronome. Dorothy took a deep breath, closed her eyes, and started counting backwards. Her breath fell into rhythm. Her formative years played like shadows in her mind but having the power to evoke strong emotions. She, a little girl, trying to tell her mom how Sister Constance sent her to the rectory daily with notes for Father Ben. Everybody knew that Father Ben was the nice priest. Most of the time, Father Ben would laugh, write a note of his own, and send Dorothy back to class. The worst part for Dorothy was her classmates calling her a teacher's pet. *How come she gets to miss penmanship and we don't,* she'd heard someone whisper behind her when Sister Constance sent her on her way. Then one day, while reading the note, he told Dorothy to stand closer to him. There was something different about this note. He absently (as if he wasn't really doing it on purpose) stroked the front of Dorothy's uniform from the top of her peter pan collar to her neatly pressed pleats and hem while reading and then writing. He acted strange, excited in way that made Dorothy uncomfortable. She stood paralyzed by his side. One thing she did know, what he was doing was wrong.

Somewhere in the distance, Dorothy could hear Dr. Keith encourage her to keep going, you're safe, no one will hurt you in hushed tones. Tell mom, tell mom, but mom was too busy cleaning and Deirdre was screaming like a banshee from the top of the stairs. *Just do as your told, Dottie. You always think you're so smart.* The scent of Clorox was overpowering.

For the most part, Dorothy trusted that the grownups in her life were there to obey but also to protect. Her mother was too busy to listen. She couldn't ask Sister Constance. Dorothy never read the notes. Sister Constance knew she wouldn't. It was clear even to an eight-year-old that something was going on between Sister Constance and Father Ben. The only adult left to tell was Father Mayer. She was very nervous around Father Mayer. He was always grouchy. Still, she mustered her courage and told on Father Ben during confession. Her last confession before her sister died. All Dorothy had remembered until now was getting dragged from the confessional by Father Mayer.

How dare you say such a thing about Father Ben and Sister Constance! Get your mind out of the gutter, you little slut! We'll hear nothing more of this. All she'd accomplished by doing the right thing was to make an enemy of Father Mayer. From then on, he'd find any excuse to chastise and humiliate her in front of her peers.

Little Dottie had to find a way around her dilemma all on her own now that Tess was no longer around to protect her. Sister Constance treated Dorothy with more kindness and favoritism, which didn't really help Dorothy's cause among her peers. She continued to trust Dorothy with notes to Father Ben. Rather than deliver them, Dottie walked the long way around the school to get to the rectory. She threw the notes away in the trash barrels near the eighth-grade classrooms before returning to her classroom. *Father Ben didn't give me a note today, she'd lie. He said he'd read it later.* Dorothy wasn't sure if Sister Constance knew Dorothy was lying or if she felt sorry for her because Tess died. Regardless, she never said anything but eventually stopped sending Dorothy to the rectory. Instead, she found a new errand girl, Leslie Anders.

"That's an awful lot for a little girl to go through, Dorothy," Dr. Keith said kindly. I can understand why you've had such strong negative reactions to George. Can you tell me what's the worst part for you?" he asked.

Dorothy didn't even have to think about it. "The worst part is knowing that I wasn't protected even before Tess died. Deirdre took up so much emotional space. My mom couldn't or wouldn't listen to me. I always thought my family was loving and stable until we fell apart after her death. But most of this happened before Tess died."

"What strikes me is that you tried to speak up. You thought your parents and the pastor would help you."

"Yes, and all I got for my trouble was incur Father Mayer's wrath for the rest of my life. He even yelled me when I was a bridesmaid in my sister's wedding."

"Anything else stand out?"

"I feel guilty."

"Guilty? Why?"

"I was glad Leslie Anders took my place. But then I wonder if I've switched the timing. You know, like what came first the chicken or the egg?"

"How do you mean?" he asked.

"In my memory, she was mean to me before Tess died and it was after that when Sister started sending Leslie to the rectory instead of me. It makes me wonder if it was my idea to send her instead of someone else."

"What makes you say that?" His tone remained calm and non-judgmental.

"Because I was glad that Sister sent her. Does that make me a shitty person?"

"Dorothy, you were an eight-year-old girl. And human, I might add."

"Will you reassign George to a different therapist?" she asked.

"I can't imagine a better therapist for George," Dr. Keith said, genuinely surprised by her assumption.

"Really? I thought you'd want to take me off his case." She sat up, shaking off the grogginess of the hypnosis.

"Not at all, look at your willingness and courage, I dare say, to look at your wounds in service of your client. They don't say wounded healer for nothing," Dr. Keith said.

"Thank you," Dr. Keith, "I appreciate you saying so."

"Are there any other insights you garnered from the hypnosis?" he asked.

"Not that I want to share," she said with a smile. *How embarrassing*, was what she was thinking. Her issues with sex and Kenneth touching her were the first "insights" that came to mind. Although she felt confident that Dr. Keith would keep confidentiality, she worried that he'd think less of her as a doctor, if she shared her neuroses. So, no, she didn't have any more insights.

"Let me know if anything else comes up. I'm here if you need me."

"I will," she said, "thanks again, Dr. Keith." Her step was noticeably lighter than when she'd walked in.

CHAPTER TWENTY-ONE

RUTH

MUSIC THERAPY

Dorothy was wrapping up her day, finishing her notes, and tidying her desk. The day had been long, and she felt drained, but the warm light of late autumn sun threw a kaleidoscope of color throughout the office. She'd promised Kenneth she'd get home in time for a walk before dinner to take advantage of the remaining warm days. Just as she was putting on her coat, a rapid knock on her door startled her. This was not a nurse. Thomas's voice whispered urgently on the other side.

"I hope she's still here," she heard him say. She slid the coat off one arm while she opened the door to Thomas and Marcella, an unlikely duo to her mind. "We need to talk to you," Thomas said. Marcella nodded.

"I'm assuming this is an emergency?"

"That it is," Thomas said. "We think Ruth wants to kill herself."

"Did you leave her alone?"

"We're not morons," Thomas snapped. "George is with her."

"Why didn't you bring her straight to my office?" Dorothy asked.

"She wouldn't come," Marcella said.

"Let's get moving," Dorothy said, throwing her coat on the loveseat. "You can fill me in on the way."

Thomas immediately embarked on the events of the afternoon. "I was minding my own business when I heard all this commotion coming from the hallway. Someone was yelling and slamming something against the wall. Honestly, I was almost afraid to come out, but then I realized it was Ruth, and for once, she wasn't singing. I couldn't resist. I had to go see what all the fuss was about. Marcella here," he waved toward Marcella as if Dr. Morrissey didn't know her, "was trying to drag Ruth away from the payphone. The receiver was a hair's breadth from broken with her slamming it like she was. I've never seen such a spectacle." With Thomas's flair for drama, Dorothy couldn't gauge the seriousness of the situation.

"I'll admit, I thought she was just looking for attention," Thomas said. "You know how she always has to be the star of the show. But even I could see Ruth wasn't playing. She was carrying on something fierce, 'Get off the phone, Jerome, I wasn't talking to you,'" he mimicked Ruth.

"She wanted to talk to her mother without her brother butting in," Marcella said sympathetically. "Poor thing. She just wants her mom to come and visit."

"Even I felt sorry for her," Thomas said. "And for once, she wasn't singing."

"You already said that," Marcella said.

Thomas shot her a nasty look. "Bears repeating."

By then, they reached the room Ruth and Marcella shared. As promised, George sat there calmly, keeping her company.

Dorothy was prepared to see Ruth disheveled and slumped in a chair. Instead, she sat upright on the bed, and though her face was lined with tension and sadness, she also had on lipstick and blush. Blue eye shadow stood out on swollen lids. But her hair was what really stood out, tied in multiple mini ponytails by brightly colored bows. For Dorothy, the effect defined cognitive dissonance. The two just didn't fit. The hairdo on Ruth was charming but gave the impression that the situation wasn't as severe as Thomas and Marcella had led her to believe. The bows and eye makeup made Ruth look youthful but could not conceal that she'd been sobbing. Thomas's face tightened with every bit of foundation and lipstick that transferred from Ruth's face to the tissue as she wiped her nose.

Marcella noticed Dorothy's astonished face. "I put the bows in her hair. We were trying to cheer her up." The hairdo was indeed playful yet not overdone.

"Nothing makes a girl feel special like a new hairdo and a little makeup," Thomas said. Ruth just sat there, looking as stunned as Dorothy. "My expertise wasted, as you can see. And I used my good stuff." With a huff, he set about gathering his makeup and brushes as if she'd personally insulted him by not feeling better immediately.

"Can you all give us a few minutes?" She said to the three as she motioned to the door. Turning to Ruth, she said, "Ruth, would you like to stay here and talk or come down to my office?"

"I just want to die," Ruth said. She began singing softly under her breath.

"I'm sorry, Ruth, I can't ignore what you just said. Are you having thoughts of suicide?" Ruth mumbled incoherently but didn't respond. "Ruth, I need to know." One of Ruth's hands was clutched around something that Dorothy couldn't see. "Can you open your hand for me, Ruth?" Ruth opened her hand. All that was there was a foam hair roller. Dorothy breathed a sigh of relief. "What's upsetting you?" Ruth had consistently denied thoughts of suicide, even at her worst. Last time they'd met, Ruth had been discussing job possibilities.

"I finally got the pathology report."

"And?" Dorothy prompted.

"I lost my babies because I had chlamydia."

"I've never heard of chlamydia, what is it?" Dorothy held her breath because she had a suspicion that it was from Calvin.

"It's a venereal disease," Ruth said. Surprisingly, she looked Dorothy in the eye when, once upon a time, she would have hung her head in shame.

"There's only one person to blame, I'm guessing," Dorothy said, exhaling frustration.

"Yep. I've got my answers. I don't even care about that anymore. What's done is done." She paused for a long moment. "I picked a song," Ruth said. "Like you told me to."

"Okay, what song was that?"

"Sometimes I Feel Like a Motherless Child."

Dorothy pulled up a chair. "Oh, I'm sorry, Ruth."

"As soon as I found out about the chlamydia, I asked my mother to come to see me. I figured she'd feel sorry for me now."

"And, what happened?" Dorothy asked.

Ruth wiped away a tear but continued without returning to singing, which Dorothy viewed as a positive development. "We got into a huge fight. She didn't even say she was sorry for me." The first thing she said was, 'Shame on you, Ruth. You know I don't like hospitals.'"

"After twelve children, I would think she's used to hospitals by now?"

"She had us all at home. But that's not the worst part. You won't believe what she said next."

"What's that?"

"My mother had the gall to say to me that I lost my feminine power."

"What? That's a horrible thing to say." All her efforts to empower Ruth could be swept away by one negative comment from her mother. "What could she possibly have meant by that?"

"That's what I asked," Ruth replied, sitting up straighter. "Since I don't have a uterus anymore, I've lost my feminine power. She's in a women's consciousness-raising group. A woman's power lives in her uterus, she tells me."

"That's nonsense, Ruth. I'm sorry, but it seems to me that if your mother was in touch with her 'feminine power,' she would not wield it so thoughtlessly. Ironically, she talks about feminine power while you feel like a motherless child. Feminine power isn't just about the uterus. Caring for others is very much a part of our feminine energy, even though I know it's undervalued. And you have already spent a lifetime caring for your brothers." Dorothy could see the wheels turning in Ruth's contorted features as she weighed whose words to believe, her mother's or Dorothy's.

"You know what else?" she said. "I think my family believes I've been faking it. Like, why don't I just get over it?"

"Is that what you believe, Ruth? Or did someone in your family say that to you?"

"Well, both, more or less?" Ruth responded.

"Sometimes, we internalize other people's judgments," Dorothy explained. "After a while, they don't have to say anything directly. Most of the time, we aren't aware that we are repeating what was said to us."

"My mother said, you're not the first to suffer and you won't be the last, so why am I so needy?"

Dorothy was fuming inside. What she wanted to say was *Are you feckin kidding me?* Instead, she said, "your mother's judgments are particularly hurtful because you are vulnerable right now." Discussing patients' families with them was a balancing act. She wanted to show Ruth that she could disagree with her mother but still love her without minimizing Ruth's feelings.

"I think it's safe to say that your mother knows a lot about having babies, but she doesn't understand what losing them feels like. She probably doesn't know what to say. Secondly, I believe you are courageous to know when you need help."

"I don't feel courageous."

"Your resilience was the very first characteristic I noticed about you. You've withstood a lot of loss, and you're still standing. It feels unfair and hurtful that your family doesn't understand how great a loss this is for you. Rather than providing support, they're acting judgmental. Would that be accurate?"

Ruth blushed. "Yes, I feel like my mother is no better than Calvin. She kicked me when I was down."

"Yes, she did. And she tried to make you feel guilty for needing her. Rather than saying, 'I can't handle it, I'm sorry, Ruth.' She made you feel bad for asking. It sounds like, as the oldest child and the only girl, you aren't allowed to have hurt feelings."

"That's exactly what I mean! My drug-addicted brother and his drug-addict girlfriend can move in, but I lose my baby and find out my husband gave me a venereal disease but that's not enough to get a visit from my mother? When I asked her, she said, 'We all got to stick together,' skipping right over my problems. Then she said, 'You know what a sensitive child, Darren is, Ruth. He needs our help.'" Ruth searched Dorothy's eyes for the hidden knowledge she might possess. "So, they aren't sticking with me because I'm not sensitive?" Ruth's voice rose in frustration.

"You're one of the most sensitive people I've ever met, Ruth," Dorothy said.

"You know, after Marcella did my hair, she said, "you look so pretty, Ruth.' I realized no one has ever told me that I am pretty. In my whole life. Maybe I'm not as sensitive as Darren, but just once I would have liked to hear my mother say I was pretty or smart or a good singer."

"So, you feel like your mother is not one for compliments, eh?"

"No, it's always 'the family this, the family that' or like I said, 'we got to stick together,'" Ruth said, "until I need them."

"I wonder if that's a big family thing," Dorothy said, "my mother always says that sort of thing. And, God forbid, if you tried to stand out, she pushed you right back down." The comfort and safety in numbers outweighed any yearnings toward individuality. Needing to be seen and heard was selfishness.

Ruth's face lit up with the validation. "Yeah, it's like that game whack-a-mole," she said. "Stick your head up too high, and she'd knock it down. If my mother thought I was getting uppity, she'd say, 'Who do you think you are—?'"

Dorothy finished the sentence, "—the queen of Sheba?"

They both laughed.

"It sounds to me, Ruth, that you wish the people you love would return the love you show them. You would visit if a member of your family were in the hospital because that's who you are." Ruth's need for love and affection was found in taking care of others. Intentionally or unintentionally, her family's absence when she needed them reinforced Ruth's belief that she was unlovable on her own. "Unfortunately, not everyone is the same as you."

A faint smile illuminated Ruth's dimples.

"I have to say, Ruth," Dorothy said. "I'm proud of you for asking your parents to visit even if you didn't get the response you desired."

"At least now I know where I stand."

"You know, that makes me think that perhaps your Aunt Sylvie would visit you if you asked. Of all your family, she's the one who might understand what you're going through."

"You're right, she might be better for me anyway."

"And she's visited before, right?" Ruth nodded. "So why don't you ask her again?"

"That's a good idea. Thanks, Dr. Morrissey. Marcella and Thomas were so sweet to try to cheer me up, but I need my family."

"They did do a very nice job on your hair and makeup," Dorothy said. "I love it." She smiled and felt relieved and rewarded when Ruth returned with a widening smile of her own. "I think they are worried about you."

"I'm okay, I won't kill myself. I just wanted my family to understand. I don't think they ever will."

"Perhaps not," Dorothy replied. "I'm not surprised that you chose the spiritual 'Sometimes I Feel Like a Motherless Child.' I don't doubt that your family loves you, but they haven't been doing a very good job of showing it. In the meantime, ask your aunt to come to visit." She glanced at her watch. "I will need to have a nurse check up on you tonight, and I'll check on you tomorrow."

"Okay, I understand."

"Can I send Marcella and Thomas back in?"

"Sure, I need to thank Thomas properly, or he'll hold a grudge."

The pair of them, sans George, hovered near the door when Dorothy walked out.

"Well done, you two," Dorothy said. "She'll be okay. You can go on in."

✦

Dorothy went back to her office to write her note. She'd just sat down at her desk when another knock interrupted her, softer this time. "Yes, come in," she called.

Nurse Martin, clad in street clothes and raincoat, poked her head in the office. "Get a drink?" she asked.

"Sure," Dorothy said, "let me just write a note and give Kenneth a call. Do you mind if he joins us? We were supposed to take a walk but now it's too late."

"The more, the merrier."

09/12/74 Therapist contacted by two patients regarding suicide ideation in Ruth J. When the therapist entered Ruth's room, Ruth was sitting on the bed. The other two patients had given her a new hairdo and applied makeup to "cheer her up." Ruth stated, "I just want to die," but after some discussion denied suicidal thoughts. Ruth endorsed feeling sad due to hurt feelings. She indicated that her mother had made some very hurtful remarks about Ruth 'losing her feminine power,' due to the hysterectomy. The therapist will follow up tomorrow and has informed evening nurses re: Ruth's statements to monitor for SI overnight. Also, ask for pathology report.

✦

Dorothy and Rebecca Martin walked to the pub together, where Kenneth would be waiting for them. Basking in the lingering bits of warmth from the setting sun, they slowed their pace so they could process the events of the day.

"I feel so bad for Ruth," Rebecca said. "Weren't you just thinking about moving her to intensive outpatient?"

"I was hoping to broach the topic," Dorothy said. "Before today, I thought she was getting stronger. We'll have to wait and see now."

"Where will she go?" Rebecca said. "She said there was no way she was going back to Calvin."

"That's music to my ears. But I don't think she can go home either. Did she make it to the life skills group?" she asked her colleague.

"Yes, but she doesn't have a lot of confidence," Rebecca said. "I think she underestimates her gifts."

"Life hasn't been good to her, that's for sure."

Witnessing Ruth's struggle to consider alternate plans outside of motherhood, Dorothy felt grateful for the nuns in her life. They had traveled the world and had master's degrees. They encouraged her to dream big. Nowhere else did she receive that kind of encouragement.

Yet Dorothy did not want to equate her struggles with Ruth's. Dorothy could weigh her options. Traditional doors had all slammed in her patient's face, and no one was there to encourage a different future. Even with all the talk of civil rights, for a black woman, the obstacles were daunting. No wonder Ruth was depressed and overwhelmed. She hoped to nudge Ruth to find solutions that Ruth believed feasible, and Dorothy was glad to hear she had joined the life skills group where a representative from Lansing Community College would come to show them what options were available.

"If all else fails, she could sing in a nightclub," Rebecca said, brightly.

"She's such a kind person. I love working with her," Dorothy said. "All I know is, I really, really want her life to work out."

"I couldn't agree more," Rebecca said as they walked up to see Kenneth standing in front of the pub. "Geesh, Dorothy, is that Kenneth? Where have you been hiding him?"

She wrapped one arm through Dorothy's and held out her other to Kenneth in greeting.

CHAPTER TWENTY-TWO

GROUP

THOMAS PERFECT, TEA MASTER

Thomas and Dorothy set about preparing for the tea ceremony. She outlined two important caveats leading up to the next group. Thomas needed to stay on his medications. "The best way for you to maintain your equilibrium and focus is to comply with treatment," she said. Secondly, he should not seek perfection. "Neither you nor I can guarantee how your fellow patients will respond. So please, don't take anything personally. Just do your best."

"We're using Lipton Tea; you think I don't know that?" He laughed.

"Are you sure? I want this to be a good experience for you."

"I get it, I promise. Can you at least find me loose leaf?"

"I'll do my best," Dorothy promised. "But it might involve opening up tea bags.

"I might need you to help with welcoming our guests," Thomas said.

"I'd be happy to." He instructed Dorothy on the spiritual underpinnings of the tea ceremony. He asked if she could narrate these points while he prepared for the ritual so that he could welcome his guests, as host, in silence. "Once our guests are seated around the mat, will you join us?" he asked.

"I wouldn't miss it." They reviewed what other elements needed to be included besides her tea set, and the other items that Thomas requested she pick up, including two more serving cups, a square bamboo mat, and a teakettle and tea.

"Loose-leaf, no bags." Dorothy smiled.

"Unless you want to drink dust. And now, I must prepare myself spiritually," Thomas said.

"And how will you prepare?" Dorothy asked.

"I will meditate on the spiritual principles," he replied.

"Then I will too," she said.

✦

The day arrived. Fortunately, late October was blessing them with a spate of warm, sunny summer-like days, so Thomas asked Dorothy if they could hold the ceremony in an enclosed courtyard usually co-opted by the hospital staff to enjoy outdoor lunches and breaks. He explained that being sensitive to the changing rhythms of the seasons induced harmony with nature. Dorothy appreciated the sentiment and believed that any opportunity for her clients to get some fresh air would be beneficial. She worked her magic and reserved the space for two hours in the afternoon.

Dorothy stood at the door like a sentry as Thomas prepared for the ceremony. Then she welcomed each guest, one by one, instructing George, Ruth, Marcella, Mary Claire, and Krystal, to wash their hands in preparation before they entered.

"Keep your voices low," she told them.

Elliot Singer was wheeled in and parked near the bamboo mat, which Dorothy and Thomas had arranged over a large blanket. To the uninformed eye, it looked like they were preparing a picnic. And, indeed, she had brought in a dozen chocolate chips cookies for the guests to enjoy after the ritual. Much to her surprise, the patients complied without grumblings or smart remarks as they situated themselves around the mat. Thomas, dressed in his most elegant kimono, bowed to each and directed them to sit. The opportunity to bask in the warmth of the sun was a welcomed bonus, while they remained attentive to Thomas's careful ministrations. Dorothy was pleased for Thomas because the chance to be outdoors could have elicited jubilant disruption rather than hushed reverence.

Dorothy stayed where she was at the door like an offstage narrator, expounding on the spiritual aspects and history of the tea ceremony in soft tones, as Thomas had instructed, and on which she had meditated all week. Meanwhile, Thomas lined up a basin with water alongside the utensils, teapot, and teacups, which were to be cleansed during the ceremony. Standing offstage also served a practical purpose, since, in their effort to make do, a nurse had to bring Dorothy the teakettle from the kitchen once it boiled.

Once in her possession, she joined the group and knelt beside Thomas, resting on her heels as he was doing. Thomas poured the hot water over the leaves. Thomas lifted his face toward the sky, soaking up the warm rays of the sun along with the aroma of the steeping tea. Everyone, including Dorothy, followed suit. One could not help but take a deep, cleansing breath. Thomas quietly explained how the four directions symbolized by the square mat, north, south, east, and west stood for the four principles of harmony, respect, purity, and tranquility. He extolled, bowing first to the north.

"When we are one with nature, we understand harmony. We are attentive to the changes in the seasons. We change, and we are unchanging, and we come to understand the evanescence of all things." Then he turned and bowed to the east. "We learn respect when we discover gratitude. We are grateful for the tea, for the utensils, for the cups, for the teapot. Most importantly, we are grateful for each other."

Following in this manner, Thomas turned to the south and bowed. "Purity stands for the order of all things in our physical and spiritual life. We take care of everything we touch, even the most mundane. In this, we find enlightenment." Thomas demonstrated by carefully cleaning the cups and utensils. He then gestured to his guests to wash their hands in the basin. "We purify ourselves of the dust of our lives." Lastly, he bowed toward the west. "Only through our practice of harmony, respect, and purity, can we hope to experience tranquility." He bowed again. Dorothy noticed confused admiration play over George's face as Thomas turned to pour the tea.

Thomas solemnly poured a small amount of tea into each cup before quietly handing one to each of his guests, holding each person within a loving gaze, however briefly, before bowing before them. He then nodded to them to take a sip.

He served; he imbued the lowly courtyard with gravitas, he was dignified, respectful. He was unlike the Thomas they'd all come to expect—selfish, self-centered, dramatic, and boastful—and more than he or they could ever have imagined was in him. He was attentive to his guests and didn't seek their attention, yet all eyes were on him. He quietly commanded the room without uttering a sound as he performed the ancient rite. A gentle spirit shone through his concentration. A hush hung over them, with only birdsong in the air, as his guests waited and watched while Thomas just as carefully cleaned the utensils and cups with the hot water over the blue hospital-issued bedside tub typically used for sponge baths, which in his hands might as well have been porcelain. He bowed again to each person to signal the tea ceremony was over. Ruth and Sister Mary Claire unconsciously made the sign of the cross as if they'd been in church.

Dorothy could only guess what her other patients were thinking, but she was awestruck. Better to save whatever processing she might do with them for another day. Not wanting to dispel the wonder of the moment, or Thomas's time in the sun, the doctor tiptoed away so her patients could enjoy each other's company.

As she was walking toward the door, she heard Ruth comment to Thomas, "That was cool, Thomas, and you look really nice." She felt a tug on her elbow. Turning she saw that Marcella was on her heels like a wayward puppy.

"What is it, Marcella?" She asked, inching discreetly away to give herself a bit personal space.

"Do you think we could have a group session for me?" Marcella's eyes bore into Dorothy's, pleading and eager.

"Actually, I think that's a great idea," Dorothy said. Marcella grinned. "I'm so impressed, Marcella. You've found your own solution. But we'll have to talk about it later, okay?"

"Sure, thanks Dr. Morrissey," Marcella said, still grinning.

Dorothy felt like celebrating. The tea ceremony had gone better than she'd expected, and the day was still warm and sunny. She called Kenneth. "Hey, Hon, I'm feeling like a walk along the Red Cedar. Want to join me?"

"Perfect timing, Dot," he said. "I just stood up to stretch. I've been holed up here all day, writing. It was killing me to miss such a beautiful day. How about I grab a pizza on the way?"

"You read my mind," she said. "I'll grab a bottle of wine."

"Oh, crap, I forgot, my parents beat you to it. They want to know if we'd like to join them at the country club for dinner. We can take a stroll around the grounds before they get there."

"I suppose that works. I'm hungry anyway. I'll pick you up in fifteen."

"I'll need to shower first, and you may want to change—dresses only."

"Seriously? It's 1974!"

"The country club set is a little slower to get with the times, I'm afraid. The food is delicious and so are the cocktails, so worth the strict etiquette."

By the time Dorothy and Kenneth made it to the country club, his parents were already waiting for them at the bar. She'd hoped she and Kenneth would have some time alone, so she could share her excitement about the tea ceremony. His parents greeted Dorothy and Kenneth warmly. Dorothy looked around and said, "I've never been to the Lansing Country Club. How long have you been members?"

"Oh, it's called The Country Club of Lansing, Dear," Mrs. Nelson said, ever so politely correcting Dorothy. "We've been members since before Kenneth was born. Let's get you a drink," she said brightly.

"I got it," Kenneth said. "Gin and Tonic?"

"Sure," Dorothy said.

Mrs. Nelson nudged Dorothy. "You must watch the bartender in action. It's a performance. Kenneth should have ordered something fancier. Even a gin fizz would have been more fun. When we went to Peru, we had a pisco sour. Now that was a tasty drink." Dorothy's mind wandered to the tea ceremony and how elegant and sacred the whole experience was under Thomas's command. "I'm sure we can change your drink to a pisco sour if you'd like," she heard Mrs. Nelson say somewhere in the distance. You simply must experience this."

"Oh, sure," Dorothy replied noncommittally. She really didn't care. Nor did she want the elation and gravitas she experienced from the tea ceremony diluted by a bartender's antics in service of Lansing's rich and famous.

Kenneth returned with the pisco sour and a martini for himself. "Dad got to me before I ordered a gin and tonic. We'll order the next round together, so you can watch the bartender. He really is something," he said. Never in her life did Dorothy understand that bartending could be a spectator sport, but she'd try to keep an open mind, if only to keep the peace. The problem was, she couldn't help but feel like she was betraying Thomas somehow, like eating before communion. Thankfully, her disinterest went unnoticed because the Nelsons were distracted by the many people who greeted them. They were like the mayors of The Country Club of Lansing. She sipped her drink, which was delicious, and looked about the club. The décor reminded her of the Nelson's home, and she realized this was where Mrs. Nelson found her inspiration.

"The Country Club of Lansing is one of the nicest golf clubs in the world," Mr. Nelson informed Dorothy. "Do you golf, Dorothy?" he asked as they took their seats for dinner.

"I'm afraid not," Dorothy said.

"Kenneth will have to teach you," he said. "Why haven't you taught Dorothy how to golf, son?"

"It's a little thing called a dissertation, Dad," Kenneth replied. "I haven't golfed in two years."

"Well, there's still plenty of time to hit the links," Mr. Nelson said cheerfully. "If the weather holds."

Dorothy ordered lamb chops, lemon risotto, and a spinach salad for dinner. The meal was so good, she almost forgot about feeling guilty for being there in the first place. "Does the country club have a pool?" she asked the table.

"The Country Club of Lansing doesn't but we also belong to the Grand Ledge Country Club," Mrs. Nelson responded. "They have a nice pool. I'll take you there next summer. Honestly, Kenneth, if you knew Dorothy likes to swim why on earth haven't you taken her?"

"Again, I've been busy," Kenneth said. "And she swims in an indoor pool at MSU."

"I do," Dorothy assured them. "They have an Olympic size pool, which is wonderful for lap swimming."

"I can't imagine," Mrs. Nelson said. "I won't even put my face in the water. How do you protect your hair?"

Mr. Nelson filled their glasses from the second bottle of Bordeaux he'd ordered. "There's nothing like swimming off the coast of Copacabana Beach in Rio de Janeiro, and she wouldn't so much as stick a big toe in the water," he said about his wife.

"All that salt water can't be good for my hair or complexion," Mrs. Nelson said. "It takes far too long to put my face on just to have it washed away into the ocean."

Dorothy could see from the slight smirk on Kenneth's face that he found his mother amusing and that he'd heard it all before. "Needless to say, my mother doesn't enjoy the water," he said.

"To answer your question, Mrs. Nelson, I rinse my hair thoroughly and I use a swim cap to protect my hair. And I don't wear a lot of make-up."

"So, I've noticed," Mrs. Nelson said. Dorothy wasn't sure how to interpret. "You may be able to get away with that now, but you won't always. And you want to watch those shoulders. Those girls who swim in the Olympics are built like men."

"I don't think that will be my issue," Dorothy said. "My hefty thighs and calves do all the work, or so I'm told by my sisters."

"Those are some sturdy legs," Mrs. Nelson observed. Dorothy took another swallow of wine if only to keep her mouth shut.

By the time they returned home, Dorothy was too drunk to do anything but fall into bed. She hadn't forgotten about the tea ceremony, but she no longer felt like sharing with Kenneth.

CHAPTER TWENTY-THREE

RUTH

MISSISSIPPI APPENDECTOMY

"Oh, hello, come in, come in," Dorothy said when she opened her office door to greet Ruth and two older women whom she presumed were Ruth's mother, Delta, and her Aunt Sylvie. The last time she and Ruth talked, Ruth was adamant that her mother wouldn't step foot in a hospital. Yet here she was. Dorothy's face visibly shifting from total surprise to warm welcome; she invited them in.

"Please sit down over here." She directed the older women to the love seat and pulled the lounge chair next to it for Ruth. Looking at Delta was like peering into Ruth's future, so close was the resemblance between mother and daughter. Both women had pulled their afros into identical buns on top of their heads. Ruth's Aunt Sylvie was both taller and thinner than her younger sister and her niece, but still bore a strong resemblance to her niece, especially when she smiled, revealing the same dimples as Ruth.

The sisters' styles were worlds apart. Delta dressed much like Dorothy's sister, Sheila, wearing a peasant dress, floor-length and flowing. Sylvie's look took a page from Mary Tyler Moore's stylebook. She wore a sleek navy pantsuit, beige turtleneck with a silk scarf, and high heels. She was clearly in charge and pleased that she'd made good on her promise to get Delta to a session. She stood behind Delta and nudged her through the door.

Ruth was beaming. The bows had long since been removed, but Ruth's hairstyle pulled into the bun, revealed a smooth forehead that sorrow had previously creased for months. Her honey brown eyes shone, and her dimples were on full display.

"Mama, this is the Dr. Morrissey I've been talking about."

"I'm so pleased to meet you both," Dorothy said, shaking each woman's hand. "Please sit." Delta appeared nervous, eyeing Dorothy with suspicion and only nodding by way of hello. Sylvie appeared confident and relaxed and returned Dorothy's greeting. She nudged Delta to sit and then sat beside her. "I've heard so much about you," Dorothy said. "Thank you, for coming in. I know it means the world to Ruth." Ruth was still beaming. "I think we should jump right in since we only have an hour. Ruth, where would you like to start?" Dorothy asked. Normally, Dorothy would have rehearsed with Ruth about what she wanted to address with her mother, but neither she nor Ruth had believed Ruth's aunt would convince her mother to join them.

"What I really want to know is why my mother is afraid of hospitals," Ruth said.

Delta looked directly at Dorothy for the first time. "I didn't come here so you all could gang up on me. Not once did my mother come to Michigan for a visit. You don't hear me crying about it." Ruth's face fell.

"I don't think Ruth means to put you on the spot," Dorothy said.

"I really want to know, Mama, that's all," Ruth said.

Sylvie spoke for the first time. Her accent was distinctly southern whereas Delta sounded like a Michigander. "Grow up, Delta, it's time you told Ruth the truth about what happened. She deserves to know."

Sylvie looked at Dorothy and then Ruth. "Delta and I have been through some things, Ruth. Delta doesn't like to talk about it." Ruth's eye's widened with curiosity. Dorothy too was itching to hear more. Delta stayed silent.

Sylvie shot Delta a disgusted eye roll that Dorothy was well acquainted with having received the withering look many times from her older sisters. "I'll start," she said. "Dr. Morrissey, have you ever heard of a Mississippi appendectomy?"

"No," Dorothy replied.

"That's why I can't have children. I got pregnant at fifteen. We were poor, our father had died some years before, so somehow that gave the officials of Georgia the right to take my child away and sterilize me."

"Oh, my God, I'm so sorry," Dorothy said, stunned. "That's horrifying."

"Aunt Sylvie," was all Ruth could say.

Sylvie brushed off their concern. "I've been through years of therapy. I'm also suing the state as part of a class action lawsuit. Delta and I have been writing down what happened just so we could tell Ruth someday. We just never got around to telling her. Go on Delta. Just read what we wrote."

Sylvie turned to Dorothy. "We wrote some notes, so we wouldn't forget anything important."

"You're the smart one," Delta said to her sister.

"Go on," Sylvie said. "You've read it to your Women's Lib group. You can read it here. Are you ready to hear this, Sweet Pea?" She asked Ruth.

Ruth nodded somberly the incomprehension of her aunt's ordeal still written on her face.

Sylvie handed the notepad to Delta. Delta took a deep breath and situated herself more comfortably on the loveseat. Clearing her throat, she began to tell her story haltingly at first but growing stronger as she went on.

"I was seventeen on the day I took my first Greyhound trip to Michigan from Georgia," Delta began. "I stood outside the Greyhound bus depot with my mother. Rain poured down on us in cold sheets soaking us both as we said our goodbyes. I felt that was a bad omen. Why weren't you there?" Delta turned to Sylvie. "I always wondered."

"Mama wouldn't let me," Sylvie said. "Keep going."

"I was shivering something awful. I was so scared and the rain pelting my cheeks didn't help. That was the only hint of winter coming in Georgia, but Mama told me there would be snow in Michigan. Neither one of us had ever seen snow or could imagine a cold worse than the one we were enduring just then. I remember I was whining and carrying on about having to sit on the bus, soaking wet for the long trip to Michigan, but Mama said that was the least of my problems. She handed me a brown paper bag filled with three peanut butter and lettuce sandwiches wrapped in wax paper."

"'This should tide you over until you get to Uncle Dave's,' she said. 'And make sure you finish them. You're eating for two now.'"

"'I don't want to go, Mama,' I said. I was crying pretty hard by now. 'I love Drew. We're going to be married.'"

'Hush!' Mama said. 'I won't have them do to you what they did to Sylvie. The caseworker gets a whiff of you being pregnant, and next thing you know, they'll be dragging you off to that hospital and stealing that baby right from your arms. They're not touching you. And do not go to the hospital to have that baby. Next thing you know, you can't have children at all. You'll be safer in Michigan. Drew can follow you as soon as he finishes high school.'"

"I should have known better than to argue with my mother, but I tried. 'That was four years ago, and Sylvie was only fifteen,' I said. 'If I tell them I'm getting married, surely they won't do that to me.' I was so naïve. I had no idea what happened to Sylvie. I only knew it was terrible. Like Sylvie said, her status as an unwed mother gave the doctor license to make sure she'd never get pregnant again. Sylvie hadn't been the only one who'd had her baby taken away and her uterus taken too. South of the Mason-Dixon, we called it a Mississippi appendectomy."

Dorothy found it hard to breathe as she listened. A hard lump of shame grew in her throat.

"My mother wasn't about to let those doctors lay a hand on me. And I understood precious little of what I would be facing myself come summer. My mother said that her brother, my Uncle Dave, was married to a midwife in Michigan who would deliver my baby girl. My mother was sure the baby was a girl." Delta nodded to Sylvie to add to the story.

Sylvie took up the narrative. "Even before I got pregnant, we had few misconceptions about the perils of being a poor Negro family with no man in the house in Georgia in 1939. Our father had died when I was ten years old. Our mother believed that if he'd been alive, none of the ensuing tragedies would have befallen us. We'd always been poor, but our parents meted out a living, piecing together odd jobs. Their work paid off. They managed to keep food on the table and nosey case-workers from our door. But then Papa died, and our mother shouldered all the responsibilities of our household. I was ashamed that I went behind her back like I did. If I hadn't gotten pregnant in the first place, none of this would have happened. From then on, our mother didn't put her trust in anyone."

She turned to Delta. "That's why she never came to Michigan. It got so bad. She was afraid of her own shadow."

Then Sylvie turned to Dr. Morrissey. "You have to understand, Doctor, the hospital, to our mother's mind, was where poor black people went to die or get mutilated, and she'd be damned if she allowed her baby and grandbaby to suffer the same fate as I had."

Sylvie turned back to Delta. "Sorry, Sis, do you want to tell the rest?"

Delta nodded than started up again. "My mama said, 'Get on that bus, sit in the back, and don't talk to anyone. Do you hear me? A pretty girl like you can attract all kinds of trouble.' I should have known she was saying good-bye for good when she cupped my face in her hands and used her thumbs to wipe away my tears and the raindrops. 'This is for the best, Little Girl,' she said."

"Stupid girl that I was, I thought I was in love. 'But what about Drew?' I asked her."

'If he loves you, he'll get his behind to Michigan before you can say lickety-split. Now, what did I say?'

'Sit in the back, don't talk to anyone,' I repeated."

"'I love you, you know that, right, little girl? We're doing the best we can. Drew will be there before you know it.' She shoved some magazines in my hands before nudging me toward the bus. 'These will keep you busy.'

"'I love you too, Mama,' I said. I was blubbering by this point.

"I was too upset and scared to do anything but stare out the window of the bus for the first hours of the trip. Green hills stretched as far as the eye could see. Flocks of birds were flying in the opposite direction, fleeing the very conditions into which I was heading. I had the two seats all to myself, so I set my lunch bag and magazines on the other so no one could get any bright ideas about sitting next to me."

"Mama had ten ways to Sunday to explain a simple instruction. 'If anyone asks, and they shouldn't because you won't be talking to them in the first place, you're going to help a sick aunt in Michigan, do you hear?' she said. When the bus stopped for breaks, I was told to stay far away from the 'whites only' bathrooms and fountains at the depots and get back on the bus quickly again to make sure I kept my seat. No talking, no trusting, no sharing one iota of my circumstances."

Ruth interrupted her mother's narrative. "What about Drew? Did he follow you?" she asked, anxiously, as the knowledge that her father wasn't her biological father was dawning on her.

"I wanted to believe that Drew would follow me to Michigan, but I knew in my heart that he wouldn't. He was a big talker, but he would be too chicken to leave his family to start one of his own at eighteen with his pregnant girlfriend. I fell for him hard after hearing him sing in our church choir. He sang with the angels but played like a devil. We only had sex the one time. Drew said he found it hard to believe that I could get pregnant after one time. He accused me of 'going round the block' before I'd been with him. I didn't face facts until I found myself alone on a bus to Michigan with you, Ruth, my only companion."

As riveted as she was by Delta's story, Dorothy had eyes on Ruth and noticed the light dimming from them with this new information.

Delta inhaled deeply. "During the first leg of the journey, I was just plain scared. How in the name of the Lord was I going to support a child? I was certain of only one thing. I would not be going to a hospital. I'd never met my Uncle Dave but was grateful that he was willing to take me in, and to his wife, my Aunt Sally, that she could deliver my baby girl. I vowed I would not be a burden. I'd help out any way I could, clean the dishes, do the laundry, anything to keep a roof over our heads. I only hoped they wouldn't ask me to cook, or all they'd be eating was peanut butter and lettuce or fried bologna sandwiches." Delta looked over at Ruth. "Isn't that right, Sweet Pea?"

Dorothy thought it was endearing how the two older women called Ruth Sweet Pea. Ruth had never mentioned the nickname.

Ruth laughed. "Believe me, Mama, I've told Dr. Morrissey all about it."

Delta continued. "Watching the colors change from the lush greens of the south to the brilliant red, orange, and gold of the middle states, to the barren browns as the bus neared Michigan was like watching a magic show. I was either mesmerized by the beauty or brooding over the potential catastrophes that could threaten me, and my new baby. I'd never known my thoughts could turn so dark so suddenly. For instance, when I saw snow for the first time out the window I was enthralled by the beauty. But the next minute I imagined myself homeless and wandering across the cold white fields, carrying a newborn as some sort of karmic revenge for my stupidity. Back and forth I went from hope to despair until my head lay exhausted against the window. Before I knew it, I'd fallen asleep, only waking when the brakes screeched to a halt for the next stop and a slew of new passengers. The trip went by quickly that way.

"The last stop before Lansing was the depot in Detroit. I felt proud of myself that I'd done as I was told. I was stiff from sitting for so long and I needed to use the bathroom. I kept an eye open for the 'whites only' sign. More people were milling about at the Detroit station, and they came in all shapes, sizes, and colors. Mama had prepared me for a possible change in the northern depots. The situation in the big city might be different, and she had instructed me to follow a trustworthy looking older woman of color, so that's what I did, stepping in behind a grandmotherly woman toward the restrooms."

"When I got back on the bus, it was crowded. I made my way back up the aisle after I showed the driver my ticket. Whites and blacks were interspersed throughout front and back for the first time, but my stuff was in the back, and I liked it back there. I was more than a bit put out when I noticed a young man sitting in my seat against the window. His face broke into a broad smile when he saw me."

"'You're in my seat,' I said to him, unable to conceal my irritation, but also unable to ignore his deep brown eyes, framed by lashes fit for a beauty queen. Honestly, I'd never seen a face as open and trusting as his. You know I'm talking about your father now, don't you, Ruth? It's like he'd been so well-loved that the harsher realities of life never fazed him. I felt jaded in comparison." Ruth's eyes opened wide; she didn't interrupt.

"'I'm sorry, Miss,' he said. 'This was the only seat left. Looks like someone is saving the seat beside me.'"

"'Those are my belongings,' I said."

"'Well then, if you'll allow me to join you, I'd be happy to give you the window,' he said, making to stand and offer the window. I couldn't help but notice his long legs and torso. He let me by and handed me the magazines. I looked around and saw that he was speaking the truth. I slipped by him and took my seat by the window. He stuck out his hand.

"'My name is Guy. Guy Fitzgerald. And yours?' He wore a green threadbare wool coat opened to reveal the stripes of his shirt, horizontal in pink, white, and blue, while his pants flaunted a black and white vertical pinstripe.

"'My name's Delta,' I said. 'You look like a riot in a dye factory.' Guy laughed out loud, a genuine belly laugh full of joy without a hint of taking offense. He looked at his outfit. He had on brown loafers over white socks to finish the riot of color he wore.

"'Beggars can't be choosers,' he said, still smiling. 'Hand-me-downs from my brothers. When you grow up in a houseful of boys, you don't get to pick your outfits. Where you headed?'

"I knew I was supposed to lie but lying to this young man seemed to me like committing a sin. 'I'm going to my Uncle Dave's in Lansing,' I said."

"'That's funny,' Guy said. 'My boss is named Dave. I'm just returning from a trip to Detroit to pick up parts for him. He runs a gas station and car repair. I'm a whizz at fixing cars.' He smiled a broad smile, melting my heart. Drew, schmoo, I thought. 'What's your uncle do?'"

"'He runs a gas station,' I said, grinning right back at Guy."

Delta turned to Ruth whose face had stayed frozen in stunned silence. Only by the glassiness in her eyes could they tell she understood the ramifications. "I suppose we should have told you sooner," Delta said. "We just thought, what you don't know won't hurt you."

The three women turned their attention to Dorothy. She too was speechless. She was overwhelmed with emotion for all involved. There was so much to talk about from the injustice and brutality of Sylvie's trauma through the multiple repercussions down the generations. "Honestly," she said to Delta and Sylvie, "I don't know where to begin, but I want to thank you both for sharing your stories with me and for Ruth. I'd never heard of a Mississippi appendectomy. I'm sickened by the very thought, and I have to say, I will never cease to be shocked by the cruelty humans can inflict on each other. I, for one, have loads of questions. I wish we had more time to process. But I want to ask Ruth, how do you feel about all this?"

Ruth burst into tears. Dorothy handed her a tissue and Ruth wiped her nose. "So, Pops isn't my real father?" she asked Delta.

"Oh, he's your real father," Delta said with an edge in her voice. "Don't ever try to tell him otherwise. He claimed you from the start as his little Sweet Pea." She leaned toward Ruth and nudged Ruth's nose with her own.

After briefly acquiescing to the familiar sign of affection, Ruth sat back.

"Still, my father isn't my father. My brothers are only half-brothers. Why didn't you tell me? What about Drew?"

"I never heard from him again." Delta was matter of fact. "If Guy hadn't shown up when he did, our lives would have been very different. He was sent from God. I turned Drew back over to God."

"Drew was a good-for-nothing," Sylvie added. "The only thing you got from him was your singing voice. Look here, Sweet Pea," Sylvie said, "think of the sacrifice your mother made for you. She left the only family she knew, and she never returned to Georgia. You might not have been born at all otherwise. Worse, you could have been given to some other family like my child."

"Did you ever find your child?" Ruth asked her aunt, chastened.

"I tried for years. I haven't been able to track down any records. Don't worry about me. I've had a good life. I went to Spelman College. I was the first alumna to teach there. Now that our mother has passed, I get to retire up here near my sister and her children. I've led a fulfilling life, Ruth. You can too."

"So much loss in your family history," Dorothy said, "for everyone." She was struck by the similar themes that played out from one generation to the next. "It's also beautiful to witness how much love you have for Ruth. Your willingness to set aside your own trauma to be here for her is remarkable."

Ruth suddenly stood up, bent over her mother, and wrapped her arms around her. "I love you, Mama," she said.

"I did the best I could, Sweet Pea," Delta said, looking relaxed for the first time since they got there.

"Well, now I know why you're afraid of hospitals," Ruth said. She then turned to her aunt. "Thank you, Aunt Sylvie."

"You know I love you, Sweet Pea."

"I wish we had more time," Dorothy said. She turned to Ruth. "I hope you all will pick up where you left off. Ruth and I can continue to process as we move forward."

"When are you letting her out of here?" Delta asked.

"Actually, very soon," Dorothy said. "We're working on the practical tasks of living."

"Ruth can stay with me while she looks for her own place," Sylvie offered.

"And I applied for a job at St. Vincent," Ruth said to her mother.

"We're checking off all the boxes," Dorothy said. With that she stood to signal their time was up. "Thank you both for coming in and telling us your story. If there's anything I can do, please let me know."

"Thank you, Doctor," Sylvie said. "See, Delta," she said. "That wasn't so bad, was it?"

"Speak for yourself, Sylvie," Delta said, but she smiled at Dorothy. "Before we go, we have to tell Ruth one more thing," Delta said.

"There's more?" Ruth asked.

"Darren and Margo left home. Can only mean one thing."

"Did you call the police?" Ruth asked.

"Of course, we did, but the police don't care if a pregnant, drug-addicted black girl has gone missing, especially one who's a repeat offender. They said she's eighteen that makes her an adult. If they find her, they'll throw her in jail."

"Where are her parents?"

"No one knows. From what Darren said, her home life was unstable. They kicked her out when she was only fourteen."

"I'm so sorry, Delta." Dorothy said. "I'll talk to our social work department to see if they can help. In the meantime, keep me up to date. I worry about the baby."

"So, do I, it's not right." Ruth said. With that, the women stood and headed for the door.

✦

Dorothy's head was spinning when she sat down to write her note. Was it possible to be happy and horrified at the same time? Ruth had finally gotten her mother in here but couldn't possibly have guessed at the grisly truth behind the fear. This proved once again to Dorothy that there is always a backstory. Now Dorothy could be confident in Ruth's family's love and support for her, and she would proceed with discharge planning. Ruth had come so far. The news her mother and aunt disclosed today had been earth-shattering yet not once did Ruth avert her eyes and start singing a spiritual.

10/23/74: Ruth Fitzgerald Johnson. Ruth arrived on time and accompanied by her mother and aunt. She appeared pleased to have them there as she smiled broadly. Ruth's mother, Delta, and her aunt, Sylvie described in detail the trauma that explained Delta's fear of the hospital and included Ruth's birth story. Delta revealed that Ruth's father was not her biological father, but her adoptive father. Sylvie and Delta reported that Sylvie had been sterilized without consent after giving birth to an illegitimate child who was also taken from her. Ruth's aunt stated that people in the south called it a "Mississippi appendectomy." This therapist is appalled by the abuse. Ruth has made positive strides in treatment, so she will proceed with the discharge with the caveat that she remains in treatment with undersigned as an outpatient. Treatment goal to continue to process Ruth's birth story revelations. Overall, Ruth doing well, no psychotic episodes, depressive symptoms decreased, denies SI.

CHAPTER TWENTY-FOUR

MARCELLA
FAMILY CONSTELLATION THERAPY

Dorothy worked over many weeks trying to help Marcella retrieve and process childhood memories, using the letter-writing exercise. Marcella practiced breathing and relaxation exercises to ward off panic, but rather than calm her, the writing seemed to trigger her even more. Not only that, but, like Thomas, Marcella was a social creature, so it made perfect sense that she'd want a group session to treat her needs. After consulting with Dr. Keith, Dorothy thought she'd try a new approach. Dr. Keith's eyes smiled with Dorothy's request. "For someone who says she hates group therapy you seem to do an awful lot of it."

"Necessity is the mother of invention," Dorothy laughed. "But I'll need your help."

"Okay, everyone," Dorothy said to the assembled group, "if at any time, you become uncomfortable or overwhelmed, step out of character, and Dr. Keith or I will take your place."

Dorothy had prepped the others about their roles for a group therapy session that centered on Marcella's trauma. Dorothy had not led a Family Constellation session before and worried that as powerful a healing modality as it was, it could just as easily go south. She was taking the risk because she had come to accept that writing, for Marcella, was not helping her—quite the contrary. Marcella needed people to help corral her wild stallion emotions. Isolation was the worst possible situation for Marcella, even if in service of healing.

Trial and error taught Dorothy that writing was too isolating for Marcella, so, Dorothy asked Dr. Keith to supervise her conducting the session. Given their own vulnerabilities and the sensitivity of the issue, she wanted to make sure no one felt pressured to participate. To a person, her patients whole-heartedly agreed to support Marcella.

As Ruth said, "she's been there for me, I'll be there for her." Dorothy was particularly sensitive about Ruth because she would be acting the role of Marcella's pregnant mother. "Don't you worry about me, Dr. Morrissey," Ruth said. "I can handle it."

Thomas enthusiastically embraced the idea of playing the role of four-year-old Marissa, Marcella's twin. "The tragic motif suits me best," he said. "Besides, you know I'll borrow heavily from my own family dynamic. Added bonus, I can pretend to wear patent leather Mary Janes!"

All Dorothy could do was smile, understanding well his flair for the dramatic. "I'll admit," she said, "I loved my Mary Janes when I was a little girl."

George would play the role of Marcella's father. Dorothy suspected he too could borrow from his experience. Finally, Marcella would narrate and direct. Once they took their places, Marcella began.

"My dad was outside sewing grass seed at our new house. We hadn't moved in yet," Marcella started. "So, if you could pretend to be outside doing that, George," she trailed off, lost in the memory. Dorothy pointed George in the right direction. George took up seeding the carpet, pushing the invisible seed thrower like a pro. "Our new house was built on a hill, so it looked like a ranch from the front and a two-story from the back. Marissa's and my bedroom, the playroom, the laundry room, and a bathroom were all in the basement. We were in the playroom and my mother stood at the sliding glass doors that went to the back yard. It began pouring rain—no, storming, thunder and lightning, and my mom stood by the window yelling at him to come in. My mom was very pregnant."

George moved back and forth along the wall acting like he was sewing the seed while Ruth stood as if looking out a window, hands on her belly cradling the life within.

She furrowed her brows in worry, her eyes going from intently watching her "husband," to searching the "skies," above. Dorothy was amazed at how seriously they took their roles. Marcella moved on. "Marissa and I played behind our mother. She was muttering to herself about Daddy. She was angry that he wouldn't come in. Mommy hated thunderstorms. We even had a storm shelter in the basement she said."

Ruth interrupted, "What was your dad's name?"

"Nolan," Marcella responded.

"Okay," Ruth quickly got back into character. "Nolan, get in here!" she shouted toward George.

"I'm almost done," he shouted back pushing vigorously.

"I don't know if I'm making this up, but I feel like there was a lot of water. That's how hard it was raining. Anyway, Marissa and I didn't like when Mommy was upset, so we went exploring." Thomas immediately took his cue and started skipping around the room as if discovering hidden gems. "We found our bunkbeds and Marissa called the top bunk first. I was upset about that."

Thomas jumped in. "I get the top bunk!" He asserted with enthusiasm. "'No fair!' I said."

"I called it first," Thomas said matter-of-factly. "C'mon, let's play hide-n-seek."

"Oh, my God, that's exactly what happened," Marcella said. "Marissa wanted to find the storm shelter. Mommy said it was in the laundry room. The laundry room was right across from our bedroom. We opened the door and peeked inside. There was the incinerator blocking our way past. At the time, we didn't know what it was. It just looked scary to me. But Marissa wasn't scared. She plowed right past it, dragging me by the arm."

Thomas took his cue again. "C'mon, Marci, don't be a scaredy cat. Mommy said the storm shelter is in here. Let's hide and see if she'll find us." Marcella stared at him with amazement as if he'd just read her mind. Thomas crouched down as if he were hiding.

"We got bored. Mommy never did come looking. She was still standing in the playroom shouting at Daddy to come in."

"Nolan, so help me," Ruth said. George acted as if he couldn't hear her.

"We went all over the house. We checked out Mommy and Daddy's bedroom, which was upstairs and the new baby's, which was right next to theirs. Marissa and I would be the only ones in the basement until the new baby got old enough to sleep downstairs. Mommy said there was room for my grandparents when they were ready to move in but that never happened. We went through the kitchen to the garage. We found a place that looked like a jail."

"Let's play cops and robbers!" Thomas said with childlike enthusiasm.

"'Daddy said not to go into the garage,' I told Marissa."

"Poo on you! You're such a goody-two-shoes," Thomas said.

"Just then there was the loudest clap of thunder I ever heard," Marcella said.

"One Mississippi, two Mississippi," Thomas said in a little girl's sing-song voice.

"Our mother shouted for us to get to the basement."

"Girls! Get down here," Ruth shouted.

"We ran down there as fast as we could." Thomas acted out running like a scared child in search of her mother.

"Some change fell out of my pocket as we ran. Our grandfather had given us his loose change for penny candy. We were going to Tugs on the way back to their house." All the west-siders nodded, having been to Tugs many times.

Thomas bent over and acted like he was grabbing the money. "Find a penny pick it up, all the day you'll have good luck," Thomas sang.

"Marissa, give me back my money!" Marcella grabbed at Thomas's hand.

"Finders keepers!"

"That's when I noticed the sockets and had the brilliant idea to play bank. I didn't know that they were electrical outlets. Daddy hadn't put the covers on them yet."

Before she could explain too much, Thomas sat crossed legged on the floor as if getting it right away. "I'm going to make a deposit!" he said.

"'Me first!' I said."

"Oh, alright," Thomas huffed. "But I still get the top bunk."

"We hadn't played long before Mommy noticed and then she yelled at us."

Ruth took her cue. "What in the name of the Lord are you doing?"

"Playing bank," Thomas said, impishly.

"Knock it off," Ruth said, then turned back toward where George was still pushing the seed sewer faster than ever. She patted her belly. "That man knows better than to upset me when I've got a third baby on the way," Ruth grumbled. Then she shouted as if into a strong wind, "Nolan, so help me, God!"

"Marissa and I both had our fingers in the socket trying to get the last penny." Marcella paused, trying to remember. "I thought she'd put my thumb in her mouth because she was scared. But now I don't know. When I think about it, Marissa was never scared. I was the scaredy-cat. But it was my penny," she said, tears forming.

Thomas knew just what to do. Still sitting cross-legged close to the wall, he swatted his pretend sister's hand away as if they both fought over the penny still in the socket. Marcella watched him. "It's mine," he snapped, elbowing his sister out of the way as reached inside the open socket.

"I thought I'd already heard the loudest clap of thunder in my life. But that was nothing compared to this one. A deafening blast was the last thing I remember before I woke up in the hospital without my sister or my thumb."

Thomas slumped to the floor. Ruth cried out. George came running. Dorothy stood frozen, lost in a moment back in time when she was told her sister had died and feeling like she'd been struck by lightning.

As if he'd sensed she'd dissociated, Dr. Keith gently touched Dorothy's knee and took over the session by saying, "Okay, how about we all take a deep breath and process what we are feeling."

Marcella said, "It was all my fault. It was my bright idea to play bank."

She hiccupped back a sob. "I always thought she was sucking my thumb and that she died feeling protected. But we were fighting!" She couldn't hold the tears back any longer. "No wonder my parents hated me," she sobbed.

Thomas put his arm around her. "I felt like I just wanted what I wanted when I wanted it. I literally didn't know what hit me. It wasn't your fault at all. We were just kids."

"I agree," Ruth said. "I felt like I was so worried about Nolan that I wasn't watching my girls. The last thing I said to my baby was 'knock it off.' I felt so guilty."

"You felt guilty? I was the one who should be blamed," George said. "If I'd just come in when you asked instead of needing to get the damn grass in." George wiped a tear and hung his head in shame.

"Dorothy?" Dr. Keith prodded gently. "What are you feeling?"

Dorothy took a deep breath. "I felt like I lost my sister all over again. You all did so well that I could really feel my loss." Her patients made eye contact with each other surreptitiously, not sure if she was speaking for Marcella or herself. "But you know what also struck me besides feeling like I too was hit by a bolt of lightning? I felt like we're just doing the best we can."

"I wanted to say that too," George said. "As Nolan, Marcella's dad. I just want to say, I did the best I could but I'm so sorry."

Ruth chimed in. In almost a whisper she said, "Can you forgive me, Lamby?"

Marcella was sobbing. Both hands pawed at her eyes to wipe away her tears. "Why did you leave me in the basement all by myself then?" All eyes were on Ruth and George who happened to be sitting next to each other.

"What do you mean?" George spoke up first.

"After I got out of the hospital. Brianna was born and you had already moved into the new house before Grandma brought me there to live with you. I remember you were holding Brianna tightly against your chest like I would hurt her or something. We were looking at our bunkbeds. I asked you if Marissa was hiding on the top bunk."

Marcella couldn't leave the scene, but Dr. Keith motioned the group to keep quiet. She went on staring blankly at George and Ruth seeing her parents. "Grandma said, 'You can't be serious. She can't sleep down here all by herself.' You just shook your head and said, 'she'll be fine.' You never talked about her!" She accused them.

Ruth looked at Dorothy helplessly. Dorothy fought back tears and racked her brain trying to remember the issue with Marcella's mother. She remembered the valium but wasn't that Marcella's choice to disclose in front of the others? Dorothy spoke quietly. "I'm so sorry, Pumpkin, every time I looked at you, I saw Marissa. The doctors told us it was best not to talk about her. They said you were so young you'd forget her soon enough."

"But I never did," Marcella cried.

"Thank you for not forgetting me," Thomas said, touching Marcella's shoulder. She seemed to come back to the present with his gentle touch.

"I could never forget you," she said, smiling through her tears.

"I want to draw attention to what you said, Marcella," Dorothy said. "You said, 'no wonder my parents hated me.' I'm picking up something different from everyone here. Can you think of something else your parents might have been thinking?"

"Maybe they thought it was their fault?" Marcella asked.

"They didn't hate you they hated themselves," George said. "I was thinking, if only I'd covered the damn outlets or not left the seeding to the last minute."

"Maybe that's why my mother started taking Valium," Marcella said with the new comprehension showing on her face.

"Or why your father worked so much and didn't come home," Ruth said.

"We all had our roles to play," Thomas said matter-of-factly. Dorothy couldn't have summed it up better herself. She was so proud of them.

"All I knew about life, like a real flesh and blood twin sister, was swept away in that storm," Marcella said. "Today for the first time I feel like I got my life back."

"Group hug!" Thomas shouted. Dr. Keith took this as his cue to sneak out of the room, so Dorothy could bask in the glow of healing with her patients.

Minutes after her patients left to go to the cafeteria, Dorothy realized it was Tess's birthday. Feeling both drained and elated, she walked back to her office where she picked up the phone and called her mother.

PART THREE: WINTER–WOUNDED HEALER

CHAPTER TWENTY-FIVE

THOMAS

"I had a dream about Regis last night," Thomas said to Dr. Morrissey as soon as he sat in his corner on the loveseat.

Thomas had experienced relative calm since the tea ceremony, and he had not caused any disruptions on the floor for quite some time. By the time the nurses erected a small Christmas tree festooned with paper ornaments and icicles in the common area, Thomas had been working with Dorothy for almost a year. Between the benefits of talk therapy and lithium, Thomas's mood swings stabilized, and he reported only moderate ups and downs.

"Would you like to tell me about it?" Dorothy asked.

"In the dream, I'm sitting on a bed, and Regis comes in and lays his head on my chest. I think the dream means he's still out there waiting for me."

Dorothy was loathe to take that interpretation away from Thomas, especially at Christmas, but she didn't like where this was headed.

"With his head over your heart, it does seem to me that you felt truly loved by him," she said. "Do you mind if I add another layer of interpretation?"

"Can I stop you?" Thomas said, but he smiled and nodded. "Go ahead."

"I think the dream is also saying to combine your head and your heart in whatever is going on."

"You know me, Dr. Morrissey. I'm not one to reminisce about the ghosts of Christmas past, but the thought of spending Christmas in this place is just too depressing."

"Are you considering a change?" She looked at him skeptically.

"Now that you mention it, yes. I've been thinking a lot about my life lately. Have you ever felt that how you feel on the inside doesn't jive with how your life is turning out?"

"Yes, to answer your question. But tell me more about what you mean."

"I guess I always thought my life would be bigger than it is. You can't get much smaller than this." He laughed and waved his hand around her room.

"Bigger, how?" She asked.

"I should have been an actor or performer like my brother. Even as a child, I thought I was destined for greatness. I always imagined I'd live in a big city. I'd be on stage or screen or designing clothing for the runway. I'd be glamorous," he said, striking a pose. "I feel like Cinderella before the ball, and this was not the plan at all."

"Very clever, Thomas, and an apt description."

"I'd like to move to Detroit. Start over. I could audition for the theater there, live in a loft in an artists' community. Find other people like me."

"Do you know anyone in Detroit, Thomas? It's a big city."

"Isn't that the beauty of moving there? I could start fresh. I've been looking at apartments in the *Detroit Free Press*—easily affordable if I can get a job right away. I'm sure there are plenty of Spencer Gifts stores there. I could finally go to art school or work in a library."

"You know, I am glad to hear that you are feeling ready to start anew, Thomas, but I am worried that once you're discharged, you will not comply with the treatment protocol. Continuing the medication is of utmost importance. Also, you will need to remain in outpatient therapy." Thomas waved off her concerns.

"I know, I know. I'll be fine. I can handle myself. I know I can do it. It'll be my second chance. I can start over. Besides, I heard Regis moved to Detroit. I'm sure I can find him. Just imagine, by next year, Regis and I strolling down the city sidewalks enjoying the Christmas decorations. Maybe we'd be looking at the displays I've created. I'd be good at that."

"Yes, you would."

"I think it's time I find JW. My roommates told me he was in a movie—like the big screen. Will wonders never cease?"

"How did they know it was him?"

"How many Perfects do you think there are?"

"You've got a point there." She smiled. "Have you heard from JW or your parents?"

"No, how would I when I'm stuck in here? So, do you agree I can leave?" Hope lit up his face.

"I have a few concerns about this idea, Thomas. For instance, what if you don't find Regis? What then? I worry about you being alone in Detroit." *I sound just like my mother,* she thought.

"I'm a big boy, Dr. Morrissey. I can live alone, or I can find a roommate."

"And what about JW? What if you can't find him? How will you feel then? I'm also worried that hearing that JW was in a movie is what has gotten you thinking about a need for a bigger life, as you put it."

"Honestly, you worry too much." He batted away her concerns. "I'm not all that interested in contacting JW or my parents. I've done without them this long."

"But a moment ago, you said you want to find him."

"I'd rather find Regis." He volleyed.

"It's a long shot, Thomas."

"I'll never know if I don't try."

"I still have reservations about discharging you, Thomas, especially during the holidays." She leaned toward him, employing her best persuasive techniques, genuine concern for his well-being infusing her words with urgency. "The holidays are a challenging time to be alone for anyone. We can discuss this again soon, I promise, but I don't think you are ready yet. Let's review after Christmas. I'll discuss your case with our discharge planner to see if we can set up services for you in Detroit."

"OK. But I'm serious, Dr. Morrissey. I can do this." Thomas glowered at Dorothy for good measure before flouncing out of her office.

"Merry Christmas, Thomas!" She called after him.

CHAPTER TWENTY-SIX

DOROTHY

There was a soft knock on the door. "Come in," Dorothy called.

Nurse Martin poked her head in. "Your mother called the nurses' station. She asked me to remind you not to forget to pick up your brides-maid dress and shower gift." Nurse Martin smiled at her colleague. Her smile always spread from dimpled cheeks to her eyes. "We're starting to place wagers about how many reminders you're going to get. Care to make a bet?"

The nurse stepped further into the office. She wore a white pant-suit uniform but had pinned a Christmas wreath brooch to her top and wore red loafers in the spirit of the holidays. Becca Martin could always find a way to brighten the staid uniform.

Dorothy rolled her eyes. "I'm so sorry. She called me three times during my last session. I finally unplugged the phone. If I had a nickel for every time I've asked her not to call me at work, I'd be rich."

"She also wants to know when you'll get home. I told her I really didn't know."

Dorothy placed her hand over her face and groaned. "They just don't get it. Do you know, they didn't come to my graduation when I got my doctorate? But, God forbid, I'm late for Louise's bridal shower."

"Geesh, that had to hurt," Becca Martin said, sympathetically. "I mean, my parents are the same way. My sister married a total loser, and you'd think she'd won the Nobel Peace Prize, but even they managed to come to my graduation from nursing school."

Dorothy dismissed her friend's sympathy with a wave. "I'm used to it. Marriage is the end all be all."

"I give you a lot of credit, Dorothy," Becca said. "When I told my parents that I wanted to go to college, they said I could be a nurse or a teacher. That was it. The very thought of being stuck in a room all day with other people's children..." She trailed off. "Well, let's just say, nursing it was. I didn't think to question. I really admire you. You didn't give in. And you've been a great addition to our staff."

"Thanks, Nurse Martin. When my mother calls again, can you tell her that?" They both chuckled, feeling a bit closer suddenly.

"Honestly," Rebecca said, "I hate when people have Christmas weddings almost as much as I hate when my friends call me Nurse Martin." She smiled.

"Sorry, Rebecca," Dorothy said. "Certainly, Louise can't be blamed for wanting a Christmas wedding, but I shouldn't be taking the time off." She avoided telling Rebecca that her sister died on Christmas.

"You have a right to go home for Christmas, Dorothy," Rebecca said. "Your patients will survive."

"I know. I just hate to think about how lonely they might feel."

"That's true for a lot of people," Rebecca said. "I'm working most of that week. I'll keep an eye on them for you."

"I'm going to head downtown for the afternoon. I need to pick up the damn dress. When will I ever wear a red velvet floor-length dress with fur trim again?"

Rebecca Martin laughed. "Oh my. I'll take it off your hands. I bet I can find some use for it."

"I bet you can. Dr. Smith is on-call, but I'll stop back before I go home."

"When your mom calls, I'll let her know." Rebecca laughed at her own humor as she headed back to the nurses' station. "But, really, Dorothy, don't worry about our patients. Enjoy your time off."

The holidays were the worst time to be away from the hospital, especially the week between Christmas and the New Year. There were more new admittances, more suicide attempts (Christmas season was notorious for suicides), more acting out in general. People felt more bereaved about their losses, lonelier for family, and more abandoned by loved ones during the Christmas season. Moreover, she had grown attached to her patients over the past year, and she certainly did not want them to feel abandoned by her.

Dorothy decided to walk downtown, so she could take in the sights and sounds of the season. Most of her Christmas shopping was finished, but for two presents, which she'd been avoiding. This was the first Christmas in many years that Dorothy could afford to buy gifts, so they had to be special. For her sisters, she'd bought sets of cashmere scarves and gloves in different colors. For her mother and grandmother, she'd found Irish wool shawls. For her younger brothers, boxed sets of Ian Fleming's 007 novels, and for her father, a whiskey decanter. She was pleased with her purchases. All that was left were the bridal shower gift, and something for Kenneth. She had to find something today, come hell or high water.

Walking along Pennsylvania Avenue, she fell to brooding. There was a brisk wind coming out of the west, and the thickening clouds were taking an ominous hue, which meant snow would follow soon. The cold air bit at her cheeks and nose. She could already feel her lips chapping and wished she'd remembered her Chapstick. Her grandmother's lamb's wool overcoat provided an impenetrable barrier against the wind but was heavy on her shoulders. She had to face her procrastination. Whatever was behind her resistance about buying a wedding gift for her sister and a Christmas gift for her boyfriend stirred waves of pain in her abdomen.

Dorothy was more than a little surprised that Louise chose a Christmas wedding. Talk about hanging out the family's dirty laundry! Louise may well have believed that a Christmas wedding would heal the wounds of Christmases past. More likely, the wedding would set off the unspoken but simmering tensions beneath the surface.

The impending marriage already caused tension between her and Kenneth. His patience worn thin as she ran out of excuses for why still hadn't introduced him to her family. He wanted to make them official. No more sitting on the fence. He wanted to spend Christmas with Dorothy. And not just Christmas. His plan was for the two of them to spend Christmas with her family, followed by New Year's with his.

Dorothy had been invited to Sanibel with the Nelsons, but she couldn't see taking that much time away from her patients. As it was, Sunday was Louise's bridal shower. Monday, the Morrisseys would host Louise and Mike's rehearsal dinner. Tuesday was the wedding. Christmas was on Wednesday. Leading up to the holiday every day was filled. His parents' gala was the following Tuesday. The Nelsons would leave for Sanibel Island, Florida early on New Year's Day.

Dorothy's excuses drew only frustration from Kenneth anymore. He felt that a wedding was the perfect opportunity to be introduced to Dorothy's family. "C'mon, Dorothy," he said. "Louise knows we're together. With so much family around your father will barely notice me." They had both grown tired of this argument and the wedding was the last straw for Kenneth. "Really, Hon, you need to shit or get off the pot. Don't you want to be together?"

"Of course," Dorothy sputtered.

"Then, no more lame excuses. I need to meet your family."

Dorothy didn't think her excuses were lame. The push and pull from both sides made her insides churn. Christmas was complicated for the Morrisseys and not the joyful holiday he'd expect. To introduce him on Christmas would upset the apple cart for her mother even more than Louise's wedding. There was no separating out Christmas from the day Tess died.

"I just don't think Christmas is the right time to introduce my live-in boyfriend," she said, irritably.

"When is the right time, Dorothy?" Kenneth asked.

She became flustered and defensive, the color reliably rising in her cheeks. A sudden pain shot through her abdomen at the very thought of facing her parents with Kenneth at her side. She bent over, clutching her belly.

"I'm not trying to upset you, Dorothy. But it's now or never."

She took a deep breath, and the pain in her abdomen eased. *I must be getting my period early.* She thought. "Okay," she relented surprising herself.

"I'm going to hold you to that." He could barely contain the grin that spread from ear to ear.

"I need to get to work and then I plan to do some Christmas shopping. Can we talk about this when I get home? We'll need a good strategy if I'm to introduce my Protestant boyfriend to my staunch Catholic parents."

"Maybe they'll surprise us," Kenneth said. Dorothy exhaled a huge sigh of relief. Her shoulders came away from her ears. Finally, she'd made Kenneth happy.

That was this morning but by afternoon, she began to regret the decision. So, now Kenneth was happy, but her father will be furious. All Dorothy wanted was to enjoy the season with a little spending money in her pocket for a change and free of family drama. Despite Tess's death on Christmas Day, Dorothy loved the spirit of the season, and just now, all she wanted was to recapture a bit of its magic. Downtown Lansing did not disappoint. The Salvation Army volunteers jingled their bells at every storefront. Street vendors peddled warm bags of roasted chestnuts along the sidewalk, filling the air with a mouth-watering nutty aroma. And groups of shoppers bustled up and down Grand River Avenue. Evergreen wreaths hung over lampposts imbuing their fresh scent and color to the drabness of winter. She couldn't help but love the festive atmosphere.

She also enjoyed buying gifts for her loved ones. She headed for Kosichek's for Kenneth's gift. All that was left for him was to defend his dissertation. Maybe that's why he was pressuring her to meet her family. He wanted his ducks in a row. He'd been very hush- hush about his prospects. If she were to venture a guess, he'd likely take a postdoc in the economics department. He knew how much she loved working at St. Lawrence, and that she wanted to stay in Lansing. Kenneth enjoyed the pomp and circumstance of academic life. His parents also tethered him to Lansing. They had already bought him a suit and sprung for his doctoral attire. She thought a white buttoned-down collared shirt and tie with some fancy cufflinks would be nice to wear with the suit.

Dorothy browsed for too long among the men's clothing, obsessing over variations in white dress shirts. Finally, she chose a green and white striped tie and MSU emblazoned cufflinks to go with a crisp white button-down. No doubt, Kenneth would look fetching in a white shirt and green tie. She had Customer Service box up the gift in their best wrapping paper. She added a pair of leather driving gloves for her father and had them gift wrap them too.

With Christmas shopping completed, Dorothy commenced brooding over the morning's conversation with Kenneth and how to devise a good plan. In her heart of hearts, she knew why she avoided introducing him to her family. Though Deirdre was the obvious reason her father posed the bigger challenge. She loved her father, but in the years since Tess died, he had changed, and she did not want to add to his pain.

Dorothy always wondered how they would have all turned out if her sister hadn't died that Christmas. The large family gathering, the laughter, and singing, once the stuff of every Morrissey holiday, snuffed out if her father was around. (Dorothy suspected the rest of his family still sang when they got together). After Tess died, his dreams died too. Her father never recovered. He kept providing. He took lots of overtime just so he could stay out of the house. He was overjoyed when his little miracles, the twins, Declan and Aidan, were born. Still, even they weren't enough to resurrect the lovely tenor, to lift his voice alongside his siblings at Christmas.

Dorothy remembered a time when her father never said a mean word about anyone. Now, he was always angry. He had to blame someone. He blamed the WASPs, aka the Protestants. Tapping into the Irish hatred for the British, he complained bitterly about the WASP. The WASP's had their hands in your back pocket, cutting your wages, taking everything for themselves, undermining the unions, stealing your pensions, and worst of all duping his fellow working-class citizens with their empty promises. The more he drank, the more vitriol he spewed. And who would call him out?

Tess had been the apple of his eye. His brothers and sisters, wife and children, even Grandmother Morrissey, who typically had no trouble speaking her mind, all felt too sorry for him to confront him. They knew where his anger came from and that he needed someplace to put it. The Vietnam War and the prospect of his boys getting drafted had only made him worse.

"They"—WASPS were always the impersonal THEY—"can send their own damn kids to fight their wars. They're not taking mine!"

One look at Kenneth, and her father would sniff out in a minute that he wasn't Catholic. Kenneth's father was an executive at General Motors. All her father would see was a union-busting WASP. He would detail loudly and line by painful line the history of GM's history of poor working conditions and undermining workers' rights. Kenneth didn't stand a chance. It wouldn't make a hill's bit of difference to her father that Kenneth had, in fact, been drafted and served in Vietnam. Her father would never accept him.

How could she possibly admit this to Kenneth? Her father, a very stubborn man, would willfully refuse to warm up to Kenneth, no matter how loving or hardworking or even religious. Walking among the shoppers, she inwardly rehearsed introducing Kenneth to her father without revealing he was a Protestant or that they lived together. And how many times had she replayed her explanations about her father to Kenneth before she gave up before ever opening her mouth? Kenneth was a man of reason. The thought of holding generations' worth of resentments was not reasonable. He would look upon her father with disdain, or worse, he'd try to convince her father of the error of his ways. Maybe, she needed to have more faith in Kenneth. He was able to hold his own in any situation. He was confident that her family would welcome him once they met him. And he was right, if not now, when? Still, she broke out in a sweat just thinking about it.

Dorothy strolled down Pennsylvania Avenue, taking her time as she headed to Knapp's, to look at the competing Christmas window displays of all the department stores. She breathed in the sights, sounds, and aromas of the Christmas season as she moved up the street. The department store windows were filled with animated Christmas themes, which brought out the kid in her. First up was Arbaugh's where parents and children stood in wonder watching Clara and the Nutcracker traverse the interior in a circular dance. Dorothy loved the mechanical movement of the Nutcracker and pajama-clad Clara and the whirling fake snowflakes matching the real flurries commencing on her side of the pane. She watched dreamily, taken in by the fairy tale, long after one crowd dispersed, and another group of children squeezed in front of her. Hudson's competed with a Frosty the Snowman themed window, while Knapp's theme this year was Santa's Workshop. She enjoyed them all.

Lansing's department stores achieved the same magical effect that she remembered from her childhood. When the girls were young, her mother dressed them up in matching dresses, coats, and mufflers to take them to Downtown Detroit to see the Christmas windows before having lunch at Jacobsen's. So, what if she was by herself, she could keep the tradition alive. She decided to treat herself to lunch at Knapp's in-store restaurant.

Gone for good were the outings to see the Christmas windows after Tess died, along with all the other Christmas traditions. The Morrissey girls were not about to complain and upset their mother further. Their grandmother cooked and the girls decorated as best they could. Dorothy couldn't even remember a tree in those days. Only with the birth of Declan and Aiden did Christmas become magical again. By that time, Dorothy and her sisters gladly helped their mother transform the living room into a wonderland for their cherished baby brothers.

Dorothy found a seat at the counter in Knapp's dining area. The Christmas decorations throughout the department store extended to the dining area in ribbons of gold, silver, red, and green. Faux Christmas presents adorned corners and windowsills, and a massive Christmas tree lit up in the center. She relished the hustle and bustle, shoppers and waitstaff alike in good cheer in anticipation of the holidays; the hum of Christmas tunes overlaying the clanging of silver and dishware. The anonymity of the crowd gave her a place to hide in plain sight and collect her thoughts.

No sooner did she settle herself at the counter than she began to ruminate again.

Louise's impending nuptials put all the Morrissey girls on high alert. The problem of Deirdre was the most likely, but her uncles were known for acting up once the alcohol started flowing, picking fights, keeling over, just plain raucous "fun," leaving the rest of them to clean up the mess. There was bound to be drama. If not from Deirdre, then some other extended family member. Every Irish-Catholic wedding had drunken drama. Anything could happen at Louise's wedding and Dorothy was sure to be mortified with Kenneth there to see it.

The more she worried, the gloomier she became. She decided to go all out and ordered a plate of biscuits and gravy. This time of year, Knapp's topped the buttered blobs of warm dough with turkey rather than sausage. Dorothy's grandmother used up leftover Thanksgiving turkey in much the same way. She made a filling of turkey, onion, and celery seasoned with summer savory, simmered it in gravy, and put the filling into a pie or on top of bread, biscuits, even leftover stuffing. She served the glorious concoction with lots of mashed potatoes slathered with butter and freshly ground pepper from her favorite teak pepper mill. Dorothy's mouth watered at the very thought. Much of what Dorothy considered comfort food was thanks to her grandmother. And Dorothy needed comfort now more than anything.

When the food arrived, she dug in, savoring every bite. As full as she was after cleaning up her plate, she ordered a peppermint chocolate shake for dessert. Not until she slurped the last minty goodness, did she remember she still had to try on the bridesmaid dress for a final fitting. On her way out of Knapp's, she saw a display of their famous Christmas cookies. She bought a dozen, a sweet treat for Kenneth that they could enjoy together with tea after dinner. That she was eating her feelings was not lost on her.

Before heading home, Dorothy stopped into St. Lawrence to check on her patients. To her surprise, her favorite four patients were in the common area, watching *Mister Rogers' Neighborhood* of all things. A flood of tenderness filled her as they sat in rapt attention like a bunch of children. None of them noticed as Dr. Morrissey entered quietly and stood behind the bedraggled group gathered around the black and white on mismatched furniture. Thomas sat imperiously on an office chair, his long dirty-blonde hair brushing atop his kimono-clad shoulders, hand on hip, his chin tilted as if camera ready.

He looked over to George and asked, "Is this the Mr. Rogers that Dr. Morrissey quotes all the time?"

George's dark curls were mussed as if from sleep. His hair was getting long, and he had a cigarette tucked into his ear like a barrette holding back his curls. He wore a ratty robe over a tee-shirt and pants. *He must be depressed*, she worried. "No, you idiot, that's Carl Rogers. This is Fred Rogers."

"They must be brothers, then." Thomas said. George just shook his head.

Ruth quietly sang along with Mr. Rogers as if to uplift her own spirits. Thomas shot her a glance of scorn. Ruth ignored him. Marcella, whose long straight black hair obscured her features, had her feet tucked up close to her body with her chin resting on her knees, hugging them tightly. Dr. Morrissey could only guess at whether Marcella was in a space to accept Mr. Rogers' loving message, but she appeared to be listening intently. How well could she accept that she was loved just as she was? He sang on. Dorothy's eyes filled with tears. She turned on her heels and walked briskly away.

CHAPTER TWENTY-SEVEN

DOROTHY AND KENNETH

Dorothy and Kenneth busied themselves with packing while she laid out all the minefields of meeting her family for the first time. Wet snow came down in sheets outside the window, making Dorothy nervous about the drive ahead. She had no choice but to leave today, so she packed frantically while putting Kenneth through every possible eventuality that could go wrong when he met her family. "Whatever you do, don't mention that we live together," she said.

"I know, I know, stop worrying, Dorothy," Kenneth said.

"And don't mention that you're a Protestant," she said, shoving the gifts she'd purchased into the suitcase.

"Here, let me do that," Kenneth said. "You'll wrinkle everything." Kenneth always concerned himself with the little messes. Dorothy had bigger fish to fry.

"Now, remember, Deirdre will be a challenge," Dorothy had a tough time describing her to Kenneth without making her sound like a monster.

"Stop worrying," Kenneth said.

"The quicker we get out of there, the better," she said. "I say we stay at the reception for two hours tops."

"I think we should stay for Christmas Day if all goes well," Kenneth said.

"Did you book the hotel?" she asked with sudden panic. Staying with her parents was out of the question.

"I did, will you relax already?"

Dorothy's mind started to wander with thoughts of Christmas at home. As nervous as she was, a part of her was glad to get the dreaded introductions over with. Did she dare invite him to stay through Christmas? Kenneth would finally see how Christmas was done in her family. She loved Kenneth's parents. They were very kind to her and did everything right, but it wasn't the same. As much as her family drove her nuts with all the talk of marriage and children, they were a lot more fun, especially when all the aunts and uncles were around.

"One step at a time," she laughed. "Just remember to come to the Church. I'll be busy with bridesmaid duties." She shoved the rest of her clothes in the suitcase and pressed down hard to latch it, her back to Kenneth.

"Listen, Dorothy," he said, turning her toward him. "I've thought of a way to get your parents to like me." He handed her a gift-wrapped box. "An early Christmas present," Kenneth said.

Dorothy opened the gift. Inside was an envelope and a smaller gift box. She opened the letter first. Kenneth watched her, scarcely able to contain his excitement. Dorothy immediately noted the United States Government symbol on the letterhead. She skimmed the job offer, taking in all the momentous, life-changing implications of the position for Kenneth and, by extension, her, including a move to Washington D.C.

"You're moving?" she asked, stunned.

"Open the box," Kenneth said.

In the velvet ring box was a diamond flanked by emeralds. Dorothy didn't know anything about carats but noted that neither the diamond nor emeralds were of a size afforded by a graduate student with meager finances.

"What's this?" she blubbered.

"This was my great-grandmother's ring. Do you like it?"

Dorothy didn't know what to say. She tried on the ring. It felt heavy on her hand and was about two sizes too big.

"We can have it sized," Kenneth reassured her. "Dorothy, will you marry me?" They both held their breath as Dorothy absorbed what was being asked of her.

"This is too much," she blurted. "I can't accept this ring."

Kenneth turned sober. "Are you saying you don't want to marry me?" The room felt like it was closing in on her, trapping and suffocating her.

"Well?" Kenneth asked, waiting for Dorothy's answer. Tears streamed down her face, the weight of the ring reflecting her indecision, her loneliness for what, she didn't know, her reluctance, all of it.

"I'm not saying no," she stumbled, trying to find the right words. "I just wasn't prepared for a Christmas proposal. We can't steal Louise's thunder by going in and announcing our engagement. And I wish you'd told me about the job offer."

"I thought you'd be happy." Kenneth's voice rose to a high pitch. Dorothy began weeping in earnest. "I'm sorry," he said. "I thought you'd be happy about this. We can get out of Lansing. I know you'll love D.C. I wasn't expecting to have a job offer so soon. I assumed I'd start after graduation, but they said I can finish my dissertation from there. I hoped we could move there together. I wanted to surprise you."

"I'm surprised, alright," Dorothy said. "What about my job? Shouldn't we have talked about this first?"

"I've been trying to talk about this." Now it was Kenneth's turn to sputter as he noted how upset she'd become. "A move to D.C. will be good for both of us. You can finally get away from your family, and we can think about starting our own."

"Are you feckin serious? I really don't know what to say. I thought you understood how much I love my work. What do you think I've been doing here, place holding until I can get married and have babies?"

"Of course not," Kenneth said. "I thought you'd be happy for me. I'm sure you can easily find a good position in D.C."

"I need to think about this," Dorothy replied. She handed him the ring.

"Are you turning down my proposal?" Kenneth asked.

"I need time to think. Can we talk about this after the holidays?" she pleaded.

"Okay, okay, but the position starts at the end of January."

"What? So, you've accepted the position? I really don't know what to say, Kenneth," Dorothy said.

"I hope you'll say yes," he said.

"I've got to get home. Let's just keep to the plan. No mention of marriage until after Louise's wedding."

With that, Dorothy gathered her things to go home to her family. The time had come for her to get off the fence. Kenneth had thrown down the gauntlet. A move to D.C. only complicated the matter for her. She didn't know whether to be happy that he proposed or angry at him for assuming she'd just quit a job that she loved. Hopefully, she'd have some clarity by the time he joined her at the reception. Her bags packed, she turned her back on him, ran out the door and down the stairs to her car. Once outside, she took deep life-saving breaths. She shoved everything she needed into the trunk, then drove off crying all the way home to Detroit.

CHAPTER TWENTY-EIGHT

DOROTHY AND KENNETH

CATHOLIC CHRISTMAS

"I'm not wearing this dress!" Deirdre screamed from the top the stairs. "I look fat!" The high-pitched cry issuing from Dorothy's older sister sounded more like a three-year-old's tantrum.

Dorothy had just walked through the front door of her parent's home and the tension that rose in her with Deirdre's greeting struck her in the gut. She wasn't feeling well. She was angry with Kenneth. His proposal felt more like an ambush. Her abdomen throbbed with pain. God, she hated Deirdre. She couldn't help it. Now even her body protested.

Elsewhere, the house was a bustle of chatter and even laughter as the Morrissey women cooked and cleaned in last-minute preparations for the bridal shower. She placed her gift on the side table where a pile of wedding presents overflowed, the larger boxes underneath. She had settled on champagne flutes for the wedding gift and a lace floor-length nightgown for a shower gift. A Christmas tree was up in the front window and decorated with tinsel, popcorn, multi-colored bulbs, and traditional ornaments collected over the years. Santa would be coming for Sheila's children this year, reviving some merriment to the holiday.

Once upon a time, her family's version of an Irish-Catholic Christmas was a joyful, much-anticipated event. Dorothy's patients weren't the only ones who felt sad and lonely during the Christmas season. For Dorothy, Christmas would always signify before and after. The Morrissey family before Tess died versus the Morrisseys after Tess died. Before Tess died, Christmas Eve was always at Grandma Morrissey's. The large extended Morrissey clan meant family, food, and drink were plentiful, laughter filling every corner of the house. The best part, besides waking up on Christmas morning, was when her father and his sisters and brothers would sit around the fire and sing on Christmas Eve. Theirs was a family of lilting tenors, altos, and sopranos whose voices melded into sweet harmony. They started with Christmas carols and ended with Irish ballads. The more they drank, the more sentimental the ballads became until Grandma Morrissey scolded them. "If I hear one more song of the famine, I'll croak."

After singing came storytelling. Big belly laughs had the siblings bent over, as the brothers looked to outdo each other with funny anecdotes from their childhood. Tears of joy spilled down rosy cheeks made hot from the alcohol and the combined heat emanating from the fire and all those warm bodies. As a child, Dorothy and her sisters snuggled up alongside aunts and uncles, laughing on cue as if they'd shared the memories. They were of such good cheer, and the stories never got old. Grandma Morrissey served platters of ham, Irish soda bread, cookies, and mini mince pies. A Christmas fruitcake that had been made months before and fed with whiskey every day since was the centerpiece. Before the night was over, all but the fruitcake was polished off, which was reserved to be finished in small bites with cups of tea throughout January.

Even better than the Christmas Eve celebrations at Grandma Morrissey's in the years before Tess died, was the sense of wonder she felt waking up on Christmas morning. The anticipation was excruciating, as she and her sisters lined up in the hall because Mother wanted everyone to gather and enter as one. Then with the first peek into the living room, a gasp of excitement rippled through the girls due to the intoxicating effect of so many gifts in neat little piles strewn about the place. Each heap was small, but that didn't matter because taken as a whole, they might as well have been at the North Pole in Santa's workshop. That was before. Before Tess was rushed to hospital with a burst appendix on Christmas day. Dorothy was eight years old. Old enough to remember how joyful Christmas had once been.

Her mother shouted at her from the kitchen. "Take your bags upstairs, Dorothy, then come help make the punch."

Dorothy climbed the stairs and went to push past Deirdre, whose complaints were largely being ignored by everyone else in the house. Remembering Tess, she thought better of it.

"Follow me," she said to Deirdre. "I brought an extra shawl that will look perfect with your dress." She opened the small suitcase where she'd packed a couple of winter shawls. "Try them both. Pick the one you like."

"Are you sure?" Clearly, Deirdre was as surprised as Dorothy by the kindness.

"Of course," Dorothy said, already questioning the impulse.

Mrs. Morrissey shouted up the stairs. "Dorothy, be a dear and clean under Deirdre's bed. I don't want anybody snooping around up there." Before Dorothy could ask Deirdre why she couldn't clean her room herself, Deirdre skedaddled down the stairs. Dorothy rolled her eyes knowing what awaited her. She wished she had nose plugs. Dorothy followed her sister, not to waste her breath on convincing Deirdre or her mother that Deirdre was perfectly capable, but to grab the kitchen broom.

Back upstairs, she got on all fours to assess the situation. Gagging, she took the broom and with long sweeping motions, she pushed the garbage out from under the bed. Out came cans of Tab and Fanta, candy wrappers, empty Burger King or McDonald's bags with ants crawling all over them, tampons and pads some with dried blood on them, used tissues, and dust an inch deep. She tried and failed several times to sweep the trash into a garbage bag.

If, Dorothy thought, Carl Jung was looking at this heap, he would remind Dorothy that Deirdre carried the family's shadow. Dorothy wasn't exactly the best at managing clutter. She stuffed her bureau and desk drawers with a myriad of items or papers she didn't want to deal with at any given moment. Wasn't that just as bad if only on a smaller more acceptable scale? *Maybe the messes were symbolic of the mess of our lives,* Dorothy mused. She didn't spend time sorting through the contents of her desk or life, preferring as she was doing now to sweep it all away and throw it out. Maybe Deirdre's mess represented all the shit the family didn't want to see. So, who was she to judge?

Two bags of trash later, she felt sick to her stomach the pain in her abdomen throbbing again. She laid on the floor on her left side knees to chest surveying her work. I don't think Mother would take kindly to losing another daughter to appendicitis on Christmas, she thought. "What are you doing?" Deirdre said, startling Dorothy out of her pained reverie.

Dorothy jumped up. "Nothing, just making sure I didn't miss anything. Go ahead and keep the shawl," she said.

The shower and rehearsal dinner went off without incident—two down and one to go. Louise enlisted her sisters to decorate the church basement for the reception. Deirdre begged off, claiming a flare-up that presumably only scotch could cure. The rest of the girls, Sheila, Dorothy, Norah, and Nell, worked all evening after the rehearsal dinner and returned the next morning for the finishing touches. They set up a large table for the wedding party and divided the rest of the tables around the perimeter to create a space for dancing. Christmas lights were strewn about where they could access outlets, and red and white tea candles were placed on all the tables surrounded by mistletoe. The head table was also set apart with the addition of a lace tablecloth, whereas the guest tables had paper tablecloths. Dorothy's gift to the couple, Waterford Crystal champagne flutes, set off their places of honor.

"Well done, Dorothy," Sheila said, admiring the flutes. "I wish you'd had money when I got married." They both laughed.

"They look lovely, if I say so myself," Dorothy said. All in all, the Morrissey girls' concerted effort made the cafeteria look beautiful, not elegant like the Nelson's, but festive nonetheless.

Louise and Mike had kept to the traditional Catholic wedding ceremony, surprisingly, given their tastes ran more for folksy John Denver themes. The Norman-Gothic-styled St. Ambrose Catholic Church was an imposing structure. Its grand nave was decorated with Christmas foliage and red bows. Christmas trees flanked each side of the altar. On the right, a life-sized creche obscured the lay readers piously waiting their turn. Afternoon light filtered through huge arched stained-glass windows, imbuing the ceremony with sacred yet festive grandeur.

Louise came down the aisle as the pipe organ rang out Walton's "Crown Imperial." No wonder Louise wanted a Christmas Eve wedding. She kept to Catholic tradition in everything but her attire. She wore a high-neck lace gown with bell sleeves, and instead of a veil, she wore a broad-brimmed hat covered in lace, a nod to John Denver, after all, Dorothy thought. Other than that, Louise looked every bit the glowing bride. Michael beamed as she walked on the arm of their father toward him. Dorothy glanced toward the front row where her mother and grandmother flanked Deirdre, who had not showered, but she wore the pretty rose-colored shawl that Dorothy had let her borrow and would now let her keep.

The new couple genuinely appeared smitten and delighted to be marrying each other. No one was more surprised than Dorothy when she began to cry tears of joy for her sister and even found herself entertaining thoughts of marching down this very aisle someday soon. All she needed to do was say yes.

As if on cue, she noticed Kenneth come in the church and sit in a back pew. As her father strained to see who dared come into a wedding late, Dorothy thought, *Let the games begin.* She resisted any temptation to look toward the back of the church to see how Kenneth was faring, lest she give it away that he was with her. Then after communion, the bridal party took their seats in the front pew.

The choir began to sing "Panis Angelicus" transporting Dorothy immediately to Robert Kennedy's requiem mass. She remembered how her father wept watching it on television. As the sopranos' voices rose to a crescendo, Dorothy felt the notes wash over her like when she'd lie on the beach of Lake St. Claire as a little girl, right at the water's edge, and let the waves crash over her. Like her father had, she wept. She quickly knelt to make it look like a burst of piety impelled her to her knees, covering her face with her hands as if in deep prayer but really to hide her tears. She thought, *You can take the girl out of the Catholic church, but you can't take the Catholic church out of the girl.*

The Morrisseys had strict orders from the very ancient Father Mayer to close up shop by eleven o'clock to make room for the cars for midnight mass. As it was, he was annoyed by Louise Morrissey's request for a Christmas Eve wedding, and he suspected she and her fiancé had reason to be in a hurry. He also didn't attend the reception as the couple had chosen the new pastor, Father Rob, to preside for the ceremony.

As it turned out, there had been something going on with Father Ben and Sister Constance. They'd long ago given up the charade, left their vocations, and got married as Ben and Connie. Ever since they left, Father Mayer had had difficulty keeping associate pastors around. The older he got, the more irritability became his closest companion, and true to form, he would rather nurse his resentments alone with a good glass of scotch than suffer the cheap stuff the Morrisseys would likely serve to their guests. The cafeteria was named for him, and his portrait hung prominently over the serving line, so he'd be there in spirit. His picture was so large, Dorothy, who was feeling particularly guilty for bringing a Protestant in the room, felt like his beady eyes followed her every movement about her childhood cafeteria.

Since she was part of the wedding party, she couldn't sit next to Kenneth. She was not closer to accepting his proposal and was glad for a bit of distance. She thought it better to introduce him after the formalities. She sat him next to her brothers, who were too self-absorbed to ask questions. No one had yet to notice that Dorothy was walking about with a blond, handsome man, so certain were they of Dorothy's future as a single woman. Once the dancing started, Dorothy summoned her courage, grabbed Kenneth's hand, and headed toward her mother, who was chatting with her Aunt Maeve. Introducing him to her grandmother first would have been the safest bet, but for some reason, Dorothy avoided her grandmother who was chatting with Louise and Mike.

Oblivious, Kenneth squeezed her hand, pleased that she was finally owning up to their relationship. "We can do this, Dorothy, don't worry."

"Don't count your chickens before they hatch," she said. "You don't know my family." No doubt, her godmother would assail her with a barrage of questions about her date. Still, she felt like Aunt Maeve would help as part of the trial run of introductions before facing her father. The pain in her abdomen throbbed. Was it her imagination, or was the pain getting worse as she approached her mother and aunt? Making matters worse, Dorothy had been feeling anxious and ill since seeing Kenneth come into the church earlier, as if she believed he'd be struck down for doing so. The knots in her stomach grew as she approached her mother and aunt. "Here goes nothing," she whispered to Kenneth.

"Who have we here?" Dorothy's mother and aunt said in unison, staring down Kenneth.

Kenneth preemptively stuck out his hand. "Hello, I'm Kenneth, Dorothy's boyfriend."

"Boyfriend? You've never mentioned a boyfriend, Dorothy," Mrs. Morrissey said, eyeing Kenneth with suspicion.

"Calm down, Mary Frances," Maeve said. "You should be happy Dorothy is dating, *finally*. My Patsy is six months younger, and she's been married five years already. They're over there talking to Norah and Nell," she said pointing toward Dorothy's cousin and husband. Dorothy hadn't seen her cousin since she was married.

Maeve did a quick appraisal of Kenneth, "I'm Dorothy's godmother, Maeve. We are so pleased to meet you." She was practically gushing; she was so surprised that Dorothy was dating and a handsome one at that.

Aunt Maeve went on cheerfully. "I took care of Dorothy when she was just a baby. I'll never forget taking care of you after Patsy was born," she said, turning to Dorothy. "I called you and Patsy my twins. Remember? Of course, you don't, you were only two months old. Your folks went to Florida for two weeks to help your mother heal from that depression. You got so sick...I'm the one who nicknamed you, Dottie."

"Wait, what?" Dorothy turned to her mother. "You went to Florida? When I was only two months old, and Aunt Maeve had a new baby?" Twist, twist went the knots in her abdomen.

"Oh, don't get your panties in a bunch," her mother chided. "I had the post-partum thingy."

That explains a lot, Dorothy thought. Kenneth was smiling broadly, apparently enjoying this bit of Morrissey lore.

"Oh, she could hardly look at you; she was so depressed," Maeve said. *No wonder there are no baby pictures of me,* Dorothy thought.

"Maeve," Dorothy's mother paused to give her sister the evil eye, "was perfectly capable. She could handle a two-month-old and a new baby."

"Well, that was until Dorothy got so sick with the flu that she turned green, God's truth," Aunt Maeve said turning to Kenneth. "She was inconsolable. I felt terrible."

"And you had a new baby!" Dorothy was incredulous. *Who in their right mind would put her own baby down to pick up another's and a crying, sick one at that?* She thought. "She probably stuck me in a corner," she whispered to Kenneth.

"You wouldn't look at me when we came home," her mother stated. "She was always difficult," she said to Kenneth. "But I guess you know that, seeing as you're her boyfriend. And don't go quoting Dr. Spock on me. Your generation is so uptight," her mother said, appropriating, in an impressive way, Dorothy thought, the lexicon of the very generation she sought to insult.

"I suppose you're one of those so-called doctors," Dorothy's mother said to Kenneth. Before he could open his mouth to respond, she continued defending her decision to abandon baby Dottie to the care of her aunt. "Besides, you know how much your father likes the sun. I thought you knew about our *one* family vacation." Sprinkling in a little guilt in hopes that Dorothy would stop making an issue of her one-and-only maternal transgression in front of the handsome young man. Dorothy would do no such thing if it kept her mother from peppering Kenneth with questions about himself.

"You don't look so good right now," Maeve said. "Are you feeling alright?"

"You do look a bit flushed, Dorothy," her mother said. She reached into her small handbag, reserved for special occasions, the crystal bead trim glittering. "Here's a couple of aspirin. Have you introduced this young man to your father? He won't be pleased to know you're dating..."

Suddenly Dorothy couldn't breathe. *How did she know?* She thought, panic rising. Then her mother finished her sentence, "...another psychologist." Dorothy, who was feeling relieved, hysterical, and in pain, laughed out loud, tears streaming.

"Bad enough she's always telling us we have to open up about our feelings," she said to Kenneth. "We don't need two of you."

"Oh, I'm not a psychologist," Kenneth said, looking at Dorothy with some concern.

"That's a relief, what is it you do then?"

"I'm an economist."

"A what?" she said, just as Dorothy's father walked up and took his wife's hand.

"Fancy a dance?" he asked. Dorothy's mother blushed.

"How many of those have you had?" she said, taking his scotch and placing it on the nearest table, not about to introduce Dorothy's boyfriend when her husband was asking her to dance.

"Thank God, sentimentality wins the day," Dorothy said as she swung Kenneth around and away from her father. "I need a drink.". They went to the bar, ordered a Jameson and Vernors, and stood watching the crowd. Dorothy sipped but Kenneth downed his and ordered another.

"I love Vernors," he said. Dorothy's insides churned. She chalked it up to the roiling anxiety of the situation. Who should meet Kenneth next? As if on cue, Deirdre approached them.

"Who are you?" she said, somewhat rudely Dorothy thought.

"I'm Kenneth, and you are?" he asked, holding out his hand. "I'm Dorothy's boyfriend."

"That'll be the day," Deirdre said. "Dorothy's too stuck-up to have a boyfriend." Deirdre turned to the bartender and asked for a scotch. Dorothy having a boyfriend didn't fit into her world view, so she dismissed the man in front of her like a mirage. Dorothy could see Deirdre had already had plenty of scotch.

Deirdre addressed Dorothy as if Kenneth wasn't standing right there. "You'd never introduce a boyfriend to us low lives. You think you are so much better than the rest of us what with your highfalutin Ph.D. in God knows what." She was slurring her words. Deirdre stumbled away toward the dessert table.

Stung into silence by Deirdre's mean words, Dorothy sighed as she watched this ghost of Christmas walk away, somehow believing that her unhappiness gave her permission to say whatever she wanted. Soon Deirdre would be facedown and drooling on some table before she could rise up and scare the bejesus out of Kenneth.

"Now you've met Deirdre," Dorothy said to Kenneth.

Kenneth downed his drink and ordered another. "I guess I'm more nervous than I thought," he said.

"If you can get past my mother and Deirdre that easily, then my father will be a walk in the park," Dorothy assured him, trying to convince herself in the process.

Taking pains to avoid her family for as long as possible, she and Kenneth drank and danced. Eventually, they made their way over to Sheila, who, Dorothy figured, would be the easiest on Kenneth, mostly because she fancied herself on a higher plane. She was the one sister who embraced the counterculture movement from its inception.

As soon as their bridesmaid duties were completed, Sheila changed into a flowing, brightly colored sari and sandals. Given their mother's strict adherence to tradition, Dorothy was amazed that, even as an adult, Sheila got away with the liberties she flaunted in their mother's face. Dorothy wished for an ounce of Sheila's moxie. She and her husband, Ned, were the definition of earth mother/father, with plans to populate the world with baby hippies. Sheila was pregnant with a third child. She was in the corner, nursing her two-year-old. Dorothy was a bit embarrassed by this but figured her discomfort was a small price to pay to get the introductions over as quickly as possible.

"Namaste, sister," Sheila called, as Dorothy approached.

Namawhat? Dorothy thought. Sheila pulled part of her wrap over her son as if sensing Dorothy's embarrassment. Still, as she was entirely confident in her choice to nurse a toddler, she was not worried about Dorothy's judgment. Sheila rarely, if ever, questioned her own decisions.

"Well, hello," she said, sticking her free hand out to Kenneth. "I saw you sneaking in the back of the church during the ceremony. No offense, but you've got an air of Nazi youth about you." Kenneth laughed with genuine heartiness, but Dorothy was mortified.

"Jesus, Sheila!"

"I'm Kenneth, Dorothy's boyfriend," Kenneth warmed up immediately to Sheila's frank assessment. "I do have German roots," he said, "but no Nazi affiliations, I assure you."

"That's a relief," Sheila said. "Boyfriend, you say? Dorothy's never mentioned a boyfriend." Just then, her son came up for air, gave his Aunt Dorothy a big smile then went back in.

Dorothy wanted to get off the subject of her boyfriend status. "Sheila, I wanted to ask you about Florida. Mom mentioned—"

"Mom knows about Florida? How?"

"Knows what?" Dorothy asked, confused. "I have no idea what you're talking about. I was just talking to Mom and Aunt Maeve. Aunt Maeve said Mom and Dad took you, Deirdre, and Tess on a family vacation to Florida right after I was born. I was left with Aunt Maeve."

"I don't recall a family vacation to Florida, but that explains why I feel such a strong affinity with the place." She switched her toddler to her other breast then covered him back up with the shawl. "Ned and I are joining a Buddhist commune in the Florida Keys." Dorothy burst out laughing. This was too much. "We haven't told Mom and Dad yet, so mum's the word, Sis."

"Are you kidding? When do you plan on telling them?" Dorothy asked with thinly veiled mirth.

"What's so funny?" Sheila asked.

"A Buddhist commune?" Dorothy laughed, but she could feel her abdomen seize. "How do you plan to inform our staunch Catholic parents that you're joining a Buddhist commune? Kenneth being a Protestant will pale in comparison," she let slip. By this time, the combination of pain and alcohol had muddied her brain so much that she hadn't noticed her mistake.

Now it was Sheila's turn to laugh. "So, has your WASP boyfriend met Dad yet?"

"What's going on?" Norah said, stumbling over onto Nell's arm. Clearly, they'd enjoyed themselves, but they were cheerful drunks, unlike Deirdre.

Dorothy looked from Sheila to Norah to Nell. Sheila's demeanor remained passive, but she apparently had not told their younger sisters about her plans and she could see by their appraisal of the new man that Dorothy had not introduced them to her Protestant boyfriend.

"Dorothy's got a boyfriend," Sheila said.

"No way," Norah said enthusiastically giving Kenneth the once over. "I thought you were a dyke," she said, looking at Dorothy.

"What?" Dorothy asked. "What is that supposed to mean?"

Norah ignored her. Nell responded as if she knew precisely what Norah was thinking.

"You're all about the women's lib stuff, you act like a man, you have the drive of a man, you've never had a boyfriend until now apparently, you don't want to get married, and you don't want children. I hate to break it to you ..." She paused, realizing she didn't know the name of the new fella.

"Kenneth," he said, before taking a gulp of his drink.

"I hate to break it to you, Kenneth, but isn't it obvious? She's a lesbian."

Dorothy watched Kenneth's face, knowing by the churning of her stomach and the burn moving up her cheeks that he harbored such thoughts many times of late.

Now it was Sheila's turn to laugh. "Well, Dorothy? Are you?" she said.

Dorothy did not want to dignify their ignorance with a response. Their teasing was humiliating to her, especially because they were hitting on her fragile sexuality. She was never very good at defending herself against the onslaught of her sisters' group effort to take her down. How they could possibly think this was funny, she didn't know. From their large family of scarce emotional resources emerged a harsh reality of sibling rivalry couched in humor. That was just the nature of being dethroned at fifteen months, but their timing was atrocious.

"Dorothy probably doesn't know if she's lesbian or straight. She's been so busy trying to be a man, how on earth would she know if she likes them or not?" Sheila asked, standing her little fella on his feet and patting him on the behind. "Go find your father, so Mommy can chat."

"I assure you, I am not a lesbian," Dorothy said, "and Kenneth is my boyfriend."

"Fiancé," Kenneth said, also too tipsy to realize his mistake.

"What?" Dorothy and her sisters said in unison. Dorothy shut her eyes. She knew Kenneth was just trying to defend her, but this was not how she wanted her family to learn about their relationship. Norah ran off like a child hellbent on tattling. Dorothy braced herself, knowing her parents would be on this like white on rice.

"By the way, Nell," Sheila said, "Did you notice that Kenneth didn't come up for communion?" Nell looked from Sheila to Dorothy to Kenneth. Dorothy hoped she wasn't getting the gist of Sheila's comment. Sheila smiled placidly at Dorothy.

"Thanks a lot, Sheila," Dorothy said, dragging Kenneth toward the bar. Aiden and Declan stood in front of them, ordering beers. They laughed good-naturedly at some inside joke before turning back toward the dance floor.

"Hey, man," they said to Kenneth, recognizing him from their table. "Hey, Dorothy." And they were off. She couldn't have loved them more than she did at that moment. Why couldn't her sisters take so little interest in her? She ordered two Jameson with Vernors and a squeeze of lime.

"We need to brace ourselves," she said to Kenneth. "I'm sure Norah will be dragging my father over here any moment."

"I've already cut your father off," the bartender, who was a distant cousin, said cheerfully. "On orders from your mother."

"Oh, great," Dorothy said, taking a big gulp of her drink and moving Kenneth away from the prying ears. "Do not mention the word fiancé," she whispered.

"Kenneth took a long swallow. "Don't worry, I'll be fine."

"And don't listen to my stupid sisters," Dorothy said. "They don't know what they're talking about."

The pain in Dorothy's abdomen throbbed. She closed her eyes and took a deep breath. She was just starting to relax when she heard, "What's this I hear about a fiancé?" Her father chummily clapped Kenneth on the back. Kenneth visibly relaxed or was drunk, Dorothy wasn't sure.

"Dorothy, you never mentioned that Kenneth is your fiancé," her mother said. Dorothy didn't bother to answer. Norah stood behind them, quite pleased with herself and soon Sheila and Nell joined the fray, not wanting to miss anything. The only good news was that most of the extended family were out on the dance floor surrounding the bride and groom.

Kenneth stuck his hand out to Mr. Morrissey. "Kenneth Nelson, Sir," he said. "I only just asked her. Technically, she hasn't agreed yet."

"I suppose at her age, you don't need my permission."

"I don't need your permission at any age, Father," Dorothy said. *God get me out of here,* she thought. A wave of nausea swam over Dorothy that had nothing to do with alcohol.

Sheila elbowed her and whispered. "Don't be stupid, Dorothy, if you want Dad to like him."

"Now you're sticking up for me?" Dorothy whispered back.

Dorothy couldn't concentrate. Kenneth appeared to be holding his own, so far, with her father. At least they were both smiling as far as she could tell. But she knew Kenneth had plenty to drink and certainly her father had.

"Nelson, that's an Irish name, isn't it?" Her father said more than asked.

"Yes, Dad," she answered for Kenneth, as if to say, isn't it obvious? As long as her father doesn't ascertain that his family hailed from Northern Ireland, they'd be okay. She heard her father ask Kenneth what he did for a living and Kenneth answered. Her father called him an egghead but in a slap-on-the-back way. "I wouldn't expect any less from my daughter," he said with a wink. "Where are you from?"

"Lansing," Kenneth said, "But growing up, my family traveled all over for my father's job."

"Military?" her father asked. All Dorothy could think, but feeling too preoccupied with stomach pain to say, was *please say yes, please say yes*. His father had served, of course, but that was not why they traveled.

Kenneth went on amiably, drunkenly unaware of the land mines. "Oh, no, he worked as an executive for the international branch of GM."

"I thought your name sounded familiar, Nelson, is it? The only Nelson I know in the automobile industry set the police on our men from the UAW when we went on strike for higher wages."

"I don't know," Kenneth responded hesitantly, suddenly aware of the land mines. Not even Dorothy could have prepared him for this. She had no idea. Kenneth looked to Dorothy to save him. He took a giant swallow of his drink, coughing up the gingery Vernors. "That sounds more like my grandfather. He worked for Ford Motor in the early days."

"What parish do you belong to?" A seemingly innocent question full of menace. Even through the fog of pain, she could see her father's drunken ire rising. She looked around frantically for her grandmother. The only person of reason in the whole Morrissey clan. She spotted her dozing in the corner, her head balanced precariously on the wall.

"We're not really churchgoers, Sir," he said. Why hadn't she prepared him for this question? *Dummy, dummy, dummy.* Her father seemed to let this go, but Dorothy knew that was a trap.

"Were you raised in a barn?" The menace obscured by drunkenness.

Her Uncle Marty elbowed his way forward. "Hellman's or Miracle Whip?"

"What?" Kenneth shook his head in bewilderment.

"Answer the question."

"Okay, Miracle Whip," Kenneth sputtered. Dorothy covered her eyes. *The jig's up,* she thought.

"I knew it." She heard Nell whisper to Norah. "He's a Protestant."

"What?" Mr. Morrissey asked, giving Dorothy the evil eye. "Good Catholics go to mass every Sunday. If I know my daughter, she'll go home right after mass to a fried egg sandwich with mayonnaise, not Miracle Whip." As if they could smell trouble, her uncles suddenly flanked her father like a bunch of schoolboys on the playground ready for a brawl.

"Do we need to beat him up, John?" her uncle Marty asked. Her other uncles pressed in, ready to defend the family honor.

"Not really, tell him Dorothy," Kenneth looked to Dorothy to back him up. Dorothy froze. Was the DJ really blasting "Nothin to Lose" by Kiss? Thomas had played the song for her just this week. She couldn't hear herself think. She saw Aidan and Declan jumping in time to the music. All was lost. Her father could ensnare the best of them like a bear in a trap. Pain and fear gripped her abdomen. She had never overtly crossed her father. Poor Kenneth, throwing caution to the wind, he charged ahead.

"We have different Sunday morning rituals, Mr. Morrissey," he shouted above the music. "We get up, we buy the *New York Times* and *The Detroit Free Press,* a box of donuts and we sit around all morning reading the paper."

"What the hell? You're living in sin?" Mr. Morrissey roared.

Maybe he was just trying to be heard over the music, she reasoned. But his brothers looked as if they were being held back from jumping the poor unwitting Kenneth, drunken arms and legs flailing about but never hitting the target.

"If you think, I'm allowing the son of a union busting Protestant with no shame marry my daughter, you've got another thing coming!" He was inches from Kenneth's face. Dorothy stood frozen in place though the cafeteria bathroom of her childhood beckoned, the need to vomit or hemorrhage in urgent competition. Kenneth tried to sound reasonable. "We're grown-ups, Mr. Morrissey. We can live as we please. Like Dorothy said, we don't need your permission. Let's go home, Dorothy."

Louise and Mike pushed toward the center of the crowd. "What's going on? Dorothy is this, Kenneth?" Louise asked, unsure of what had just transpired.

Dorothy stood frozen in place. She was shivering from what she didn't know. Now was not the time to spike a fever. Kenneth looked at her with sad-eyed disappointment.

"I see," he said, and he walked out.

Satisfied, her father and his brothers dispersed but not before her father said to her, "I thought you were better than that."

Her mother also looked at her reproachfully before following them. "You should have known better."

She'd barely heard what Kenneth, or her mother, had said to her. But her father's words cut like a knife. The knots in her stomach intensified, sending piercing pain through her abdomen. Her forehead was beading with sweat, but chills shook her entire body. She'd been ignoring the oncoming symptoms for a couple of days in the flurry of emotions and activity. Now she was doubled over. Her sisters went from vindictive to solicitous in a heartbeat.

"Dorothy, are you alright?" Norah and Nell peered closely at her.

"What the hell?" Nell said. "Dorothy, you're bleeding."

"She's burning up," Sheila said, her hand gently on Dorothy's forehead. She tried to guide Dorothy over to a seat. Searing pain seized Dorothy's abdomen again, making her dizzy.

"We need to get her to the hospital," Nell said, putting her LPN to good use. Norah rushed off to bring their mother back. Dorothy fainted.

✦

Dorothy woke to the whispering voices of Norah, Nell, and her grand-mother. The last thing she remembered was doubling over in pain. The room was dimly lit, and she couldn't see out the windows, so she wasn't sure if she'd been out for hours or days. For a moment, she was perplexed about what they were doing in her bedroom in Lansing, where undoubtedly, she lay curled up next to Kenneth. *The jig's up,* she thought. Dorothy didn't realize how right she was.

"I'm still shocked she has a boyfriend," Norah said to their grand-mother. "No wonder Mom is so angry. A Protestant boyfriend is one thing but living with him? And birth control? The nerve of her." That would explain why her mother's voice was noticeably missing.

"I feel so bad," Nell said. "We thought she was a lesbian." Dorothy kept her eyes closed, trying to assess what happened. Her abdomen ached, but she was no longer in severe pain. She listened carefully as her grandmother, always her staunch ally had a say regarding what happened.

"She'll be okay. In my day, we all knew who to see if we didn't want to get pregnant." The sisters gasped. "For crying out loud girls, do ya think I was born yesterday? As long as men can't be trusted, women do what they need to do. This has been going on since the beginning of time. Not all men are as true as your father. Your own mother has wondered at the wisdom of having so many children. I don't know why she's on her high horse. She should be glad Dorothy knows how to take care of business." Even in her drugged state, the irony was not lost on Dorothy that she'd never had sex. Of course, now none of them would believe her.

"Dorothy might not be able to have children at all," Nell whispered.

"Only time will tell," their grandmother asserted. "I just hope she'll be alright."

Dorothy opened her eyes. "Is it Christmas?" She was very hoarse.

"Oh, no, Dear," her grandmother said, taking her hand. "It's already the second of January. You've been very ill. They just took you off the ventilator yesterday."

"No," Dorothy moaned, that must be why her throat felt raw. "What happened?"

Norah and Nell flew from their seats, practically shoving their grandmother aside to get to Dorothy. They clamored to inform her of the unfolding of events.

"Just to let you know, Louise said that you ruined her wedding. Deirdre said she'd be here, but she's too ill with the Lupus. She can't risk catching something. Sheila was here, but then she and Mom started arguing about a commune in Florida. And Mom isn't speaking to you or Sheila. She said you both ruined Christmas."

"They waited until they knew you were okay," her grandmother clarified. "Louise had to leave, or they'd miss their flight, but she waited as long as she could. And your mother stayed until you received the all-clear. She left word at St. Lawrence for you, so you don't lose your job. Give her time, she'll come around."

Nell was the only one who could clearly explain what they'd been told. "The doctor said you have pelvic inflammatory disease, which is a terrible infection from the Dalkon Shield you had implanted. They had to take it out. You were hemorrhaging something awful, and then you had a blood infection. They had to induce a coma and load you up with antibiotics. You're lucky to be alive. There was a lot of scarring, but he saved your uterus. Still, not likely you'll be able to have children. He said that time will tell. In the meantime, you'll be in the hospital for a while as the infection clears your system."

Dorothy was too drugged up to absorb all the bad news. The most she could muster was, "I can't," in a hoarse protest. "I have patients..."

"So, Mom thinks you've been sleeping around," Norah said. "Why else would you be stupid enough to bring a Protestant home to Dad? She ate a whole box of Hostess Cupcakes while she waited to hear if you were going to live and another after she found out you were alright." The sisters chuckled because they had all withered under their critical mother's judgment if they overindulged in anything.

"Well, obviously, you're not a lesbian," Norah said.

"Where's Kenneth?" Dorothy asked, in a weak whisper. She was grateful for her sisters' support, but she was exhausted and weak and needed to process what had happened. In her dazed state, she had yet to piece together that Kenneth would have had no idea what happened to her after he stormed out.

Her sisters were more interested in indulging their curiosity than answering her question. "Why didn't you tell us about him, before?" they asked.

"Isn't it obvious?" she sighed.

Thankfully, her grandmother noticed Dorothy's listless appearance. She shooed her sisters from the room and hoisted herself from the chair. She kissed Dorothy on the forehead.

"Everything will be alright, my bonnie lass, you'll see," she assured her granddaughter. "Get some rest."

Just then, Dorothy realized, no one had mentioned whether Kenneth had been in to visit.

CHAPTER TWENTY-NINE

NEW YEAR: 1975

DOROTHY

Enter the ruins of your heart. –Rumi

As if to draw out what had been a much longer visit home than she'd anticipated, sleet and snow slowed traffic to a crawl on Dorothy's drive from Detroit to Lansing, turning the two-hour drive to three and half. A feeling of doom weighed heavily on Dorothy throughout. Kenneth was obviously upset with her. He'd expected her in Sanibel the day after Christmas. Why hadn't she thought of getting a phone number in Florida? Regardless, she had been in no condition to make a phone call. She'd been in a coma for God's sake. He'd never believe her after all her excuses.

Everyone was angry with her. Once her mother realized she'd be okay, she stopped talking to her for having premarital sex and using birth control. Dorothy didn't even bother to explain that because she was so uptight, they'd not had sex. She'd had to stay with Sheila and her family to recuperate. Sheila's growing belly and children were a constant reminder that she would likely never be able to have children after the damage done by PID.

Dorothy dreaded having to tell Kenneth. She'd tried calling the apartment multiple times each day, but he never picked up. She knew his parents were in Sanibel. Did he go with them? In all the flurry and anxiety before Louise's wedding, she hadn't registered where in D.C. he'd been offered the job. She was overwhelmed with worry and grief about all that had transpired. It was one thing when she'd been choosing not to have children, but now that it was no longer her choice, she grieved. One more thing she'd have to explain to Kenneth. Just like he assumed leaving her job to follow him to D.C. would not be an issue for her, he may have been harboring hopes that children were in their future.

✦

The skies overhead looked like grey wool blankets folded over one another, darkening the horizon and assuring heavy snowfall all the way to Lansing. Her thoughts filled with doom and gloom, Dorothy felt desperate to get home yet afraid to drive any faster as she might hit black ice and spin out of control. Before she left Sheila's, Dorothy tried the apartment one more time, trying to reach Kenneth to let him know she was on her way. He had not answered. As she replayed the night of the wedding, dread enveloped the car as if those blanket clouds descended atop of her. *You may find you are feeling more sensitive and fatigued,* her doctors had explained to her after the surgery. *Don't make any significant decisions or do any heavy lifting.* So, Dorothy, still feeling tentative and discomfited about her abdominal area, attributed her premonitions of doom to the psychological toll resulting from the trauma of the medical emergency.

As she approached the entry to her apartment, the sinking feeling intensified. Something was amiss. The absence of light or warmth emanating from underneath the door as she approached and no hint of movement from inside suffocated any hope.

Still, Dorothy was slow to absorb the emptiness of the home when she walked in. She shook off the snow from her hat and coat and hung them in the front closet, not noticing that Kenneth's overcoat, jacket, and boots were gone. A few beats later, walking past an armchair and coffee table, Dorothy did not register that the couch was missing. Entering the bedroom, empty but for the bed and a lamp placed on the floor, she finally absorbed the meaning of the deafening silence. She circled back toward the living room. There was a note on the coffee table, the only evidence of Kenneth's existence in the apartment.

Dear Dorothy,

When you didn't follow me after the way your father treated me, I had my answer. You will always choose your family over me. I do believe you want to get married and have children. Just not with me. I hope you find the love you seek. Always, Kenneth.

She moved about the apartment numbly. The fog of drugs, conflict and sorrow unmooring her, so much so she reached out blindly to find her balance but there was nothing to hold her up. She stumbled against his missing presence as if he'd taken her life away with him. The clearing felt like a death in the family, but also vindictive. Gone were his coffee mugs, the furniture he'd contributed, which, of course, had been much better than the cast-offs she inherited from family. Every scrap of evidence of their love for each other gone, as if up in smoke. Even the knickknacks and a mirror in the entryway were gone. Dorothy went to the bookcase to check the photo album, and sure enough, he'd taken all the pictures of the two of them. He left her pictures and took any singles of him or of his family out. He knew her well enough to know that she'd counted on the particulars of their relationship, how he'd be waiting for her with a cup of tea or glass of scotch at the end of a long day, or how he'd bring her coffee in the morning. The comfort she took in his presence was all she had ever needed, the fact and habits of their shared daily life.

He must have been furious with her when she didn't follow him. Her sister said they tried to track him down at all the nearby hotels to tell him that Dorothy had been rushed to the hospital but there was no sign of him anywhere. There was no denying the vengeance in the emptying of their apartment. Precisely what was the message he was trying to send? Did he wish her to know just how much he'd contributed materially or emotionally to their relationship? She could only believe that underneath his patience, resentment simmered until finally boiling over. When she hadn't returned to their apartment, he'd had lots of time to speculate before he emptied it of his belongings. Explicitly clear was the message that her almost fiancé was never coming back.

Patience was Kenneth's long suit, and she had taken his patience for granted. He had been patient with Dorothy's fence-sitting. He had teased her about compartmentalizing her life into neat, manageable, but very distinct components. Unlike her, Kenneth believed that they would be able to overcome her Catholic family's opposition. But then, he got a full dose of her family's baggage.

What could she have done from her hospital bed? She'd had no way of contacting him. Her mind was a jumble of *if only.* If only I had not hesitated when he asked me to marry him. If only I had left with him. If only I had stood up to my father. If only, then maybe, he'd still be here. She even berated herself for getting Pelvic Inflammatory Disease when she knew full well the infection was out of her control. The litany of woulda, shoulda, coulda was endless as Dorothy blamed herself for anything and everything that had ever gone wrong in their relationship.

Countering her logical mind, the women-shaming beliefs of her Catholic upbringing added to the chorus of self-blame. *You should have known better.* The worst part? She and Kenneth had not had premarital sex in the first place, yet she had all this shame heaped on her. Dorothy could hear her mother's *I told you so* as if she was standing in the room with her.

But she didn't cry. She wandered aimlessly about the apartment, not knowing what to do, picking up the phone to call him at his parents' dozens of times, only to put it down again. There was nothing to clean or pitch. He'd taken care to assure all that was left for his love to do was face the emptiness. Beneath it all, Dorothy felt a little voice rising in the back of her brain. *How dare you all. You all judge me?* Every one of them, her mother, father, sisters, even Kenneth. Dorothy thought, angry now too. Emboldened, the little voice growing stronger, she tried his parents' home and let it ring through.

Still on shaky ground, she became discombobulated when Kenneth's mother answered, having assumed the Nelsons were still in Florida. "Hello," Mrs. Nelson said.

"Mrs. Nelson, it's me, Dorothy. May I speak with Kenneth?" Her voice was weak and wobbly.

"I'm sorry, Dorothy. Kenneth has already moved to D.C., but he left strict instructions that we do not provide a forwarding address, and I don't think he has a home phone as yet."

"Could you send him a message for me, please?" Dorothy said.

"Certainly, though, I don't think it will make a difference."

"Please tell him I was in the hospital. I was very sick, and I had no way of contacting him. And that I'm sorry."

"I'm sorry to hear that, Dorothy. I trust you're feeling better. I will be sure to let him know."

"Thank you, Mrs. Nelson. I'm sorry I ruined Christmas."

"Goodbye, Dorothy."

With that, the line went silent, yet another person refusing to let Dorothy off the hook. Shattered, she went into the kitchen to see if he'd left anything to eat. The refrigerator was empty of all but a stick of butter, a bottle of catsup, and a jar of pickles. In the cupboard over the fridge, she found a bottle of scotch. There was nothing left for her to do but pour a scotch before going to her bedroom alone, flop face down on the bed, and wait for the next morning so she could go back to work.

The next day, Dr. Smith was waiting for Dorothy outside of her office. He was wearing a serious expression that was a stark contrast to the baby blue leisure suit that, Dorothy thought, made him look like he was headed for a disco. His manner was uncharacteristically solicitous as he ushered his colleague into her office and shut the door.

"Welcome back, Dr. Morrissey. How are you feeling?"

"I've been better," Dorothy said.

"I have news," he said as Dorothy removed her coat. She sat behind her desk to remove her winter boots and discreetly slip into high heels.

"What is it, Dr. Smith?" she said, hung over and sad from the night before, and impatient to get started on checking up on her patients after her long absence. "Do you have a patient you'd like to discuss?"

"I'm sorry, Dr. Morrissey. I would have called, but I didn't want to disturb you at home as I was told you were ill." Dorothy felt he was hedging, and she wished that he'd get to the point.

"I was, yes, thank you, but I'm here now. What is it?"

"Your patient, Thomas Perfect, checked himself out against medical advice. The clinical note is in his file."

Dorothy closed her eyes and took a deep breath, holding back tears.

"I should have seen that coming. When?"

"Right after the New Year." For once, Dr. Smith did not appear to gloat, as he was curious about her absence, which, he assumed, must have been severe since Dr. Morrissey had missed so much work. He stood awkwardly near the door as Dorothy had bent over her desk, head in hands.

"He'll be back," he said, edging his way closer to the door. "Let me know if there is anything I can do."

"Thank you, Dr. Smith. I will," Dorothy replied.

After Dr. Smith left her office, Dorothy walked over to the door and locked it. She moved to the love seat with a view of the tea set that they had used for the tea ceremony. After a few moments, Dorothy hung her head in despair and wept.

CHAPTER THIRTY

DOROTHY AND REBECCA
DID SOMEONE CALL A NURSE?

Dorothy spent the next few days going through the motions. She'd go to work, try with all her might to stay attentive to her patients, consult on others with her colleagues, and attend psychopharmacology in-services, numbly listening about the latest medications being developed. Swimming would have provided emotional relief but was against doctor's orders for three months. So, she spent as much time at work as possible, stretching the hours, reading psychology journals or books, and reviewing Thomas's file to see what she'd missed. She had hoped he had trusted her enough to wait until they could map out a plan together. All she could imagine was that he thought she abandoned him. She pored over the data looking for evidence.

Once in her apartment, she'd sit on the floor with peanut butter and jelly or cheese and mayo sandwich, and one glass at a time, she polished off the scotch that Kenneth had left. Most nights, she'd either sit contemplating her mistakes or mindlessly watching television on her black and white TV. Tonight, Dorothy numbly read and reread the note he'd left her while listening to the morose lyrics of Gilbert O'Sullivan's "Alone Again Naturally." Still, she couldn't bring on the tears. Kenneth had been the only serious relationship she'd had in her life. Where were the tears?

There must be something wrong with me, Dorothy thought. Sipping her drink, she thought back to her early experiences with boys in high school. Inevitably before every weekend was over, Dorothy would be flopped face down on her bed, bawling her eyes out after some guy broke her heart, despairing that she'd ever find true love. Dorothy's mother had little patience for a teenage girl's histrionics by the time it was Dorothy's turn. Deirdre and Sheila had more than used up a family's worth of theatricality. Mother dismissed her daughter's heartbreak as silly and self-indulgent. Dorothy's father would be sent to buck up the wretched daughter. He'd stand, shuffling awkwardly in the door to his daughter's bedroom, waiting for a pause in her sobs, to get a word in.

"Dottie," he'd say, "boys are like buses. If you miss one, you'll catch the next." The sweet absurdity of his logic, to say nothing of the stilted delivery, achieved what Dorothy assumed was the intended effect—laughter.

Her father's words floated up from her childhood and into her apartment, as she sipped the last bit of scotch, shoving aside Gilbert O'Sullivan as whiny self-indulgence. "Boys are like buses," Dorothy said out loud. "If you miss one, you'll catch the next." As if on cue, there came a knock on the door. Dorothy had just pulled the peanut butter from the cupboard and was actually looking forward to a tall glass of milk. *Kenneth?* She thought. Who else could it be?

Nurse Martin stood at the door with a Domino's pizza. A bottle of wine stuck out of the large black suede satchel with fringe hanging from three sides, which was slung across Rebecca's left shoulder to right hip. Dorothy wasn't so numb to notice how stylishly Nurse Martin was dressed. Out of context of the hospital and bundled against the cold in an ensemble of wool that held up to the elements, it took Dorothy a beat to recognize her work-friend. She wore a tartan-plaid overcoat with velvet collar, navy knit scarf and hat, and black suede gloves. She also wore black suede knee-high boots over her jeans.

"Did someone call a nurse?" She smiled at the startled Dorothy.

"Nurse Martin, what are you doing here?" Dorothy asked, already in pajamas and slippers at six in the evening. "How did you know where I lived?"

"Doesn't take a rocket scientist," Rebecca quipped. "I know, I should be mad. You've never invited me over. And now, you're not asking me in. I'm roasting in this hallway," she said, peeking around Dorothy into the apartment. Dorothy reluctantly opened the door to allow Rebecca to enter. Rebecca looked around. She turned to Dorothy.

"Oh, please, yes, come in," Dorothy sputtered. "Don't judge, there's been a change in circumstances, which involved a taking of furniture." Even heartbroken, Dorothy's instinct was to match the humor Rebecca brought with her and tried to make light of the empty apartment.

"Will you stop with the 'Nurse Martin'? We're not at work. I had a feeling something was going on," Rebecca said, making her way past Dorothy to set the pizza on the coffee table. "If you promise to call me Rebecca, I'll share this with you," she said, pulling a bottle of wine from her satchel. "What happened here?"

"Kenneth left. He took almost everything with him, as you can see."

"Good thing I brought wine," Rebecca said. She knew Dorothy was extremely private, but she would have none of that. "Why didn't you say something? Damn psychologists don't know when to ask for help."

Rebecca ushered Dorothy to the one chair. "I knew something was wrong," she said. "I know you care for Thomas, but to be so distraught over a patient, well," she said, appropriating a phrase of Dorothy's, "I figured it wasn't about what it was about. Even if you are more devoted than is reasonable. Dig in, I'll go look for glasses." She headed toward the kitchen. "And don't worry about plates. We can eat out of the box."

Over pizza and helped by wine, Dorothy found she could confide in her friend about her heartbreak. In Rebecca, Dorothy found a good listener and an unapologetic dispenser of advice peppered with "I know you're the psychologist, but..." If Rebecca hadn't shown up when she did, there was no telling how long Dorothy would have sat on the floor of her apartment, ruminating over every misstep she had taken toward the demise of her relationship with Kenneth. With Rebecca, Dorothy could hear herself, and Rebecca felt like a sister who didn't judge or resent her. She confided in Rebecca about her father and Deirdre because Rebecca reciprocated with her own crazy family stories.

"Every family has 'em," Rebecca said, dissipating Dorothy's shame with one throwaway sentence. "Wait till you meet my brother, Mark. Well, after we find him. He's been on a bender for weeks." She was an open book. She didn't hide her family's shortcomings in shame. Instead, she put them on display with humor.

Nor would Rebecca allow Dorothy to take the blame for every last problem between her and Kenneth. "It takes two to tango," Rebecca repeated over and over. "I don't much like how he accepted the job offer without consulting with you. Just like a man to assume you'll drop everything and follow him." Rebecca emphasized acceptance, as in Dorothy accepting who she was and accepting the inevitable. "So, what, if you didn't bring him home? You know as well as I do that your parents would have had a conniption. My daily communicant parents would never allow me to marry a Protestant."

"Kenneth never understood what I was up against."

"Do what I do," Rebecca suggested with a laugh, "go to church just long enough to find yourself a good Catholic boy."

"I'm not ready," Dorothy responded, "but I'll take your advice under consideration."

"Have it your way," Rebecca teased. "Baby steps."

Before the evening was over, which lasted until two in the morning, Dorothy learned that Rebecca rarely took no for an answer, but her good cheer and enthusiasm made you want to do her bidding. Her bidding was usually in your best interests anyway. Dorothy had always respected Rebecca's professionalism and bedside manner. An astute nurse, she could quickly and accurately assess whatever ailed her patients and was capable of intervening in a caring, compassionate, yet efficient way. And, as Dorothy learned during her time of need, Rebecca did not leave those abilities at the door of the hospital. Rebecca was a woman of genuine good cheer, able to see the silver lining in any situation.

✦

Into the spring and summer, the details of that first night, when her intrepid friend showed up at her apartment, altered such that Dorothy saw her heartbroken self in a better light, not the mess Rebecca had encountered when Dorothy opened the door. The gist was the same, however. Rebecca wheedled her way into Dorothy's heart with humor and tenacity. And Dorothy was grateful for Rebecca's enthusiasm, nudging her back to life.

As Rebecca successfully persuaded Dorothy to take one baby step at a time to move past the heartbreak, she was emboldened to push her further. "There is nothing but sad memories here," she said. "You shouldn't be holed up in this apartment. It looks worse than you do."

The dismal state of Dorothy's apartment and seeing firsthand how Kenneth had emptied the place of all that had made it home was all the impetus Rebecca needed to orchestrate Dorothy's move out of there. Within a week, Rebecca convinced Dorothy to buy a place of her own.

"There's a cute house in my neighborhood up for sale on Mitchell Street in Edgemont. There's a family of eight in there now. I don't know how they all fit in that tiny house. They had twins a couple of months ago, so I think they finally realized they need a bigger place." Nothing could squelch her friend's excitement. "You can even walk to work. Hey! We can walk together!"

During the day, Rebecca wore her nursing scrubs with pride. After work, she rivaled Dorothy when it came to style. In fact, with their dark hair and freckles, they could have passed for sisters, two sides of the same coin—Dorothy reserved and quiet, Rebecca fun-loving and gregarious. In the following weeks, as the friendship deepened, their personal styles became a confluence of their mutual admiration. Dorothy "got with the times," as Rebecca teased her, even going so far as to wear jeans on occasion, and Rebecca discovered a new interest in vintage styles from the forties and fifties.

"You're like a dog on a meat wagon," Dorothy said to her friend, appropriating George's analogy about people like Rebecca once an idea entered their heads, they didn't let go.

"That's me in a nutshell, all right," Rebecca laughed as she corralled Dorothy to "just take a look," at the Mitchell house. Before she knew what was happening, Dorothy was signing a mortgage for the small red brick house with the carport on the side and small garden in the back. There was a large unfinished basement with a washer and dryer ("lucky you, no more going to the Laundromat"), a pink-tiled bathroom, and a kitchen with green linoleum countertops ("okay, so it needs some work"). There was even a white picket fence.

"All that's missing is a husband and children," Rebecca beamed, hands-on-hips, as she surveyed her handiwork, and Dorothy was finally settled into her new home. Undaunted, her friend assured Dorothy she'd meet a new man as soon as all the necessary upgrades were finished.

Dorothy had to admit, buying the house on Mitchell, proved, as her new friend had insisted all along, to uplift her sagging spirits. The new home, which involved many upgrades, followed by the need to fill each room with furniture, cemented the two women's friendship as they decorated and shopped, cleaned, and painted, and turned Dorothy's house into a home.

And they walked. Two miles each way from Edgemont to St. Lawrence, they walked and talked about everything under the sun, beginning with Kenneth and ending with their shared patients. With each conversation came acceptance that Kenneth had done what they had both known had been coming for a long time. As Rebecca said, he needed to "rip off the bandage. Nobody's fault." Dorothy knew she was right.

As the weeks went by, Rebecca wouldn't let Dorothy leave any room in her new house unfinished. There would be no ghost echoes off empty walls, as Dorothy had allowed in her old apartment. When she was alone after work, and she didn't feel like painting or cleaning the grout, Dorothy implemented the practices she used with her patients. She bought a turntable and began purchasing albums to fill her new home with music. She had ample time to catch up on all the music she'd missed out on while she'd been in graduate school (another way for her to get with the times, according to Rebecca). Sometimes, she worked around the house while she listened. Other times, she danced along to the music behind the new curtains she'd hung immediately. Despite Rebecca's best efforts, Dorothy would, first and foremost, fiercely guard her privacy.

As the warmth of late spring began to reliably hold, the two women toasted their work with glasses of wine at Dorothy's new kitchen table.

"Well done, us!" her friend said. "Just in time for a family visit."

"That'll be a cold day in hell," Dorothy laughed. "My parents have never visited me in Lansing. My mother hasn't spoken to me since I left the hospital in January."

"You never know," Rebecca insisted. "She'll have to get over it eventually."

Sure enough, Rebecca's intuition was on the mark. Just as Dorothy and Rebecca put the finishing touches on the spare bedroom, Mrs. Morrissey called.

"Hello, Dottie, it's Mom," she said. "I've heard from the girls that you've bought a new house. So, I take it, you're in Lansing for good?"

"It would seem," Dorothy responded, assuming the worst. Before January, she couldn't get her mother to stop calling. Since her surgery, her mother hadn't called once, and when Dorothy called her, she said she didn't have time to talk. "Is everything alright? How's Grandma?"

"Actually, that's why I'm calling," Mrs. Morrissey said.

"Oh, no, what?" Dorothy asked crestfallen. Her mother paused just long enough for tears to well up.

"Oh, she's fine, better than fine," her mother said. "You know your grandmother. She'll outlive us all." Dorothy detected bitterness in her mother's assessment of her mother-in-law. "I'm calling because I need you to look after her."

"What?" Dorothy replied. "I just bought a house."

"Precisely why I ask. Sheila, Ned, and the kids need to move in with us. I guess the commune wasn't all it was cracked up to be. And we're getting a hospital bed for Deirdre. Her Lupus is getting worse. The boys are going to the University of Detroit in the fall but living at home to save money. I don't have enough room for everyone. Grandma likes you the best, and your sisters said you bought a three-bedroom. So, I need you to take her."

Dorothy did not know how to react. Not because she didn't want her grandmother. She was delighted about the prospect. Grandma Morrissey would be great company. Dorothy pictured her grandmother puttering around the garden while Dorothy worked during the summer. If she was still there for the winter, a pot of chicken soup would be simmering on the stove when Dorothy came home, and the two of them would chat about their lives over dinner and a glass of wine. Her grandmother had stories to tell that Dorothy was eager to hear, and unlike Dorothy's mother, her grandmother was easy-going with an open mind.

With her grandmother to come home to, loneliness would no longer plague Dorothy. What made Dorothy's blood boil about the request was her mother's nonchalance about asking for a favor after not speaking to her daughter for months. There was no point in challenging her mother, however, unless Dorothy wanted to invite a good dressing down. Mary Morrissey could outmaneuver anyone when it came to laying blame. Never wrong, her mother would make mincemeat out of you if you dared suggest she had been.

"Of course I'll take her," Dorothy said.

"Your father and I will bring her to you this weekend, if you don't mind."

"I'll have a room made up for her," Dorothy said, knowing that was the end of that conversation, but pleased nonetheless that her parents would have to visit.

CHAPTER THIRTY-ONE

RUTH

In the end, all manner of things shall be well. – Julian of Norwich

Ruth came in for her last session with Dorothy. She had come straight from her job at St. Vincent's Orphanage, and still wore her uniform and had her hair tucked into a hairnet. Late afternoon light streamed in through the open blinds. The therapist and client knew their time had come to an end. Ruth had come so far. She had steady work at St. Vincent's, where she honed her skills as a cook and was surrounded by children. Her supervisors had already commented about how well Ruth interacted with the children and suggested that she return to school for education.

She enjoyed living with her aunt for the past three months. During that time, her Aunt Sylvie helped Ruth and her mother mend fences. The three women talked about their trials and joys over dinner once each week. Once Ruth's mother could see for herself that Ruth could handle the truth, she opened up more about her history. For Ruth, learning about her mother's story had helped heal the hurt feelings, especially when she considered how frightened her mother must have felt moving away from her mother for baby Ruth's sake. Not only that, but the news that her father insisted his name be on her birth certificate despite knowing he was not her biological father was "icing on the cake," Ruth said.

"I was always wanted," she said. "That's how I see it. I think they are just overwhelmed with so many children."

"Twelve is a lot of kids, all right," Dorothy said. "And I like your new perspective, Ruth. Although, I've always believed a naturally optimistic person was buried beneath your grief. The losses you've endured would knock anyone down."

"I have other news," Ruth said, grinning. "My aunt helped me pay for a lawyer, so I've filed for divorce. And, get this," she said. "My brothers pitched in and paid for my first and last month's rent on a brand new one-bedroom apartment. Once they heard about Calvin's latest shenanigans, they didn't want me to go back to him. He's not fooling anyone anymore. Jerome ran into him at Scotty's and punched him in the face." She laughed, her dimples on full display.

"I am so happy for you, Ruth. It sounds to me like your brothers *do* appreciate all you've done for them." Dorothy couldn't help but return Ruth's contagious smile. "Is your aunt okay with you moving out?"

"Oh, yes, she loves me, but she's made it clear she needs her own space. Her apartment is small for two people. Not only that, but the place I'm moving is right up the street." Everything about Ruth expressed her delighted surprise that she could come out on the other side of her grief. Some of the light had gone out of her eyes but she basked in the love of her family.

"Are you truly ready to move on without Calvin?"

"I believe I am. That zebra will never change his stripes. Besides, I don't feel so alone now." With this new outlook, Ruth became more excited than scared to build a life independent of her soon-to-be-ex-husband.

"Your family has backed you up more than we could have imagined, wouldn't you say?" Dorothy's smile too reflected the warmth of the love Ruth was receiving.

"I feel blessed. I still get really down about losing the babies, but between you and my Aunt Sylvie, I've been able to talk about it. That's helped a lot. And my mother is doing the best she can." It took a long time but the skies had finally cleared for Ruth.

"Any news on your brother Darren and his girlfriend?"

"All we know is she should have had the baby by now." She said, worry for her brother tamping her enthusiasm. "We don't know where they are. Speaking of Darren, I've been dreaming about him again."

"Would you like to share? As you know, dreams and music are symbolic expressions of our inner life. And you've been making a lot of changes lately."

"Just think, I wouldn't have believed a word you were saying a year ago," Ruth smiled broadly.

Dorothy hadn't stopped smiling the entire session, buoyed that their journey together had brought Ruth to this place.

"Anyway, in the dream, I'm standing next to Darren, except now I'm taller than he is. That was interesting because he's the tallest in our family. He's almost six feet, but he's small in the dream like he's still a little boy. We are heading to the same rundown building, and we hear lots of noise inside like there's a problem, so I go around the side and look in the window. I shout to Darren to call the police because I see a woman tied up inside. He's slow to react. I get frustrated with him, and finally, I find a payphone and make the call. In most of the dreams, I usually wake up at this point. This time, instead of the dream ending, the police arrive after I call. But, by the time they get there, the woman is untied, and everything is fine."

"What do you make of it, Ruth?" Dorothy asked, leaning in.

"I was hoping you could tell me." Ruth shrugged her shoulders. "It was so weird."

"I find it remarkable, frankly. It reminds me of the first time I met you. You were at the lowest point in your life but singing a song of optimism. Remember?"

"How could I forget? Pretty embarrassing."

"Just like back then, this dream seems to be telling you that everything will be all right for you and Darren even though he's lagging behind you. Where once you were all tied up in knots, you no longer are. You know how to find help, and maybe you've shown Darren it's okay to ask for help when he doesn't know what to do. How does that sound?"

"I like that," Ruth said. "I hope you're right. I'm worried about him."

Dorothy found the dream remarkable in its representation of Ruth's inner life and foundational optimism. Like the woman in the dream, she'd been tied up, and in trouble, but believed everything would be all right.

Remarkable was an understatement as only Ruth's unconscious mind had the prescience to see what was coming. After their session, Dorothy walked Ruth to the door of the hospital. They stood there quietly shoulder-to-shoulder, hesitant to say their goodbyes.

"Can I give you a hug?" Ruth asked.

"I was just about to ask you the same," Dorothy said. "I'm really going to miss you, Ruth." The two women hugged, and Ruth turned to go when suddenly she said, "Darren?" at the young man who burst through the doors carrying a bundle in his arms. He looked about wildly, frantic, but holding tightly.

"Darren," Ruth said. "What's going on? Is that your baby?" Darren's eyes alighted on Ruth. The relief that crossed his face was palpable. Dorothy noted he was a youngish man, but his drug-ravaged face had all but stripped him of youthfulness.

Like Ruth had just said, Darren was very tall and very thin. He appeared to be highly agitated, strung out on God knows what, but very protective of the small bundle in his arms. His eyes were bloodshot as if he hadn't slept in days. His whole body bounced with nervous energy.

"Ruth!" he shouted. "I've been looking all over for you." He started circling around as if lost, "What'll I do, what'll I do? I can't do this."

"Okay, okay, calm down, Darren. I'm right here." She spoke in soft, soothing tones as she might have when he was a child. A small cry rose from the bundle.

Dorothy moved closer, hoping to take the baby, but he clutched the bundle closer to his chest, guarding against her prying eyes, much like Ruth had done when Dorothy first met her. He looked around as if he might flee. She and Ruth made eye contact.

"Darren, can I take a look?" Ruth asked calmly so as not to upset him. Darren handed the baby over to Ruth. Dorothy skirted the sister and brother and baby out of the lobby and toward an empty room, usually reserved for intakes. There was a desk where they could lay the baby and a phone. Dorothy called the ER while Ruth inspected the baby.

"Ruth, my baby. I need your help. Don't hurt her," he said. "I think she's sick." His anguished cries accentuated his ill health. His body wracked with shivering so violent they could hear his teeth chatter.

"Don't worry, I'll be careful," Ruth said, barely above a whisper. She laid the bundle on the desk to get a look at her. He'd wrapped her snuggly in a tattered blanket. He'd also tucked a still warm bottle into the blanket with the baby. Dorothy stood by her side.

"Oh, my," Ruth crooned. She bent, tending to the infant as Darren hovered over her shoulder. She was underweight, but beautiful from the looks of her. Her eyes were tightly closed as if to shut out the glaring lights of the hospital. A full head of coal-black hair topped her little head. Ruth inspected fingers and toes and delicately ran a finger over the tiny ears. The baby opened her eyes to peer into Ruth's as if she knew that she was now safe. Her eyes matched her hair. Ruth breathed in every inch of her. The infant let out a piercing wail.

Darren turned frantic. "Ruth, please, my baby. You've got to help her."

Dr. Morrissey found a wheelchair and a couple of blankets. She tried to get Darren to sit, but he batted away her efforts to help him. She handed a blanket to Ruth. A nurse and orderly arrived from the ER.

"We need to get him to the ER and the baby to NICU," the nurse said. Ruth picked up the baby and cradled her in her arms. The nurse looked at Ruth. "Is this your baby?"

"No, she's my brother's baby." She turned to Darren. "Okay, Darren, I need you to focus. What happened?" Ruth said.

"I need you to help her, Ruth. She's sick," he said. "She doesn't sleep. She hasn't stopped crying since she was born."

"When was that?" Ruth asked.

"Two or three days ago, a week, I can't remember," Darren replied.

"Where's the mother?" the nurse asked.

"I don't know. She took off. She was strung out. She said she's never coming back. I can't take care of her. She's sick. You've gotta take her." His words slurred and jumbled together, revealing that he too was strung out. His gaunt features exaggerated by worry emphasized that he was in no shape to care for an infant. His eyes were bloodshot, and he scratched obsessively at his arms as if he had bites all over them. Yet here he was doing right by his child, however late.

By now, Ruth had let go of her initial resentment to the news that Darren would be a father after many sessions with Dr. Morrissey discussing the unfairness of it all. Dorothy now noticed the soothing effect Ruth had on her brother.

"What's her name, Darren?" Ruth asked without a hint of judgment or anger.

"I named her May," Darren said. "I want you to be her mom."

Everything happened so fast. The nurse bent over the infant whose wails became more pitiable in their intensity.

"We need to get her over to NICU immediately," she said. "I think she's withdrawing from cocaine. The agitation is a sure sign. See how she's shaking, and those high-pitched wails all signs of withdrawal."

Dr. Morrissey made the call to the NICU to prepare for the emergency. The nurse turned to explain to Darren what was needed. He was gone. She looked at Ruth as if she could answer for his whereabouts.

"He'll be back," Ruth said. "Will she be alright?"

"It's not going to be easy, but she's gotten this far, so I'm guessing she's a fighter. Poor little thing, all tied up in knots, but she'll be all right."

Dr. Morrissey returned to the group. "We can go right up. The nurse in NICU said to keep her warm." She bent over Ruth and the baby. "Here's another blanket, Ruth."

"She's shivering like the dickens," Ruth said, pulling the baby to her chest. "You don't suppose Darren meant what he said, do you?" Ruth implored Dr. Morrissey. She rocked back and forth gently and softly sang a lullaby. The infant's wails turned to a whimper.

"We'll have time to figure that out while she recovers, Ruth. I'll contact the social worker to set about the process for you if you'd like. Whatever happens, I think you'll have a case for guardianship until we know what Darren and his girlfriend want."

The nurse helped Ruth to the wheelchair and covered her little May with another blanket. Ruth looked up at Dr. Morrissey. "I guess you're not getting rid of me just yet."

"Gosh, that already feels like ages ago," Dorothy said.

She asked if she could accompany Ruth and the baby to the NICU. "I won't stay long, just long enough to see that little May gets situated."

Ruth beamed at her therapist and held tightly to her niece. "And then, I'll contact the social worker. I should probably inform them about the missing mother. She is probably very ill herself."

✦

Two days after the baby's admittance to the NICU, Ruth came to see Dr. Morrissey.

"We haven't been able to find Darren or Margo," she informed Dorothy. "So, I've been given temporary guardianship. She'll be coming home with me when she gets better. I'll keep looking for him, though. Strung out as he was, he loved her. We can figure it out. I've got to go shopping. Damn, I wish I hadn't gotten rid of the crib. I was so upset after losing my last baby I told Calvin to clear out the nursery we'd set up."

"Any chance he hung onto the stuff?"

"No, but that reminds me, I bet my parents have an old one in the basement. Oh, well." She laughed, delight filling her voice. "And guess who wants to babysit little May?"

"Who?" Dorothy asked. Nothing would surprise her now.

"None other than Delta, but she'll be fighting off a long line of relatives. This baby will have no shortage of love."

"I'm not surprised, Ruth," Dorothy grinned. She couldn't have imagined such an outcome when she first met Ruth. "I like May for her first name. Are you thinking about a middle name?"

"I like Magdalene for a middle name," Ruth said. "Like the Magdalene in *Jesus Christ Superstar*, this girl will be strong and true, just like Mary Magdalene."

Dorothy smiled, appreciating Ruth's affirmation for Dorothy's use of the album in therapy.

Ruth's singing on the floor had inspired Dorothy to use music as part of therapy sessions. All of that seemed so far away just now.

Ruth spent as much time as was allowed, sitting up in the NICU holding and soothing baby May Magdalene with lullabies, and ushering her back to health. Once May withdrew from the drugs, her pitiful crying calmed, and she put on weight. The infant's face relaxed, and she opened her big black eyes to find love in her aunt's face.

"The doctors told me that only time will tell, but that they feel confident May will thrive with my loving care. If I've heard, 'she's lucky to have you' once, I've heard it a million times. But I know better."

Dorothy agreed.

The entire staff at St. Lawrence was rooting for Ruth and May and taking a little piece of ownership in the serendipitous turn of events. Dorothy just hoped that Darren would relinquish his rights and allow Ruth to adopt baby May. Though Ruth wanted Darren to return and get healthy, she harbored hopes that he would give May to her to raise. Dorothy marveled at Ruth's courage to risk loving the infant with the possibility of losing her too. Ruth wouldn't abide any naysaying. Ruth had become the woman Dorothy had imagined she'd always been before so much sorrow had befallen her. Smiling and optimistic, she spoke of miracles, and love, and the goodness of God. Dorothy liked to believe that their work together was at least partially responsible, but the arrival of the baby girl was just the miracle that Ruth had prayed for.

"God did not abandon me, just showed me that when one door closes, a window opens," she said the last time they met. "Just like I told Marcella. 'Keep the faith,' I told her. God will show you the way."

CHAPTER THIRTY-TWO

1983

MARCELLA

Journey within yourself ...
and bathe in the splendor of your own light. –Rumi

The ER was crowded for so early in the day. Dorothy imagined they'd had a long night, or there was a change in shifts delaying admittance. Tired, anxious faces looked about, hoping to catch the eye of a helpful nurse or doctor. Others stared blankly at the morning news on the television. There was no sign of Marcella anywhere. Her condition must have been grave to receive such immediate attention. Dorothy walked over to the reception desk, where a paramedic stood chatting with the intake supervisor. She wore a baseball cap, and a dark bun was neatly pulled through the back opening. Dorothy tapped the woman on the shoulder to see if she had any information about her former patient. Dorothy was stunned.

"Marcella," she cried. "I can't believe it's you. Nurse Martin told me you came in by ambulance, so I came running down."

Marcella laughed. "I'm sorry, Dr. Morrissey. I wanted to surprise you. Look at me. I'm the one bringing in the patients now. I guess I couldn't stay away."

"I'm just glad you've figured out a healthier way to visit," Dorothy said. "How is everything?"

"I'm doing great. I'm so grateful for all you did for me. Like you suggested, my parents, my sister, Brianna, and I went to family therapy. Turns out, my mom's addiction was much worse than we thought, but she's been clean for a couple of years now. Between my mom and me, Brianna's issues kind of got missed. I never thought about what she might have been going through. Turns out it's tough stuff to be born after your sister dies. Anyway, we get along great now."

Dorothy smiled. "I'm so happy to hear that, Marcella. Were you able to finish school?"

"Yes, I finished up at MSU, but you know me, I still needed drama. So, I trained as a paramedic, and here I am." She splayed her hands up in a happy shrug, pulling her shoulders to her ears. Smiling broadly as she explained.

"That's perfect," Dorothy replied. "I'm so happy for you! Have you been to Sylvie's, the new bakery yet? Guess who owns it."

"Have I been to Sylvie's?" Marcella teased. "Who do you think Ruth enlisted to work the cash register? I get as much day-old baked goods as I want!"

"You do look a lot healthier," Dorothy complimented.

"Ruth said that if I see you, to let you know there's a chocolate crois-sant with your name on it."

"How's little May Magdalene?" Dorothy asked.

"She's growing like a weed and becoming Mama's little helper at the bakery. Her dimples rival Ruth's. And, you know Ruth's got her singing."

"I'm not surprised," Dorothy laughed, pleased.

"Well, listen, I've got to get back to work. I just wanted to say hi, and let you know I'm doing well. Thanks again for everything, Dr. Morrissey."

"Thanks for coming in, Marcella. It's so nice to hear good news," Dorothy said. "Tell Ruth I'll come by Sylvie's soon."

"Will do," Marcella smiled and, with a wave, ran off to the ambulance where her partner waited behind the wheel.

CHAPTER THIRTY-THREE

GEORGE

I have spread my dreams under your feet;
Tread softly because you tread on my dreams. —Yeats

There were many pivotal moments of George's therapy with Dr. Morrissey while he was at St. Lawrence Asylum, but the one that stuck with him, in the end, was probably not the one she would have guessed. He was both embarrassed by it and grateful for it. Dr. Morrissey let him down gently. She made a positive reframe, he has since learned.

"It's called transference, George," she said. "Now that you know you'll be released, you're able to imagine all the possibilities life has to offer, including the possibility of a loving partnership."

"Right," he said, "with you." He was sure that he loved her. Without Dr. Morrissey, he would never have uncovered the abuse. He had never opened up to anyone in the same way.

"It's only natural to imbue our relationship with amorous feelings, George," she said. "In our sessions together, we have cultivated an intimacy, unlike any other relationship."

"Then you feel the same way," George replied hopefully, leaning toward her from his usual perch on the sofa. Dr. Morrissey had been trying out an experimental "musical approach," as she'd dubbed the new stereo she'd brought into her office. She told George he could choose any song that resonated with his experience. They'd commiserated over all the counterculture they'd each missed—so much great music out there. He'd chosen *Young Americans* by David Bowie. He'd heard the song on the radio in the common area. He wanted to hear more. Dr. Morrissey put the album on the turntable and sat down with him to listen, her head nodding along with the beat of the music as she tilted toward the speakers to listen carefully for his benefit. He noticed how she blushed as she began to comprehend the lyrics. George took that as a positive sign.

She tread lightly for the appropriate words to address the delicate issue without damaging their bond. "Transference shows us both what is inside you. You have love to share with someone," she said, "but you'll want to find someone with whom you can have an equal partnership." He had been sure that he loved her then, but now he was grateful for just how gently she'd rejected him.

✦

"Happy Father's Day!" Margaret said. She was on top of him, face flushed from their concerted exertion, strands of her long red hair sticking to beads of sweat on her forehead and chest, every cell imbued with the flush of well-being, to say nothing of the unseasonably ninety-degree temperatures.

He grinned broadly, looking up at his wife as if meeting her for the first time. He never tired of his unabashed pleasure in his new life and good fortune. "Oh, Mags, I love you." Every day was like the first day he heard the news of his release. George had quickly shed the prickly armor he wore around his heart once he absorbed the full knowledge of his new lease on life.

He raised his torso to kiss the small cleft (she called it a dimple) in her chin, the place where her finger rested when she was deep in thought.

She gazed back at him. "George?" She waited a beat.

He looked at her quizzically. "Am I missing something?"

Had she read his thoughts? How embarrassing would that be? Thinking about his psychologist immediately after intimate relations with his wife was worth analyzing and revelatory of the closeness he'd felt with Dr. Morrissey.

Dr. Morrissey had explained the concept of transference to him and how "it happens all the time, as does countertransference, which was why there are ethical standards to serve as safeguards to ensure patient welfare and prevent an abuse of power." He had quickly backed away, embarrassed by his overture and misread of the situation. Dr. Morrissey again remarked about how the nature of the therapeutic relationship can easily lead to misinterpretation. Did he understand?

At the time, he'd felt crushed, but now, happily married, and about to begin his post-doctoral internship, he was grateful for the experience and lessons learned firsthand.

"I suppose we should get a move on if we want to spend time with both our fathers," George said, coming out of his reverie. Margaret climbed off her husband and lay next to him. She smiled.

"Like I said, Happy Father's Day!" She grinned. "I'm sure they will be excited for us."

"My dad will be happy for us, but I don't know about my mom. She'll be sad to see us go," George said, thinking Margaret was talking about their move to Illinois. "Mom will always be trying to make up for the lost time. But Dad will be over the moon to hear I'll be training at Great Lakes."

George and his father had been slowly mending fences over the years. After he was released, George and his parents followed up with a family therapist that Dr. Morrissey had recommended. His father had a difficult time, at first, believing that Father Miner had been capable of molesting children until the evidence that piled up against the priest had become irrefutable. After that, his father felt angry about the time stolen from his family and George's childhood by the abusing priest, and guilty that he'd not figured out what had happened to George. Many an evening's conversations, aided by a spot of bourbon and cigars for father and son, involved a rehash of remorse and outrage for George's father.

"I can't believe that pompous son-of-a-bitch sat at our table expounding on Canon Law like he did," George's father would fume. "He was such a stickler, making people feel guilty for the smallest transgression, and there he was abusing our children for Chrissakes! I will never step foot inside that church again!"

By this time in his life, George had taken the long view. His specialty in graduate school had been post-traumatic stress disorder. Coupled with all the therapy he'd done, George understood so much more about why he had behaved as he had. He and his parents worked hard to forgive each other. He'd surprised himself with how easy he was able to forgive his father. Forgiving Father Miner was another story.

"Well, at least he finally got what was coming to him," George would say.

"I should've known better, George. You were always such a good boy. Why didn't I ask you what happened?"

"Water under the bridge, Dad," George responded in kind, even tones. "The priests' authority was unquestioned. He had a good racket going."

"All that time wasted in an insane asylum," his father said.

"Not really, Dad," George said. "Without that time wasted, I wouldn't have given psychology a thought, and, more than likely, Mags and I would not have gotten together."

Multiple iterations on this theme were discussed while George's father worked through an issue that was incomprehensible to him and had dealt a severe blow to his once blind faith in the Catholic Church. George hoped his father felt reconciled enough to suspend the conversations with his son, so George could embark on a new chapter in Illinois with his wife. The fact that his internship was at Great Lakes Naval Air Station would undoubtedly help.

George's wife was still looking over at him, smiling but shaking her head in disbelief. "To think that I thought you were so smart! You are not a quick study, my dear." Mags laughed.

He loved his wife, his long-ago nemesis in grade school. The two over-achievers vying for the top spot in their teacher's heart, which, of course, young Margaret won. Little had he known the resentment Margaret had harbored against the indignities suffered at the hands of Father Miner. She hadn't forgotten a single moment of his attempts at public humiliation. That compounded by the abuse inflicted by the priest on her brother Matthew, George, and the others, fueled her passion for seeing justice done, like a dog on a meat wagon, as George teased her. She smiled again at her uncomprehending husband.

"I guess I need to spell it out for you. Your mother will be thrilled when we tell her that another freckled face will be waiting for her to visit in Illinois, Papa," she added pointedly.

George propped himself up on his elbow and gazed into his wife's smiling face. He was still dripping sweat from their exertion. *Wait a second, did my wife just wish me a Happy Father's Day?*

"Papa?" he asked cautiously.

"Or Daddy or Pops, whatever you'd like our child to call you." George scooped Mags in his arms and squeezed her tight, planting kisses all over her.

"Really? I'm going to be a father? You're pregnant?" George jumped from the bed and ran to the living room, woohooing on the way. He grabbed his favorite album. This one he gave Dr. Morrissey as a thank you and a do-over after the embarrassing incident occasioned by his first choice. He still loved "Young Americans," he did, but "Solsbury Hill" summed up his experience with Dr. Morrissey and where it brought him better than any other. He cranked up the volume and went to grab his wife to dance around the room.

Husband and wife sang out, holding hands, jumping around naked in their living room, buoyed by the words of their favorite Peter Gabriel song. The one, as Dr. Morrissey once instructed, that resonated best with his experience. The news of Margaret's pregnancy, just one more example in a long list of late, to George's mind, that he had been saved. Saved by his mother, by his wife, and the insightful prodding toward awareness by Dr. Morrissey. All three women willing him to see beyond the protective armor he'd erected against the wounds of his childhood toward the unabashed joy he never believed he'd be capable of feeling.

"George," Dr. Morrissey had asked him when he was finding it so hard to believe that his life would ever get better, "if your life can be ruined suddenly, why can't it also be saved suddenly?"

CHAPTER THIRTY-FOUR

THOMAS AND DOROTHY

You are now the Sun. What need have you for a crown? You have vanished from this world. What need have you to tie your robe? —Rumi

This was about as playful as she got. Every morning her fellow lap swimmers tentatively stick a big toe in the water or sit on the edge of the pool adjusting their goggles, waking up, legs dangling acclimating them to the cool water. Not Dorothy, goggles on and swim cap covering wet hair, she swings her arms like a ten-year-old at a backyard pool on a hot summer's day, and jumps in. Every morning at six—best way to start the day. Without coming up for air, she kicks off and completes her first length under water, flip turns before taking a breath, proud that she knows how to do one, having taught herself for her fortieth birthday. Her body rolling slightly, always to the right, she rests into the rhythm of lap swimming where she can count and think.

Swimming is her Church like her father's daily communion, her grandmother's Sanka and newspaper, her mother's daily washdown of the kitchen counters with Clorox. The steady pace allows her thoughts to rise from the deep to the surface where they float alongside her counting—one, one, one, flip, two, two, two, flip. And, like church, there is something of the divine in what floats to the surface, inklings that inevitably manifest before the end of the day. So, on this morning, when on lap twenty-four, her thoughts turn to a former patient, Thomas Perfect, she knows she will see him again.

✦

Dorothy entered the stark, brightly lit room. If she hadn't known better, she never would have guessed that the motionless occupant lying in bed, hooked up to the monitors and IV drips, was Thomas. He looked ghastly, she thought, frighteningly so. His brother John sat in an armchair, reading a magazine. He stood to greet her when she entered the room.

"Hello, Dr. Morrissey," he said, shaking her hand. "Thanks so much for coming up. Thomas has been asking for you. I'll leave you two alone. Can I get you anything from the cafeteria?"

"No, thanks," Dorothy responded. John Wayne Perfect was so handsome she had trouble looking at him. "I get my fill of cafeteria food. I'll find you when we're finished if that's all right?"

John nodded and walked out, stretching as he did. Color rose to her cheeks, and she was suddenly warm.

"Hello, Thomas," Dorothy said, turning toward her patient. She put on the mask that she'd been advised to wear. "I brought you the obi that was confiscated the first time we met." She laid the obi on top of Thomas's chest. He placed his hand over it but was too weak to lift it into his line of vision. Muscle memory guided his hands to stroke his favorite accessory.

"Still swimming," Thomas said weakly. "Eau de chlorine." He smiled at his own joke. Soft brown eyes protruded from gaunt features.

After JW brought in Thomas to psychiatric, Dorothy sent him for a medical evaluation to rule out physical conditions that could explain his deterioration. Once there, he was diagnosed with pneumonia. Large doses of antibiotics did nothing to improve his health, so he was currently undergoing tests for cancer. She sensed a great deal of tension and uncertainty among the medical staff regarding his condition and prognosis. Wearing the mask was precautionary until his doctors could determine the means of contagion and what type of infectious agent they were dealing with. They had not yet decided if his symptoms stemmed from tuberculosis, another virus, or an unknown bacterial infection.

There were rumors of a new deadly illness, and even the doctors admitted to their fear of contracting what ailed him. She was grateful for the mask as it muted her involuntary gasp at the sight of him. The bright lights seemed to be hurting his eyes, and the television was turned up too loudly as far as Dorothy was concerned. Perhaps she was projecting, but nothing about his room felt comforting or healing.

"Did you see JW came home?" he said, mustering as much excitement as he could convey given his weak state.

"I did, Thomas, I'm so happy for you," she said. "I'm sorry about the mask, doctor's orders." She did not want him to detect any fear in her.

He nodded. "JW told me. I know."

Dorothy's experience as a patient in the hospital, some years ago now, had indelibly scarred her emotionally and physically, but she thought she'd never seen anyone as ill as Thomas. Tubes poked from his skin attached to IVs. Parched lips and raspy voice hinted at a sore throat or great thirst, but listlessness discouraged even the short reach for the water near his bed. His breathing was labored, and his pallor dull. She noted sores on his forehead. She was surprised he had any energy to talk. Nonetheless, he insisted that he needed to confide in her. She turned off the television and dimmed the lights.

"Is that better?" she asked.

He nodded, settling into his pillows with a ragged sigh. "Did I ever tell you I played football in high school?"

"You mentioned it once or twice," she replied, smiling. She couldn't help but find it amusing that even a gay man would cling to his high school glory days.

"My father always wanted me to play football," he croaked in a whisper. Dorothy moved closer to hear better, although she remembered some of this story. "Dad thought playing football would 'cure me' of my propensities. I'm sure you remember what those were." He gave her a hint of his old impish grin. She nodded. "I wasn't half bad. Football got me through that year after JW left. Of course, football didn't cure me of anything, quite the contrary. I did enjoy being surrounded by all those guys." He managed a noise that sounded like a cross between a laugh and a croak. "Up until then, all I knew was that I liked dressing up in my mom's kimonos. I didn't know I liked boys. I couldn't have named what I was feeling then if you'd spelled it out for me. Football was a great cover for me. I took some perverse pleasure in getting hit. I felt a little bad because playing football was the only way I made my father proud of me, and his butt was sitting in jail, so he never got to see me play. JW told me Dad died. Did you know that?"

"I did," she responded. "I'm sorry." He waved her sympathy away.

"I don't miss him. Anyway, did I ever tell you about Regis?"

Dorothy nodded. "Yes, go on."

"He was my only real boyfriend. We met playing football." He chuckled, which triggered a coughing fit. Dorothy rose to get him some more water, but he stopped her. "I'm fine, really." But Thomas began to cough uncontrollably.

Dorothy poured him a glass of water, waiting for the coughing to subside. She held up his head while he took a sip.

The mere effort of taking a drink of water appeared to deplete him, but he was determined to press on. When he regained his composure, he continued, hushing Dorothy's overtures to let him rest. There was a confessional tenor to the urgency in his storytelling, as if he felt he did not have much time, and he needed absolution.

"After I discharged from here—feels like ages ago, doesn't it?" Dorothy nodded. "I moved to Detroit, just like I'd planned. I'd had all I could stand of Lansing. Detroit had more gay bars at any rate. And of all people, guess who I run into in my favorite bar? Regis. Can you believe it?" He asked her as if still marveling over the wonder of his rekindled love. "I was overjoyed to see him, and somehow we were able to pick up right where we left off. I thought, finally, my life will have a happy ending. Regis introduced me to a whole gaggle of closeted men who would never, in their daytime lives, admit to being gay, but who at night caroused in an orgy of drugs and sex. Most of the 'guys' were much older than us and more successful. I'm talking doctors, lawyers, engineers, buttoned-up types by day. On the other hand, Regis and I were piecing our lives together, working odd jobs. I had a particularly hard time finding work after I was—"

"You mean after you released yourself against medical advice," Dorothy interjected.

"Potato, potahto," he sighed with some of his old exasperation. "The point is, I couldn't explain what I'd been doing during much of my twenties. Plus, I went off the rails again when I stopped taking my medication. Regardless, the men we were meeting stood a lot higher on the social ladder than we did, and they had a lot more power. They could shield me from the police and get their hands on the medications I needed. I imagine they went back home to their wives and children to play at being upstanding citizens, moralizing on the wages of homosexuality or abortion, and no one guessed what they were doing at night in downtown Detroit. I'm sure that they would never in a million years consider themselves to be homosexual. The first time Regis and I got together, in high school, I knew I was gay. I couldn't have named it before then, but I never looked back once I was with him, but for some of these men, you could see how they wrestled with their conscience immediately after they wrestled with us. There were others, of course, who had no conscience at all." He took a ragged breath.

"We became too careless, not understanding at all that there could be any danger to our escapades. One night these two men invited us to an exclusive 'club,' in the heart of Detroit's business district. I'm talking somewhere near the big three, but I wouldn't be able to take you there if I tried. We were driven there in a limo with dark windows. Immediately, our hosts poured us glasses of champagne. We thought we'd hit the jackpot. We hardly thought to take notice of where we were going. From the outside, the place appeared non-descript, but as soon as we walked through the foyer, we might as well have been in a 1920s speakeasy. I wouldn't have been more surprised had we run into Al Capone. I'm talking scary bizarre." Thomas shook his head as if he still could not believe such places existed. He took another labored breath before continuing his story.

"Alcohol and drugs flowed, which, trust me, usually, I would have enjoyed to my heart's content. But there was something very off in there—predatory. For one thing, this was not a place strictly for gay men who did not want to be found out. There were women in there too, and I shouldn't say, women, I should say girls. We were still young-looking bucks, enough so that I wasn't sure if we were among the predators or the prey. The 'patrons' were men much older than the ones we'd meet in bars. I'm talking 'Hotel California'. We could check-in, but we could never check out. Dottie…" He paused. "Did you know we called you Dottie behind your back?"

"I had an inkling," Dorothy said. "But go on, so you don't tire."

"Ah, yes, anyway Dottie, my alarm bells had never rung so loud before or since. I felt a shiver up my spine. I kid you not, Dr. Morrissey. There were teenage girls and boys in cages dancing in the middle of the room, ostensibly of their own free will, but I had my suspicions. For one thing, they had chains around their necks, loosely, mind you, but why? I don't know. I knew I had to get us out of there. Regis was agog, taken in by the men's fancy attire, the sparkling chandeliers, the waiters in tuxes, and the endless flow of drugs and alcohol. All I could see, on the other hand, were shadows. Dark hallways, shadowy characters, shadows under the eyes of the dancers. I whispered to him that I had a bad feeling about the place. He wouldn't budge, no matter how much I pestered him. He was drawing the attention of this one old guy, who you could tell had a thing for the younger men. Regis walked off with him, so I stood by the bar, pretending to drink.

"For once in my life, I had the presence of mind to keep my wits about me. I begged off the advances of some older gays, saying I wasn't feeling well, all the while keeping an eagle eye on Regis. When I saw the old geezer directing Regis toward a dark hallway, I burst into action. I quickly walked over to them, drink in hand, and said, 'Reeg, before you go,' but I acted like I tripped and 'accidentally' spilled my Manhattan with lots of cherry juice all over the geezer's crisp white shirt. He was pissed, furiously daubing his shirt with a napkin. I tried to grab Regis's arm. I said, 'Reeg, we gotta get out of here.'"

"'You're just jealous,' he said. 'Find your own Sugar Daddy.' He winked at me as if he was just kidding, but I wasn't laughing because I genuinely feared for him. He wouldn't budge. I was making a scene, and before I could say jack be nimble, they were on top of me. Two bouncers grabbed me by my arms, led me out the door, and stuck me in a waiting cab. I had no choice. I left him there. Reeg didn't show up at our apartment that night. I didn't know how to reach him. I called all of our 'normal' friends to see if he was camped out on a couch.

"I was frantic. There was no telling what happened to him. I was heartsick. I had no idea how to find the place. And, I don't know how to explain it, but it was as if an eerie radio silence descended upon me."

"I'm pretty sure Regis was lured or coerced into staying there because he didn't even return to pick up his things, not that he had a lot. I didn't see him at the bars, and he didn't show up to work, no sign of him. I'm telling you this because, after that night, I felt like I was a marked man. We stumbled upon a secret society of some sort, and I hadn't played along."

"That is very scary, Thomas," Dorothy said. *And hard to believe*, she thought.

"Cross my heart and hope to die," Thomas said as if he read her mind. "But I'm telling you this in confidence. It's not that I want you to do anything about it."

"Then why are you telling me, Thomas?" She believed him enough to feel scared. How many places like this existed?

"I need to tell someone, so I can let go," Thomas replied. "I've been carrying this around for so long. Here's the worst of it. You know how I have a knack for finding trouble? Like getting beat up?"

"How could I forget?" She sighed in memory and anticipation.

"One would have thought I'd learn to avoid such things, but there you have it."

"Isn't that how you ended up in here in the first place?" *Repetition compulsion*, she thought. Never ceased to amaze her.

"Exactly. Well, since I've been sick, I've had nothing to do but lie here and think. All kinds of memories are flooding back." His eyes implored her to understand how very sad for him the next part of his story would be, like a homeless puppy waiting to be rescued. He continued though his head seemed to loll.

"Sometimes, I wonder if I looked for trouble like I was reliving my childhood." Dorothy had to smile. Sometimes the therapist had to wait a long time for the client to gain insight. "Believe it or not," Thomas continued, "I was beaten up again on yet another night before Thanksgiving. This time, however, I swear they came looking for me. I was still reeling from the break-up with Regis. Can you imagine my confusion and pain that he would choose some ole geezer over me? I just remember thinking, *what did I do?* Yeah, I was out at the bars, but I was only trying to stay busy and distracted. Man, I hate Thanksgiving. It's like my unlucky charm.

"All of a sudden, I'm being dragged from the bar out to an alley. I had no idea who these guys were or what I had done to offend them. Their grip on my arms was eerily familiar to those of the bouncers from the club. One was particularly enraged, but that's not what hurts the most. What hurts is that someone had to have told them that I would be in that bar. Someone who would know for sure and who would be able to describe me accurately. I don't feel that the assault was random at all. I didn't recognize the men who inflicted the blows, but I swear I know who was behind them."

Dorothy was stunned. "When did all this happen, Thomas?" She was confused about his sickly appearance that did not appear related to a beating, no matter how brutal.

"Doesn't matter," Thomas replied weakly. "I was heartbroken. I thought Regis loved me. I had no choice but to keep moving forward, or else I'd lose my apartment. I was barely making ends meet. Then one day, not long after that, I received a call from Detroit Mercy. Regis had put me down as next of kin on his admission form. What could I do? Of course, I went. When I saw him lying in that hospital bed, I was both horrified and elated. I was horrified because he looked so ill, but I was elated that he had asked for me. I was perversely overjoyed that he requested that I be at his side during his time of need. The rapprochement was sweet but short-lived once again because my love died soon after. It didn't take me long to realize that my new aches and pains were not in my head, but that I too was suffering from the same illness."

They sat quietly for a while, letting his story sink in. Dorothy felt overwhelmed with sadness for Thomas and the unfairness of his life story.

"Frankly," Thomas said, breaking the silence, "I didn't have the heart to be angry with him. He looked so pathetic. I knew he was sorry. I have forgiven him. I can only imagine what kind of life he had."

"I wish I knew what to say, Thomas," Dorothy said. *Harder than yours?* she thought.

"Can I ask you something, Dr. Morrissey?" His eyes beseeched hers.

"Of course, but call me Dottie, Thomas," she responded.

He smiled. "Do you think anyone ever loved me?"

"Yes, Thomas. I love you. And I think Regis loved you, and JW loves you, and your mom. Human beings are flawed, though, and we mess up. I've been reading Rumi again. Can I share a line with you?"

"Can I stop you?" He winked. She wanted to cry. Here he was at death's door and he winked.

She smiled. "Speaking of," she said, "this poem reminds me of our time together." She opened the book on her lap and read from a translation of Rumi's poetry. A thirteenth century poet and mystic perfectly describing her work and people's struggles with mental illness. Thomas, who always seemed to draw the short straw in life, his words coming to an end in death. Such a privilege that he chose her to be with him at the end of his journey. Dorothy choked up as she read barely making it through the end of the poem. He was like her prodigal son come home. She did love him.

As if on cue, John Wayne returned to the room. "Oh, you're still here?" he asked, seeming pleasantly surprised, Dorothy noted. "Is that the obi you'd mentioned?" JW noticed Thomas stroking it ever so gently.

"It is," Dorothy responded. "We're just wrapping up," she said. "I'm so glad you asked me to come to see him. Thomas, I need to get back to work, but I will come back to see you tomorrow, okay?" She pulled off her mask, bent over him, and kissed him on the forehead. Thomas's eyes were closed. He looked very peaceful as if he'd said all that needed to be said. With tears in her eyes, Dorothy turned to say good-bye to JW.

"I'll walk you out," JW said, placing his hand at the hollow of her lower back. As they reached the hallway, he added, "Would you like to have a cup of coffee later?"

Dorothy blushed, despite her weariness and sorrow over Thomas. "I would love to," she responded.

CHAPTER THIRTY-FIVE

THOMAS

Now the words are over and the pain they bring is gone.
Now you have gone to rest in the arms of the Beloved. –Rumi

As Thomas lay dying, his mind began to play tricks on him. He wasn't sure where he was. Sometimes, he thought Regis was speaking with him. Sometimes, he felt JW's presence, or was it the other way around? Maybe he was just talking to himself. He drifted between the only two worlds he knew—past and present. No point in worrying about the future. He thought about Regis and his father. He wondered if there really was a better place where they would be reunited and happy for once. He remembered how his mother always said, *"the inmates are running the asylum"* about life inside their home, but then he wondered, did she really say that or was he mixing her up with Dorothy? Sometimes he wished he had stayed put in the asylum. He tripped down the lane of woulda, shoulda, coulda. He had not heeded Dr. Morrissey's clinical advice to stay put until she'd returned. He wondered if she worried about him. Did she think about him? He was also curious about what happened to her in the interceding years. She hadn't said. If he hadn't ignored clinical advice years ago and stayed in the inpatient unit, he'd likely not be staring death in the face right now.

Don't be so melodramatic, Thomas, he thought. But really, he hadn't thought it through just like all the other bad decisions in his life. He shuddered when he pictured the look of disappointment crossing Dr. Morrissey's face when she learned he was gone. Anytime he brought up discharging from the hospital, she had dissuaded him; the tell-tale worry flicking in her eyes even as her tone remained even. He could hear her now, like it was just yesterday, exhausting him with admonitions regarding his difficulties with compliance and self-care. He remembered his dismissal of her pointed question, "*How will you stay out of trouble, Thomas?*" She hadn't meant to be hurtful. She really wanted to know if he'd had a plan.

He shouldn't have gone, sneaking out during her absence like he did. But would he have wanted to miss out on those couple of years of pure joy with Regis? He thought not. Behavior and consequences, as Dottie always said. Dottie, he and his fellow inmates all loved her like a mother, and hadn't they felt like family? George was his pesky brother, a fill-in for his real brother, JW, albeit a more irritating one. Ruth was his sanctimonious older sister; Marcella, the baby. Had he made them up, or were they all still living in the asylum floor of St. Lawrence? Even if they were, they couldn't visit, but Dorothy came to see him. She reminded him, as she was wont to do, that she couldn't speak about the others. In the end, he felt closer to her than he did his own mother. And JW came back.

The illness was terrifying, he knew that much. He could tell they all were afraid. He was no longer afraid. He just wanted to go. Some nights he dreamed of Regis. How he missed him. His death never seemed real to Thomas. He never dreamed of his father. In fact, he prayed that he would not. He remained as afraid of him as he'd been as a boy. All that was in the past. Tonight, he dreamed that Regis sat by his side holding his hand. They'd be together at last.

Thomas thought about the last time Dorothy sat with him. She read him a poem by Rumi called "We are Not a Caravan of Sorrows." Then she said, "Sounds like it was written for our Home for the Bewildered family." Did he dare call them family? Maybe Dorothy was right. He would miss her. He could hear her say, "Let go now, Thomas. I am here. You are safe." Was that JW he heard just now? "Now's the time, now's the place, little brother. I love you."

ACKNOWLEDGEMENTS

First to my husband, Gerry who has lovingly supported the ups and downs of my creativity with enthusiasm often to his own detriment. His willingness to pick up extra work to keep us afloat gave me the freedom to pursue this dream. And to my three children, Elizabeth, Daniel, and Conor who have been loving witnesses to my long journey toward book publication and who have supported me even if they are afraid to know what goes on inside my head. To my two sisters (or should I say two of my seven sisters), Elise and Maria, who throughout years of shared interests in mental health, writing, and teaching, and mutual love and support, do know what goes inside my head. Thank you for your thoughtful feedback through many iterations. To my son, Daniel, who also provided invaluable feedback and called me out when the story didn't ring true. I couldn't have done it without the three of you.

To my first draft editor, Mary Nolte, many thanks. To my friend, poet Beth Gylys who gave it a thorough going over before I submitted. To my early readers and friends whose support I cherish: Sue Martin, Sue Field, and Laura Lewis. Special thanks to a Dr. John Neafsey and Dan Mulhern for their generous time. And to Jonathon Star who so generously allowed me to borrow from his Rumi translation. Thank you to Jessica Bell, Amie McCracken and all the editors and staff at Vine Leaves Press, especially Elaina Battista-Parsons whose feedback was invaluable, editor extraordinaire and birthday buddy, Melanie Faith, and copyeditor, Ash Crantas. You don't know how much your kind words meant to me.

To my eleven siblings whose shared experience has shaped our lives and contributed greatly to this book. The whole often seemed greater than the sum of its parts but we each have a unique place and perspective within our family of fourteen. And in loving memory of our brother Patrick whose death in 1974 changed the trajectory of our lives.

To all the chefs and friends at the Ballymaloe Cookery School who helped give me the courage to undertake this project. I wrote a blog about my adventures at Ballymaloe called Noleftovers: Cooking up mental health.

Finally, to all my clients over the years from whom I've learned so much and whose stories I honor and carry within me. As Daniel Patrick Moynihan said, "I don't think there's any point in being Irish if you don't know that the world is going to break your heart eventually." Though your stories break my heart sometimes, it is my privilege to walk part of the journey with you.

VINE LEAVES PRESS

Enjoyed this book?
Go to *vineleavespress.com* to find more.
Subscribe to our newsletter: